The Iron Thorn

Honor White Jackson was a human being. But his planet was not Earth, nor his time Now. His world was dominated by a giant Iron Thorn. Beyond the reach of this tower there was, supposedly, nothing – except a frozen, airless desert where huge winged beasts called Amsirs roamed.

Michaelmas

Michaelmas and Domino, man and computer, were linked to each other … and to the complete database of Earth. There they virtually ruled the world. For by making the right subtle manipulations, they had the power to change the course of human destiny.

Hard Landing

The body was found dead on the tracks, electrocuted. The autopsy confirmed what some had always feared, that we are not alone in the universe - and that even now, some visitors are still at large.

Also by Algis Budrys

Novels
Man of Earth
Who?
The Falling Torch
Rogue Moon
Some Will Not Die
The Iron Thorn
Michaelmas
Hard Landing

Collections
The Unexpected Dimension
The Furious Future
Blood and Burning

Non-Fiction
Benchmarks

Algis Budrys

SF GATEWAY OMNIBUS

THE IRON THORN
MICHAELMAS
HARD LANDING

GOLLANCZ
LONDON

First published in Great Britain in 2014 by
Gollancz
An imprint of the Orion Publishing Group
Orion House, 5 Upper St Martin's Lane,
London WC2H 9EA

An Hachette UK Company

A CIP catalogue record for this book is
available from the British Library

ISBN 978 0 575 10833 2

1 3 5 7 9 10 8 6 4 2

Typeset by Jouve (UK), Milton Keynes

Printed and bounded by CPI Group (UK) Ltd, Croydon, CR0 4YY

www.orionbooks.co.uk
www.gollancz.co.uk

CONTENTS

ENTER THE SF GATEWAY . . .

Towards the end of 2011, in conjunction with the celebration of fifty years of coherent, continuous science fiction and fantasy publishing, Gollancz launched the SF Gateway.

Over a decade after launching the landmark SF Masterworks series, we realised that the realities of commercial publishing are such that even the Masterworks could only ever scratch the surface of an author's career. Vast troves of classic SF and fantasy were almost certainly destined never again to see print. Until very recently, this meant that anyone interested in reading any of those books would have been confined to scouring second-hand bookshops. The advent of digital publishing changed that paradigm for ever.

Embracing the future even as we honour the past, Gollancz launched the SF Gateway with a view to utilising the technology that now exists to make available, for the first time, the entire backlists of an incredibly wide range of classic and modern SF and fantasy authors. Our plan, at its simplest, was – and still is! – to use this technology to build on the success of the SF and Fantasy Masterworks series and to go even further.

The SF Gateway was designed to be the new home of classic science fiction and fantasy – the most comprehensive electronic library of classic SFF titles ever assembled. The programme has been extremely well received and we've been very happy with the results. So happy, in fact, that we've decided to complete the circle and return a selection of our titles to print, in these omnibus editions.

We hope you enjoy this selection. And we hope that you'll want to explore more of the classic SF and fantasy we have available. These are wonderful books you're holding in your hand, but you'll find much, much more ... through the SF Gateway.

www.sfgateway.com

INTRODUCTION
from The Encyclopedia of Science Fiction

Algis Budrys was the working name of writer and editor Algirdas Jonas Budrys (1931–2008), who was born in East Prussia (now Russia), but at an early age was taken with his exiled parents to the US, where he remained from 1936. Budrys began publishing SF in 1952 with two more or less simultaneous releases, 'The High Purpose' (in *Astounding* for November 1952) and 'Walk to the World' (in *Space Science Fiction* for November 1952), and very rapidly gained a reputation as a leader of the 1950s SF generation, along with Philip K. Dick, Robert Sheckley and others, all of whom brought new literacy, mordancy and grace to the field. From February 1965 to November 1971 he wrote regular, incisive book reviews for *Galaxy*, and from September 1975 to January 1993 he contributed 160 'Books' columns to *The Magazine of Fantasy and Science Fiction*; for these reviews, and other critical work, he received a *Pilgrim* Award in 2007.

During his first highly prolific decade as a writer Budrys used a number of pseudonyms on magazine stories, none of which however were preserved in book form. He wrote few series, the most memorable of these being the Gus stories, as by Paul Janvier, which include 'Nobody Bothers Gus' (November 1955 *Astounding*) and 'And Then She Found Him' (July 1957 *Venture*). They are early examples of a story type which would haunt Budrys's work throughout, in which an Alien (or foreigner, or exile) must disguise his eternal exile from the normals around him.

Budrys's first novel has a complex history. It first appeared in abridged form as *False Night* (1954), then was much expanded as *Some Will Not Die* (1961; this edition being further revised in 1978). In all states of the text a Post-Holocaust story is set in a plague-decimated America and, through the lives of a series of protagonists, a half century or so of upheaval and recovery is described. *Some Will Not Die* is a much more coherent (and rather grimmer) novel than its predecessor. His second novel, *Who?* (1958), which was filmed as *Who?* (1974), grafts an abstract vision of the existential extremity of mankind's condition onto an ostensibly orthodox SF plot, in which it must be determined whether or not a prosthetically rebuilt and impenetrably masked man, difficult to distinguish from a Cyborg, is in fact the scientist vital to the US defence effort whom he claims to be. The ultimate indeterminacy of his Identity gives this novel a decidedly un-American resonance (as far as SF goes), but its analytical dissection of 1950s Paranoia is very telling, though some of the later plot-heavy detective work in which the tale becomes embroiled somewhat distracts the reader's attention from what seemed Budrys's main intention: to write an existential thriller about identity (it is rather similar to the later work of Kōbō Abe), not an SF novel about the perils of prosthesis. Similarly, *The Falling Torch* (1959) presents a story which on the surface is straight SF – several centuries hence, with Earth dominated by an Alien oppressor, the son of an exiled president returns from exile in the stars to liaise with the underground – but can clearly be read as an allegory of the Cold War with specific reference to Eastern Europe. Like *Who?*, it asks of its generic structure rather more significance than generic structures of this kind were perhaps designed to bear.

Much more thoroughly successful is Budrys's next novel, *Rogue Moon* (1960), now widely regarded as an SF classic. A good deal has been written about the highly integrated symbolic structure of this story, whose perfectly competent surface narration deals with a Hard SF solution to the problem posed by an alien Labyrinth, which has been discovered on the Moon, and which kills anyone who tries to pass through it without obeying various arbitrary and incomprehensible rules. At one level, the novel's description of attempts to thread the labyrinth from Earth via Matter Transmission – which works as a form of Matter Duplication, generating multiple versions of the protagonist – makes for excellent traditional SF; at another, *Rogue Moon* is a sustained *rite de passage*, an existential confrontation (through the Doppelgangers generated) with the mind-body split, and a death-paean. There is no doubt that Budrys intends that both levels of reading should register, however any interpretation might run; in this novel the two levels interact fruitfully. His last early novel is *The Iron Thorn* (1967) (see below).

After some years away from fiction, Budrys returned in the late 1970s with two final tales: his most fully engaging and longest novel, *Michaelmas* (1977) (see below); and the much shorter but densely compact *Hard Landing* (1993) (see below). They are both entirely accomplished works of art; but they were his last. In the 1980s, Budrys controversially associated himself with the L. Ron Hubbard Presents Writers of the Future programme for new writers which had been initiated (or at least inspired) by L. Ron Hubbard, arousing fears that the Church of Scientology might be the source for the programme's apparent affluence. It was, however, evident from their willing participation in the programme that many established SF writers felt these worries to be trivial, and the workshop can indeed claim to have introduced several authors of note to the field, including Karen Joy Fowler and David Zindell.

In pieces like *Writing Science Fiction and Fantasy* (1990 chap), composed originally for the Writers of the Future, Budrys fascinatingly couched his sense of what it meant to be a professional. The Hubbard school absorbed most of his energies for the remainder of the decade, although in 1991 he announced his semi-retirement from Writers of the Future and soon published *Hard Landing*; in 1999, however, he resumed his editorship of the annual Writers of the Future sequence of anthologies assembling stories from the workshops. During the same period however, from January 1993 to August 1999, Budrys published, edited and wrote for *Tomorrow: Speculative Fiction*. Columns on writing from the first ten issues were revised and assembled with related nonfiction as *Writing to the Point: A Complete Guide to Selling Fiction* (coll 1994). His shrewd sense of the genre informs this didactic material, as it did the earlier sequence 'On Writing', comprising seventeen instructive columns which appeared in *Locus* from 1977 to 1979.

His SF criticism – now assembled in the ongoing Benchmarks series, *Benchmarks: Galaxy Bookshelf* (1985) and *Benchmarks Continued: The F&SF 'Books' Columns Volume 1: 1975–1982* (2012) – is almost unfailingly perceptive, and promulgates with a convert's grim élan a view of the genre that ferociously privileged the American magazine tradition, though this focus was softened in later reviews. Budrys was in fact that rarity, an intellectual genre writer, which his shorter work also demonstrates; his best short stories were assembled as *Entertainment* (1997). From his genre origins stem both his strengths (incisiveness, exemplary concision of effect) and his weaknesses (mainly the habit of overloading genre material with resonances, so that earlier works can seem top-heavy with meaning). But these difficulties were transcended. Budrys's last three novels demonstrate how effective this kind of pressurized narrative can be. It is to be regretted that he wrote no more at novel length.

The first novel selected here is *The Iron Thorn* (1967), a tale told with a deft lightness of touch that might deceive the incautious – there are always depths within any story Budrys ever brought to book-length, and there are certainly some depths here. The narrative opens on Mars, where members of a straggling human colony hunt what seem to be Aliens for their meat and other bodily products. This sounds rather like a Planetary Romance, of the kind Edgar Rice Burroughs founded; but it emerges in *The Iron Thorn* that these winged, beaked 'Amsirs' are in fact adapted human stock. The action now shifts, through the use of a long-dormant Spaceship, to a somewhat decadent Earth, where the protagonist's adventures are regarded as an artistic, aesthetic experience. Under the vivid action, however, we're being told, almost with a smile, that eating people is wrong.

The next novel reprinted here may be Budrys's finest; certainly it is his most humanly complex and fully realized version of things to come. *Michaelmas* (1977) describes in considerable detail a Near Future world where the information media have become the dominant shaper of society, a creator of news that the owners of the world turn into reality, in a highly cogent pre-figuration of the Internet (which had not of course been invented in 1977). The Michaelmas of the title is a man who moulds news. Unusually, however, the book does not attack him, or treat the world he controls in terms of satire. Michaelmas is a highly adult, responsible, complex individual, who with some cause feels himself to be the world's Chief Executive or Secret Master; beyond his own talents, he is aided in what he thinks of as a task by the immensely sophisticated AI named Domino with which or whom he is in constant contact, and which in turns accesses and instructs all the Comput-ers in the world-net, not to mention peripheral devices including lifts, automatic doors, household electronics, etc. As usual with Budrys, the plot is exciting and perhaps not quite up to carrying the burden of the tale: Michaelmas must confront and defeat mysterious Aliens who, with human connivance, are attempting to manipulate *Homo sapiens* from behind the scenes. As Michaelmas assumes more and more responsibility, Budrys draws him more and more warmly. In the end, we trust Michaelmas. We trust him to take care of us.

Budrys's final novel, the third selected here, is *Hard Landing* (1993), which concentrates into relatively few pages a tale whose implications resound in the mind's eye. A small band of spacefaring Aliens has crash-landed in America in the early 1950s. Three of the survivors live surreptitious lives as humans, disguising their culturally destructive super-powers; but one betrays his vow of secrecy and exploits his scientific knowledge to gain power and money, in cahoots with an American Congressman who is never named but (as Budrys makes pretty clear) we are almost certainly meant to identify as Richard Nixon. The tale, complexly told, conveys a hard dry mature mel-ancholy irony. In its brief compass, it is a true recipe for wisdom. It is as always. Inside every Budrys tale hides a treasure trove that is meant for us.

For a more detailed version of the above, see Algis Budrys's author entry in *The Encyclopedia of Science Fiction*: http://sf-encyclopedia.com/entry/budrys_algis

Some terms above are capitalised when they would not normally be so ren-dered; this indicates that the terms represent discrete entries in *The Encyclopedia of Science Fiction*.

THE IRON THORN

This is for Jeff, who told me why it was possible, and for Barbara who told me how it ended.

CHAPTER ONE

I

The floor of the world was rippled like the bottom of an ocean. The setting sun inked each ripple with violet shadow. Striped and dappled, the low dunes lay piled one beyond the other like stiff people in blankets filling the world to its edges.

Those edges stood high and cruel. The eastern horizon was a blue-black wall below a flaring shallow arc of eaten rust whose ends sank out of sight far to the left and right. Occasional nearer masses of rock glowed, their sunward faces orange, pitted and bright against the featureless shadow under the rusty edge. Above that horizon, tiny flecks of unwavering light were stabbing themselves through the black windings of Creation.

Towards that horizon the Amsir sped, its clawed, wide-toed feet thumping and hissing among the ripples as they kicked up momentary bursts of coarse sand that fell flat quickly. Each time it topped a dune, the Amsir emerged from thickening shadow and, like the rocks, glowed briefly, before, unlike the rocks, it cavorted down out of sight to pop up again on the next rise. The Amsir was half a dozen feet tall. It gripped a metal-shafted javelin across its chest with the little hands that grew halfway down the main bones of its wings.

Honor White Jackson was honning it and had a different opinion, but the Amsir was beautiful. Its beaked face was all angles and slits, like a knight's visor, and it had its great, translucent, flightless wings extended for balance. Graceful as a goblin bride, it curvetted in a flutter of lacy pennons growing from the horn of its puffed-up body and its spindled lower limbs. These made good insulation for Amsirs at rest, and were also quite useful to the humans of the Iron Thorn. Their effect now was to make a shy wonder of the beast – a pale, tossing creature that soared on in skittish, possibly joyous, quick steps.

The wings, spanning twelve-odd feet from nail-hard tip to tip, glowed pale coral in the waning sunlight and were excellent for infuriatingly shrewd changes in direction. Many times as he ran after it White Jackson had changed over to his casting stride, the brutal glass-headed dart nocked in the socket of his Amsir-bone throwing stick. Just as often the Amsir had tossed up one shoulder in a motion fraught with disdain, pivoted around the resistance of the fifteen square feet of braking surface, and been off again on a slightly altered tack. Behind the slitted, round turrets of horn in which its eyes were veiled, glittering pupils twinkled back over its shoulders.

As they traced their paired wakes of magenta dust over the great desert, White Jackson and the Amsir together made a certain beauty greater than their individual own. Jackson was thinnish, long-limbed, tall and burned brown. You would never have known he came of people who had evolved to swing from limb to limb and never hold their backs quite straight. Like the Amsir, he had a lean face and glittering eyes. Like the Amsir, he ran daintily, touching the surface just long enough to gain traction for his next stride, striving never to come down flat-footed. He wore a very old bright metal cap with a pointed spike and a new chinstrap made of Amsir lace. He had a half pint of water in an Amsir-bubble strapped to the small of his back, and carried his spare dart in his left armpit. As wiry and as taut as the Amsir was ethereal to the eye, he was very much aware that this whole scene depended on a suspicious sloth in the quarry just as much as it did on the Honor's energy.

White Jackson was also aware that the Amsir's exasperating jigs and jogs had a common baseline that was leading him steadily away from the safety of the Iron Thorn. The damned bird was trying to lure him. White Jackson was new to being a Honor and if this was the sort of thing he could expect to have happening in his chosen way of life, he wanted very much to investigate it while he was still young enough to learn. Accordingly, though he now and then came down on his soles in the jolting, slower bounds designed to transfer momentum to his poised throwing stick, he expected nothing more for his pains that what he got – a series of sharp nudges of his cap's rim against his scalp. He saw no reason to doubt that he was tougher and smarter than any Amsir or man in the world. If he wasn't, now was none too soon to learn it. He was content to keep running all day – barring one limitation he couldn't help – and he expected the Amsir would spring its trap whenever it was dark enough for it. He was even willing to help spring it, if the trap was what he suspected it was.

As they ran on, playing their charade on each other, the Amsir undoubtedly had its own motives for being where it was. Meanwhile, Jackson was thinking that if he brought in the Amsir, his brother, Black, would treat him one way, and another if he did not. Though his brother was always very good to him. He was thinking that it would be pleasant to sit down to the community table with the demeanour of one who has killed what is being eaten. He imagined this would have its effect on women, and might go some distance towards getting elders off his back. But all this was coloured by the simple joy of being tirelessly strong and a Honor in a world bounded by sand and Amsirs, populated mostly by dull farmers, and centred on the Thorn to which the farmers clung.

He looked back over his shoulder to locate the Thorn. He had got very far away from it. Only the top several dozen feet of its black silhouette were visible over the horizon. There was no doubt that if he lost his cap now, there would be a few very bad moments of death for him and damned little else. What puzzled him was that the Amsir was not giving him enough credit for intelligence.

Honor White Jackson, even more than the wise old farmers who knew better than to want anything off beyond the fields, had a clear understanding that it was bad to get out of sight of the Thorn. It was also bad to go beyond the perimeter of the fields without a cap. The proposition about the cap had been proved to him by his brother, who had taken him to the desert and pulled his cap off. The air around White Jackson had instantly turned into thirsty burning ice. The sun had become a pale, cold hammer that left his skin itchy for hours after the cap was clapped back on his head, and would have blackened his frozen corpse given the chance. The proposition about never getting out of sight of the Thorn, cap or no, Jackson took on faith in Black's word as an established professional Honor. There were also the elders, of course, who knew so bloody much that only their constant open-mouthedness prevented its running out their ears. And there were the elders' women, whose job in life seemed to lie in giving girls all sorts of useful tips on how tricky life was.

With all this information being passed around the humans since time began with the creation of the Thorn, it was inconceivable that the Amsirs hadn't deduced how much of it was true and how much of it the humans believed enough to act on. The Amsirs after all had been in the desert beyond the fields since time began, and had seen many a farmer turn his plough, and many a Honor popping up from his night-laid ambush in a dune.

The story was that the world hadn't been made for Amsirs; Amsirs had been made for the world. Either way, it was surely no world for men, and men could be presumed to know it. Therefore, thought White Jackson as he skimmed across the sand, with faint swirls in the space immediately around him, as if the air were nearly boiling water, what was the Amsir's plan? Did it honestly expect him to follow it over the Thorn's horizon and drop dead for its benefit?

That seemed to be the idea.

It really did. Having seen a Amsir get away from an ambush and carefully maintain half-speed with all the appearance of going full out, White Jackson was prepared to believe there was more to honning Amsirs than had ever been spelled out for him. A while ago, the beast had started working him around behind one of the rare-rock outcroppings, and Jackson had been ready to expect three or four more Amsirs, waiting to jump him. But nothing like that was happening; the shallow curve of their course was now far beyond the spongy up-thrust of bloody orange rock, and just beginning to turn in behind it. Their distance from the rock gave him a clear field to see that he and the treacherous bird were the only two live things working here.

All right. They were about as far from the Thorn as Honor White Jackson cared to go. He was going to have to nightwalk back to the Thorn, solving the navigation problem by reversing his memories of every change in direction and every stage of distance he had covered since leaving it. He was, hopefully, going to have to do it with the Amsir's eighty pounds across his shoulders, and he was about ready to start. In another eight strides, he was going to stumble, lose his stick and dart, paw at his face and try to crawl back along his track, for all the world as if the Amsir had lured him over the horizon. If the bird didn't go for it, that was just too bad. If he did, he was due for Jackson's spare dart right in the throat.

But it was only three strides before the world was cold and his throat was full of splinters. He had been moving forward at a pace that covered twelve feet per second, comfortable and planning ahead, and now he was flailing forward, incapable of stopping until he fell, or of doing anything but trying to squeeze breath out of the breathless air. He thought his eyeballs would freeze. He searched indignantly for the sight of the Thorn and he couldn't understand why, if you were still inside the Thorn's horizon, an outcropping of red rock between you and it was the same as losing your cap. Black Jackson had never said a word about that, and neither had anyone else.

And now that damned Amsir was turning around.

II

The Amsir came in like fury; nothing in the world moved faster than one of its kind when it wanted to, and it wanted Honor White Jackson very soon. Its wings were flung up like a hook for each moon. The javelin was caught half-way up its shaft in the bereft little right hand that grew where the wing folded in mid-span, thumb and all three fingers making a bony fist. The Amsir was gathering speed as it ran, and its strides were growing longer and more urgent. It was almost as near to flying as it could get. The wings were folding into leathery cups for the thin air, and beating with a rattling thrum that raised wakes of dust beside its springing knees. Now White Jackson could see its full face – the delighted grin of its beak, the adrenalin-exaltation of its eyes. Its talons chuckled through the sand.

Jackson almost didn't care. He knew what was doing it to him – it was the cold and the choking that were making him all concerned with what went on inside. After Black had shown him the trick with the cap, he had thought for a long time about what had happened, and although several old women had told him it was a kind of sunstroke and perhaps impiety's simple reward, he had decided it was cold and lack of air. Sudden lack of air, that caught a man halfway through drawing a breath, and made his heart nearly stop with fear when an everyday useful action suddenly got him nothing but savage disappointment. So he could understand why his body wanted to double over on itself and his hands wanted to beat on his throat.

He had tried it out, getting one of the neighbour kids to hit him in the stomach, and it had been a feeling a lot like that – no cold or burning in the eyes and nose, but the same helplessness until the spasm had passed and he could begin to pant. He guessed if he thought about it long enough, he could reason it out about the cold, too, and the thing that made bloody cracks inside his nostrils. But the Amsir was coming on. White Jackson's stick and dart were lying away on the sand just as if he'd thrown them deliberately, and he was dying.

In spite of all reasoning, he would have been helpless if he hadn't already been planning to fake this same thing. He had no air – no air at all, and you can't go long with not trying to breathe if your lungs are empty, even if you know there's no air around you any more. But he had that other dart, and as he folded he got a hand up to his armpit with a very natural motion. The Amsir had reached him. It was up in the air, at the height of a great leap, bucket-winged, and he couldn't understand why it wasn't flirting those feet like knived clubs, ready to shred him up as it came down. He would have been. But it was up there, falling at him from a height equal to its own length. Now the ends of the wings were tucked down and back, and the hand with the javelin was bent towards him. The gleaming metal point was going to hit the sand right in front of his eyes, and the Amsir shrieked, 'Yield! Yield!'

White Jackson only looked as if he was all in a heap on his knees and chest, with his face in the sand and his eyes rolling up sideways. He had the dart in the hand under his body, point sticking out of the bottom of his fist for more punch. 'Yield, wet devil!' the Amsir shrieked while Jackson got his open hand on its ankle, which was hard like a cockroach.

There was a lot of noise and flurrying, and Jackson had the Amsir down on the sand at his level. He jerked himself across the body, which was hard the same way, and wrapped in flapping stuff, and he was himself wrapped in wings and fingernails, with his head down between his shoulders as far as it could go, with the beak carving him. It was *punch* through the side of the Amsir's throat and through the spinal cord, and a feeling like a stick coming back out through a jabbed parchment window, and then, for the life of him, *punch* through the Amsir's chest and into a bubble – one of the two big, main ones down inside there under all that horn and stuff – and hug the Amsir with all the affection in the world, mouth to the chest-hole, and breathe in, in.

The Amsir flopped and flailed, wings drumming, legs dancing, back arching, but White Jackson stayed with it. The stuff coming out of the Amsir was hot with life and puffed like hollering; when his lungs were bursting full of it, he had to lock his throat against its pressure. Nor could he move his head, for his mouth was the only stopper he had to save it with.

He didn't have to breathe; he didn't have to breathe. He could go on doing this forever. It was altogether different from being out of air. It was being free of having to breathe, like the Honors he had seen dancing around the Thorn with the bubbles from their fresh kills, dancing all night, hey, and gulping the Amsir-wind from the bubbles, but never breathing, just blowing out once in every while and mouthing the disembodied parts of Amsir chest again, laughing and whooping, like the dead were said to whoop with joy on Ariwol.

The Amsir's body was dying now. Its head might be dead, or it might live forever, but who could tell when nothing but skin connected it to the body and it had no wind to shriek with? The eyes were shut. There was something thick and clear seeping out between the closed lids and drying immediately to a crust. The wing tips were still quivering. But Honor White Jackson was a hell of a lot more alive than it was, and he picked it up. Staggering, and grinning as much as he could, he stumbled quickly to the javelin, his throwing stick, and his darts, the one far away and the other near to hand with fresh gouges up the short Amsir-bone shaft. He got them clustered into his hands with his arms around the Amsir, and then he wandered out from beyond the outcropping's shadow, still cold but not caring, riotous as a tickled child, happy on pure oxygen, with his first Amsir like the world's most awkward bucket of cool water on a blazing day.

CHAPTER TWO

I

When he had rested for a long time in the cool sand, watching nebulae and moons wheel by beautifully without his knowing what they were, he raised himself on one elbow and fondly stroked the Amsir's long thigh as it lay sprawled beside him. The hunting bird, wings folded, was only a dim, cover-letted shape, but Honor White Jackson could have named every curled rim of horn, every trailing pennon, every nail, every tooth. He unfastened the trimmed and harnessed water bubble at the small of his back, unstoppered it and raised it to the corpse before sipping from it himself.

As his neck and back muscles stretched, sand cracked free of his wounds and tickled him as it slipped down his spine. He grinned at the Amsir and patted its hip. He stood up, hooked and tied his gear into place, and oriented himself to the shadow of the treacherous rocks against the stars. Now that he knew where he was, he could go where he had been. And now that he was standing up, he could no longer hear approaching Amsir feet if there were any such in his vicinity. So he must go.

Stooping, he hefted his first conquest, eased it down across his shoulders, and began a steady, fast and comfortable walk, broken with pauses for listening closely and looking around as well as he could. Amsirs did not seem to move much at night – hence the Honor tactic of slipping away from the Thorn at dusk and picking a good ambush in the morning. But Honor White Jackson was more than ever in an iconoclastic mood, and he wondered why, if Amsirs did not haunt the darkness, so many of those ambushes failed.

His grip on his slain enemy was needlessly rigid; he knew that, but he did not slacken it. He could have carried him more easily if he'd relaxed, but he did not do that, either.

Nobody had told him Amsirs could talk. Nobody had told him they carried metal spears, or any weapon but claws, beak, and wing tips. He had been told – all children of the Thorn were told, even before most of them drifted into farming and a very few tried to be Honors – that the Amsirs would get them all if the Honors did not watch out. But he had not been told how they would be got.

He would not let his Amsir go. He thought it was because he had had to learn so much to get him.

9

The gritty, sharp-faced grains of sand made noises like gentle screams beneath his trudging feet. The Amsir rustled and rattled. It was full of ridges and pointed places that goaded White Jackson's flesh. The wings were full of joints along the main bone. It was conventional to speak of the hand as growing out of the elbow, but in fact there was a joint between shoulder and hand. From the hand down, the remainder of the wing was supported by what would have been a monstrously long little finger in a man. The ribs that stiffened the wing were of hard cartilage growing from the joints of that finger, of the wrist, and of the true elbow. It was like a broken awning. No matter how Jackson folded the wings and tried to tuck them into each other or pin them under the Amsir's hard chest, the nail at the end of that little finger on one wing tip or the other would flop down and swing teasingly across his ankles as he walked. He put the Amsir down, and trussed it with its own lace. Now it was a rolling bundle on his back, stiff and contrary. An edge on it found the deepest place Jackson was cut – a beak-furrow across the top of his shoulder, its edges stiff and gaping, crusted dry with sand, open down to the rubbery twist-surfaced muscle. Jackson was fascinated with the cut – it was unusual to be able to touch his own inside, to dwell on the thought that if he were not a victorious Honor he would be wincing pitifully. He understood perfectly well that all men would rather not put their flesh in peril. He knew from himself that even a small hurt could nag a man with reminders of why reluctance was wise. But he had noticed that it wasn't the size of the wound, it was his feeling for himself that made a man cry or not, and that was why he had become a Honor. Now he was a Honor who would have a white Amsir-beak scar across one broad shoulder; a Honor who put his Amsir down from time to time and stretched out on the sand beside him, ear to the grit, listening, with the stars and small moons giving him little to light his night by, and going back to the Thorn where he would live differently from before.

II

It was very nearly dawn when he caught the loom of the Thorn against the low stars. At the same time, he noticed a human step on the sand. He thought it might be Black Jackson coming towards him around the shoulder of a dune.

The way it was supposed to go, a Honor was discovered sitting beside his kill on the Sun side of the Thorn when the people got up in the morning. Successful Honors had been known to stay out on the edge of the desert all night, even when they didn't have to. People who accidentally came across a Honor before dawn pretended the man didn't have a carcase across his back. The idea was to create an effect that it had all just somehow happened, like a meteorite shower. The Honor was supposed to play it very cool too, and not notice that anybody was paying any attention to him – at least until there was enough of an audience for him to suddenly break out in a big happiness.

All that guff got more comment than it did attention. It seemed to be a hangover from some time maybe half a dozen generations back when some nut had whipped up a lot of pious ritual. The trouble with any of this stuff that was supposed to make life better and more interesting was that life plain never did get any better, and a man still had to find his own interests. After a while even a community of farmers could notice that. So White had half expected, especially on his first kill, that a live head like Black Jackson would be around to give him a personal handshake, or something, before discovering him all over again in the morning. To say nothing of the fact that just maybe, even though it wasn't like a Honor was supposed to be, Black might be worried.

The Amsir was suddenly beginning to get that characteristic smell Jackson had studied from boyhood. He pulled his cap off cautiously, and sure enough he was inside the comfortable radius, even if it was still very much like desert underfoot and breathing took a little work in the chill air. It was a lot farther out than the farmers cared to come. Farther in, there would be a good four dozen feet of weedy grass around the perimeter before the fields began. Winters, that strip shrank to something that was still wider than two dozen. For a part of the year, when the days were long, and the high sun beat down sharply on the glistening gridwork atop the Thorn, the strip might be close to five. The fields never crept out into it. A farmer, White Jackson had decided early, was anybody who would scheme nights to edge an inch off his neighbour's boundary but wouldn't reach for the title to all Ariwol if he'd ever cut his finger on an edge of parchment.

It *was* Black Jackson, tall and with muscle around his stomach and waist that White Jackson envied the hell out of, his short hair marking him as a made Honor. His bare face showed up in a paler patch against the dark contrast of his mouth and eye-pits. White stopped, but didn't let the Amsir slide to the ground, and stood easily.

'Welcome, Honor,' Black said. There was something unusually breathy in his big rumble of a voice, which, for many years, White had been thinking of as strong but friendly. Black came forward and touched White on the shoulder – the sound one, as it happened. Although it was still pretty nearly full dark, at this distance White could see the sober set of Black's broad mouth. This was beginning to relax as Black touched the Amsir. White had noticed long ago that people believed only what they touched – the rest they believed conditionally, on the testimony of people who claimed to have touched. 'You all right, kid?' Black touched him again.

'Uh-huh.'

'Well. Well, you got one, didn't you? And you're O.K.' Black was walking around him, displaying more and more of a species of relief, studying the Amsir, poking the carcase. 'Young one,' he said, appraising the callouses on the pads of its toes with a rasp of his thumb. He had been carrying his dart and stick. He put these down and looked at White. 'Give you a lot of trouble?'

White shrugged.

Black had found the javelin across White's shoulders under the Amsir's body. It slid easily into his hands.

'Come at you with this, did he?'

'Uh-huh.'

Black's glance came up fast from under his lowered brows. 'Say anything?'

'Nothing much.'

'What did he say?'

'Something about how he had me, I guess. I was busy. And he called me a wet devil.'

'Any more?'

'No. I killed him about then.'

Black bent to examine the Amsir's neck. He fingered the edges of the dart punch. 'Nice work. Caught him clean.'

'Well, that's how Black Jackson taught me.'

'Kid?'

'Yeah?'

'Feels good, doesn't it?' Black Jackson was grinning. Whether he knew it or not, he looked as if he was remembering, not as if he was enjoying now. And it looked as if he was working hard to remember. 'Going out there, getting your first one ... finding out just how tough you are?'

'You mean, it felt good for you when you did it.'

'Well, yeah. Yeah, kid. I remember how—'

'How tough am I, Black?'

'I don't follow you.'

'I mean, you're the one that's making happy about what I found out. Do you know what I found out?'

'Well, sure. I ... Look, I didn't hold it against anybody they didn't tell *me* Amsirs had spears and could talk.'

White Jackson had been thinking about this ever since the first screech out of the Amsir's mouth. But he had never seen his brother this way before. He studied Black as closely as he had studied the Amsir who had taken off from the blown ambush but hadn't really tried to outrun him. 'I figured maybe we could pass a few words about it.' He was thinking about a throwing spear that had at least as much range as a Honor's dart, and a Amsir who nevertheless hadn't pulled out to a safe distance and then picked him off – and also hadn't stood and fought until he was ready.

'Point is, you didn't need to be told, did you? Got him anyhow, right?' Black had the javelin head-down in the sand beside his foot, and was leaning on it. That way, it looked like a stick of some kind and not much of a weapon. 'And I told you they were tricky. Remember?' he said as an afterthought.

'Uh-huh.' He held tighter to his Amsir. He believed this was because he had a stupid feeling Black might try to take it away. He believed he had the stupid feeling because he had suddenly realized Black wasn't going to give the spear back. He waited for Black to say something. It was Black who obviously knew what was going to happen here next.

'Well, ain't it something to go out against something that's that tough, and come back carrying it?'

'It's something.'

Black was wrapping and unwrapping his thick fingers around the javelin's shaft. The sharp metal head gritted down, sinking deeper. 'It gives you the feel of being a man, right?'

'It gives me the feeling of something. I was a man before I went out there.'

Black tipped him lightly, awkwardly with his clenched fist, this time on his bad shoulder. He couldn't see it was bad. 'You always were tough. Never gave an inch. You'd cut me down just as soon as you would one of those kids you used to bloody up. If I wasn't your brother, I mean … And bigger, I guess.'

This was not the view White had had of himself through his brother's eyes. And this wasn't the talk he had expected. It was teaching him a lot more about Black than it was about Amsir-honning, and he didn't want to be taught any more about his brother. He had been perfectly satisfied with what he had believed up to now.

'Black, it's getting on to first light,' White said softly. 'I have to go sit by the Thorn. Come mid-morning, the Eld Honor's got to look over my Amsir, see it's real, call me a Honor, chop my hair, name a winning man to shave me; that'd be you, I guess. Be a busy day for both of us. Why don't we just call me a made Honor for now and let me pick up any other tricks of the trade as I go along?'

A foot of the javelin's length was buried in the ground. It occurred to White that Black only had a third of a dozen feet to go before he had it out of sight entirely. 'No, look – kid, it could of been somebody else waiting here to meet you. We all get met the first time. It's – hell, you can see it's necessary. But it could have been Red Filson or Black Harrison or one of those other guys that hang around the Eld a lot. It didn't have to be me. But I trained you – same way I was trained; we all get trained the same way – when you get back, you see the good in tha—'

'If you get back.'

'*You?* Hell, I knew *you'd* get back!'

'Sure.'

'Well, I figured you had a good chance.' Black twisted the javelin; White couldn't decide whether he was really trying to bury it right here or whether he was so wrapped up in his words that he wasn't even thinking about his hands. A trait like that could get a Honor killed. White had to assume it was rare. '*Good* chance,' Black said stubbornly.

'All right,' White said, feeling the cracks in his lips where the edges of the Amsir's chest wound had cut them.

'Listen, kid, there's a lot more to growing up besides getting your hair chopped!' White noticed that Black was getting angry in the same way as when somebody refused to believe it about the caps. 'You think we're gonna let a bunch of punk kids – even Honor kids – run around tellin' the farmers all about what it takes to be a Honor? You think those farmers don't all believe *they* could be Honors if they could spare the time? You think it don't make a difference to a Honor, taking a piece of a farmer's loaf, to *know* he couldn't be?'

'Because he's a Honor who got back from his first time.'

'That's right. Now you're getting it. It ain't what you're taught – it's what you *are* that makes a Honor!' Black looked proudly across at his brother, at a man whom he could consider a man like himself. He jerked the spear out of the ground and brandished it. 'Because you went up against *this*.'

That, and talk from animals, and caps that didn't work, and brothers who spent years getting you ready for the night they lurked to check you out on the way back in. White Jackson looked at this powerful simpleton who had raised him. He didn't know whether he was supposed to swallow this line because he was dumb enough to believe it or because Black was dumb enough to believe it. Either way, Black was not the man White had thought him, and in that case what brains did White have to brag about?

'All right. I've got it.'

Black looked at him sidelong in the growing greyness. 'You sure, kid?' He was begging for the right answers. He was being very gruff and tough about it, but he was begging. White guessed that in his own simple way Black loved him and was sweating out the payoff for the years in which he had prepared the greatest gift he knew to give. 'I mean you're not going to say anything different, are you? I want you to be sure in your own mind you're not going to pop off to the people until you've had a chance to talk to the Eld Honor about it. Lots of times, the Eld Honor can explain it all in a minute or two. Explain it a hell of a lot better than *I* can, that's for sure,' he realized.

White shook his head. 'I'm going to play it the way every new Honor plays it. I'm going to tell a story about ambushing him and having a hell of a fight and winning out in the end, and that's all.'

'You sure?'

'You're damned right I'm sure.'

14

Black began to sigh with relief, but White was mad at him now, and wasn't going to let him off the hook.

'Now you tell the Eld Honor something for me. You tell him I want to know about a metal spear even a Amsir can throw farther than I can flip a dart. Hell, a human could throw it eight dozen yards into an eye, and just how many of 'em do we have cached away? I want to know why my hat didn't work when I was behind a rock. I want to know about Amsirs that talk. You tell him for me I think he's got rotten brains for letting a brother come out to talk to me. You're so shook up I *could* take you – even if I wasn't expecting you to try for me.' He finished slowly: 'You got that last part all sorted out, Black? I do. I got it sorted out fine about a Honor out here with weapons but no hat. There's only a couple of things a Honor could kill out here with that rig. One of them's poor slob Honors tryin' to crawl back with spearholes in 'em that couldn't be explained, and the other one's young Honors that won't shut up about what kind of people we're sharin' Creation with. On the short end of the share. Now you just go take that spear and put it wherever all the other spears are; I'm not gonna go around upsetting the Honor racket, especially now I made my way into it, but don't you mess me around until I'm over this.'

He swung away and his Amsir rattled on his shoulders, smelling like hell. He realized he was simple for giving Black so many excuses to just give that spear a little toss in the name of whatever Black thought was decent. But whenever White got mad and didn't show it, he was always crying sick inside for days. He figured if he just kept walking away from his brother who loved him, he had an even chance of getting off.

CHAPTER THREE

I

It was warm and pleasant in the sun. He sat cross-legged with his back against the warm black-and-brown flank of the Thorn. His eyes were slitted into the sunrise, and he was only a little bit conscious of the people filtering out of the low cement dwellings that ringed the Thorn, beyond the running track.

The running track made a clear space of bare dirt a couple of dozen yards wide around the Thorn, and was a dozen times a dozen dozen yards long from start to start. Red Filson, long-legged and looking like he knew everything about anything – from the scar that lifted his mouth and the corner of his left eye – was running a group of young Honor-types around it. As they went by White Jackson, the sound of bare feet thudding first in his right ear and then in his left, the young ones rolled their eyes sidewards at the spread-winged Amsir sprawled beside him.

Filson, sun-bleached lank blond hair all spiky with sweat, just grinned his grinless grin and kept eating up ground with his feet, with that smooth, scissoring motion that had run down a lot of things. One of the things had been Black Olson, who had been Black and White Jackson's father. Still was their father, White supposed, but was dead, run down with his throwing arm stabbed through and his eyes blinded from a cut across the brows.

Truth to tell, White hadn't seen an awful lot of the old man after his naming day. It seemed like he'd no sooner found out Dad's first name was Jack than he was part of a Honor candidate class like this class of Filson's. White was supposed to be mojoed by the worry that between a running father and a farmer mother no Jackson could stand up with Red Filson. White wasn't ready to swear what went on in Black Jackson's mind, with all its side steps, but as for White, he had noticed long ago he wasn't either his mother or his father. He sat smiling faintly into the Sun, his arms dangling over his thighs. The class went on by in its circuit, the young ones sweating and grunting, Red sweating and grinning. White was thinking that being strung out mad about being mojoed would be a handy excuse if he ever decided there was something he didn't want to share with Honor Red Filson.

The sun did feel good. Now that he was sitting down and didn't have to do anything but wait for other people to do things, White could let himself feel sleepy. And he was where he had spent a lot of time wanting to be. Up against the Thorn, feeling its pitted warm surface comfortably rough against his back, and the sweetish scent of the Amsir rising around him. He could turn loose of things he had held tight for a long time. He gazed through his lashes at the half-focused sight of the green fields and orchards beyond the houses, with the shadows of gathering people moving across the corners of his eyes.

Listening to them talk to each other – like a cross between things crackling far away and a mumble like the sound of whatever went on inside the Thorn – a man felt as good as a baby in his crib. His back was safe, and nobody in front could do anything to him right now. A lot of them would never dare to do anything anytime from now on, just because he had killed something and would be short-haired. The rest of them would think long and hard about messing around a Honor's goods or women. The idea was, Honors looked out for each other. It worked out they did look out for each other, when it was between Honor and farmer, so from now on there wouldn't be a farmer or even a Honor-type who would buck him to his face. And damned few who would go for his back, even when they had a good chance.

He had really messed up that Amsir, too. Given him one hell of a shock, with all the plans of that horned brain notching into each other, and the wet devil lying there helpless, and all of a sud—

What was it like to die? White wondered. Get cut off like that, in the mid-dle of being alive, in the middle of thinking you had it made. Did you have time to know you were a chump? And just suppose there was an Ariwol. Suppose you were a human and a Amsir had done that to you, and you turned up among the happy dead with all of that chumpiness slopping around inside you. Yeah, sure, everybody laughing and singing, feast going on all the time, but man, the ones who hadn't died chumpy would have an extra laugh on you, and all the chumps would try to buddy up. Thing to do was not go to Ariwol being a chump. But that was a tricky idea to live up to, because sure as there was sand in Creation that Amsir hadn't thought he was being a chump, he had thought he was on top right up to *punch*!

Well, how could the Amsir know White Jackson had watched the Honors around the Thorn with their fresh bubbles? How could he know White Jack-son would remember that, would trust that, wouldn't try to breathe what couldn't be breathed, would wait for what his enemy had to give him? Was it being a chump to be happy when your plan worked out? It was, White Jack-son decided, when you didn't know all about what it was having to work against. And how do you know all about what's inside a head?

There were more people gathering around him. Just standing there, with their farmer tools in their hands, the women with their water buckets, their kids … farmers not going out, women not lining up at the taps in the side of the Thorn, kids playing Honor behind the crowd, hanging on to grownup legs up front.

What do they know? White Jackson thought to himself, watching the Sun, smelling his Amsir, letting himself notice his shoulder and his other cuts just enough to remind himself. All they see is me and a dead one. No – all they see is the outsides of the two of us. What do they know about that we found out? And if they had been there and watched us do it, would they know any more? Touch me – any one of you, touch me or touch him, and you'll find out the last thing there is. How's about it, you muckers – anybody want to ride to Ariwol on the end of a dart this morning?

Filson and his candidates came around the Thorn again, Filson in front now, not running sweat but with a nice all-over bead worked up, the candidates pale as lace and soaking wet, their eyes blind. They were one less – somebody had turned farmer after all, lying sucking wind somewhere around the curve of the Thorn with dirt in his Mouth and water in his eyes. White Jackson thought bout that scar on Filson there; Red had come back from his first hon with that on him. Filson knew. White wanted to grin at him as he went by. But he wouldn't have known if he was really getting an answer. He'd have had to figure out what was inside that head. And, hell, Black Olson hadn't been able to figure that, had he? Welcome to Ariwol, Olson.

Petra Jovans came walking up to the edge of the crowd, making a little space around herself, as usual, and stood there with her hands folded in front of her abdomen, just looking at him with all of that quiet in her eyes. What do you know? White Jackson thought, testing it on her, and then he wished he knew the things she knew; how to look at somebody without speaking and say, Not now ... but someday for sure. Keep your hands off, but eyes are all right. Yes, I'm going to be damned good for you when you're what I expect.

He wondered whether it would really be with her that he first exercised some of his new rights as Honor Secon Black Jackson. Well, anyway, with somebody. Then sooner or later a son would be old enough to name, and people would learn his own name was Jim. Then someday he'd leave off honning and be Honor Gray Jackson, and maybe there'd be a Honor Jimson or a farmer named Jim Petras to scatter his bones and maybe not. Somebody'd scatter 'em, that was sure, because whether they did it out of grief or anything else they felt, the idea was to make damn sure that the old man was dead. Sitting there, looking at it that way, White Jackson could see that if he was lucky enough to have all of this happen without ugly interruptions out in the desert, it was still a short damn list of important things left to have happen in his life.

It came to him he'd spent a lot of years running around the Thorn and pitching darts to come to the moment he realized it was all downhill from here on. But it *was* all downhill, and when he thought of all the people he'd seen follow that road, and the way they did it because they'd all heard the elders telling them and telling them how to do it, White Jackson realized that the track to Ariwol was beaten many times as hard as the track around the Thorn.

What do you know? he thought to all the people. I could die sitting here, all punched out inside like Red Thompson was that time last year. The first anybody knew was when the Eld Honor touched him and he fell over just as stiff as his Amsir. I could be doing that, and when you found out you'd say, Oh hell, what a shame. But when I get up in a minute you'll make all kinds of noises except that. And just the same I'm dying. I wish there was a puddle of blood under *me*. You'd say the right thing then. What *do* you know?

Petra had drifted into the crowd in such a way that she was right in his line of vision. Because he was thinking that she knew, if anybody knew, that he was as dead this minute as the farmers had been from birth, he winked at her. He realized he was getting a little crazy, but it seemed reasonable to get that way when you were dying and you'd been fighting animals that were people inside and had a fine brother like Black who was too simple to either beg your pardon or kill you and get it over.

White Jackson was wondering where the failed Honors' graveyard was, out there beyond the fields, when the Eld Honor came through the crowd and touched him on the shoulder.

'Arise, Honor – you are home with your kill!' the old man said in a loud voice. He was all knobs and bones under his brown shrunken skin. His cheeks were in deep where his teeth had been, and his eyes were pouched. If he had had wings, he would have been fair game. 'You all right, son?' he asked in a low voice.

White could see Black hanging off around the edge of the crowd with a lot of other Honors. 'Black talk to you?' he said to the old man without moving his lips. It wasn't all that unusual to see Honors carrying their weapons around the Thorn, but there were quite a few of them doing that. White would have been happier if on this particular day he didn't see so much sun on so many dartheads.

'Yes.' For the crowd the Eld Honor said, 'The people are waiting to praise you.' His hand on White's shoulder had a lot of knuckles in it. His voice changed again. 'What do you think of them?'

White looked frankly and fully into the old man's eyes. 'As near to what you think as makes no difference.'

'Hmm. Was Black right in passing you?' the Eld Honor asked, which surprised the daylights out of White. But the rheumy old eyes were tight on his. Maybe the old man expected he could tell a liar that way. Maybe he could.

'As far as you and me go, he was right.' That might not have been quite what the Eld Honor had been expecting, either, but it was what White had for him. It was more than what White had intended to give him. Some of that stuff they told kids might really work – always give the Eld a straight answer, never do anybody dirt, that kind of thing. Parts of it seemed to stick better than others.

They were blowing time. The Eld Honor's mouth was working at the corners, and he was looking at White the way a farmer looked at his new wife's first loaf. But they couldn't keep testing each other out here forever. The pressure on the Eld was a lot worse than it was on White, as far as White could see. Seeing it suddenly as he did, he relaxed inside as happily as ever a man did when he unstoppered a bubble on a hot day and felt the cool water going all the way in to the pit of his stomach. He was ready to go on this way forever. The old man had to move, he didn't; the old man was the one who would have to think up the story if he had White killed now. And White was saying things that didn't really give an excuse. They were just aggravating.

'So you think we're equals,' the Eld said. 'You think you've lived one day longer and all of a sudden even your brother and his friends are dumb, and only the Eld is fit for a man like you to be frank with. Must be a happy day when a young man picks his peer from the decrepit.' It was hard to tell when a mouth like that was smiling faintly. 'Well, all right – you'll get your badges and tokens, and we'll talk afterwards.' The old man raised his voice. 'See here!' he cried. 'A man sits with his kill!'

That, of course, was the signal for a lot of general roaring and shouting and people pushing forward. There were things to do, and the Eld Honor pointed out people to do them – Black Jackson would do the shaving – and White Jackson found that becoming a made Honor meant you had to shake hands with people like Filson, and get punched around by a bunch of farmers who considered that touching you was the price of admission for standing around and staring at a dead Amsir, which was what they all went off and did as soon as they were through assuring themselves that White Jackson was real. 'Keep it short,' the Eld Honor said, as he led White Jackson forward to where the shaving bowl was waiting.

'Uh-huh,' White Jackson said, looking back over his shoulder. Black Harrison and Red Filson were guarding his Amsir. You still couldn't tell whether Filson was grinning, but you could tell about Harrison, and he was.

So his hair was chopped short and he was shaved by his brother's steady hand, and they called him Honor Secon Jackson to the crowd, and the crowd grinned and laughed. Secon Jackson stood there with his head chilly and thought: Oh, you people, you dumb, happy people! You're killing me.

CHAPTER FOUR

I

'Well, ah, Secon, you certainly brought back one with flesh on him,' said Mowery Sals, who was a grainy-necked farmer already. There was a time when Boy Jackson and Boy Samson, who was Mowery now, had been playmates. That was just about the same time Dorrie Olsons had been widowed and gone to be Dorrie Filsons. Boy Samson had remarked on it to Jackson, and that had lost him his name right there; you don't keep up with the other apprentice Honors when your ribs are fresh broken.

But here he was now, with his eyes big and his face sweating for the chance to touch a Honor, and there seemed to be no malice in him at all.

The idea was, there'd be a feast around the Thorn this evening, an Amsir-butchering, and Secon Jackson was now supposed to pick the people who'd eat his bird and get what parts. He was supposed to pick out people who'd been especially nice or good to him in his younger life. Leaving the feast to wait between noon and dark gave people he'd left out a chance to curry favour. He didn't know whether that last part was on purpose or not, but he'd seen a lot of Honors turn up a lot of bright new friends and riches on the afternoon of Shaving Day.

Well, Secon's father was a long time dead, and his mother had done what she did with Red Filson, and his brother had done his best to raise him, when he had time, but then there was that business this morning. He didn't have any kindly uncles or aunts, not being a farmer bred, and he didn't have any friends.

He might have had some friends this morning, but they were all going to have to go out into that desert pretty soon themselves, and he didn't want them around to listen to a pack of lies this evening. So here everybody was, looking at him expectantly, and the Eld Honor shuffling off from the edge of the crowd to go inside the Thorn where the Honors lived, and Secon didn't have a thing to say.

'Look,' he said, looking around at them, thinking he could try saying Petra Jovans' name and see how they liked having him pick her out in front of everybody. 'I got to go do something about this,' he said, pointing to the wound on his shoulder. 'I'll be seein' my friends durin' this day.' He pushed his way past Mowery, and his brother, and a disappointed sound from the people. He heard some talk about how he was auctioning off the Amsir to the highest bidders, and he didn't give a damn about that because he was expecting it. His brother pushed up next to him and walked beside him.

'Hey, that ain't no way to do!' Black Jackson said.

'If I did what I oughta do, you'd have holes in you,' Secon Jackson said and kept walking.

He went into the Thorn through the oval doorway as if he'd been doing it all his life. They taught you that; you memorized the whole layout, drawing it in the dirt with a stick, so you'd know where the Eld Honor was, and you'd know where the armoury was, and the doctor, and where you would sleep when you came back from the desert after killing your animal.

It was so the farmers would think a species of great enlightenment had fallen on you, and the kids tagging along could crane their necks and see how sure you were. They stopped short at the door, of course, because they knew anybody that wasn't a Honor would sicken and die right away if he stepped across the high threshold. White Jackson had got through the door and peeked up a couple of three inside corridors while he was a kid. He hadn't sickened and died. But he'd been smart enough not to do it on a dare, or when anybody was watching, and he'd had the idea well in mind that if he was caught he might wish he could sicken and die. Besides, all he'd learned was that the inside of the Thorn was just as much metal as the outside, except it was painted.

There was a lot of thumping and humming inside the Thorn; the metal floor shook under his feet. There were great big parts to the Thorn's inside layout that he hadn't been taught. He figured that was because those were places where the machinery was. Something had to be giving power to the ploughs. Something had to be making the water that came out of the taps, and that ran out into the fields to make the crops grow. He didn't believe that the dead in Ariwol would bother to take time out from the feasting to do all that by magic. If they could, what was there a Thorn for in the first place?

Now he had to figure the Thorn ran the hats too, and, that being the way it was, he was less ready than ever to believe in magic from something that could be stopped by a hunk of rock. Maybe they'd let him get a look at some of those mechanical insides, if he was a good boy and played along. He wondered if he could ever work things around to where they'd let him fool with it, though, and what was the good of machinery you couldn't fool with? So what was the good of playing along? And besides, Petra Jovans hadn't tried to talk to him at all while he was on his way from the shaving bowl to the door to the Thorn, and so he was pretty mad about everything as he found the Eld Honor's door and stepped inside.

'You don't knock?' the Eld Honor said from behind the table where he was sitting.

'You weren't expecting me?' Honor Secon Jackson said.

The Eld Honor grinned – there wasn't any doubt about it this time; he grinned as big as Secon Jackson had ever seen on anyone, and in some way that scared him.

'Sit down, Honor,' the Eld said, pushing a chair out to him. 'I think there's a way we can get along pretty well.'

The chair was exactly the kind of thing that everybody had in his house, except this one hadn't been used for so many years by so many people. Its wheels still rolled. Secon Jackson took it, nudged it around to where the desk was clearly between him and the Eld Honor, and sat down. 'All right. I wouldn't mind.'

'I wouldn't mind, either, if I were you,' the Eld Honor said. 'Let's not mistake the situation, Honor Secon Jackson. I've been alive a long time, and there was a day for me too when I went out in the desert and got my little surprise. Every Honor you see walking around this place – every Honor who's ever told you anything about honning and Amsirs – has gone out and had the same surprise. You don't hear any of them complaining. And you don't see me having any trouble running things. Think about that. Don't do anything that looks good to you. Whatever it is I've already thought of it.'

Secon Jackson studied him the same way he always studied things. The grin was a lot less, now, but it was still there. Secon Jackson tried to think what he'd be thinking if he had that grin; that didn't often do much good, but this time it worked. It had the feel of truth all over it. The old man was thinking what a fool Secon Jackson would make of himself, and how easy he'd be to handle, if he went ahead and did what looked like a perfectly sensible thing to him. All right, Secon Jackson thought, then I won't do it, and the next move is yours.

'So you're not going to get anything special out of me just for having done what every other live Honor in this place has done.'

I knew that a minute ago, Secon Jackson said to himself, and then he realized that the old man could have that grin and still be making a fool of himself. He knew Secon Jackson was fast, but he didn't believe how fast. There's more Amsir to you than just your looks, old man, Secon Jackson thought, feeling better, and how would you like to go up to Ariwol right now and find out about being chumpy?

'Don't plan to kill me now,' the Eld said carelessly. 'I'll die soon enough, and then you can have it all.'

II

It was like having extra distance put between him and his eyes and ears. Secon Jackson leaned back in his chair and said, 'I can.'

'Yes, you can. But I have to tell you how, and you have to learn how, and you have to learn how to make it stick.'

'All right,' said Secon Jackson, coming back to himself, 'start in on your part of that.'

The Eld Honor looked amused. 'Well, I can't give it all to you in one day.'

'I didn't expect you could, but start in.'

'All right. Look – things are very simple here. We tell the people a lot of garbage to make it look tricky, but it's simple. We live around the Thorn, here, and out beyond the Thorn is a desert with Amsirs on it. We can grow crops, and we can get some meat and some tool-stuff from honning the Amsirs. Now that's all there is to the world. The sun comes up, the sun goes down. There's summer, there's winter. There's just so much land, and there are just so many hats to give to the Honors. Now, that's all got to be managed. If we let the farmers alone, they'd do whatever was easiest, and they'd sit around having babies and planting whatever came into their heads, and there might be enough food or there might not. And even if there was enough food – which I don't think the farmers could see to – everybody'd live exactly the same. Would you like that, Honor?' The old eyes were twinkling.

'You don't need an answer for that. Go on.'

'All right, I don't need an answer. Now all you can see is the top of the system. You see the way we've been kidding the farmers, and you see the things we do to make the farmers think we're something special. That way, when we need something to keep this place running, we can have it. When we see a woman we want we can have her. Now let's talk about women. What's a woman for – besides making jokes?'

'Cooking, cleaning, keeping house,' Secon Jackson said.

The Eld Honor was shaking his head, which didn't surprise Jackson because you don't ask questions if you don't already know a tricky answer. 'No,' the Eld Honor said wisely, 'a woman is for being better than your mother, so you can have sons who are better than you. Remember that. It's the same way about everything else. When you take a farmer's loaf of bread, and you eat that bread, the reason for that bread is to make you better – to keep you strong, and to make you a better Honor. And if one farmer's woman's bread is better than another's, then you go back to that place for your bread. Even if you never take that woman – and she might be old and ugly. But she might have a daughter, and you can take that daughter. And even if she doesn't have a daughter, you're still better and stronger, from the better bread, and you can take a better woman than you could have otherwise. And even if you don't take her, but you just use her, and her kid turns out to be a farmer, he's going to be a better farmer than he would have been, 'cause we already know his mother's man wasn't good enough to stop you.'

'So we're always making it better, no matter what we do,' Secon Jackson said. It occurred to him that it was a pretty nice world where a Honor could do any damn thing that struck his fancy, and it always made things better. 'Now explain about Amsirs that carry spears and talk.'

'We'll get to that, I promise you,' the Eld Honor said. 'The reason we don't ever take a chance of anybody's finding out until he becomes a Black Honor is the same reason we don't spell any of this out where the farmers can hear it.' The Eld Honor leaned forward earnestly. 'Now this is important, boy. If you can understand and use this, there will be a reason for you to be somebody special, even among Honors.'

The Eld gestured negligently. 'Hell, I know most of the boys who carry weapons around here are just farmers with a different kind of plough. Instead of knowing how to thresh wheat, they know how to jump Amsirs, and as long as they know that, they figure it makes them special enough, and that's all the thinking they'll ever have to do. No, boy—' The Eld pointed a dried old skinny finger at him. '*You* have to be like *us* – you have to have eyes in your head, and ears, and something in between them. You know that much as well as I do. What I know a lot better than you is how.

'There's a whole bunch of people around here and every one of them thinks he's someday going to go to Ariwol the same as everybody else, and live high without working. You let him hold on to that, because it makes him work while he's here, all right. You let him be a farmer, or a Honor, but you let him keep thinking about Ariwol, where *his* kind of people are on top for sure. But you make sure he knows he's a farmer, or a Honor, because then he knows who he is, and he knows what's expected of him while he's here.

'If he knows what's expected of him, then he'll do what's expected. He won't start snooping around in the middle of the night, or in a bunch in the middle of the day, and pull the props right out from under everything that's being done for him. How many of *us* do you think there are in any generation? It's a damn small number, boy. What all of the farmers and most of the Honors aren't ever going to admit to themselves is, if it wasn't for us they'd all be dead. They'd be dead from ruining the land, or they'd be dead from eating wrong, or they'd be dead because they'd be messing around inside here, and they'd kill the Thorn.'

The Eld studied Secon Jackson's face. 'Now have you ever heard of anybody wanting to get into the Thorn that wasn't entitled to? But do you see any guards around? Have you ever heard of a farmer suddenly saying "I'm gonna go out and hon Amsirs?" Have you ever heard of a farmer saying "I want more water"? And let me ask you: if we had guards out front, wouldn't the farmers say "I wonder what they're guarding. And if it needs guards, maybe all I have to do to understand it is knock somebody out of my way"? Have you ever thought what would happen if we said to the farmers: "You can't go Amsir-honning." Wouldn't they stop to wonder "Well, hell, that's just a rule they're making up"? No, boy, you don't do that, or you have the whole mess of it milling around and figuring that all it has to do is break a few rules and it can have whatever it wants. You show it an open doorway, and you say to it

"That's for Honors". You send people out into the desert, and a lot of them don't come back. You don't have to tell the farmers that's just for Honors – not doing it that way, you don't. They can see for themselves.

'That's the way you run things, boy. And I'll tell you something else – I'll bet you there are farmers who have gone out into the desert, and I'll bet you there are people who have come through that front doorway. But they didn't tell anybody they were going to do it. And they either got all the way out into the desert, and died, or they came back from the edge of the desert, and they hadn't seen a Amsir, and they didn't tell anybody about it. I don't think any of them got very far. Not because they died, but because they knew from every-thing around them since they were kids that they should be ashamed. And even if they saw a Amsir, or even if somebody came in here and saw things, he wouldn't know what they meant because nobody ever told him. And after a while he'd just go away again. And if he didn't sicken and die, he wouldn't tell anybody about that, either, because anybody he told just might kill him to correct the oversight. Nobody loves a loner, boy— 'cause nobody knows who he is.'

Secon Jackson looked back into the old man's tightly squeezed eyes. 'Unless he's on top.'

The old man smiled and nodded. 'That's the idea.'

'All right,' Jackson said. 'Now, besides the fact that you want some of your young Honors to get killed, how come I didn't get told that Amsirs could talk and had spears?'

'Well, you would have started making yourself a shield and a long spear before you went out there,' the Eld Honor said. 'And if we had told somebody like your brother before *he* went out, he just would have had to tell some-body, to show he knew something nobody else did. Either way, it would have got the farmers pretty well worked up. Listen, boy – what did the Amsir say to you?'

'He said "Yield".'

The Eld was already nodding – it was another one of those questions he knew the answer to. 'Exactly. He didn't want to kill you – you'd have to be a lucky damn fool not to have known that almost from the start and still be alive, and you're not a damn fool. I'm not so sure you're lucky, either. Boy, there is more to the world than anybody knows—'

'I know that. Figured it out all by myself,' said Honor Secon Black Jackson, who was tired of being called 'boy'.

'Did you? And did you figure out what it means? Have you had time since it happened to do the same thinking that the farmers would do if they knew about it, and had time enough to mull it over? Listen, boy, in this world – in this *real* world that's got to be a lot bigger than just the Thorn and the desert – there's something that doesn't want to kill Honors. There's something that wants to take them away, instead. He wanted you to be his prisoner. He and every other Amsir that has let himself be ambushed out there was willing to take the chance of dying because he was playing out some plan, while all the Honor wanted to do was kill him.

'Something out there wants Honors. Maybe it just wants to eat them alive, in comfort someplace, out of the desert. I don't know – nobody does. But whatever it is, the way it looks is there's a world big enough so that Honors aren't even farmers to it – they're a crop. And how long do you think we could run this place around here if the farmers knew that was what we were?'

Secon Jackson sat there waiting for more, but the Eld was sitting back in his chair, and looking at him as if he'd expected him to be knocked over. For a minute there, Jackson couldn't believe it. The Eld had told him all this, just to make a point that Jackson had figured out for himself last night in the long walk home. All this aggravation, all this listening to an old man talk, when he could have been doing something useful, and here was the big pack the old man had unwrapped for him, and there was nothing in it – nothing – that wasn't second-hand.

You old man, he thought, you've been wasting our time. He said: 'So you figure I'm smart enough. If I learn how to keep people in line without shovin', one of these days I'll get to be the Eld Honor?'

'You could. You've got the best chance of anybody.' The old man looked at him steadily, with his lie-detecting stare. 'But you're going to have to earn it. It's a hard world, boy, you can see it's harder than you ever figured. Nothing comes easy, not even for one of us.'

'One of us smart ones,' Honor Secon Jackson said.

'One of us smart ones,' the old man agreed. 'No sense kidding yourself about that – you look at yourself any other way, and you're licked before you start.'

'You seen many smart ones in your time?'

'Some.'

'Some walking around out there now, figuring they're gonna be the Eld. Each one of them, off by himself inside his own head, figuring it that way?'

The old man smiled. 'Some. Worry you?'

Jackson shook his head. 'No.'

Now the old man grinned again. It was almost as if he were getting ready to yell 'Yield! Yield!' He said: 'Got to be that way, boy. Got to have it out – got to fight. That's what makes things better; the hammering and the stabbing. It's what gives everything its shape; it's what gouges out the weak places. Boy, this place has *got* to be made better. It has got to stand up to some day when the Amsirs figure a way to get closer to the Thorn. It has got to be that way so we toughen up enough to live here if the Thorn ever goes.' The old man stood up sharply and lightly kicked the metal wall behind him. The flat of his bony old palm spatted against it. 'This is just another damn *tool*, boy! It's got to wear out someday. Everything willing, it will be the people like *us* who have made the people in this place hard enough to do without it!' The Eld's eyes were shining. He was shaking. 'Boy, you've got to see!'

'See ahead. See what's gonna happen,' Jackson said.

'That's right! That's what makes *us*!'

I see, Honor Secon Black Jackson thought. I see what's ahead. I could be like you. 'Funny,' he said.

'What's funny?'

'I figured, maybe you'd give me something special when you saw I wasn't like the others,' Jackson said.

'I knew you weren't like the others before you ever went out there. Don't you think I would have been disappointed and mad if you hadn't come back? And I *have* given you something special – I've given you knowledge.'

'Yeah, well, that what I had in mind,' Jackson said. He stood up, reaching across his chest to touch his shoulder again. 'I better go see about this. Bad time to heal up crippled, now.'

III

He went down to the doctor's room. The doctor was a Grey Honor who'd got a long, twisty slash across his stomach a long time ago. He walked a little bent over all the time, and his mouth was always tight. But as long as he could doctor, the Eld would see he got food and anything else a full Honor was entitled to. When Jackson walked in, he grunted and looked at him with deep eyes: 'Your first, eh?'

'Got off cheap. Considering.'

'Any way you can get off at all, Honor. Any way. Nothing hurts more than not being able to hurt any longer.'

'You think so?' It looked like the idea was, the doctor had a little set line he gave you; buck you up a little, buck him up a little. Well, a Honor who didn't hon needed bucking up.

'Always here to patch you up the best we can, Honor,' the doctor said, then swabbed out the gash with a clean rag dipped in boiling water and held in a pair of bone tongs.

''Preciate it, Doc,' Jackson said, and left after the doctor had taken a couple of stitches.

He stopped off outside the Thorn, where Harrison and Filson were still guarding his Amsir, like they were supposed to. The way of it was, when a Honor brought in his bird, the Eld picked the hardest men of the Thorn to stand guard over it. The way people changed their ideas of who was the hardest man, was when a Honor decided he could tell somebody like Harrison or Filson he would guard his own bird.

Jackson looked at one, then he looked at the other. Filson grinned at him. Or maybe he didn't. 'Your mother'll be proud of you today.' The thing was, you couldn't tell from his face how he meant it.

'I guess,' Jackson said. 'You two Honors be at my feast tonight, huh?' He nodded down at the Amsir. 'Can have any part of him you want,' he said, ''cept I don't suppose you better want the same part, huh?' He walked away, and they being guards appointed by the Eld couldn't come after him if they wanted to. He didn't stop to look back at his Amsir either. It was starting to smell pretty good, which some people considered a delicacy, but he figured this particular one had given him all it could. A lot more than it had been ready to, and he figured the credit was his, not the Amsir's.

There were all kinds of people walking around, farmer women going about their chores, and kids, and the usual sort of traffic. To anybody who looked at him, and looked like he might want to talk, Jackson just said, 'You wanna come to my feast? Come ahead.' And kept walking towards the cement hut that he had been living in most of his life alone.

Inside, it was just one room, with a pad in the corner. There were bone pegs in the walls with pieces of kit hanging on them – some of it was just kid stuff; stuff he'd made when he was just learning how to make his own tools. Play stuff. Some of it was pretty useful, but he'd gone out with his best gear, and that was still either on him or in his hand. He sat down cross-legged in the corner where he usually worked, with the featureless light coming in through the parchment window he'd stretched across the frame, where maybe there'd been some other kind of lookout when the hut was first created, and somebody'd scoffed it, or maybe when the world was made whoever made it forgot to make a window.

He reset his dartheads with fresh Amsir-hide glue from the little pot he kept bubbling in a corner. He looked around. He walked over to the big blank wall opposite the window. The cement was all sooted and streaked up where he'd practised pictures and rubbed them out and practised them again, until he was pretty well satisfied.

There were things there that he'd made, oh, half, three-quarters of a dozen years ago. The wall was pretty well taken up with this kind of thing. There were pictures of kids running, and yelling, and jumping up and down. There were pictures of the houses, and the Thorn, and a few pictures of farmers walking along behind their ploughs with the desert on beyond them. There was something that looked a lot like a black blur of soot, and was supposed to be the Thorn up against the stars at night, and didn't look it. He'd tried leaving blank spots on the cement to make stars, but he couldn't make stars that way.

He hadn't rubbed it out, because it would have just made it even more of a blur.

There was a picture of his brother. Black would come around and look at it every once in a while, and shake his head, and say 'Is that me?' Well, no, but it was a picture of him; it was a picture of him all tensed up but smooth, with all his weight on one leg and the rest of his body flying forward with an arm out, and a throwing stick way out in front of him, and you could see the way his fingers were shaped to hold on to the end, and the way the muscles of that arm had just finished snapping out the dart and were changing to keep the fingers locked on the stick. You could see the look on his face, that White Jackson had had so much trouble getting right, and off – way off – in the distance you could see something grabbing itself that was as close to a Amsir as you could draw if the only ones you had ever seen were dead and you had never seen one running.

Secon Jackson looked around the room. There wasn't a thing here that he needed to take with him. You didn't expect a Honor to take anything out of his old place on Shaving Day; living in the Thorn, you had the Thorn armoury and you didn't have to have some kid come in and keep your room fire going. All you needed was what you could carry in your hand. People came in after a Honor moved out, if he'd been living alone, and they took away what they needed. Let's see you take that wall away, Jackson thought, but he didn't really give a damn whether they could or not.

He went over to where he'd made a shelf near the tool-making fire, and looked at the burnt sticks he kept there, and the little pots of coloured mud. He picked up one of the sticks, and he walked around with it in his hand for a while. It felt like something was going to come of it, and he looked over at the window that was clean with light through the translucent scraped hide.

He went over and looked at it with his fingertips and the flat of his palm rubbing over it. He leaned enough of his weight against it so he was just short of breaking through, and then he brought up his right hand with the stick held as if it were a handle to something, and watched the line of black grow on the parchment.

He moved the line by moving his body. When the line had gone from its beginning to where it was done, he put in another one, and when he had enough of those he began stroking at the parchment with the worn-down angled edge of the stick, jabbing his body forward from the waist and shifting his feet until it felt as if he were walking, as if he were walking in half-light over ground so rough that his feet had to be put down carefully. But each step was almost exactly the same as the last, as if with this walk he could go a long way and was measuring out his strength against how long it would take him to get there. He saw the Thorn from far away, way out over the dunes with sunset turning the sky, and he saw the rocks nearby with their sides towards him black and grey, and with just an edge bright where he could see the last sunlight hitting the parts that faced towards the Thorn.

Down in the sand he did a man with his hat off, just landing, with his gear coming loose, and his shoulder just rolling under. Now he saw from beyond the Amsir, who had only the tip of one toe in the sand, and one wing up, and was turning with his lace beginning to stream out ahead of him, and his weight transferring towards the leg he was kicking around. The Amsir had his neck stretched forward, and his mouth open, and he was going to do something wild and wonderful in a minute.

Now all that was left to do was the fingers of the one hand you could see from this side of the Amsir. And the thing was, Honor Jackson thought as he looked at it, that the Amsir was going to miss. That leg was going to swing around just wrong. When it hit the sand the other foot would have to slide forward – not much, but enough, so that when the Amsir went to spring back towards the man, off that leg he was positioning, he would be awkward, and maybe one step later he might even stumble. If he had that hand empty of anything to give it weight. So Jackson had to draw in the spear.

CHAPTER FIVE

I

Fine, fine, he thought, looking at it for his death warrant. Now you've really done it. He picked up one of his darts and used the tip of it to cut the drawing out of its frame as quickly as he could. He slashed fast enough to be reckless, but he noticed while he was doing it that he made straight cuts, and he didn't mess up any of the drawing.

It was funny how different the room looked when he could see out. He put the dart away in his armpit, and stood there with the parchment rolled up in his hands, holding it as if it might twist away from him and go straight into the fire. But then, he thought, what's the use? One of these days, they'll gut you whether you give them an excuse or not. You wanna gut something, just the thought of wanting it makes you feel so strong you don't need excuses.

He wished he had somebody here to kill. But he couldn't kill them all and live here by himself.

He went outside, carrying his two darts and his stick, with his cap riding loose on the back of his head, and the half-full bubble of water jogging behind his back. Carrying the drawing made it awkward, because he was used to having one hand free. His shoulder hurt like blazes, and he could have used some sleep, and some food. The skin around the back of his neck, and on his ears, was itching with sunburn.

He scowled at Petra Jovans as she came stepping up to him from where she'd been waiting. All of a sudden he figured maybe he better find out for sure just how much of her was farmer. 'You want to come to my feast, too?' he said with a lot of kill in his voice.

She looked up at him with her head at an angle. 'No, I don't want to be like everybody else.' Her voice was simple, her eyes were clear. She just said it, the way she would have said water runs out of a tap, or the Sun shines on the Thorn. Looking at her, he knew something all complete, all one piece, all of a sudden. What she was here to tell him was that she wanted to be his woman. It was the only thing she could be here for, and it was her way – the way he understood her way. It sure wasn't the way things were supposed to go between man and woman.

Now she was standing there, waiting. You could tell by looking at her, she figured the words she'd said were just as good as the words she'd been going to say. Now he was supposed to pick up on that. I mean, there she was, talking like that. Talking like that supposedly made her so good, no man like Jackson would even think before he took her up. I mean, hell, Honor, you're a strange one, and I'm a strange one, we don't stop to wonder does a strange one maybe seem strange to a strange one.

Ah, come on, he whispered to himself, you're looking for trouble. Been nothing but trouble all day – be just as sensible to figure you're due for a break.

But, yield, yield, he thought to himself, and the feeling came over him strong and hot that one of *us* at one time, on one day, for one killing, was enough.

'All right, then have this,' he said, jabbing the rolled-up drawing at her. 'You want to be different. That's different.'

She unrolled it and looked at it, and then looked up at him. 'You didn't make this up, did you? This is how it is.'

'Yeah. And now *you're* stuck with it.' He had no idea why he went on to say: 'By the way, my name's Jim.' He turned away and walked off, leaving her there.

Oh, people, Honor Secon Black Jackson thought. People. *People!*

II

It wasn't too crowded now. The farmers had gone off to the fields, and the women were doing their household stuff. The smell of fresh bread hung around the Thorn like glue. The Honors were either off sleeping or practising things. There were kids playing around, and some of them tried to hang on to him. But you can always get rid of a kid by looking at him as if he was nothing. Jackson did that as he walked along. Petra wouldn't have followed him; Petra wouldn't follow anybody. She'd wait. Or maybe she'd follow when no one was looking but she'd make it look like it was at her own good time.

Jackson walked over to the Thorn to look at his Amsir. He studied the places where it kept its wind and water stored inside itself, for piecing out to itself in the lonely ambushes of twilight. Looking at it that way, he could see how much it looked like a thin, dried-out man with big blisters under his skin. How much *he* looked like a thin, dried-out man. In his mind, Secon Jackson gave the Eld Honor another snort.

Red Filson grinned at him, rubbing his chin and jaw, which were as tough-looking as the rest of him. Secon Jackson knew his own face was flaming pink where the beard had been, and he didn't like to have Red Filson tell him he was funny looking. But he wasn't that interested in Filson just now, and it probably showed, because Filson said: 'Just about everybody around the Thorn's gonna be at your feast tonight, huh? Spreadin' things a little thin.'

'Well, tell you – you're that worried, I'll watch this bird, and you go out and get another one to throw in the pot.'

Harrison chuckled softly. Filson never much changed expression. 'Some people figure they could maybe pay off everything the same day, I guess,' he said speculatively.

Jackson found himself having to look deep into Filson's eyes, 'Now and then, I guess, one day's all the time a man might need,' he said, thinking that one of the troubles with killing a man out in plain sight was you had to hang around for the Eld's judgement on you, and there was a lot of fasting, and of sitting around cogitating, and of trialing, to be got through. A man could sicken and die, waiting for the trialing to get over. He turned around and walked away, heading off between the nearest houses. And he just kept walking.

CHAPTER SIX

I

It was hot and gritty, lying buried in the sand. Secon Jackson felt miserable. He lay trying to breathe as little as possible, just his nose out in sight, finding out about the world around him by ear. It had to be about a third of a dozen hours since he'd walked away from the Thorn. And lately he'd begun to hear stirrings in the ground – the *chucka-chucka-chucka* of quick-running feet, sometimes near and sometimes far. The sounds always moved from the direction of the Thorn, so he knew they weren't Amsirs. As a matter of fact, he was just far enough away from the Thorn to give trouble to anyone trying to find him, and not far enough out yet really to be in Amsir country.

He figured even with thirty or forty Honors to send out, the Eld would have a hell of a time finding him around the perimeter of as much radius as he had put between himself and the little concrete houses around the big metal spike.

He wasn't too worried about being found, both because there weren't enough people really to search and because whoever found him, he figured it would take more than one or two of them. Mostly, he lay there dreaming. There's a lot of stuff out here in the desert – spears, dead Honors, and very likely some dead Amsirs too, with holes from spear-wounded Honors in them, but no way for anybody to account for them in the village if the Honors couldn't come back. He dreamt about all those dead men under the sand with him. From the way the Eld had talked, things had been going the way they went now for a long time back. In that time a lot of metal spears and a lot of dead Honors must have got hidden out around here. If you could farm this well-fertilized country, the size of the javelin stalks you could raise!

But you can't raise a crop where you can't breathe, and if you're a farmer you only know one way to breathe. Well, Secon Jackson thought, come to that, if you're a Honor you only know one way to breathe. If you were a Amsir you probably didn't know any more than that. Oh, a man could find two, three different ways to get air and water, but that wasn't what he meant by that dream.

He didn't dare move much. He'd done a lot to cover his tracks and there was just enough constant rippling in the sand so that even when he wasn't hearing *chucka-chucka* sounds there was a sort of hissing in his ears. A dozen

dozen dozen dozen grains of sand, he thought, dry as life, rubbing on each other. He saw himself floating in the sand, and the sand going on down deeper and deeper. He twitched a little finger and by the thickness of one grain of sand his finger hid itself farther. By the thickness of one grain of sand, pushing out of the way underneath, filling in above, he was that much closer to sinking down to where the deepness stopped. I could float, he thought, I could float here a long time, but I'd sink little by little.

What is this stuff I'm in? Dust. Nothing. Out at the edge of the fields, beyond the weed borders of the village, it smoked up into the air like hope and then twisted in around back on itself, drifting up so thin, so fine, that you could walk through it almost without knowing it was there, and could only see it edge-on when you were passing through the middle of it. Then it had substance; a thin, dirty yellow line, curving up in an arc that probably reached just below the gridwork at the top of the Thorn, but lost itself and couldn't be seen that high. Thin enough to drink.

Chucka-chucka-chucka. Someone was coming close, but off at a little bit of an angle. Secon Jackson judged it from the way the sounds didn't get louder quite as fast as they beat on the sand. Somebody running; some Honor saying to himself he would find Secon Jackson any minute now.

He wondered what the Eld was saying to the farmers to explain what had happened to Secon Jackson. He wondered if the Eld was bothering to say anything – they all knew Secon Jackson was crazy, or if they hadn't known it, it would occur to them now. He wondered what the Eld thought. It must be a good long time since a Honor ran out on his feast, a good long time since the Eld had seen any need to wonder what a man might be doing. Secon Jackson grinned carefully with the sand murmuring on his lips, and went on dreaming.

He dreamed through the rest of the short afternoon and into the twilight. When it was full dark and cold, and it had been three dozen parts of a day since he'd slept, he slipped up out of the sand. Boy, he thought, looking up at the night, I'd sure better know what I'm doing.

He began to walk towards the edge of the world. He felt a little draggy.

From time to time he put his face down to the ground, and from time to time he could hear the sound of running Honors, *chucka-chucking* distantly. Merely because they couldn't imagine what else to do, they were quartering back and forth across the line his Amsir had led him on yesterday. That happened to be exactly right, because that was where he was headed. He figured maybe Amsirs always worked back to that line in the end, when they'd got Honors far enough away from the Thorn. But he wasn't being any dumb Honor himself. For the time being he was headed off at another angle, covering more ground than you'd cover if you only had a used bubble of water and were planning ever to make it back to the Thorn.

He'd done that on purpose. He could imagine them comparing notes and figuring out he'd never gone to one of the Thorn taps. He could imagine them figuring out they couldn't figure out what the hell he'd been thinking of, just taking off like that. He had imagined them not believing it when he walked by first one line of huts, and then the next one farther out and then the next one and then out into the nearest field and then the one beyond that, and so on. They just couldn't believe it; when he was lost from sight of the people around the Thorn, covered by the houses between him and them, he could imagine them not believing he hadn't stopped just out of sight. But he'd done all that; he'd just sloped off and gone out without enough supplies, and he'd gone off without eating, and now he was headed in the wrong direction, and those were the only reasons he'd got away.

Well, no, Secon Jackson thought. He was going to get away because he could imagine them, but they couldn't imagine him. They could never imagine what he wanted. Come to that, he couldn't either. But he could move to it.

Red Filson's dart took him in the elbow.

It spun him around and knocked him down, and it took his left arm out of the fight. He sprang for his life, throwing himself off to one side, not even knowing yet whom he was fighting, knowing only because he rolled over its head that it was a dart in his elbow and not a spear.

Now the shock was going through him. It was so bad that even the back of his neck felt struck stiff. He'd never been clobbered so hard in his life. Then he saw the shape of the man-shadow jumping towards him. It was Filson. Lucky days, Jackson thought.

'Tough luck, Honor,' Filson said, getting ready to stab. He was very fast – as fast as Secon Jackson had ever dreamed him – and Jackson could only hope to be as fast as he had ever dreamed himself. He got out of the way of the first lunge, but he couldn't make his feet grip right. When he tried to turn, his dead left arm knocked against his knee. He went down again, just as if Filson had struck him. It *was* like fighting in a dream.

Filson was good. He was like something you'd hear about from an old woman. Jackson flopped forward off his knees, knowing exactly how this would put him inside Filson's kick and knowing exactly what he would try to do to Filson after that. But Filson kicked him anyhow. And one more time Jackson was down.

He had his stick, but he didn't have either of his darts – the best he could do was grab his left wrist and scratch at Filson's side going by, using the head of the dart sticking out through his elbow. He might even have cut the other man some – he thought he'd felt the point dragging momentarily – but that was a hell of a defence to put up, wasn't it? He struck out at Filson with the stick, missing; dropped it, grabbed sand and threw it at the other man's face, and didn't seem to have any effect on him. 'Boy, you messed it,' Filson said. 'I would have figured you for my best enforcer when I became Eld. Your mother would have liked that a lot. Now look what you're doing to your family.'

Will they at least give me any peace in Ariwol? Secon Jackson thought as he twisted out of Filson's way again. He tried to think of things to do with one arm. He could pull off Red's cap, he supposed. But his own was loose and jouncing around his skull; he was in no shape for any game that two could play. He tried for a grip on Filson's dart-arm, but it was like trying to hold a piece of the Thorn come to life. The best he could do was drag his nails across Filson's biceps as the hold broke. He figured it would only take him two or three days to scratch the man to death.

He spun away and tried to drag the dart out of his elbow so that he would have a weapon too, but all that did for him was nearly make him faint.

They were scuffling and fluttering like two kids under a blanket out here; whirling and groping for each other in the dark, raising dust, making slapping sounds as they tried for each other and made each other miss. But it couldn't be much longer before Filson got that other dart in. Jackson knew it, and Filson knew it. Filson was doing it like a practice. He even found time to talk. 'Where did you think you were going?' he panted. 'It's all right being crazy, but I never figured you for dumb.'

Maybe he thought that would be a finish line. His arm hooked down and came up again, and his forearm snapped over as he punched his dart towards Jackson's face. Jackson dropped under it, but he was off his feet again. He made a try at knocking Filson's knees together, and then dropped sideways, barely getting out of the way of the other man's return stroke. The side of Jackson's face was in the sand.

That made all the difference. He could hear the new sounds coming up fast … *chicka-sip, chicka-sip, chicka-sip*.

In his mind – but very quickly – Secon Jackson laughed like crazy. It was working out after all. Turned out he'd damned near died before he could know for sure. Maybe he still would, if he couldn't stall Red off.

He had to interrupt himself to flounder out of the way of the next rush.

But it was nice to know he'd been figuring it all correct, from the minute that he had been sitting there in the Eld's room in the Thorn and had been beginning to think on it, because where else was there any hope for him.

He pushed the laugh out into the cold air. 'Huh!' He kicked towards Red's ankle and made him hop back. 'I know where I'm goin'.' Well, no, he didn't, but he knew whom he was going with. *Chicka-sip, chicka-sip, chicka-sip, whop!* That was the sound of the running Amsir coming down solid on both feet nearby. Up against the stars and the horizon there was a fast glimpse, for Jackson to get, of a javelined wing unfurling.

'I yield! I yield!' Jackson shouted to the Amsir, making a grab for Red, who was distracted. His two stiff fingers hooked upwards into Filson's nostrils. His arm pulled back hard, and at the same time he planted one foot and kicked Filson in the crotch. Filson bent double, with both his hands still clapped to his torn, shocked face. Jackson plucked Filson's second dart from between the man's limp fingers and then made one move more, with the dart held for cutting windows. He dropped the dart and stood holding his right thumb and forefinger tight around his left arm above the elbow. The Amsir stood looking at him, its spear ready, only the lace stirring on its body.

'I do yield,' Jackson said, looking down at Filson all huddled up. He kicked a little sand towards the dead man. 'My name is Honor Red Jackson.'

II

'You will come with me, wet devil?' the Amsir said in its high, puzzled voice. You could tell it – he felt proud, but you could tell he couldn't understand what had happened. Well, that was all right, too, Jackson thought.

'I better had,' Jackson said. 'Or there's been a lot done for nothing. My mother's a widow twice over for nothing.'

'You're wounded, devil. You're spilling moisture. Come with me quickly.'

'Right behind you.'

'Before me.'

They ran over the night desert, *chucka-chucka-chucka, chicka-sip, chicka-sip*. The Amsir gave Jackson his directions with light little touches of the spearpoint, until finally they reached the place the Amsir wanted, and the leathery bird said: 'Stop. Dig here.'

Crouching down, Jackson did his one-handed best. A sixth of a dozen feet down, he felt something hard and swollen under his fingertips. He pulled it out. It was a bladder of some kind, twice as thick through as a man's head. It felt as if it were made of glue-varnished leather; he could feel the edges of seams, and then a folded-in gut stopper.

'That is breathing-stuff,' the Amsir said. 'You will need it soon; the iron cap is almost useless to you now. Dig deeper – there is a moisture-bottle, and there are wrappings for warmth. There are patches for your hide.'

Jackson dug them out. The water bottle was a lot like the Amsir-bubble at his back in size, but it felt like the oxygen bladder. The robes were some kind of leather, tanned soft. They'd used leather for the body-patches, too. They thought of everything when they cached one of these bringing-in-the-pris-oner kits; they knew they weren't likely to get many without holes in them.

He still couldn't get the dart out, so he tied off his arm, using his good hand and his teeth to make the knot. The Amsir wouldn't come anywhere nearer him than the length of the spear.

There were sling-straps for the oxygen-bladder and water bottle. He unhooked his own bubble, drained it dry, and tossed it away in the dark before he replaced it with the Amsir bottle. Then he said: 'Set,' and they began moving again towards where once upon a time his in-curving horizon had been.

As they travelled, he asked: 'You bring in any other prisoners in your time?'

'You're my first.'

We sure have lost a lot of maidens today, Jackson thought. He was getting very cold. After a while, he had to pull out the length of tied-off intestine into the oxygen bubble, stick the end of it in his mouth, and use that for air, pinching the gut between two fingers to keep himself from swelling into broken-lunged sickness and death, as the Amsir warned him.

When the sun came up, they saw it sooner than almost anybody Jackson knew, for they were at the top of his world's rim.

Jackson was bone-pulling cold. He had to peek out between his eyelids. He hurt in his nose and his ears, and behind his ears. He saw his robes were made of stitched-together human skins, and for a minute he was scared and furious, but then he remembered the thrown-away Amsir bubble, and he told himself it didn't mean much. Or maybe it did, but not now.

'Hurry along; you will die here, but it is not much farther to comfort ... of a kind.'

Jackson squinted ahead. He saw below him another great dish-shaped world. But this one was blue-green from rim to rim; fences, light as stretched strings marking out plots, divided the land. High houses on stilt legs shone pink and ochre and glistening blue; bright yellow and sharp green, flashing in the sunlight. Lacy lines, fragile as the fencing, traced from house to house, swaying down in free arcs, webbing the whole town together. And at the centre of this world, far away, he could see a Thorn. A tall, massive, shining Thorn, not the blunt, tilted, rust-streaked thing he had been born under. A fairy trap of gridwork twined in the air around its peak. And everywhere everywhere, in the air, curving, curvetting, disporting, the Amsirs trafficked with the early morning air.

Air. Thick, lustrously clear, it reached out to envelop him as the Amsir pushed him forward.

Ariwol! Jackson thought, Ariwol, by all that's pious! He arched his back and stared up into the sky again. Shouting and singing and laughing, he thought. But I don't see you, Red.

CHAPTER SEVEN

I

'You will have to climb down,' the Amsir said, showing Jackson a place on the rim where you could see something that looked a little like a path. 'You can leave those things here. They will be taken.'

Jackson dropped the stuff on the ground, and when the Amsir negligently knocked his spear point against the iron cap, Jackson took that off too and set it down on top of the pile. All he had left now was the dart still trapped in the joint of his left elbow, and the human leather tourniquet. He shrugged and began to scramble down. It was six or eight times his own height to the ground.

The Amsir did something that must have given him a lot of pleasure. He stepped off a steep place in the rim, cupped his wings, and pivoted luxuriantly so as to be able to keep watching Jackson while he drifted downwards. Every so often he beat his wings once or twice gracefully and kept himself from sinking too quickly.

For Jackson, climbing down wasn't any picnic. He had to do it all one-handed, which meant that often enough he had to brace himself by leaning his face or his chest into the broken grit so as to help keep his feet from sliding. It was just too damn bad, wasn't it?

He began running into patches of the pretty blue-green stuff that he had seen filling the bottom of this world so attractively right up to the rim. It was cheesey and brittle. It broke off and smeared on his hand and body when he rubbed against rocks it was growing on. It smelled sharp, the way old bread dough tasted, and it came apart in little leafy chips. Jackson had never seen anything like it before. While it had looked fine from up there on the rim, down here it looked a little bit like something that had made somebody sick.

He got down to flat land with a half-twist of his body that left him leaning against the rocks at the bottom of the rim. From down here it was only a gentle slope for maybe a dozen dozen strides, and then everything flattened out. Already, from this angle, most of his view of the Amsir Thorn was blocked by the Amsir houses stilting their way into the air. It all looked different, not as spread out, and pretty crowded.

His left forearm and hand were turning purplish white. The Amsir came down lightly a few strides away from him as he stopped to loosen the tie above his elbow, and leaned watching the blood squirt out around the dart. He tried to work his fingers. Finally he reached over with his right hand and pushed against the crooked stiffness in his fingers. A little bit of that and he was able to make his thumb and forefinger twitch towards each other. They were also beginning to feel like he was holding them in a fire. Give and take. He tied the leather band tight again.

The Amsir said curiously: 'How long will that take to heal.'

'I don't know. Long time, I guess. Tell you better after somebody helps me get this dart out.'

'We have people who can do that. But I don't mean how long until it is perfect; in your experience how long until it can do work?'

'Look, I don't know. Six, nine days. Maybe twelve. Maybe three.'

'Three ...' the Amsir repeated to himself thoughtfully. He looked Jackson up and down. 'No sooner?'

'Look, I *told* you—' Jackson stopped and let it go. People never believed anything they hadn't touched, and the Amsir didn't have any dart in his elbow. The Amsir was just standing there with his lace drifting perkily around him in the breeze that swept towards the rim along the floor of the world and vanished up the rocks. Jackson knew there was something different about his face, and then he saw that there were two wrinkle-edged holes open there, where a man's nostrils would be if his upper lip was an Amsir beak. And he could hear air hissing in and out. The Amsir was upwind of him, too, and now that he noticed, Jackson could smell the old breath emptying itself out of his chest bubbles.

'Come along,' the Amsir said, motioning with his spear. 'We don't have time to waste. You have to walk to the tower.' He pointed with one wing tip. By that Jackson could tell he meant the Thorn. 'You'll have to just walk through the fields,' the Amsir said as he sprang up into the air to circle watchfully around Jackson. 'We don't make paths.'

You don't take many prisoners, Jackson thought. It's a big day.

They stopped briefly once, at the nearest of the stilt-legged houses. The house was made of something tough like horn, but scratched up and very old, looking as if it had once held a lot more particles of its bright yellow colour. The Amsir sprang higher into the air and clung to one of the uprights with his claws and one hand. He reached up over his head to tug on the downswinging loop of the line that connected this house to the next one. Jackson could hear a bell clang inside. Clang, long pause, clang clang, short pause, then more clangs and spaced-out pauses.

It got mixed up in Jackson's ears. As soon as the line had transmitted the Amsir's pulling up to the next house, he could hear another bell in there echoing the sound. Then he could hear it again faintly from the house beyond that, and then very faintly off in the distance, always moving in the direction of the Thorn. The Amsir stopped pulling and waited. After a little while, Jackson could hear a sound coming back along the ropes from the direction of the Thorn. It was a short answer, whatever it was. The Amsir nodded in satisfaction and waved Jackson on with his spear.

'All right, hurry up, now,' he cried down. 'They are waiting for you.'

They were getting notice from other Amsirs now, too. Some of them popped out of the doorways of the houses, jumping into the air and swooping to get a look at Jackson. Others – women and young kids, or anyway acting like women and young kids would have acted if they'd been farmers – clinging to the edges of doorways.

It began to make something of a procession, Jackson down below and all the inhabitants overhead. The Amsirs called to each other and back to their families in their homes. And the families back to them. It made a hell of a racket in the air, and shadows and gusts down on the ground. Jackson tried baffling them a little by walking under the houses instead of around them, but there was too much manure on the ground there, and he didn't try it twice. He walked along with his head down, holding his arm out of his way, humming a little song his mother had taught him and had liked to hear him sing:

'Ah, when I am a Honor,/And go for my game,/The people of dirt will report my new name./The Eld he will shave me/And name my new name/And the people of iron will feast on my game./The beasts of the sand/Will grow fearful and tame./The Honor of iron will have a new name!'

CHORUS: 'Talordims zasheparda/Ishalna twan ... /Talordims zasheparda /Ishalna twan!'

By the time he got to the foot of their Thorn, the Amsirs were worked up nearly out of their minds; with the crying and the calling, and the flurry of wings, he could have thrown his head back and hollered at the top of his lungs, and who would have heard? Exactly. Who would have heard? Humming was good enough for him, and, besides, he was disgusted with the way they were behaving.

There were guards and things at the entrance to the Thorn, hooting and shaking their spears in deference to his particular Amsir's dignity as a bringer-in of people. There were thumping, rustling crowds of Amsirs jumping down out of the air and mobbing around behind him and his Amsir, pressing forward towards the entrance. But only Jackson and his Amsir got let through the doorway, which got swung shut behind them, leaving the two of them standing there in silence, before Jackson got hustled forward again, and up a corridor towards a room where they were being waited for. It certainly was suddenly quiet. He was given a nudge into the room, and besides other Amsirs of various sizes and kinds, there was one who crouched and turned his head on a bent neck.

'You'll find us quicker than your kind. What do I call you?' this one said. '"Wet devil" is too respectful, and "Man" is ambiguous. What's your personal handle?' Well, if he wasn't their Eld, he would do.

II

'My name's Honor Red Jackson,' he said to the crouching old Amsir. Maybe not too old. Crouching wasn't right, either – it was more like leaning bent-legged, with some of his weight on his wing tips.

'They have a complex system of naming,' quickly said another old, skinnier Amsir. There were quite a few Amsirs in the room, including a doctor-like one. That one stepped forward and began peering at his elbow. Then he began studying it, in part by twisting the naked dry human arm bones he'd been holding in one hand. Jackson hoped he'd soon figure out just how he was going to tinker this thing up, and get around to doing his job.

'Honor is his community status,' the skinny one was still explaining. 'It signifies that he lives exclusively by hunting our sort of creature. Red means that in addition to having met the hunting requirement, he has also performed the optional office of killing a creature of his own kind. Jackson simply means that he is the son of another male creature named Jack. For creatures in sparse circumstances, they have a most amazing variety of rituals. I can't imagine how they distinguish between brothers of identical status – I do not say they don't so distinguish. I'm sure they do.'

The Amsir Eld grunted at the skinny one. 'Do not, I pray, give me any more labels for him. They may have to distinguish, but we never have so many of them that we must. Tell me what he is, not what he stands for.'

'I am telling you. It's significant that he should be so obviously young; that he should carry the very fresh scars of combat with one of our own kind – which means he brought one of our own kind to the last extremity – and then the even more recent scars of combat with one of his own kind. This was an odd one, even before he did the oddest thing of all and yielded voluntarily.' The skinny Amsir looked at Jackson proudly, as if he'd produced him himself.

'The odder the better,' the Eld Amsir snapped. 'We've had no luck with the usual run.'

'Precisely my point,' the instructing Amsir said.

'Then why didn't you make it to begin with?'

'Pfah! I did!'

'Only in hindsight. Get out. Wait where you're needed.' The Eld Amsir jerked his head towards the doorway and the instructor shuffled out. The Eld Amsir turned all his attention towards Jackson's end of the room. 'You, Doctor – get on with it.' He came a few steps closer and he wasn't old, now that he was in some kind of better light coming in through the narrow Thorn window-slits. The tattering of his lace, and the crumpled look of the wing Jackson could see best, were accounted for by damage. He was pretty badly scarred up, and discoloured. He looked as if he'd been picked up and knocked hard against something rough, had left big patches of his hide against that rough thing, and had had a lot of bones broken for it. But he threw his weight around like an Eld, and that bothered Jackson. He didn't like the idea of somebody being mean enough inside to be an Eld, but still not slowed down in his head very much.

'You, Jackson – I am above all others here. No one of my kind of creature will tell you we have any time, so give me straight, fast answers. The report is you were ready to yield when that young one by the doorway found you. This is something new. Explain it.'

The doctor put one hand on Jackson's biceps, the other on his forearm and closed his beak on the lace-feathered end of the dart in Jackson's elbow. His claws made little purchase-hunting sounds on the metal flooring.

Jackson figured it would be best to pay him no heed. 'Didn't like it where I was,' he said to the Eld. 'Figured I'd go to where the lies were all about. Make up my own if I had to.'

'Pfu. Lies require life. You won't live.'

'Right up to the minute I die, I will. Oh, hell!' he hollered as the doctor jerked his head back while twisting his arm. The dart sucked out of Jackson's wound and hung for an instant in the doctor's beak until it was dropped. The doctor's hand closed as best it could above Jackson's elbow – the fingers couldn't make it all the way around the flesh. Jackson reached over to help him, his eyes swimming.

'I think perhaps you thought you could hunt us as we hunt you,' the Eld said shrewdly. 'I think perhaps you thought out that there was another world in which our sort of creature was prey. I think you thought you knew a way to get breathing stuff. You are young. Your judgements are romantic. You thought that because you were a little bit odd, and you frightened your own kind, you would frighten us too.'

Jackson just kept gripping his arm, swaying with his eyes closed. He did have room enough inside himself, though, to think how wonderful it was that *everybody*, Amsirs included, could think they knew everything just because they knew something.

'Well, that's not how it is, creature,' the Eld Amsir went right on, while the doctor unstoppered a stone bottle of something that looked like water but burned like fire when he poured it over Jackson's running elbow, and then began winding a long, tight strip of shaved-thin hide around Jackson's left arm in a spiral from shoulder to wrist. 'In some ways here for you it is the way it is for our kind of creature with you. We cannot breathe the breathing stuff around your fields. Muck from that stuff you grow is in every breathful. We die – you would say prettily – with our first breath of it; our muscles knot so hard our bones break; our backbones snap; green fur fills our lungs. Or so the instructors say, from the times long ago when we still tried.

'Haw! We die of breathing the air that blows across the stuff you eat. *This* is the stuff we eat.' He pointed a wing at a corner heaped with the blue, crumbly stuff from the fields. 'That is rock-stuff. That is the food for creatures of wing and spirit. Can you eat rock? No others of your kind have ever been able to. You will die, prettily. Your stomach will sink in, your bones will show through the meat on you; towards the end, you will try to fang us and we will kick you away. You will bite yourself. You will try to get away back to your poison Thorn, and we will kick you back to your work. You will live altogether perhaps thirty days, perhaps less. Only *perhaps* perhaps will you live any longer than that. And only perhaps perhaps perhaps will you ever be happy again before you die. It depends how quickly and how well you can do things. On how odd you are, and most of all on whether you are luckier than any other creature of your own kind that we have ever had here. Now—' he jerked his head towards Jackson's bound-up arm. 'How soon do you think you will be able to do work with that?'

Jackson raised his arm experimentally. It throbbed when he did that; it felt like something made out of one solid stick of bone. 'Thanks, Doc,' he said to the doctor, who was standing off to one side watching him critically. Jackson tried to make his hand work. It wouldn't work. He began knocking it against his thigh, trying to get some circulation into his fingers. 'What kind of work?' he said to the Eld Amsir.

'I'll show you.' The Eld gestured towards the doorway. 'Turn towards your right hand after you leave the room.'

III

Jackson did that. The Eld Amsir and the young one who'd brought him in followed him. The doctor tried to go with him too, but the Eld just looked back over his shoulder and said 'Not you.' The doctor turned around quickly, and rustled out towards the daylight Jackson had come from.

The way Jackson had been told to turn led him deeper into the Amsir Thorn. It was a narrow passageway, and at widely-spaced distances there were lights glowing behind translucent panels in the metal ceiling overhead. It was like walking through something's ribs; every so often they'd come to another oval ridge that ran completely around, up the walls and across the ceiling. There was always an open door folded neatly back against the wall. Halfway between two of these doors there'd be another one like it, but set directly into the wall at Jackson's left side. These were closed; sometimes there was light behind them, coming through a little bull's-eye window, and sometimes there wasn't. Sometimes there were particular sounds of machines going; sometimes there was just a general sound of the Thorn, which was louder and healthier than Jackson's Thorn. But not one of these doors leading to the inside told him anything.

The passageway curved this way and that; sometimes it turned sharply. From the sound growing louder and louder, and then beginning to taper off behind him at more or less the same rate, Jackson guessed it was some kind of path they'd set up for getting through the Thorn to the other side without having to go around it. Three times they came to ladders taking up half the passageway's space and going up to round doors set in the ceiling. Two of them were closed, and the metal rungs of the ladders were dull and softly smooth. At the top of the third ladder was a round black opening, and the ladder was scratched up. There were bright, polished places on the wall, going up beside the ladder, where Amsir wings had dragged against it a lot of times. He tried to imagine an Amsir working his way up one of these ladders, just as he could see how they had to inch and shuffle to get around the ladders and keep going down the passageway. It wasn't handy for them, this place. Well, it wasn't handy for him either, but it was what they had.

They came to another room that opened outside. It had a couple more Amsirs in it; a plump young one, and the instructor, again.

'Are you going to show it to him now?' this one asked the Eld.

'He won't get any stronger.'

'No – or at least, none of them have. But you know, they do have this ability to store energy. Amazing really, when you think of it; at least, we've never observed any of them taking nourishment out into the desert with them, and we know they've certainly been able to function unfed for significant periods of time here. Whereas we're hard put to it to find individuals with the endurance to omit feeding for as much as a day—'

'—What the learned one who is well above me refers to,' broke in the instructor's young Amsir, 'is the surmise that perhaps these creatures are trading time for energy. They may be going into some sort of survival mode that permits a stretch-out of energy consumption by maintaining a low level of physical and mental activity. As you know from the learned one's witnessed discourses, he would very much like to attempt stimulating one of these creatures, as for example with pain, on the supposition that this may force it to re-enter a more energetic mode, of shorter duration, perhaps, but much more productive of over-all results ...'

Nobody listened with interest. Not even the instructor Amsir, who was doing his best not to pay attention, or at least to look as if he were someplace else entirely. He looked at the walls, the floor, and the ceiling while the novice instructor's voice got lower and lower. Jackson didn't want to hear anything about pain, whatever a mode was. The young Amsir who'd brought him in was looking at the instructor novice the way a Honor would look at a farmer his own age, except he wasn't measuring him for the kill. Finally, the Eld Amsir said 'Shut up,' gently, and the novice instructor did. Looking at Jackson the Eld Amsir said 'Do the young practise as much where you come from?'

'Only honning. The farming takes care of itself; the Thorn spreads the water in the fields, and the ploughs run straight no matter what you try to do.'

'Well, we are better than you,' the Eld said. 'Both of you shut up,' he added towards the instructor, who'd begun to open his beak. 'This one's enough experiment for me just the way he is.' He nudged Jackson towards the door with the tip of one wing. 'Step out and look at that,' he said.

Jackson found himself looking from the doorway at something a lot like a small Thorn. It tapered up into the air, maybe a dozen times as high as a man. But it was spikier, and it had other spikes curving down – it rested on three of them. It had openings, too, like throats yawning down towards the ground. It was made of the same kind of metal as the Thorn; in that shape, though, spikey and open-mouthed, it looked mean and twisty.

'What is that?' Jackson asked.

'It's the Object. It's been here since the beginning of the world. You see that?' the Eld pointed up the side of the thing. There was a ladder coming down to within, say, three feet of the ground. Jackson squinted; up at the head of the ladder was something that looked like another one of the closed doorways, but that had no familiar circular handle to turn. It was just an oval crack in the metal. Turning his head, and shifting his feet back and forth, Jackson could see glints from scratches up there; shallow ones, it looked like, no more than futile scrapes.

'That's a doorway, isn't it?' the Eld Amsir said.

'Looks like one,' Jackson agreed. 'Don't you know?'

'It says it's a doorway. It has a voice, and the instructor tells me that's what it says.' The Eld cast a glance aside at the instructor: 'There isn't anyone who will tell me it says something else,' he added dryly.

'I've spent a long time deciding that's what it says,' the instructing Amsir said vehemently. 'I have given witnessed discourses—'

'Shut up,' the Eld Amsir said.

Jackson looked the Object up and down again. There wasn't anything new left to notice, except maybe for the burnt, black splashes on the ground right under it, that the spikey legs rested on. That looked a little wrong – as if somebody had been building fires under it not too long ago; certainly not as long ago as the beginning of time. Otherwise, it just sat there. He certainly didn't hear any voice saying 'I am a door.'

'What do you want me to do with this thing?'

'Climb the ladder and open the door,' the Eld Amsir said.

'Just that?'

'*Pfu!* Every one of our kind of creature who's tried it has been killed … except for a very few of us who have only been hurt and made very angry. And too wise to try again. Every one of your kind of creature who's tried it has failed. But he hasn't been killed. He's had plenty of time to try anything he pleases, until he's finally starved to death.'

CHAPTER EIGHT

I

Oh, haw, Jackson thought, feeling weak and disgusted. He looked up towards the door in the Object again, and then at the ladder. It seemed to him that a bone-weary, one-armed, light-headed, sleepless, foodless, hopeless man could get up it all right. Considering everything. He looked at the door again. But the damn thing didn't have any handle. Well. He got himself moving and sauntered towards the ladder.

Standing there right under the Object, he could see two things; one, that it was pretty big, the other that it had been there long enough for the three spikes it rested on to have become very nearly a part of the soil. It no longer looked as if it had been set down on the ground. It had the look that the walls of the huts at the home Thorn had – or that the Thorn itself had, come to that – of having poked up from underneath, and of the ground bulging just a little bit at the torn edges, as if maybe a dozen dozen years from now it would finish reacting to this growth and would finally lie flat.

He put his good hand on the ladder two or three rungs up. He gave a little tug followed by a harder one. There was no give in the ladder. He could see that it came out of the side of the Object, up there just below the doorway. And he could see a sort of joint at each rung, as if the ladder were made to be pulled up and to fold inside a small space somewhere up there. Or to be kicked out and let hang this way when needed. But if those were hinges, they had no give in them now. He put his ear to the ladder, which was as warm as his own flesh, and he could hear things humming. Well, anything that could talk had to have a heart.

He looked over at the bunch of Amsirs. All of them were watching him with considerable interest. There were other Amsirs gathering overhead – passers-by and just loungers who'd noticed that a new creature of his kind was about to try for the talking door.

One of them swooped down and came no more than his own height over Jackson's head. 'Haa, Wet Devil! Climb! Climb!' He hovered up at the level of the door and made scrabbling fake-desperate grabs towards it for as long as he could hold his altitude, then fell away, got his wings straightened back around the way he wanted them, and buffeted up into the air again. Jackson noticed that it would have been a much better piece of mockery if the Amsir had dared actually to touch the door. Jackson took a little jump into the air, grabbed the ladder, got one foot up, and began to climb.

It was peculiar the way the metal felt neither cold nor hot. Although he had to do all the work with one arm and his legs, it was nothing like when he'd had to slip and slide down the rim into this place. He felt pretty good, as a matter of fact. There were worse things a man could do with his time than climb this ladder. He wished he knew what the Object was.

Pretty soon he was up high enough to look down at the Amsirs on the ground. They were all watching him, their faces turning up, gridwork-like, to follow his climb as if each of their bodies were a Thorn and he was the Sun.

Up to now, the ladder had been hanging reasonably far away from the side of the Object. But the higher he got, the closer the bulge of the Object got to the straight-hanging ladder. Now his eyes were only inches away from the side of the thing itself, and he could see something that didn't cheer him up. It was grease-smears, rainbowing in the light, from all the hands that had rubbed here before him as he stopped to lean his weight on the comfortable, neither warm nor cold humming metal.

Oh, pfu, he said to himself, and kept climbing, until finally he was at the top of the ladder. Here there was a little open door, not too thick, but not too thin, and strongly hinged, positioned under the slits so as to protect it against anything being thrown up from below. When the ladder was pulled up, probably the little door closed behind it and left no more seam than the door above it did. When his eyes came level with it, he noticed that there was a broken-off, fleshless fingerbone trapped in the crack between the little open door and the main side of the Object. At the same time, a voice over his head growled hollowly: 'Ouwwtenshownnn. Dhayss dwuuhrr uhhpnnss owwn-nuhhli t umm-nn pehrrsowwnnuhll. Awwll ouwwthrr uhluff-ffouwrrmms wuull be dhaysstroydd wieyethouyut dhaysscriyeshunn.'

Jackson looked up at the door. Nothing was happening. The door began to say again: 'Ouwwtenshownnn. Dhayss dwuuhrr ...'

Jackson climbed back down the ladder.

'Shakes you, doesn't it?' said the Eld Amsir, at the foot of the ladder.

'It sounds like somebody's stomach,' Jackson said. He looked over at the instructing Amsir. '*What* did he say it says?' The Eld followed his glance and raised a wing tip. The instructor Amsir came forward, brimming over and ready to spill.

'Do not be misled by the growling, rumbling, sounds. I have said them to myself at any number of speeds and pitches of voice, and I have had many below me say them to me in various modes according to my instructions. I have had witnesses in great number judge the various effects, and arrive at agreement among themselves as to the meaning of this sort of speech. It is the consensus,' he said with proud conclusiveness, 'that what the door is giving is first of all a sound much like our word "Display alertness". This is followed by a sound which is very definitely the word "object". Then there is a sound very much like our word "hatch"—'

'Shut up,' Jackson said to the shock of some, and the amusement of the Eld. 'You mean that's just a funny way of talking straight.'

The instructing Amsir looked at Jackson almost tearfully, as if it were a farmer whose daughter had just gone off with a Honor, laughing. 'That's right.'

'I want to get this straight. It talks like we do but it has a funny mouth, is that it?'

'That seems to be the case,' the Eld Amsir said.

'Well, now look,' Jackson said. 'That's a big thing. There's your kind of creature and my kind of creature, and now all of a sudden there's a third kind. And if it's all connected up with things that have been here since the beginning of time, then it could be that this thing talks for whatever made time begin. Maybe it *is* whatever made time begin.'

'Listen, you stinking wet – You keep *your* mouth off theology!'

The young Amsir who'd brought him in had been hanging around all this time, without saying two words or even boo. It made Jackson twang a little inside, having him come on this strong all of a sudden. But he rolled his eyes over at the youngster with enough cool to make it stick. 'Now what are *you* talking about?'

'Don't pick at it,' the Eld Amsir said to the young warrior. Saying it that way was maybe the fond substitute for 'Shut up!' 'It's just an ignorant creature. Listen, I think things are pretty well controlled here – you can go home and tell your flock you are well above many for this day's work. Go home. Now.'

The young Amsir jumped for the air. 'I am rewarded,' he said thankfully to the Eld, before he flung himself straight up like a thrown dart aimed at the Sun, shouting at the top of his lungs 'I am above many! I am above many! High, high up, he flung himself out flat and went tearing down at a shallow angle for a particular one of the stilt-legged houses, still shouting. Jackson could hear his voice shrinking into the distance for a long time.

The Eld Amsir looked at Jackson and shrugged. 'You have one or two things to watch out for besides the condition of your stomach. One of them is the fact that if you nudge superstition hard enough around here, you won't live to starve. And there's not much chance any of the few enlightened persons will be able to do anything to help you.'

'We have a very tricky situation going here,' the instructor Amsir explained. 'You see, we know there are two Thorns, two worlds, two kinds of creature, and we know they were all made at the same time. One must be good, and the other evil. But you see, beyond that point we leave rational logic behind, and begin trespassing on matters of faith.

'A great prophet, one of whose last discourses I myself was privileged to witness as a very young man, tells us that since we must make evaluations of our Thorn's worth on faith, then it is just as logical to believe that each individual makes either good or evil of his own place. But for this the great prophet was flung from a great height with his wings broken, by those who avoid such complicated patterns of ethics. The simple view consists of knowing that it is our place that is good and yours that is evil, and that the mob are therefore good, for living in the good place.

'We, speaking together here, are all reasonable creatures – granting you a certain shrewdness. Being reasonable, we know it is probably only an accident of creation that your kind of creatures and mine cannot live in each other's places. But you see how difficult it could be to perceive that this one is of a tender and uncultured turn of mind.

'You can see, too,' the Eld Amsir added, 'how brave that young fellow was, being as emotional as he is, and yet willing to risk waiting around the fringes of your world for something as unutterably evil and repulsive as yourself to come into contact with him. That's besides the risk of death – but then, no one really believes in death.' The Eld looked at Jackson significantly.

Jackson just looked back at him. For one thing, he didn't even know what 'theology' meant. It was the apprentice instructor who said: 'Look at him! He shows no sign of understanding! I propose the thesis they have no concept of original evil!'

'And are therefore innocent?' the instructor cried furiously. 'Shut up! Shut up!' He waved his wings, spastically hopping from one foot to the other, raising dust. He was pretty old and stiff, and didn't impress Jackson much, but the apprentice instructor quailed and ducked away, his head bowed. He acted as if he'd fallen out while running around the Thorn behind Red Filson – tireless, wise, dead Red Filson. What makes you dumb, Jackson decided, is what scares you.

II

'You see,' the Eld Amsir said to Jackson, 'we do feel we must discover whatever is within the Object. We feel this with different degrees of involvement.' He glanced aside at the instructor, who was busily running his fingertips through his lace and getting it untangled. 'Feel it for different reasons that are very close to our emotions. But it's our only clue to the nature and purpose of Creation. We've studied the Thorn for generations, of course, but it's only a machine. All we learn from it is how it works and in what parts it seems to be wearing out. It does seem to be wearing out in a number of parts. Now the Object, on the other hand, talks. Perhaps there is something inside. Perhaps one could talk to the inside something, with the right kind of mouth.'

'In what kind of talk?' Jackson asked.

The Eld Amsir nodded. 'Well remarked. Nobody is saying there won't be problems. Nobody is saying the answer will be easy to find. But we've got to begin. Things are not getting any better. They can only get worse. We can't just let them go. Oh, there are many of our kind of people who would never care, until the last moment when the sky fell down upon them. All they care about is getting their food to eat, water to drink, room to fly. And there have always been these things, so they can't imagine they could end. But we know the Thorn can end. So these things can end – there can be a last day for this world.

'There are some of us who cannot live content, knowing this, even though we may also know that we will be able to die content long before it becomes necessary to really have the answers we seek. There is a certain quirk – a restlessness, in certain minds, which does not seem to understand the passage of time. What will be real someday to everyone is very real to them now.'

Jackson listened politely.

'Now, I bear you no malice, boy. If we had food here that you could eat, I would give it to you – provided. Provided I thought you would work just as hard at opening the door as you would if you were starving. Others may bear you malice, but I don't. I understand that we are really very much alike inside. And I like the idea of your being an odd one. I am an odd one too, among my own kind.' He pointed towards the Object. 'That's where I was mangled.

'I wouldn't leave it alone. I tried to crawl up one of its throats, but I was clumsy. As all of us who don't need the ground all our lives are clumsy when we crawl. My clumsiness saved my life. I fell to the ground. Fire burst forth from the throat, to clear me out, I suppose. But I was already crawling away. Still, it caught and threw me a good distance. Haw, they called it the reward for foolishness. I lay there screaming, and they gathered around laughing and exclaiming. That's when I understood I must either rule them or not live here any longer.

'I owe a good deal to the Object. I owe a good deal to being odd. And I tell you, odd one, that you'd better owe much to it, too.

'I'll do whatever needs to be done to force the most out of you. I will remind you, if you haven't thought of it yourself already, that it treats your kind of creature better than it treats my kind. My kind can't climb the ladder to its top, nor touch the door. When we try, something goes into my kind of creature from the door, flattens its insides, boils its eyes, throws it dead instantly earthward. Your kind of creature it merely permits to starve while attempting to crawl through the throat, or while picking at the door seam.'

The Eld grunted painfully. 'There's another thing. Let it give you hope. If the Object was made with the Thorn when time began, it was made, like the Thorn, for creatures with your kind of body.' The Eld glanced briefly at the places where the three-fingered hands grew out of his wings. 'Therefore, what's inside and makes that noise will probably not treat you like an enemy. It may help you. Why not believe there's your sort of food in there? What's a friend for, if not to offer hospitality? And I think you'll do well. You're very much like me, and if my body were like yours, I think I would do well.'

I'll bet you do think that, Jackson thought. He said: 'You know, I think you're right about how much alike our kinds of creature are. There's some-body who lives in our Thorn that I think you could spend a lot of happy hours with. Just talking. Comparing problems. Sharing thoughts.'

But the Amsir Eld didn't seem to understand. He looked at Jackson the way Jackson looked at people who used words like *theology*. Well, Jackson decided, it was possible to talk, talk, talk about how alike they were under the skin, but if you had become the Eld of the Amsirs, you couldn't really think there was anyone else who'd made out as wonderfully as you.

The way, when I was a kid, Jackson thought, I thought there was only one world, and the only thing in it was honning. He looked around at the Amsirs, the blue food he couldn't eat, the stilty houses, the sky filled with flapping creatures, and the Object. And I wish, he thought, I wish I was still like those farmers and Honors back there who still think that's all there is.

He felt pretty tired. 'I'm going to get some sleep,' he said, lay down, curled up, and closed his eyes around the throbbing of his arm.

III

Wow, his arm hurt. He scraped his eyes open and looked down at it. The flesh of his hand was swollen up in a doughy ring around the lower edge of the wrapping. When he reached up to touch his shoulder he found another bulge like it there. He rolled over in the dust near the object, rubbed his hair and face, pawed his open mouth, licked his teeth. He saw it was morning again. His skin felt dry. He couldn't get his face to work. He sat up, and saw the Amsir Eld sitting there. 'Huh! Been guarding my rest?'

'Mine, too. I've been wondering what effect a long rest would have on your energy supply. You don't seem to have become any more alert.'

Jackson moved. He had it pretty well planned, the next step was to get around behind the Eld, hook his arms under the Eld's wings, whatever good the left arm might do, and get his right thumb on to the front of the Eld's throat, while his fingers curled around the back of the Amsir's neck. From there, he figured, he could start setting himself up a little more comfortably around here. He didn't know exactly what the Amsirs could really do to get him something to eat, for instance, but there was a whole world here, full of brave, strong, big-mouthed, edible people, who were used to doing what the Eld told them. And if the Eld had to do what Jackson told him …

But the Eld had had the thought to hobble Jackson's ankles with a loose leather strap while he slept, and Jackson fell down.

The Eld grinned. 'In a few days, it won't be necessary to do that, or anything like it. Then you'll be waking up with only one thought. If need be, I may remind you that breakfast is inside the Object. Then you'll turn to with a will.'

Lying there, thinking all kinds of top-of-the-head, fast-answer thoughts, Jackson said: 'I believe a lot more in you for breakfast than in any guesses about what's inside that thing.'

The Eld said: 'It's truly amazing what you may believe in a few days. It's not a pretty condition. I think you'd disgust yourself. I don't think you would like that any more than I would. We have let you sleep. Here's some water,' he said, setting out one of those sealed hide bubbles of theirs. 'That we can give you. We won't be shocked – I won't be shocked – if you smear some on your skin. Does your arm hurt?'

'Thanks.'

The Amsir nodded off over Jackson's shoulder, and the doctor came up again. He unwrapped the bandages while Jackson drank and stared off at the rim of the world through the legs of the houses. When the doctor was done putting fresh wrappings on the arm, and was restoppering his bottle of liquid he said: 'Your arm's not healing. You'll lose it.'

'I knew that yesterday,' Jackson said. He tossed the water bubble down. 'There's something you can work on me with,' he said to the Eld 'Maybe there is something in the Object that can fix my arm. Some kind of real doctor. Why not? If there's a feast for me in there, there might as well be healing, too.'

The Eld was untying the end of the thongs between Jackson's ankles; his wings got in his way a little, and he was clumsy about it, but he got them off anyhow. There were a couple of spearmen standing around, Jackson noticed now. It hadn't mattered before if they were there or not, because when you make that kind of play there's no point counting odds. But he had shot that one, and he noticed them now. He held still.

'And if not healing, why not anything else, too?' the Eld was saying as he worked. 'Indeed, why not? Why not females, why not any other pleasures that might appeal to you? Why not weapons? And you've thought of weapons in there, haven't you?' The Eld looked up shrewdly, his eyes twinkling. 'Oh, haven't you!'

The Eld shrugged too. 'And why not? Why not? If you crack open a mystery from the beginning of time, why not have it contain all lore, all rewards for the shrewd and the odd? Then you can look down on us from the doorway every morning and poke fun. Pfu! Let me show you the answer to that.' He gestured with a wingtip, and a couple of spearmen hustled something forward from behind the Thorn.

The creature smiled winningly at Jackson. It smiled at the spearmen, it smiled at the Amsir Eld, at the instructor, and in fact at everything. Jackson had never seen anything so easily pleased.

It was a shame it didn't look all that pleasant. It stood just about his size, and it walked – at a guess – like a man. But it was a little hard to tell, because it sagged so much. It was like dough, and the colour of dough. There was no part of it whose skin did not hang down in sloughy folds, except at the very top of its head, where little fleshy pseudopods spangled half-erect, about where an Amsir's crest of lace would have begun. The rest of its flesh hung on its frame of bones and meat, half-closed its eyes, dropped around little beginnings of ears, made a flabby ruff round the neck, hung in a brief, scalloped cape around its chest and upper arms, made another fold below its waist, and fell on down its legs. It was, if it was dough, some Amsir housewife's too-watery bit of kneading from which an Amsir pastry might have been baked.

All this delighted it. Its soft flap-fingered hands – the little finger rather longer than the others – twiddled constantly at its thighs, its shoulders, and its face. It seemed to love playing with its mouth. How it smiled was by stretching its lips upward with its forefingers, quite frequently.

The Amsir Eld looked crookedly towards Jackson. Jackson obliged: 'All right – what is it?'

'Oh, this is Ahmuls,' he said. 'He's of a kind of creature born to us now and then. He happens to be one of the few who does not die while still very, very young. Well, his mother was a foolish woman and fond of him. And I'm very grateful to her now. You'll see why. Ahmuls is very lovable,' the Eld said as the creature shuffled up to him still twiddling. The Eld reached out and lightly stroked Ahmuls's cheek. 'Good morning, Ahmuls. I love you.'

'Good morning. I love you,' Ahmuls said rather clearly. He hummed some sort of contented sound and stroked the Eld's cheek.

'Ahmuls – this is Jackson,' the Eld said, pointing.

'Jackson ...' Ahmuls said reflectively, opening his eyes with thumbs and forefingers as he focused his attention.

'Ahmuls, I want you to show Jackson something.'

'Oh, yes.'

'Very good,' the Eld said, stroking Ahmuls's face again. 'Ahmuls, hit that for me.' The Eld pointed to the leg of a house a dozen dozen running strides distant. The Eld threw in an aside to Jackson: 'Like many odd ones, Ahmuls has had to be special, or go under. He's very proud of things he's taught himself to do. They show he loves himself, and since we all love ourselves so very much, when we do something for that sort of love we're superb. Ahmuls ...?' The Eld looked questioningly at Ahmuls.

Ahmuls turned to one of the spearmen, floppy-fleshed arm extended. He said neither please nor I love you. The Eld's sudden uplift of his arm did all the necessary asking for him. The spearman didn't seem offended. He gave his javelin a bit of a toss and Ahmuls caught it in mid-air, thumb down, with his arm crossed in front of him, still turned three-quarters away from his target. The next Jackson saw him clearly he was already stepping forward, his muscles already relaxing again, and the javelin was going through the air in an absolutely straight line, whirring. Jackson had never seen anything thrown that didn't curve down towards the end of its path. A dozen dozen running strides away the head of the javelin went into the house-leg with a *klat!*, a whip of its metal body, then a crack as the shaft snapped away from the immovably dug-in head. Up above, indignant voices boiled out, and heads and bodies showed at the doorway. Then a voice came faintly down, pleased as well as scandalized: 'Oh, Ahmuls!' And Jackson had been shown what love could do.

The Eld said: 'I love Ahmuls,' and Ahmuls grinned and grinned.

Pfu! thought Jackson.

The Eld stepped forward and took gentle hold of Ahmuls's arm. 'Watch, Jackson.' He pulled the flesh tight, for just a moment, and there was the outline of the human arm trapped under the uncooked-Amsir skin.

'You see,' the Eld went on to Jackson, 'this is also why I love Ahmuls. But let me show you that, too. Ahmuls – climb the ladder. Show Jackson you can climb the ladder, Ahmuls.'

Ahmuls held his eyes open again, hunted, found the two things he had to know about. 'Jackson,' he discovered. 'Ladder.' Satisfied, he was beside the Object with two strides, halfway up the ladder with one jump, and at its head immediately thereafter.

He stood with his feet curled over the top rung, and the only thing that kept him from falling backwards was that he leaned forward with his arms outstretched, oozed tight against the curving surface. While the door growled, he rubbed his face against the metal and moved his flattened palms in little caressing motions. Jackson raised an ear with a twist of his neck that reminded him about his arm, and could hear Ahmuls very faintly: 'I love you.'

'Come down now, Ahmuls,' the Eld cried. 'So you see,' he said to Jackson, 'the door thinks Ahmuls is your kind of creature, for it doesn't kill him. True, Ahmuls is very stupid, and so there's no hope of his ever opening the door. But that's good for you when you think of it, for if Ahmuls weren't stupid, I wouldn't need you. Anyway, Ahmuls goes in with you, if you open the door. He knows enough to hit you if you pick up a weapon. He's been told all about it many times in the past. He will understand something if it's said to him a few times. He's too gluey inside to forget it after that.'

Ahmuls had come back to the Eld. They exchanged touches again. 'Love you,' both of them said.

Jackson studied them.

The Eld said to Jackson: 'There's only one way you can keep Ahmuls from waiting just below you on the ladder while you try the door, and then following you in. That would be to cripple him now. I still need you, and I have no replacement for Ahmuls. You wouldn't be punished, and you'd have a much better chance once you got inside. So I'm perfectly willing to let you try your luck right now.'

Jackson shook his head at the Eld and walked over to Ahmuls. He looked straight into Ahmuls's slitty eyes as he fondled the spongy thing's cheek. 'I love you.'

But Ahmuls wasn't having any. He caught Jackson's hand with something that felt like a five-fingered machine inside a cloak of blanketing. Somewhere inside all there, Ahmuls's sense of touch got a message through to his head. 'No good,' he said, rubbing Jackson's hand before throwing the arm aside. 'Soft.'

CHAPTER NINE

I

It was hot up at the top of the ladder with Ahmuls humming happily a few rungs below him. Jackson ran his hands over the door again, and again found that it was exactly like any other door, except that it didn't have a handle, and it talked. He had got used to the growling. There were those scratches around the edges, where various hands before him had tried to pry. One or two of the scratches actually went maybe a fingernail-thickness deeper than the surface. The Eld had told him they were places where everybody sooner or later came to scratching in old scratches, trying to just plain wear through. The Eld's best estimate was that the deepest scratch had taken about a dozen men, working day and night, for maybe two weeks a piece. And it was as thick as a fingernail. The doors in the Thorn were as thick as two arms. But it was possible, Jackson thought, that a week or ten days from now he might start telling himself maybe this door wasn't that thick – maybe it was only a finger thick. Probably, the last two or three days he could hang on up there, he'd be telling himself he'd wear through any minute now.

The door was easy to get mad at. It was just another oval seam in the metal. A sensible man with other things to do would tell himself inside of an hour that it wasn't a door – it was some kind of fake wrinkle in the metal. He could climb back down the ladder, and never try again. There wasn't even any place for the voice to come out. It was the first time Jackson had ever met anything that could talk but didn't have a mouth.

He put his ear up to the door, trying to hear the heartbeat he could feel through his fingertips, but when he did that the voice went right through his head, and he couldn't hear anything but it. He leaned out as far as he dared, and looked it up and down again, and then he said: 'Hey, Ahmuls, let's go down.'

'Down?'

'Down. Let's go down.'

'You're stupid,' Ahmuls said, but he moved obligingly down, one rung at a time, making sure Jackson came with him. The instructing Amsir, who'd been keeping a sharp eye on this public tooling, came hurrying up to them. 'What's wrong?'

Amhuls grinned and pointed at Jackson. 'He came down. He's stupid.'

'I've learned all I'm going to, up there,' Jackson said.

'Where else are you going to learn anything?'

'That's the real problem, I guess – answering that one. But I've learned everything I'm going to, up there,' Jackson said, and walked towards the Thorn.

'Don't you leave me!' Ahmuls cried, taking Jackson's good arm.

'It's all right, Ahmuls dear,' the instructing Amsir said hastily. 'You wait here – I'll bring him back. He'll be with me.'

'All right. But you bring him back,' Ahmuls said dubiously.

'What are you going to do?' the instructing Amsir said, rustling along beside Jackson, his eyes glittering with intense curiosity.

'Study doors,' Jackson said. He jerked his thumb towards the Thorn. 'Quite a few of them in there.'

He stood in doorways all that afternoon, bracing his feet and elbows inside the oval door jambs as best he could, trying to understand how it felt to be that thick, that tall, that flat. He growled grudgingly out of various Amsirs' way whenever they came shuffling and scraping up the halls through him. He swung himself flat against a wall and stood that way for a long time, his fingers and toes curved around the jamb, being hinges. By the end of the afternoon, he had a pretty good idea inside his head of how a door would think and act and feel about people. But, always, only a door that had a handle through its middle.

By evening, the little hollow place that he dreamed through his middle, where the handle's works would be, had grown into something that he had to admit resembled the faint beginning of hunger in a man who let himself think about food. That was the only gain he had to show for the day, and he had to admit it was a loss. Towards evening, Ahmuls came looking for him, unhappy because the instructor didn't love him or he would have brought Jackson back, unhappy because Jackson still wouldn't go back up the ladder, unhappy because the Sun was going down and it was time to go back, to sleep, to wait for morning and the ladder, and Jackson again, and meanwhile not be loved.

II

In the morning, Jackson climbed back up the ladder. Ahmuls patted him approvingly on the shoulder as he stood aside to let him by. 'Now you're smart.' he said.

'Glad to hear it,' Jackson said. The doctor had re-done his arm again, with the usual results. Jackson could feel that arm all the way up his neck and into the inside of his head this fine morning in the bright sunlight with all the happy Amsirs flopping in the sky above him, and Ahmuls slurring and slapping up the ladder below him. When he got to the top, he sat down facing outwards, leaning his back and the back of his head against the metal, his feet resting on the next rung down, letting himself warm up. He kept his arms crossed over his up-bent thighs.

He began to talk casually. 'You know, door, I spent a long time last night trying to be like you.'

The door said: 'Ouwwtenshownnn. Dhayss dwuuhrr uhhpnnss owwn-nuhhli ...' and so forth.

'Didn't do any good. Man can't be a door. Can pretend to be a door – can tell himself he is a door. But a man doesn't have hinges. Anyway he doesn't have the kind of hinges a door does. And a man can't be a door like you at all, because a man has handles.'

'... dhaysstroydd wieyethouyut dhaysscriyeshunn,' the door said.

'Then I got to thinking to myself, door,' Jackson said, paying no mind as the door began again.

'Hey! You talkin' to me?' Ahmuls said peevishly from below.

'No.'

'Awwll ouwwthrr uhluff-ffouwrrmms ...' said the door.

'I got to thinking that if a man can't be a door, can a door be a man? And I guess we both know the answer to that. You're stupid, door. You tell the difference between my kind of creature and a Amsir; you're supposed to keep Amsirs out, so it figures maybe you're supposed to let men in. I mean, even the instructor has got that much figured out. And their Eld has it figured out, so that clinches it. But you won't let me in. You don't knock me off, but you don't let me in. You don't knock Ahmuls off either, and that's a mistake. No, no two ways about it – you're stupid. So I got to thinking, how do I make myself as stupid as a stupid door that thinks it's a man.'

'... wieyethouyut dhaysscriyeshunn.'

Jackson turned his head in a way that looked pretty casual and idle, and would have been casual in somebody whose arm didn't hurt all the way into his head. Ahmuls was right there, looking up at him. Over the many times Ahmuls had had this kind of duty, he'd learned that if he hung his head back and twisted his shoulders so that he was looking upside-down, he didn't have to hold the loose skin away from his eyes. 'Love you,' Jackson said.

'You're awful,' Ahmuls answered decisively.

'Well, I was saying, door – you're stupid. But you've got ears, and you can feel, and I guess you can see, too, even if you can't talk straight.'

'... t umm-nn pehrrsowwnnuhll.'

'Now the thing is, door, if you won't let me in, and you won't let Amsirs in, what did you ever let out that you *would* let back in? It would have to be something that talks like you, but looks like me, wouldn't it, door? Or, anyway,' Jackson said, listening to Ahmuls hum through the sound of the door going on talking, 'anyway something soft. But you've been here since the beginning of time. What happened to what you let out, way back then? Door, I figure somewhere you've got a picture of what you should let back in. A picture that talks, I guess, but I figure that's what you've got to have. Something to let you compare. Something you're too stupid to forget.'

It was getting hot again. Jackson wiped his face.

The instructing Amsir was getting all excited down below. He cupped his beak in his hand and shouted up: 'Ahmuls! What's he doing up there?'

'Nothing.'

'Then why has the door stopped growling?'

Jackson took a long, deep breath. He turned around and looked at the door, holding it tight with his good hand and with the best he could do with his bad one. It would be no time to fall off now. 'You dumb door!' he said. 'This is only the first thing I thought of to try.'

Down below him, Ahmuls was shifting his grip too, forgetting he couldn't see as well right side up as he could upside down.

'All right, door – if I've got you started thinking again after all this time – all right, if you do listen better than you talk, then you figure out what you let out would look like by now, and you figure out what it would talk like. It can't be that hard!' he said, suddenly irritated. 'If that instructor can figure out some of your words, then something smart enough to tell the difference between a Amsir and a man should be able to figure out my words. *Open up, you dumb bastard!*' he cried.

The beat of the Object's heart changed. There was a creak, a suck, a pop. The door jumped back the thickness of a finger, and zipped sideways, into a place made for it to slide into in the skin of the Object.

Jackson scrambled around on the ladder. Down below him the Eld was a little slow getting things organized. There were spearmen throwing from down there, but they hadn't really got themselves set.

The whole thing was happening too fast for everybody. Jackson hadn't really figured the door would make sense out of what he said, and for all of his talking, the Eld hadn't figured Jackson would get the door open this fast, if ever. So that buggered up all the Eld's quiet, unspoken thinking about how once the door was open he didn't need Jackson at all, because he had Ahmuls or could maybe get other creatures of Jackson's kind who maybe wouldn't be as tricky. Well, all that thinking was shot, too, because Jackson was in through the door, and into a dark little room banging himself up, laughing and cursing, before the spearmen got into the air. In fact, the only one who stayed cool was Ahmuls. He'd been told what to do a lot of times, and now he did it. He came flipping in through the doorway, and stood next to where Jackson was lying on the floor. 'I come, too,' he said, happy to be useful.

Jackson let out his breath as the first couple of spears came buzzing in through the doorway from nervous, fluttering spearmen. He ducked as they clattered off the walls. 'I guess you do.'

There was this other door at the end of the little room. There was a red, bright lamp shining over it. Then the outside door closed, the light went out, yellow light came on from overhead in the little room, and the inside door opened ... *thuk, wink, wink, thum*! Past it were all kinds of things that looked like what Jackson guessed was Thornlike machinery. Through the metal around them, he and Ahmuls both could hear the outside door hollering as spears hit it. Its voice was too fast, too high. It sounded as panicky as everybody.

'Attention! Attention! This system has now been adjusted to accelerated speech mode. This door opens only to human personnel. All other life-forms will be destroyed without discretion. An intelligible warning has been given.'

'It was about time,' Jackson said.

CHAPTER TEN

I

'What's happening?' Ahmuls said unhappily, peering into the inside of the Object. He'd jerk back his head to look over his shoulder every time another spear-point hit the other side of the door, but then he'd peer again. Things were beginning to hum inside the Object. Jackson could see light getting brighter, dancing around in there; he could hear things going clickety-click. Most of all he could feel how strong the Object was becoming. All around them, a frantic voice like the voice of the door said: 'Uhhcumminng uhup t full pow'r!' Farther inside the Object the same voice cried: 'Standing by on full power! Main generators On, maintenance power supply Off!' The voice steadied down. It began to sound as if it felt normal. You could even tell it was a woman. 'Condition of vessel report: All systems functional and reliable. Maintenance Mode battery drain excessive; recharging.'

'What's happening?' Ahmuls cried.

'Don't look at me, chum,' Jackson said quickly, 'I haven't picked up any weapons.'

'You better not!'

'I know.' Jackson had his feet firmly under him and moved to the doorway that led deeper inside the Object. 'Will you look at all that machinery!'

'What are we going to do! Who'd want to stay in here!' Ahmuls wailed.

Jackson listened to the *tang! tang! tang!* of spears hitting the outside of the Object. 'Oh, I don't know,' he said.

'Is anyone going to take command?' the door-voice said.

What? What now? Jackson thought. Any minute now, this clown was going to decide something was a weapon, and now there was this. Wasn't anybody in charge?

There was all this humming and buzzing; these voices talking and doors opening; all these things happening that he maybe could have enjoyed, if he'd come on them a little bit at a time, ready to take them on or take them apart. Maybe be them, or maybe picture them. But with a stomach and an arm and spear sounds and a Ahmuls like he had, he didn't feel all that ready.

'Command must be exercised within a reasonable period of time,' the voice said.

'Huh?' Ahmuls said.

'Command *must* be exercised! Stasis wastes power!'

Nag, nag, nag, Jackson thought. Whatever stasis is. 'All right,' he yelled. 'What'll make you happy?'

'Function. Duties to perform. I cannot come to full power for nothing!'

'Listen, you quit talking to it!' Ahmuls said. 'You done enough already.'

'Listen, no weapons, right?' Jackson said to him, holding out his empty hands. 'I'm *supposed* to talk to it, remember?' He raised his voice. 'You got a name, voice?'

Ahmuls was frowning, Jackson guessed. Maybe he'd stay busy that way just a little bit longer.

'My name is Self-Sustaining Interplanetary Expeditionary Module,' the voice said. 'Call me Susiem.'

'What can you do?'

'Anything! Anything a Susiem can do.'

You wouldn't think that was a lot of help, Jackson thought. But there was one thing he knew a Susiem could do, and it was with doors. He jumped, and bounced off Ahmuls. Ahmuls fell back. Jackson fell through the doorway farther into the object. 'Close that door!' he yelled. He lay there on the floor. He found that to the now more distant, and less frequent, sound of spears against the outside, was added the soft *klop!* of Ahmuls, trapped in the little room, beating his fist against the door.

Jackson shook his head and looked around. The room he was in was full of machinery; metal and glass all over the place, humped, twisted, full of knobs and pointers, flashing and gleaming, humming—

'That's great. But I don't see anything to eat.'

'Certainly not! Do you think you're in the mess compartment?' Susiem said.

'You trying to say there's another room here? Where there's food? There's really food?'

'I can do anything a Susiem can do!' Susiem said.

Klop, klop, klop.

'Boy, he talks plainer than you do,' Jackson said. 'All right, how do I get to that other room? And don't open that door until I say so! By the way, if you've got food, you wouldn't happen to have a doctor?' Jackson grinned. After that I want a Thorn where everybody wants to be like me, and Amsirs that want to give up to me. What you got here, Susiem – so much to give, a man could run out of dreaming? Not in the life of creatures of my kind. Well, come on – come on – work up a doctor for me. Give him gallons of boiling water, and a pile of clean rags big enough to sleep in.

'Certainly I won't open the door! You're in command! Report to Sick Bay immediately.'

'They got food there?'

'Medical treatment takes precedence over rations. Report to Sick Bay.'

I'm in command, Jackson thought. 'Where's Sick Bay?'

II

Susiem led him to Sick Bay by simply having him follow lights. They kept turning on just ahead of him as he walked through a door and then down a ladder and through another door. Sick Bay was all white except where it was bare metal. The doctor was white and bare metal, and had wheels. He unstoppered himself from a doctor-shaped hole in the wall and came rolling forward like a plough. He came to about the height of Jackson's chest. 'State your complaint,' he said.

'My arm's going to have to come off,' Jackson said, looking at the doctor carefully, deciding to believe Susiem when she said 'This is a doctor.'

'You're not competent to prognose. State your complaint. How do you account for the fact that you don't match any comparison in my files? Show proof you're entitled to receive medical treatment from this station.'

'Emergency, Doctor,' Susiem said. 'This man is in command.'

'You'll have to fill out forms,' the doctor said. A hard, soft-white square on its top turned a very pale white-green. A stick popped up most of the way out of a hole beside the square. 'Take the pen.' Jackson pulled it out curiously. It was the same shape and about the same length as the burnt sticks he had left behind at his home Thorn. But it wasn't burnt – it was light, felt soft at the surface but was as rigid as metal, felt slick, but didn't slip from his fingers. At the very end of it was what looked like a little ball of glass.

'Well?'

Jackson peered at the green-white square. There were lines running across it now, bright white. At the beginnings of the lines there were shapes of some kind – patterns made out of lines, bent and crossing each other. 'Kind of pretty,' he said.

'Criticism is not your function. Fill out the forms.'

'I think he's illiterate, Doctor,' Susiem said.

'Well, let him make some kind of mark,' the doctor said impatiently. 'I'm sure there are others waiting. He's wasting time.'

'He's in command.'

'Well, then he certainly ought to be literate.'

'Look – I order you to make yourself understandable,' Jackson told the doctor. 'My arm hurts, and I'm hungry.'

'Do you know how to make a mark? Make a mark on the surface of the plate with the light-pen. I have to have some sort of identification for you or I can't file you. And if I can't file you, you're lost.'

'Oh. You just want to be able to find me again. Well, here's what I look like.'

The little ball slipped much too easily over the top of the plate, if that was what you called it, but the light-pen, or whatever, left a nice white line behind it. Jackson started turning his wrist to thicken and thin it, and that didn't work, but by and large he had a pretty good picture of himself down on the plate very soon. For good measure, he took one corner of the plate and made a drawing of his arm bones, showing where the dart had gone in. 'That's what's wrong with me. The dart's been pulled out, but the arm died.'

The doctor and Susiem didn't say anything for a little bit. Finally the doctor said: 'Your knowledge of anatomy isn't bad.'

'Draws well, too,' Susiem said. 'You can tell what you're looking at. Not like the paraphrastic stuff they do.'

'The arm,' Jackson said.

'Certainly the arm,' the doctor answered. 'Uh – Let's just have an overall look at you while we're about it.' The doctor shimmied back and forth on his wheels for a moment. There was a little humming plough-noise inside him. 'Hmm. Yes. Well – you've certainly led an active life. But it's all healed very nicely – barring some of the fresh events, of course. The only one that we need to do anything much about is in that elbow joint. 'You're going to need a restoration there. Your blood sugar is a little low. Are you fatigued?'

'Huh?'

'Are you tired?'

'Damn right. Hungry, too.'

'Well, I can introduce a little protein into your system, I suppose, while we're working on the arm, but I'd rather you had something to chew and swallow. It sets up a good reflex series. Susiem, why don't you get the Captain here some nourishment while I'm taking care of this.'

The doctor came apart, partway, with some kind of flip of his sides, which turned into a kind of chair-cradle. The seat and back, and the part that went under the legs, were padded, and so was the place for Jackson's right arm to rest. A trough that extended partway into the doctor was for Jackson's left arm. It was bare metal, and a little bar of light popped out on a stalk over it, lighting up the leather wrappings as Jackson sat down.

'Sick Call takes precedence over Mess,' Susiem said. 'I see no reason why he can't be treated and then go to where the food is.'

'I said bring him something!' the doctor snapped. 'He's undernourished, he's got one arm free to serve himself with, and besides, rank has its privileges.'

'If you record it as a prescription, Doctor.'

'I do.'

'Very well,' Susiem said. Something began to stir around one compartment lower down. 'I'm breaking out a food cart.'

'For a machine,' Jackson said to the doctor, 'you got more sense than people.'

'Damn right,' the doctor said. 'Now let's get this slop off your limb. Who's been treating you – some veterinarian?'

'Some what?'

'Captain, you need an education.'

'What's that?'

'What you need.' Maybe the doctor didn't want to go around and around any more; maybe he figured he could keep Jackson busy with something else. At any rate, something that must have been a knife zipped down the length of Jackson's arm. It laid open the wrappings as neat as any slash Jackson had ever seen. It laid open his arm too, and it sure did cut down on his desire to do much talking. He sat there staring at his own bones, pink-white, in the halved shell of his arm. All around the torn, discoloured place where Red Filson's dart had gone down in on its way to the elbow joint, it looked like something rotten.

Sparks – maybe metal, maybe light – winked and flashed around the bone. There was a cloudy white puff of fog where the joint was; there was a suck of air and that was gone, *whummph!* and then the joint was gone. The bones of his upper and lower arm didn't meet by a full third of a dozen finger-widths. More sparks, and now the ends were notched and drilled, the way a stick-maker might make a pegged splice. The rotten place in the meat of his arm was getting smaller. His whole arm was tingling. The bar of light above it seemed to be shivering.

Something like a little doctor came rolling in the door, and flipped open its top. Steaming warmth hit Jackson in the nose like the clout of a damp, hot rag. He'd never smelled anything so strong in his life. It poured right up his nose and seemed to fill his whole head. He blinked; it was making his eyes water.

Lying on a dish were some greens with something greasy-looking on them, a round ball of something white and made out of small parts that looked like maggots, and a rounded squishy-looking brown thing that looked like what you might find under a Amsir house, if it had been dried. Next to it was something with a long slim handle and four long curved points, a folded-up white hunk of something that might have been Amsir lace shaved until it was thin and crinkly, and a glass of what would have looked like milk if it hadn't been so white and opaque.

'Lunch,' Susiem said. 'Salisbury steak, with Roquefort salad, and rice. Enjoy it, Captain.' Jackson couldn't make up his mind whether to look at his lunch or his arm.

The doctor was really getting things done in there. Delicate stilty little fingers with hinges in them came popping out, from under the same overhang that the bar of light came from. They were carrying a woven white contraption that looked like an outline drawing of an elbow joint. The little fingers put pegs in place, and in a trice where his broken elbow had been was this white thing, snugly slipped into place. He could see right through its weave, of course, but it looked pretty strong and solid all by itself.

'Okay,' the doctor said. 'That's what we call a jig-splint. In a couple of days, you'll have a pretty good structure of bone cells forming around that grid, and in a week or so that'll be as good as new.'

The two halves of Jackson's arm were pushed back together as the walls of the trough gently squeezed shut around them. The trough wiggled its halves back and forth for an instant until the halves of the arm were lined up just right. Then they fell back and where the cut had been there was a very thin line, like the scratch of a playful woman, running along the seam. For the first time, Jackson saw blood. It stood up in droplets like pinheads along the scratch, already scabbed and hard. The cut lengths of arm wrapping lay in the trough for an instant and then puffed out with a flash, a fog of smoke, and a *whoomph!* 'Eat your lunch,' the doctor said.

Jackson tested his arm. The lunch still looked like what it had looked like before. The arm was great. He twisted and stretched it, making a fist, squeezing, trying to see if it would pop open into two halves again. It wouldn't. It was a good, well-made arm. He rapped his left elbow with the knuckles of his right hand. It sounded good and hard.

CHAPTER ELEVEN

I

It didn't seem possible he had eaten. But Susiem had said: 'If you think I'm going to throw away this perfectly good food, and go to the trouble of synthesizing burnt Amsir and whole grain bread, when the whole basis of your being here is that you're *human*'.

Jackson had to admit that Salisbury steak, rice and Roquefort salad wasn't bad. He licked the leftovers off his fingers. But he drew the line at what Susiem called milk; he finally got some water instead.

He sat back. The doctor was still letting him sit in him. 'You know,' Jackson said, 'it's funny how it works out.' Here the Eld Amsir had been jollying him along with lots of fine talk about maybe there was food in here, and something to do about his arm, and be damned if there wasn't. Luck. Was he getting paid off for never letting down? Who could tell that, and send the luck to him? Where was there a place from which the luck-sender could have that kind of vantage? Was there Ariwol after all? Believe in luck, believe in Ariwol, huh? Rather not believe in luck. What do you call it when it comes, then?

'What are your further orders, Captain?' Susiem said impatiently.

'Well ... I don't know. Is there some place around here for me to sleep?'

'You don't need any right now,' the doctor said.

'*Sleep!*' Susiem said simultaneously. 'Here you've got everything turned on, and you're going to *sleep?*'

'Well, it's something us humans do. Whether they need it or not. Can't tell when your next chance is going to be.'

'Humans,' the doctor said, 'sleep at set, regular times.'

'That's right,' Susiem said. 'Stasis wastes *power!*'

Oh boy, it never stops, Jackson thought, even with machines. 'Well, look – you must have had other captains—'

'I should say so!'

'What did you do when they slept?'

'When they slept, the First Officer was awake. Don't you know anything about being human?'

'He needs an education,' the doctor said.

'More than I need a First Officer?' Jackson said.

'What about the individual in the airlock? Isn't that your first officer?'

'Him?' All Ahmuls was in Jackson's head right now was a *klop, klop, klop* on the inside door. That was enough. He still hadn't decided what to do about that. But why did he have to decide now? It wasn't as if he was going to spend the rest of his life anywhere else but here. Being Captain ... whenever the machines didn't have something else in mind. 'What's a First Officer do? I got one's pretty good with a spear, I guess. But spearing don't seem to be much needed. I mean, you're made out of metal, Doctor, and I don't even know where you are, Susiem.'

Susiem giggled.

'All right, that does it,' the doctor said. 'I'm prescribing this boy a university. You do have the necessary fact library, don't you?'

'Self-Sustaining Interplanetary Exploration Modules are, self-evidently, self-sustaining,' Susiem answered, as the doctor's arm immediately, but gently, unfolded additional sections that held Jackson by the wrists. The seat changed slope, so that he was mostly lying down.

'No need to get offended about it. Just be ready to patch through into my inputs when I say the word. And no stirring around in *my* banks while we're overlapping, either – everybody thinks all *they* need to be doctors themselves is facts. Get the leukocytes and the cytoplasms in their right places and anyone can be a sawbones! That's what *you* think. So stay out and do your job, and I'll do mine.'

What the hell were they up to? Jackson made one try at getting his arms out, which taught him he couldn't do it. Anyhow, supposing he'd get loose, where was he going to run to? Outside? Through the little room with Ahmuls klopping in it? But what the hell were they up to? Round pads came from somewhere behind Jackson's head and pressed it close among them, front and back, both sides.

'All right, I'm hitting him with the predisposants now.' A little thing like a hollow spearpoint whipped out of the doctor's insides, darted at Jackson's throat, stopped short but close, and fired something cold and stinging into the place where the heavy throb of blood came near the surface of the skin. Jackson felt it just for a heartbeat, and he was still admiring how fast it moved and how keen it looked, when it flipped back and disappeared. 'Massive dose,' the doctor commented. 'With this individual, you want the same dose as you'd need to teach a horse symphonic composition.' Jackson could feel something very funny happening to his eyes and ears. Sounds were beginning to break up into little reverberating pieces. First the edges of everything he could see were blurred, and then he was weak. Moisture – great glittering streams of tears – pooled out of his helpless lids and sheeted down his face.

A bulky, warm feeling spread out from the pit of his stomach. His fingers felt as if his palms were split painlessly and smoothly along each string of bones clear back to the whites. The same time his eyes ran wet, his lips were puffy and dry, and the same time his belly was warm, his forehead was icy cold. He swallowed, and his ears popped. He blinked, and his tear-filled eyes felt sandy. 'He's ready,' the doctor said.

There was another fine, cold spray at the back of Jackson's neck. 'Inputs going in now.' Something fine and ticklish as Petra Jovans' hair came in through the back of Jackson's neck, slipped gracefully to the inside of his head, and for all he knew quivered there. 'All right, patch in,' the doctor said.

Whatever patching-in was, Jackson guessed Susiem had done it, because suddenly, inside his head, where he was, there was a feeling like— A thing happening like— Well, what was happening, was that, in there, and around there, what was being done – no; what was happening—

'Who could I tell?' Jackson hollered at the top of his lungs. 'Who would believe me!'

II

It was no different, really, than remembering what it was like being a boy around the Thorn. One day he was just another brat – just another brat, except he was inside himself – and the next day he was here in the expeditionary ship, remembering it. It was probably no different from that.

'Well?' the doctor said.

'He's done,' Susiem said.

The taste of hot dust was in his mouth, swirling up around the Thorn as he ran, and ran. The feel of the first time he swung his arm just right and the dart shot straight and true into the target, a buzzing streak of what Honor White Jackson could do. Honor Secon Black Jackson. Honor Red Jackson. Honor Red Jackson, hurting and hungry, being a door in the alien echoes of the Amsir Thorn. And now he was here. Memory had no time or space.

His head was very full.

Hey! he thought, I was right all along! It was too small – it was all too small, and it was all wrong. I was right and they were wrong.

When he thought of how they tried to keep him down, and how they kept themselves down, he began to grin. When he thought about the Amsirs, poking and prying, trying to understand it all – from where they were – he grinned even more fiercely. Oh, wow – mine is the Earth and everything that's in it.

'Congratulations, Captain,' Susiem said, 'you are now an Honours graduate in Liberal Arts from Ohio State University. You have a special Masters in Command Psychology from the University of Chicago, and three semester hours in military journalism from the Air Force Academy. You are fully qualified to command this vessel.'

'I know that,' Jackson said.

'These qualifications are now on file in my data banks, and will be listed with Earth Central Statistics immediately upon my reacquisition of contact with the Associated Midwestern University Generic Research Project communications network,' Susiem went on, tidying up the loose ends.

Jackson had loose ends of his own. He barely heard her. What he heard, through the fabric of the ship, very softly but very much on his mind, was *klop, klop, klop*.

'There's no way you can tease him out of that airlock and back down the ladder, is there?' he said, pro forma, but he didn't want to do that anyway. Poor bloody Ahmuls. If he got him out of the lock and back to the Eld Amsir's love, what use would they have for him with the ship gone? And the ship would be gone. He most certainly wasn't going to spend his life grounded aboard her now, even supposing her life support system could endure that long with his organism draining it. But that was secondary, too – in fact, irrelevant. For who, knowing him as he was now, knowing how much time there was to make up for, could imagine him going anywhere but Earthward?

Earthward to Ariwol, he noted parenthetically. Earthward to Airworld. The tongue of his mind twisted voluptuously around the ability to make the long vowels flow; he took a deep, deep breath – breath enough to make him giddy.

Klop klop klop.

Kick him out, struggling, to ridicule and scorn, to uselessness with the ship gone? How could he do that to a creature at his mercy that he did not ever need to eat?

Eat.

'What about this lichen they eat? Can you synthesize that for ... our shipmate?'

'I can do anything a Susiem can do.'

'It's a perfectly normal Terrestrial form,' the doctor said.

'Oh. Then there's no problem. Let's bring him in. We'll control him long enough for you and Susiem to do as much as you can for his brain and data file, and it's solved.'

'It is not. You're already proving a little learning is a dangerous thing. In the first place, I don't know what you mean by control, but I certainly wouldn't take on any hostile organisms of his size with one limb as fragile as that arm of yours is at present. And you don't seem to have drawn the proper conclusions from his diet. I am amazed you were able to survive out there at all. I have no predisposants that could possibly do anything useful to *his* nucleic acids. You're anthropomorphizing. To all intents and purposes, there is less kinship between him and the human heritage than there is between you and me.'

'That's ridiculous!' Susiem cried. 'He's perfectly human – he can't fly, can he?'

'If you don't want your mistakes brought up, ship, don't activate doctors.'

'All right, you two, cut it out,' Jackson said. What the hell did the doctor mean, he couldn't control Ahmuls? It was perfectly plain how he could control Ahmuls – he'd been told about it in his sophomore year. What he hadn't been told was how to like it. But he'd also been taught how to get along without liking, while going for his Masters. It was amazing the things he'd been taught. 'Doctor – all right, you can't predispose him. Can you patch him up if he's hurt?'

'No problem,' the Medico replied.

'Susiem, if we let him in, can you protect your components in that room?'

'To an extent.'

'Well, then, let's get to it – I'm sick of this place. The sooner we get this done, the quicker we can move.' I wonder how he'll like Ariwol.

He walked up the companionway to the airlock level. He put his face up close to the door. 'Ahmuls! Ahmuls, can you hear me?'

'You son of a bitch.'

'Listen to me – if I open this door, what'll you do?'

'Kill you, you son of a bitch.'

'Ahmuls, listen close. You may not believe this, but I can bust you up real good.'

'Not if I kill you, you son of a bitch.'

'Ahmuls, I'm telling you – they gave me a—' What had they given him? They'd given him a weapon, and he had picked it up.

By the time Susiem and the Extraterrestrial Life-Adaptability Technique Experiment were launched, the art of unarmed combat on Earth had reached a point of development which made practice unnecessary and the karate-ka's callouses superfluous. The system had been refined to so simple a point that a mere explanation of what places were to be touched was sufficient. Any man with a decent memory for instructions, and reasonable dexterity, could successfully apply it to an equally proficient man with slower reflexes – and to all uninitiates – with cunning rapidity and shocking accomplishment. Jackson's reflexes were not as quick as Ahmuls's but his memory was as fast as Susiem's feed to his brain, and in any case Ahmuls just had no idea—

'Aw, hell,' Jackson said. 'Susiem, open the door.'

It was amazing how fast the sport was, bags of loose flesh and all, flapping and grunting, his feet slap-slapping, his pudgy hands extended from his forearms as if he wore ragged sleeves.

Jackson extended his body, right forefinger first, and touched him as he had been told in the fieldhouse amphitheatre of the sunny Canterbury Gothic campus. It was shocking how Ahmuls's feet flew out from under him. Jackson reached down quickly, and touched the one ankle he could reach;

Ahmuls cried out. He probably hadn't often felt pain. Not since he'd got big enough.

Jackson moved back out of the way. 'Look, Ahmuls – you can't get up to catch me now. Will you listen?'

But Ahmuls could get up. People did walk on broken legs – they even ran on them, when they had to and were in shock. It was just a matter of how much actual physical incapacity was introduced into their physical structures. Until things really disintegrated, they could just keep running. It happened on football fields and in parachute jump training all the time. The uneasy part about it was, it often made them run faster. That was how Ahmuls was now.

Jackson wove around Ahmuls's charge. His reflexes were slower, but the method was foolproof against charging attacks provided the eye could register them at all. He touched Ahmuls on the ribs. After that, Ahmuls's side was like a rawhide bag of blood. God damn it, don't smear on me! Jackson thought as he made Ahmuls brush by him again. Aw, you dumb animal! 'Give up!' he yelled.

Ahmuls charged him, grunting: 'Leave me alone – leave me alone, will you!'

Jackson touched both arms. He had to take the shock of Ahmuls hitting him, but he took it on Ahmuls's bad side, and anyway, Ahmuls then had no arms to hug him with. He moved them right, but they bent in too many places, and Jackson got out through them.

'Get the doctor up here!' Jackson yelled.

'Watch out for my components!' Susiem cried as Ahmuls blundered.

'The hell with you and all your components! ' Jackson yelled as he touched Ahmuls low in the back, feeling the flesh turn to porridge as the shock travelled from where he touched, and then he touched again in the same place, just to make sure; this time he felt the same thing in his fingertip you feel when you're a kid and you nudge out a baby tooth. Ahmuls windmilled his floppy arms, but he had nothing to hold his legs up any more, and he went down, folding in the middle and folding at the broken ankle, putting out his broken arms to catch him, landing on his broken side, and then his face. He lay slumped on his knees, arms out, his face squashed flat against the deck, and only one red eye peering up at Jackson.

'All right, all right,' he wept. The tears found hidden channels in his folded cheek.

Jackson dropped to his knees on the deck beside him. 'I tried to tell ya,' he said.

'Yuh.' Ahmuls swung his neck as best he could, very fast, going for Jackson's wrist with his teeth. Jackson pushed his head down. 'Cut it out; please cut it out.'

'Yuh. Yuh, all right, all right, I've got nothing left.' His fingers crept towards Jackson's ankle, dragging his arm, and Jackson put his knee on them. The doctor came rolling up. He stood there.

'Well, goddamn it,' Jackson squalled, 'what are you waiting for?'

'I have no authorization.'

'All right – pursuant to the emergency veterinary provisions, I declare this creature is a valuable, harmless alien life form in distress. I order you to proceed with medical services as far as your knowledge and experience go!'

The doctor's sides unfolded. 'Yes, sir. No problem.'

Ahmuls had quit trying to move his fingers under Jackson's knee. Under his face, the deck was wet. 'What are you going to do? What are you going to do, all you soft things?'

'No, no, it's all right, Ahmuls,' Jackson said. His hand on Ahmuls's head was making smoothing motions up where a Amsir would have its lace. 'The doctor'll fix you. You've got to listen, Ahmuls. Why the hell can't you listen? I love you.'

'Did you have to hit me?'

The doctor gathered Ahmuls up in his arms. He was amazingly gentle. He lifted smoothly and tenderly, making Ahmuls comfortable in his arm. He was shockingly gentle.

A maintenance machine had already slipped from its wall recess. It was hovering around the three of them, jockeying to get to the deck where it was messed up.

'Just wait your turn, Susiem,' Jackson said angrily, facing the maintenance machine as if it had eyes and ears. 'You have no sense of decency, no sense at all.'

CHAPTER TWELVE

I

'Get me an audiovisual picture of the outside,' he told Susiem, sitting in the piloting chair.

Susiem swung a scope towards him. The speakers filled with the sounds of the outside; the rustle of wings, the murmur of wind, the ping and crackle of large expanses of metal in the open weather. The Amsirs were flying patrol just past the door, beating back and forth, spears ready. There was a littering of broken spears on the ground below the airlock ladder. At the doorway of the Thorn, the Amsir Eld, and the instructing Amsir, and a crowd of more than six but less than twelve apprentices of some type were clustered there, in postures that were not essentially useful. He could hear them discoursing; he motioned impatiently towards the gain control and he could make out their words. They were disputatious and bereft.

'And I tell you we must accept the possibility that we are the interlopers here!' one of them was saying.

'Shut up! I can clearly recall a witnessed discourse in which it was impeccably postulated that if the Object destroyed our kind on touch, how much more terrible must be the fate of any creature it would permit to enter its maw!'

'Shut up yourself! I'll try conclusions with *you* any time!'

'Eld!' Jackson said, and the Object growled to the Amsirs at the doorway. 'Eld – stand clear!'

'What?' The hard beak was up. The bright, dark eyes were searching where the doorway was on top of the ladder.

'Eld, I have some facts for you.'

The communicator went dead abruptly. The screen was blank, the speakers were silent. 'You are not permitted to contaminate the experiment!' Susiem snapped. 'You are exceeding your authority and directly contravening expedition regulations. You are not permitted to communicate facts to the experimental subjects. All facts required by the experimental subjects are predetermined, programmed, and were long ago introduced to the system. Any repetition of this incident will result in your automatic and immediate dismissal from command. This incident will be logged. It will be transferred to the central comprehensive files on Earth at the earliest opportunity following reacquisition of contact with the Project's communications network. You are reprimanded and are permitted to resume communication only on the basis that you make no further attempt at contamination.'

The screen and the speakers came back to life. 'Stand clear,' Jackson shouted to the Eld. He counted thirty seconds on the fascia clock. 'Let's go, Susiem,' he said, and with a bang and a roar and a flash they all went, taking the world's hope with them, while broken Amsirs crashed about.

II

Earth was pastorally green, its hillocks crowned by elms, its infrequent, low buildings starkly white. Earth was green, fair, and heady with the wine of life, in a condition not often attained since the hills of Greece were first so limned by the deft pencillings of Walt Disney.

It hadn't seemed like such a particularly long trip. He had spent large parts of it in the piloting couch. At first he'd yearned at the stars in their great glowing panoplies, bemused to think that he finally understood what they were, toying in his mind with thoughts of immensity, with notions of how vast it all was, how marvellous its creation, how unfathomable its extent. Fantasy-grasps of macrocosm and microcosm haunted his understanding. All this great clockwork, this explosion and decay, these cycles and epicycles of infinitude, distended his capillaries with shivers of delight at how vast a table had been prepared before him. For a while he thought he understood the infinitely tiny complexities that hurtled around about themselves to form each millimicrocubit of immensity.

And Susiem did much to sustain this feeling for him. She groaned and whined, thumping and jolting within herself all around him; his couch trembled to her humming. Each start of ignition, each fit of clicking busyness seemed to reflect another spasm of gobbling at the miles between where he was and the nebulae on which his eyesight rested.

But a couple of days went by and it occurred to him that the nebulae weren't getting effectively closer. He had a clear intellectual understanding of how many miles per day were being clocked on Susiem's instruments. He got the idea that he ought to calculate how many days of whining, banging, and groaning from this tireless mechanism he'd have to endure before he got to the nearest nebula. It came to him that there was just so much of that a man could put up with.

Susiem could put up with it forever, of course. Only somebody like Susiem was liable to want to.

'How's the doctor coming along with Ahmuls?' he asked her, thinking a good way to put it was that he was lonely among a myriad of stars.

'I'll check— He's reporting good progress. Considerable healing has been accomplished and the patient is resting. His manner is subdued.'

'Yeah, well. He's had a lot happen to him.'

He had Susiem close the ablation shutters on the piloting windows again. And for a while he had her run tapes of Earth. He found that it was just as he remembered it – swarming with Man and his works, beautiful beyond belief, busy in its beauty, echoing with flashes of light and sound, ashake with motion, singing of power to the morning and the evening wind.

He created little moments of naïveté for himself. He looked at the rivers tumbling down out of the mountains and rowelling across the plains while saying to himself I never knew there was that much water in the world; how green everything is, how full! He looked at the cities where the rivers forked, at the shipping complexes in the deltas where rivers and ocean mingled, and he cried out to himself *Thalassa! Thalassa!* He compared the flight of supersonic aircraft with flappings of Amsirs and he pretended to see a portable rocket launcher in terms of a demigod's throwing stick. He craned his neck at the cloud-raking spires of the mighty cities. And he made the back of his mind wail: 'Alas, Thorn!'

Ah, horse apples, he said after very little of that, being a man with a Master's, and had Susiem turn it off.

What to do? Jackson had another meal – this time it was delicious, because he knew how to order. There was even wine. Wine was considerably better than beer. But it left him moody.

He had Susiem play him some music. He read from her library, sticking mainly to entertainment; westerns, mostly, at first. Susiem's library had a first chapter précis index; by using it lackadaisically and carelessly, he tripped over the Big Little Book version of *John Carter of Mars* and from there his taste spiralled outwards. He had got as far as G-8's struggle against the Kaiser's land aircraft carrier when Susiem passed him the word that Ahmuls was ready to be talked to.

'You feeling all right?'

'He feels fine. All his structural damage is repaired and healed. It was a massive job, but what with all the things I know how to do – and three days' sleep – he's fine.'

Ahmuls was sitting propped halfway up in a Sick Bay bunk, leaning back into a corner. There were shadows across his face. But he had his hands up, framing his cheeks, and you could see light glinting on his open eyes.

'How do you feel about all that?' Jackson said.

'Feel rotten,' Ahmuls mumbled. Jackson had to stop and re-think before he could understand him – he mumbled so fast, and so many syllables of his speech had drifted loose from the cleanly Midwest that Jackson remembered from his schooling. 'That doctor machine says we're going someplace.' Ahmuls mumbled on, and Jackson deciphered it all right, improving with practice. 'Where to?'

'Yeah, well. That's what I'm here to explain. You all done trying to kill me?'

'Can't kill you, you son of a bitch.'

'Aw, come *on*, Ahmuls. I'm glad you all done trying to kill me, but I wish you wouldn't call me names. Look, it's not like it used to be, all our lives. It's all different.'

'I'm no different.'

'Well, I am!'

'You say.'

'Will you listen?'

'Gotta listen. You can kill me.'

Jackson sighed and gestured towards a chair-cubby. The chair came promptly out of the wall. He sat down on it with the feeling that he might be here a long time. 'All right. So listen. Where we were before was a place called Mars.'

'Amirs,' Ahmuls repeated studiously.

'Okay, now there were these two places where people lived. My place and yours.'

'One place, where Amsirs lived. You're not people. Maybe I'm not people. But I'm not as soft as you are.'

'There were these two places where people lived. Amsirs and humans. But they came from the same place. The reason Amsirs looked different from people is because somebody wanted to see if people could be changed.'

'Humans look different from Amsirs. Amsirs are people.'

And so on. Jackson spent the better part of the rest of the trip trying to explain genetics to Ahmuls. But Ahmuls had the idea he already knew as much as anybody could teach him. He sat on his bunk most of the time, eating little brick-shaped packets of lichen as they were issued to him by Susiem according to the doctor's menu, and every so often either he or Jackson had to stop to go to the head. But he listened because Jackson could kill him if he didn't. This seemed to be something Ahmuls had learned long before he had Jackson for a tutor.

Finally, Susiem told Jackson they were only hours away from docking at Columbus, Ohio, and that he had better start getting presentable.

'All right,' Jackson said. 'Ahmuls, you hear that? Now pretty soon you're going to get a chance to really see something. You're going to see more people and more machinery than either you or me ever had any idea of. You're going to see the place we all come from. Your folks, my folks, the Amsirs' folks. We all come from the same place. You're going to get to see people living in houses stacked up two hundred houses tall. You're going to get to see places that make the whole place that Amsirs live in look no bigger than the way one Amsir house looks compared to the whole bunch of them. You're going to see things zipping across the sky three, five hundred times quicker'n a Amsir can fly falling straight down.'

Ahmuls said: 'How many dozen is that?'

'Oh, dear God. All right. *Don't* learn. I'm trying to tell you you're going to see things that you won't know how to act about. You're going to have more chances to be happy than you've ever thought of.' Well, it seemed reasonable. Wide as the world was, and as complex as he knew it could be, there had to be something in it for the poor freak.

For the poor, dangerous freak. 'And there's going to be lots of chances for you to be stupid, and for you to get hurt. So I'm telling you one last time – you don't want to learn, all right, you don't have to learn. But, by God, at least know you're stupid. Don't go pushing into things. Watch and wait. Walk soft. Maybe after a while you'll realize I'm giving you the straight goods. Any time you're ready, you just let me know and I'll do my best to tell you the straight of it again.'

'I'm straight now,' Ahmuls said, twiddling the flesh that grew on his arms where his wings should have been.

III

Just before they hit atmosphere, Jackson came down to Sick Bay to be with Ahmuls, knowing how the noise and the changes of acceleration would upset him. Jackson was wearing his Captain's pale blue coverall with the Associated Universities shoulder patch.

'What you got on you?' Ahmuls asked.

'This is clothes,' Jackson said. 'I had Susiem make some for you, too. Here.' He passed over the specially-cut coveralls. 'You got to put these on too. It's like a blanket. It keeps the cold and the sun off you.'

'I ain't never seen you wear clothes before.'

'Well, I didn't. But I know better now.'

'I don't know any better.'

'Look, you want them all to think you're a freak?'

'What, all those soft people you said all look like you?'

'Come on, Ahmuls, put the clothes on.'

'You going to kill me if I don't put the clothes on? I ain't cold and there ain't no sun on me. Don't they know enough to go into all of those big, stacked-up houses when they have to?' He dropped the coveralls on the floor.

Jackson shook his head. 'All right, Ahmuls. All right.' He stretched out on another bunk. His skin was already chafed in a couple of places, and he was having a hard time getting used to the whole idea of being wrapped up all around the legs and crotch. But he was very badly embarrassed at the thought of stepping out in front of a spaceport full of people with a naked freak at his side. It was, when he stopped to think of it, the first time in his life that he'd ever been embarrassed at first hand.

It was the damnedest feeling. It occupied considerable of his attention while the ship was coming down in her final approach. Ahmuls whimpered and lurched around on the bunk all through the process. What's going to become of him? Jackson thought.

But Earth was pastorally green, its hillocks crowned by elms, its infrequent, low buildings stark white. 'This is the site of the Associated Universities docking facilities,' Susiem said as Jackson stared out through the open air-lock hatch, like a kid who had just watched a dart hit a target broadside on and then bounce off. 'There have been social changes on Earth since my last communication from the Project. I have just been assured you will be brought up to date on these changes by another source. You and your companion are instructed to debark from this vessel immediately, since it is no longer classified habitable. Attention, all hands! Captain going ashore!'

'Good-bye, fellows,' the doctor said as Jackson and Ahmuls slipped down the ladder. 'Don't worry, Ahmuls – your menu's on file. I'm told all you have to do when you get hungry is say so out loud.'

'Always did,' Ahmuls said.

Jackson looked up Susiem's height. She was beginning to ring. He noticed a swarm of bright, dancing insects whirling around the very tip of her prow. They were bulleted in from over the top of the nearest hillock, in a stream that thickened rapidly, divided to pass around the trunks and through the branches of the elms, and clustered more and more passionately around the tip. The ringing sound increased in volume, and he saw that Susiem was blunted. Her prow was gone. As he watched, the tightly spiralling insects ate another shaving of metal from her plates, and then came round again, cutting off a little bit more with each pass, passing very quickly. It was like a Looneytoone of termites destroying Elmer Fudd's house.

Some of the insects broke away from Susiem, and darted down towards the ground. One nearby seemed to be performing a typical action; it had a little chunk of astronautics-grade steel in its mouth, and it was spinning like an auger. It bored down two or three feet into the ground, Jackson judged by its speed, then back out empty-jawed, and immediately streaked back to snip off more.

Larger bugs came down out of the sky, burrowed into the exposed 'tween-deck spaces and the component arrays behind the stripped-out plating. They buzzed away again, trailing some few components in their grappling append-ages, casting off most of the others, which fell in a swathe beyond the diminishing Susiem with sharp thuds on the thick, clipped green grass and delicate wildflowers. Ground-moving insects and other metal creatures of that kind were waiting to pick them over, chop them up into chunks, plant some, gulp down others as if they had digestions.

'Hey!' Jackson yelled, trying to get through to Susiem before there was no one left on Earth to tell him what was happening. But it was way too late for that. She and the doctor and the food-serving robot and the maintenance robot and everything about her – except for Jackson's coveralls – were dead and useless. Well, no, not useless. A lot of valuable minerals had just been put back into Earth's soil.

Ahmuls was looking around. 'I see some people coming,' he said. 'They ain't got no clothes on.'

CHAPTER THIRTEEN

I

He was very heavy in the limbs. He wasn't slumped like Ahmuls was, but he was very heavy in the limbs. And Ahmuls was right – they didn't have any clothes on.

They were a big bunch of men and women, just less than twenty of them altogether. The first one of them – a man, with clean limbs, much more gracefully and heavily muscled than anyone Jackson had ever actually seen – had lithely walked up into sight from a hidden hollow nearby. He had stood looking at Jackson and Ahmuls, ankle-deep in the grass, with sparkling silver glints swirling around his head and shoulders like a short-lived cowl of day-time stars. Then the little insects had flown away into the sky and been lost, and the man had motioned to whatever was down in the hollow behind him. The rest of the people had come up.

They were all grown-ups, and they moved with a confidence that reminded him of Amsirs. They had apparently been doing something together down there out of sight.

Jackson felt heavy and he felt in layers, like there were two transparent picture screens laid over each other between him and them.

Looking at them, he knew what they were. They were people who had eaten right all their lives; lived right, had the right kind of doctoring. They were people sprung from the kind of person he himself had been when he was at Ohio State.

From the kind of person he had been at Ohio State, he knew how to look at himself now. He was undersized, gangling, knobbily long of leg, hollow-stomached. His skin was like the leather of a horse that has at some past time broken through barbed wire. His eyes were pits, icy blue without a trace of melanin, their whites like smooth, wet bone. His hair was a short, raggedly-cut thatch of brittle straw. In his coveralls, he was a parody.

Their men were too big; their women were too smart. They came walking in towards him and Ahmuls as if none of them had ever stepped on a cockleburr.

Well, what was he going to do? He couldn't even let them see him rip off his coveralls and be himself. It would be too gauche.

'See? Told you – no clothes.'

'Right. My apologies, Ahmuls.'

'Your what?'

'I mean I'm sorry.'

The buzzing of the insects had stopped. Now he could hear the murmur of the soft wind through the pliant grass, and take time to feel the warmth of the wonderful sun on his face and hands. He could even remember strolling along the shade-dappled groves of State in the April weather, and the slumbrous delight of baking for hours in the sun of Jackson Park Beach when he was at Chicago. I'm home, he thought, I'm home where I've never been, and I have to stake my claim upon it.

He began to feel the onset of voices, murmuring as the people spoke between themselves. He shook his head to clear it, feeling the knots growing in the muscles of his neck.

They had reached him. Some of them raised their hands in casual greeting, and smiled. They were all taller than he was. One of them said: 'Hello, there! Comp tells us you're from that genetic experiment on Mars. Both of you. Tell you the truth, Comp had never told us about the experiment before. There was a great range of new data when that space ship came down with you and prompted us to ask about it. Biggest thing in years. It's great. Welcome aboard.'

Their accent was a bit beyond Midwest. But it wasn't unintelligible. He could already feel himself sorting it out properly.

Comp would be Central Control; the thing that guided the insects, that determined the fate of spaceships, of specimens from the – abandoned? forgotten? – genetics experiment on Mars, of the landscape which no longer needed more than a minimum of serviceable features.

It had happened here some time after Susiem's expedition had left to begin the – human, superseded – experiment. They had got their services properly centralized under one comprehensive control, and here he was, among the people it serviced.

But I'm one of you, he thought. My body wasn't built among you, but my mind was. I have come back from the apes and the jungle; Simba is an ailuropod carnivore to me, and Ahmuls is a pachyderm. And how shall I speak to you that you may know me?'

'I'm glad to meet you,' he said earnestly. 'This is Ahmuls, and I am—' A wicked little relay closed in his mind. He had found a way to licence himself. He grinned. 'I'm Jackson Greystoke.'

II

He had said the right thing. They were smiling, twinkle-eyed. There was a brunette girl looking a little bewildered, but a golden-skinned blonde was scandalizedly dispelling her ignorance – Jackson could see the sweetmeat lips quickly whispering 'Tarzan, stupe!' before the blonde's mouth turned towards him and became a ripe plum.

The first man – maybe a little older than the rest, but maybe not; it was hard to tell, as it should be – was saying: 'Wonderful! Well chosen. My name is – ah … Kringle. These are my sons: Dasher, Comet, and Cupid. My daughters, Dancer and Vixen. My other sons: Donder, Blitzen, and Prancer. I'll let these other people tell you who they are – I wouldn't presume to. At any rate, come on, let's all grab a bite, and we can talk.'

It was amazing, being with people who could pick up like that. 'Come on, Ahmuls,' Jackson said, feeling better and better, lofted on a cloud of names as other people made introductions for themselves – Cincinnatus, Columbus and Elyria – Perry, Clark, Lois and Jimmy – Fred and Ginger – Lucky, Chester, Sweet, Home and Wings (who was the brunette again, and was glanced at with disappointment by some of the others when she gave her name) – Batten, Barton, Durstine, and Osborne.

He found that he got them all straight, and kept them all straight. They all fitted. Even when Wings said, shamefacedly: 'I did it wrong. Call me Pall.'

'I'm hungry,' one of them said from the back of the group.

'We're ready,' Jackson smiled. 'And thank you for the invitation. Let's go,' he said to Ahmuls again.

'Don't want to eat with you,' Ahmuls said. 'Don't want to eat with these people.'

A voice spoke in Jackson's ear. He felt the tiniest flutter of air, and out of the corner of his eye he caught a glimpse of something bright, metal, and hovering. 'This is Comp,' the voice said. 'He needn't worry. There'll be food of his kind, too.'

Ahmuls said: 'What did it say?'

'He said he loves you. Come on.'

Some of them were already beginning to walk away, back towards the hidden hollow. Jackson took a step to follow them, stopped, frowned at Ahmuls, turned his head back to watch them go, then looked back at Ahmuls. 'Come on!' He moved quickly, and it felt heavy.

Ahmuls's eyes darted to follow his hand. 'Don't.' He got himself into motion, one hand to the right side of his face, holding his eyelids so he could watch Jackson from the farthest corner.

The group of them walked over the grassy rise of ground. Durstine, the blonde, murmured, her perfume very near to Jackson: 'I wish I'd thought of clothes.' Jackson stopped looking at Ahmuls and grinned at her. She raised one eyebrow back, touched her glistening upper lip with the tip of her tongue, and laughed.

Jackson could see Kringle frown.

CHAPTER FOURTEEN

I

The breakfast things were set down waiting on the grass, arranged to look nice on a broad, cream-white cloth that had doubtless been woven on the spot by bees. The graceful dishes were earth-colours, softly glowing, delicately drawn into shapes that seemed to float, waiting for palms, fingers and lips. It occurred to Jackson they were fragile enough to appeal to insects as well as Man.

They disposed themselves in comfortable attitudes upon the grass, the people did, Jackson with them. He breakfasted on tamales, tidbits, Riesling and conversation, while Comp's bees brought Ahmuls lichen.

They made no dishes for Ahmuls. Either Comp felt his hands would break chunks from any utensils the bees might make, or Comp was disinclined to produce anything clumsy enough to be sturdy enough. Ahmuls ate grumpily, peering at them all.

Jackson's senses were pretty busy with the vivacious scent of women, with the sound of words arranged and sung, not grunted or cawed, and with a horizon of perfect blue, thornless. When he did watch Ahmuls, it was infrequently, and from the corners of his eyes.

'It's not really so much different from the way you now remember it, is it?' Kringle was saying urbanely. 'I imagine you have the picture. When Comp reached the serviceability threshold, certain gross externals were modified very nearly overnight, but the verities remain.

'We still have the same old services: food, clothing – or the control of factors which once made clothing necessary – and shelter.' He gazed around him at the prairie grass, raised his eyebrows apologetically, and smiled at Jackson.

'Well, in actual fact the distinction between clothing and shelter has disappeared; in essence, it was dependent on the distinction between genial and hostile environment, and when *that* was taken care of … But you see my point. It's really very much as it was. People are the same. We feel the same things you remember – remember from old Earth and remember from Mars, too, I'll venture. We have our joys and sorrows, our social interactions …'

Kringle glanced at Ahmuls, at Pall, at Jackson again: 'There are little difficulties and large, as always … distinctions between individuals … levels of accomplishment … we tend to think our lives have an even tenor, since the externals are so efficiently serviced. And of course we are well mannered, since we each share with Comp and none of us regards any other one as a potential source or drain of commodities; we need not cozen one another, nor speak harshly. You follow? Ah, I see you do. But—' Kringle frowned at a tamale. '—set us down on Mars and what a change you would see, I suspect! In short order, the physically weak, the slow of reflex would be eliminated, yes. But the rest; ah, the rest would *not*. The animal is tougher than all that, wouldn't you say? I imagine that in short order I would find myself at the head of a numerically smaller group. Granted that. But I think if we were to postulate a thing called a "toughness index" … *comprisi?* … the measure of a certain basic quality, which would wane in those insufficiently participant in it (as some people will always be), but would wax in the remainder – You see what I'm driving at? The "toughness index" of the numerical remainder of this little group, on Mars would total certainly not less, perhaps more, than it aggregates now for the larger number.' Kringle smiled encouragingly. 'That would be the crucial factor, would it not? The measure of humanity? One might say that so long as the index does not lessen, humanity does not lessen, no matter what humanity's number might be at the given moment.'

'Nice reasoning,' Durstine murmured, speaking from close beside Jackson. She reached forward to pluck another bite from the platter nearest Jackson's feet. She turned her head to look up at his face, her arched golden eyebrows rising in inquiry. At his nod, she lightly handed him the bit of cheese and took another for herself. She moved beautifully, bending, plucking, handing, sitting back again in one composed flow.

Jackson let the cheese soften against the roof of his mouth. He had to admit he was barely listening to what Kringle was saying. And it was probably just as well, he made out from as much of it as had registered. But, wow, he thought, what a luxury of just talking, along with eating like this. And not a blessed thing to worry about, not a damned thing to need going out and hunting up to pay for all of this.

'Even today,' Kringle was saying, 'we are in a sense the select winnowing of a larger but perhaps less sufficient number. Consider that a great deal of the procreative urge is actually a reflection of panic – not a tough quality – and of boredom – certainly a symptom of insufficiency. I would place the world's population at, oh, five percent of the number for a thousand years ago. Is this a tragedy? Well, I say in reply to that, can number be impressive where index is invariant?'

Kringle bowed his head slightly, smiled graciously, and sipped his wine, his hands cupping the goblet symmetrically, the whole gesture a declaration of structure completed. 'So now you understand us.'

Well, maybe not this morning, but I will, Jackson thought. That's the great thing about it – there's all this time and all this world. The Riesling's very nice in the morning here.

All around him were the soft voices. Who cared what they said? He was in with them.

He began to chuckle, watching Ahmuls with lichen in his mouth, and bees darting at his face. Jackson thought, who would believe it? Where are the Amsirs, and where are all the people who believed in Ariwol?

And yet, in looking back, he couldn't honestly say that he'd ever told himself there was something better than Thorns. He'd only never stopped feeling there was something wrong. And he had never even tried to change them. All he'd had was the sense not to let them change him.

That was all it took. Now go back and try and explain it to Black. Or his mother. Sure it was simple. All you had to be was Jackson Greystoke, lost among the primates, with a Tudor manor waiting for him at home on a sceptred isle.

He began to laugh even louder as it occurred to him what an incredible, marvellous, wonderful thing he'd done. He was here by right. He was one of them.

Watching him laugh, they smiled. Little Pall held out a cup of wine, her large brown eyes twinkling again as they had no doubt always been intended to. 'It *is* nice, isn't it?' she said. 'It must feel good.'

It was beyond his wildest dreams. He sat on the grass with his knees drawn up, sipping wine and feeling the heavy familiar touch of Earth upon him.

II

'So we're agreed, then, aren't we?' Kringle was saying, leaning forward far enough so there was a three-fold wrinkling of his heavily-muscled stomach. It occurred to Jackson that Kringle might be just a little slow of foot – if it ever came to running. 'There is no essential difference between you and – for example – myself,' Kringle was going on. 'With some exposure to your environment, I – for example's sake, I – would resemble you physically. And there are no essential differences of capability.'

Durstine's fingertips had found the ridge of the beak scar through the light fabric over Jackson's shoulder. Kringle frowned fleetingly, even though for the most part he kept his eyes on Jackson's face.

'I don't know. Have to have it tried, wouldn't we?' Jackson said reasonably. He looked around at the other people. They were all politely chatting with each other, nibbling, munching. Yet, now that he looked at them again, it seemed they had a reflex of looking at him the moment he looked at them. The women were about half and half; some of them seemed to be ready to play it Durstine's way, or Pall's, and others weren't. But they were ready to play it some way, it occurred to Jackson. The men … well, it was a funny thing, but they seemed to know that about the women. They seemed to know without looking at the women, while looking over towards Jackson.

'Tried?' Kringle said. 'It's been tried, hasn't it? We still have a common ancestry, you know.'

'Well, sure, but so do the Amsirs. So does he.' Jackson nodded over to Ahmuls. He flexed his shoulder under Durstine's hand, and winked at Pall. Columbus, over in among the group, there – the one who'd been so anxious to get back to breakfast – saw the wink. He looked at Jackson, slowly and thoughtfully cracking his knuckles.

Ah, so, Jackson thought. Enmity in Eden. Well, listen man, I've been going without for a long time.

And underneath that he thought with a little touch of doom that soon enough the novelty would wear off him, and they'd all be competing for their women on an even basis. Maybe a little less than even, he reminded himself, heavy in the limbs. He winked at Columbus. But soon enough ain't now, he thought.

As he turned his head back towards Kringle, he saw that lots had been going on while his attention was elsewhere. Kringle was taking little cubes of cheese and flipping them off the ball of his thumb with his middle finger. He was paying no obvious attention to what he was doing … just toying idly with his food on a pleasant morning, very much at his ease, woolgathering. But he was flipping every one of those cubes at Ahmuls. They were bouncing off the sport's chest and thighs, rebounding soundlessly, and falling into the grass, where bees pounced on them and doubtless immediately turned them into plant nutriment. Jackson looked from Kringle to Ahmuls quizzically. He took another sip of wine. Now, what the hell was going to come of this? he thought.

Gradually Ahmuls noticed. 'Hey – hey, you!'

Kringle slowly turned his face upwards, and opened his eyes wider, so that now he could plainly be said to be looking at Ahmuls. 'Speaking to me?'

'You doin' that?'

'I beg your pardon? I think, if you spoke more slowly, perhaps, then …'

'He wants you to cut it out,' Jackson said.

'Does he?' Kringle said back over his shoulder. 'Ahmuls! Is there something bothering you?'

'Yeah. Quit doin' that.'

Kringle held up his empty hands. 'I have stopped doing it. What's your problem?'

'Don't hit me with that shit.'

Kringle raised his eyebrows. He picked up another cube of cheese, and daintily holding it between his fingers, nibbled at it. 'What are you calling me?'

Jackson leaned forward to Kringle, grinning a little. 'Listen, don't let me butt in on anything, but he could tear you apart and be juggling the pieces before your feet stopped moving.'

'Could he?' Kringle's eyebrow-raised eyes looked momentarily back at Jackson again.

One of the tiny silver bees detached itself from the swarm around Ahmuls, zipped over to Jackson, and said:

'This is a Comp. Pardon *my* butting in, but I think you forget your own education. These people share it, and more. Furthermore, they know all about what happened aboard that obsolete vehicle. All the information in Susiem's files was naturally transferred to me. Therefore, it was fully available to them, and Kringle is among those who absorbed it.'

'You can always ask Comp anything,' Durstine murmured in Jackson's ear. 'He'll tell you. If you want to know a lot, one of his extero …'

'Exteroaffectors,' Comp said.

'That's right, one of his exteroaffectors will give it to you by absorption.'

Kringle flipped another piece of cheese at Ahmuls. It hit the tip of his nose. Ahmuls stood up.

Kringle stood up. 'Is there anything I can do for you, beast?' he said softly. Jackson could see Kringle's fingers taking on the appropriate tucked-in stances.

Jackson stood up. 'Let's everybody take it easy,' he said.

'But that would be against the nature of the beast,' Kringle said. He was taking time out to lick his fingertips. Standing up, his mouth was inches higher off the ground than the top of Ahmuls' head. You could collapse a spine, touching the head downward.

III

'Listen, Ahmuls, he can kill you,' Jackson said. 'Look how he's holding his hands. You remember what that does?'

Ahmuls peered intently. 'Are you all that smart?'

Kringle cast a languorous eye back at Jackson. 'I'm not certain it's nice to come entering into other people's conversations.'

'Well, I'm not sure it's nice, either. But I don't think it's nice to flick poison at people until they get mad enough for you to kill them.'

'Either it's not poison or he's not people,' Durstine murmured.

'Well formulated, my dear. *Keep* thinking clearly,' Kringle said.

Ahmuls was searching from one of their faces to the next while Durstine scornfully arched her back at Kringle and fluffed her hair away from her neck, deliberately touching Jackson on the calf as he stood beside her. Kringle was looking at Durstine, and Pall was looking from Durstine to Jackson.

Only the bees looked where they were going, but as one of them tried to pop another crumb of lichen into Ahmuls's mouth, he growled, and his hand flicked out. He caught the buzzing silvery nugget. Durstine gasped. 'He's so fast!' Ahmuls flicked it towards Kringle. The bee spatted hard against Kringle's shoulder, and he clapped his hand over the white-centred blotch of redness that bloomed in his skin instantly.

'Ai!' said Durstine.

There was a rustling in the grass behind Jackson; he turned his head to look. The breakfast people were up on their elbows and knees and feet; they had stopped reclining or talking. They had their heads up, alert; their eyes shone, and their parted mouths drooped at the corners.

Kringle was drawn up; there was just the faintest snaky ripple of the muscles up one calf and thigh as he shifted his weight, and a fine, regular jumping began under the skin just above his left elbow. He lifted his hand away from the bee-bruise, and looked at his fingers, but there was nothing on them, and the bee had flown away, of course.

'Jump me. Jump me, animal!' Kringle whispered. He got his arms and legs ready; his fingers were stiff and motionless, and the moisture glinted on his lower teeth.

'Hey, I bother you, you know it?' Ahmul said to him. 'Like around the Thorn. Was always the little and beat-out ones that made jokes on me. Only beat-out one that didn't, he was boss of the whole thing. Whyn't you lay off me? Maybe you'll be boss.'

'Just touch me,' Kringle pleaded in a whisper. 'Just lay the least little bit of a hand on me ... please.'

Oh my God, my God, Jackson thought, visualizing what would happen the instant Kringle had an excuse for uncoiling. Ahmuls, you poor dumb son of a bitch – I knew you never had a chance here. Why didn't you listen? Why couldn't you *learn?*

'I ain't gonna touch you,' Ahmuls said. 'You think I'm crazy? You just leave me alone, and I ain't gonna touch you.'

'Leave you alone? You won't leave me alone!' Kringle moaned.

'Then I'm gonna go away. I ain't crazy about you.' Ahmuls turned to go, rippling turgidly, and began to move off. Kringle stared at him in pop-eyed astonishment.

'Come back here!'

'Won't,' Ahmuls said over his shoulder.

Jackson couldn't believe it, either. Where was he going to go? There was nothing out there but grass and white Walt Disney houses, and exteroaffectors. 'Hey! Wait! Hold on!' Jackson said, standing up. 'Don't just go out there like that!'

Ahmuls turned his head, holding his face so he could look at Jackson clearly. 'What's it to you? I ain't bothering you. Never gonna bother anybody like you. You people want this place, you keep it. You people wanna push me around, uh-uhn. S'lots of room. You gonna get tired of pushin' 'fore I run out of room t'get pushed to. You think I'm nuts, gonna get myself all beat up again, arguin' with you people? You're crazy!'

Where was he ever going to find a place that was going to love him? Jackson took a couple of fast steps and caught up to him. He put his hand on a doughy shoulder. 'Oh, come on now – just wait,' he found himself pleading. 'Look, we just got here. You've got to give it a chance. You've got to give yourself a chance. I mean, these people are some good, some bad, I guess. That's not going to keep me from being happy here. You could—'

'I'm not like you. I'm not like them.'

Kringle was walking up towards them. The whole feeling of everything had changed. He was grinning cockily. The rest of the men in the breakfast group were smiling and sneering at Ahmuls.

'Stop trying to mollify him,' Kringle said. 'He wants no part of us. He knows when he's whipped. He's right about one thing. He's not like us.' His glance flickered just very briefly over Jackson. 'Or you.'

Say, thought Jackson with icy ferret swiftness, suppose it turns out I can't live with these people, and then it turns out I can't even find Ahmuls, if he gets lost out there someplace?

'Look, will you just leave us alone and let me talk to him?' he snapped at Kringle.

'Well, I don't see any need for you to be provoked into losing your patience.' Kringle walked away, back to the breakfast group. He reached down, deliberately took a tidbit from Durstine's fingers, and began chewing it with his front teeth, very delicately, while standing in front of her in such a way that she would have to reach around him if she wanted more.

'Come on, Ahmuls,' Jackson said.

'Say … Man to man on the prairie's endless waste, the sinewy Jackson Greystoke and his monstrous adversary faced each other,' Chester remarked.

Durstine laughed. She chimed in, 'The battle of two superb physical machines trembled on the brink of being joined. Here in this peaceful glade that had seen no violence in a score of centuries, suddenly there was a reawakening of Earth's age-old heritage of struggle between brute strength and trained intelligence.'

Donder declaimed: 'A still hush settled over the land, as Nature herself seemed to draw breath in shuddering anticipation of the awful onslaught.'

'What? What are they talkin' about?' Ahmuls muttered. Jackson looked over his shoulder. Durstine, and some of the others and even Kringle were staring towards him and Ahmuls, very much laughing-eyed. Some of the others had got back to just plain eating, gracefully sipping and nibbling. All of them were lounging about.

Pall seemed a little interested, but people with large, moist eyes frequently seem emotional when in fact they are merely displaying a phenomenon of physiology.

'Never mind,' Jackson said to Ahmuls. 'You just go on and do what you want.'

Ahmuls said: 'Right.' He trudged up the slope of the hollow, was silhouetted massively against the pale horizon of late morning, and began to diminish from the legs up as he lumbered down the other side of the slope and out of Jackson's line of vision.

Swift, once more, the underground pit-pattering flow of the thought. 'Comp – you'll keep track of him?'

'Oh, I always know where everybody is, of course,' a bee said in his ear. 'Even if I couldn't predict where they'll be. But I think there's no problem, predicting *him*. He'll find the place.'

'What place?'

'Room to roam around in, yet ideally suited for permanent food facilities. Places to play, and things to play with. He'll be delighted. He'll flourish.'

'What place, Comp? No, all you'll do is give me a name I don't know. What kind of place?'

'Kind of a zoo.'

'A zoo.'

'*Azoo, azoo, azoo, zoo, zoo.*' Kringle hummed, breaking into a waltz with Durstine. Chester caught up Elyria. Cincinnatus gathered Pall into his arms.

Soon they were all spinning over the grass like courting herons, humming, smiling, faces flushed, eyes laughing back over their shoulders, only Durstine winking at Jackson, only Pall looking momentarily bewildered, and yet she, too, was humming, '*Azoo, azoo, azoo, zoo, zoo. azoo, azoo, ah-zoooo, ah, ah, ah, ah, zoo, zoo, zoo*, etc.'

Well, now, what do you do? Jackson thought. Scream at them? Be a monkey while they waltz? And so what if they *are* lunatics? Aren't they kind of cute … like a motorized sculpture of seraphim made out of razor blades?

Ahmuls was quite a distance away already; the dancers had made their point, and were stopping, sinking back down on the grass. 'I don't suppose you could educate him,' Jackson said to the bee. 'All you have are the total resources of a planet.'

'Don't see the need,' Comp said. 'Can I make him happier? Can I make him human without stealing his essence from him? He has no history and no future. All his yearnings are self-contained.' Comp knew when a point was made. The bee flew from beside Jackson's ear.

They were still flushed and giggling in the breakfast group. They looked at Jackson curiously, and he looked at them.

'Has your faithful companion left you speechless, then, Masked Rider of the Plains?' Jimmy inquired. 'Got your balloon pricked?'

'The only person he was ever faithful to is back on Mars,' Jackson said tautly. 'Unless that person's been busted. He misjudged me, you know.'

'Oh, come and eat with us, Jackson,' Kringle said. 'If you wish.' He lounged back with his arm around Durstine. Durstine rolled her eyes sideways and pouted seductively at Jackson.

'Yes ... come and join us. Don't be miffed.'

Pall giggled. 'Funny old thing, galumphing off that way. And you should have seen your face when we all started dancing, Jackson!'

'Yes ... almost as if he'd never heard of civilized habits,' Chester said, 'or never knew how to communicate.'

Jackson could feel himself winding up. If these people thought Kringle was something when he was in that mood, they had something to learn ...

'Jackson communicates very well,' Durstine said.

'Yes,' Kringle said. 'I think, Chester, Jackson would surprise you in his own milieu.'

'I'd have to see that,' Jimmy said.

'Well, it's entirely possible *for* you to see it,' Kringle said reasonably, 'If Jackson's willing.'

'I wonder if he would be,' Chester said.

'Of *course* he would!' Pall cried.

Turning his face this way and that as they spoke was like running from tunnel to tunnel, all full of cross-ways and no clues.

'Of course you will,' Durstine said in his face, soft and warm, with a half-twist of her body that brought her mouth and breath poignantly near.

'Will what?'

'Fight!'

'Fight what?'

'Amsir.'

'Why?'

'For me!'

'Where?'

'Here!'

'How?'

'No problem,' Comp said.

CHAPTER FIFTEEN

I

'What?'

'I can arrange it all. I can make an Amsir for you – excuse me; a Amsir – and a throwing stick and a couple of darts. I have some very good footage of the Martian terrain from my orbiters up there.'

'Orbiters? You mean you've got your eyes on Mars?'

'Certainly. We're not talking now about accelerating something man-carrying out to that distance. Our space exploration's quite sophisticated these days, compared to what it was when the primary system component was humanoid. But what I'm saying is that I have plenty of stock background. You go ahead and hunt your Amsir. I'll run in proper background and lighting. And perfect dubbing of the terrain. I am sure we can get you one hell of an audience for it. Wait one – I'll ask around.'

'Great response,' Comp said to him a moment later. 'We have over four hundred thousand lookers-in; thirty-eight percent of the potential audience.'

'I don't think I understand. Thirty-eight percent of the audience for what?'

'The audience for your actuality, man. Look, the number of the audience and the number of the world population are theoretically congruent, right? In practice there are always some individuals asleep and some urgently occupied otherwise. So there's never been a hundred percent audience for an actuality – the live version at any rate. The record is eighty-three percent, or thereabouts, but that was for the competition between Melanie Altershot and Charles Dawn, and a very long time ago. Well, I queried the population for interest in a Amsir hon, and they're all waiting – thirty-eight percent of them are waiting now, and a number of others have expressed serious interest in taking it on the delay. It hinges now on whether you're willing. But I think you should know there hasn't been a thirty-eight percent audience in quite some time.'

'You know, we don't have all day,' Donder said.

'Well, I'd like to do it,' Jackson said. 'Right here, huh?' Besides the impatience in Donder's voice, he had also noticed Vixen and Batten. The two of them now had some kind of flying toy.

It was a pale, translucent lavender. It caracolled back and forth between them as they stood some distance apart from each other and flew it from hand to hand. The object seemed to be to make patterns, for the marvellous toy trailed a feathery lavender wake which hung in the air briefly and then distintegrated into dusty filaments.

They had begun this game while Comp was explaining actualities to Jackson, and Jackson was busy listening. One or two people in the group had stopped watching Jackson and had started watching the flight; from being a tight group around Jackson, these people had begun to spread towards Batten and Vixen, attenuating. 'Sure,' Jackson repeated. 'Provide me with the tools and a Amsir, and we'll get with it.'

'Good!' Durstine and Comp said simultaneously. Pall smiled. Jackson smiled back at her. 'I know what it is,' she said. 'You never realized you'd get a chance here to do something you must have enjoyed so much.'

'Pall, darling,' Old said, 'one of the reasons I want to watch this is because it's done in a place where people do things they don't enjoy.'

Pall put her fingers to her mouth. 'Oh, Jackson, I'm sorry,' she said.

II

In this world, Amsir bones were made by insects. They came whipping in over the tops of the soughing grass stems, in a swarm far smaller than the one that had devoted itself to Susiem, each carrying a little white speck. They buzzed, they grouped to some efficient shape, and in a trice there was the stick. The place that would serve as the handle was properly shaped as if by patient sanding; the hinge was neatly fitted, the nock for the dart's butt properly incised. Jackson picked it up and admired it.

'It's a lot like my own, Comp. Those are good scanners you've got.'

'How about the darts?'

The short, bluntly tapered hafts had been produced the same way the throwing stick had been. The head was done by burrowing exteroceptors, who came spilling up out of the ground, clustered at the head of each dart as bees held it in place, and withdrew leaving cooling, jaggedly pointed silicate heads fused into the cups that had been made there to receive them – each, for all Jackson knew, already freighted with its dab of synthetic Amsir-hide glue. He picked them up and bounced them in his palm. He rolled them around with his fingers. 'Good,' he said. 'Good, fine.'

He walked up the slope of the hollow and looked around. The landscape rolled away from him, empty. There was no sign of Ahmuls, or of anyone else. But there were a great many receptor bees clustering in the air up there.

'Look to your left,' Comp said. 'I am starting your Amsir.'

About seventy-five yards away the exteroaffectors attacked the grass. They darted down to catch stems being hurled up to them by others on the ground. They seized them and pulled them up into position. They moved with great rapidity, dexterity, and economy – it was as if the grass had freed itself of compliance to the breeze and had decided to bend its own way. It bent in all directions towards a common centre as the exteroaffectors took it, but as it bent it hurried forward rootless, and when it reached the centre it fountained up, urged by splashes of buzzing silver, and there before Jackson's eyes they wove a Amsir's bones.

Toe and tarsal, leg and knee, thigh and hip, they wove him from the inside out; spine, collarbone, shoulder joints, arms, elbows, forearms, hands – he watched the little finger extend itself like the shooting of a magic shrub. Neck and skull matted themselves into structural compactness. Now, flesh; fibrous strands wrested into place upon the green bones. In a moment, he was all hooked up together. Then they clad him; hide was fitted; bubbles swelled. Beak and talons, crest and wings; lace, fluttering … fluttering pale; as he stirred there, exteroaffectors burrowing nimbly between the fibres to give him life, he bleached.

An army of burrowers came running forward, and fused the glistening fragments of his javelin. They tossed it upward; a low cast, but his wing rippled as his right hand swooped down to seize it, and hollow-eyed, he straightened to turn his head and look at Jackson.

'Comp, your name is miracle,' Jackson said.

'My name is Comp.'

Jackson opened down the Velcro of his coveralls and shrugged out of them. Immediately, exteroaffectors clustered around him. He winced as they plated his body everywhere with themselves. But the touch was gentle, and they were gone again in the blink of an eye. 'Sunburn lotion,' Comp explained.

'Oh. Yeah, makes sense.'

He looked around to see what the breakfast group had made of all this. But there were none of them near him. They were all down in the hollow, sitting or stretched out gracefully, each with an exteroaffector on each eye, at each ear, on each hand. A little string of them, like a girdle of small jewels, lay across each stomach just below the navel. Jackson looked over at the grass Amsir standing alert in the middle of his patch of stubble. Jackson bent down, picked up the throwing stick and the two darts. The coveralls were gone, dissipated.

'Ready any time you are, friend,' he called to the Amsir.

'Ready,' Comp said in his ear, and withdrew.

III

The Amsir waved its javelined hand to him. Jackson took a few quick steps; running on grass was different, but he remembered. Remembering it gave him Ohio feet, instead of Thorn feet, but at least it gave him feet. He tried a few dry casts of the stick, slapped the spare dart up into his armpit, and was off.

He was playing it about the only way he could; as if he and the Amsir had each turned a shoulder of a dune at the same moment and had spotted each other at a distance. He ran away at an angle, down and across the slope of the land, picking up speed, ready to dive and roll straight downhill if the bird cast its javelin.

The Amsir was turning. A thousand or ten thousand exteroaffectors shifted its weight, raised its arms, cocked its hips, raised its leg. It tipped forward, planted its leg, raised the other, and was running like the wind, lace streaming, wings unfurled. It ran down and across the slope of the land, diagonally away from him, cutting across his line of flight, putting him in a position where he'd have to throw in the direction opposite to the one he was running in.

Shit! Jackson thought. I forgot how smart they were. He looked back over his shoulder. The dark, wide, empty eyes were looking along a wing at him. Jackson got his legs out in front of him and set his feet. He was sliding to a stop. The Amsir grinned, spread its wings, and hung stock-still in the air, legs free of the ground. Its knees bent; one wing dropped, the other rose. It landed faced around on a dime, claws sunk in the tough grass, javelin poised. Its legs began to scissor. It came on like an ostrich, straight for Jackson, eating up distance between them, confident it could duck.

For Jackson to get up any momentum to reach it with a dart, he would have to run straight towards it, now. If he ran to either side it would have a clear shot. And the best he could do would be to try something side-arm. If he ran away from it, it would run him down.

Oh boy, Jackson thought. All right, let's try one on you. He took three steps forward, simultaneously loading the stick, and then with the fourth step he fired.

Jesus, there was nothing on the throw. It was straight enough, but there was no whip to it; it was like throwing straight up. Or throwing with a sick arm.

I'm made of gruel in this place! he thought. The dart might reach the Amsir, but it was a fool if it bothered to break stride long enough to duck. The dart would never get through its hide, but would hang tangled in its lace. Even if the dart happened to stick into him a little, it would have no stopping power.

The dart reached the Amsir, who swayed clumsily to get out of its way. But he'd miscalculated. He ran right up on it. It took him in the chest, on the lower left, and it just seemed to keep going in past all reason. It went in up to the butt, with the sound of shocked fibres. The Amsir's legs went out from under him. He spread his wings for balance, dropping the javelin.

'The dart. Give him the other dart!' Comp said quickly in Jackson's ear.

'Right.' The Amsir was all spread out, and had no traction. Jackson fired the second one, and this time he had enough practice really to step into it. He could feel it all up and down his arm and across his back, clear down to the sole of his foot, like a rope of electricity. He threw that dart harder than he had ever thrown in his life, and to reward him it took off feeling about half as good as it should have. But it got to the grass Amsir all right; it went in below his right collarbone and it came out the other side, carrying about two or three yards beyond him, tumbling, looping down and bouncing on the grass, a trail of torn grass floating out in the air behind it. The Amsir's right arm folded back as if the hinge locks had failed on a carrier-based aircraft. He ground-looped around the surface of his left wing and nose-dived heavily to the prairie. You could hear his neck pop.

'He's dead,' Jackson said.

Comp said, 'Listen.'

The sound was incomprehensible. It sounded like what you might hear if you ran as fast as you could, dragging a spear point-down through rough sand. 'What the hell is that?'

'That's applause, Jackson. That's the applause of thirty-eight percent of the world's population – with the gain turned down, of course.'

CHAPTER SIXTEEN

I

Jackson walked over to the dead Amsir. It lay sprawled where he had dropped it, all broken, Jackson's first dart just peeping out of its chest. There was a rustling and a shaking; it slumped, its tissues separating. The little metal insects came out of its fibres, and each took its little bit of dead grass away. Others came popping up to join them. The Amsir's wings became insubstantial; its body flattened. Its skull uncurled, and quick as that the burrowing exteroaffectors were scurrying off with its components, a straw-and-metal wave, still roughly in the shape of a broken Amsir's silhouette, hurrying through the grass, back to the stubble patch, there to return its elements to the soil. A buzzing cluster chewed through the javelin and the darts; Jackson dropped the throwing stick into the midst of them, and they snapped it up.

The breakfast group came up over the crest from the hollow, their faces flushed, their eyes sparkling. Dancer broke into a sprint towards Jackson, and as soon as one of them had done it, the rest followed suit. They came springing up to him, laughing, delighted with him. Jackson was watching the stubble patch, where clear droplets of water were forming on the clipped stems.

Kringle threw his arm around Jackson's shoulders and hugged him. 'Terrific!' he said. 'Just great!'

'You were fine!' Durstine gasped. 'Unbelievable!'

'Wouldn't you like to see it?' Pall asked.

'Yes! He ought to see it,' Jimmy agreed, and the rest of them took that up, smiling and laughing, pressing some sort of feast upon him.

Comp said: 'Here—'

Exteroaffectors landed like butterflies at his ears and eyes. They touched his palms and his belly.

'All that's involved is my getting in phase with the appropriate sectors of your central nervous system,' Comp explained. 'Just relax. Many people prefer to sit or lie down, but it's not necessary.'

They were all around him. Jackson had never had that happen to him before; all of them were radiating at least ninety-eight point six degrees Fahrenheit. At that temperature, they were creating all kinds of ranges of evaporation at their bodily surfaces, and none of them were insulated, nor was he. All kinds of effluents were being volatilized in close proximity to his olfactory receptors and the thermesthetic components of his own system. He sank down to the grass, hugging his knees. They sank down with him, all around him, smiling encouragingly and watching him. He closed his eyes. 'That's right,' Comp said. 'Now – here we go …'

II

The desert faded in. First there was a long shot of the two craters and the two Thorns, from a high altitude. The edge of the planet curved, nearly undiffused, against star-filled space. Then his point of view transited into tighter and tighter focus on the human crater, until it was a tight shot of the desert at dawn, reddish-purple, rolled up into dunes, with the harsh light of morning upon it. The point of view pulled in even tighter, until all there was to see was a flat, featureless, uniformly granular, unmarked field of desert-colour. The point of view held for a beat; then a Amsir's white claw flashed down into the middle of it, thrust in running stride across the granules, scattering them, flashed up and forward, out of the frame and was gone leaving everything as before except for the pit of its print, whose sides began to crumble and flow. Light sparkled from one granule, and Jackson's attention followed it as it slid down the side of the footprint. It had not touched bottom yet when, with a *thump!-thump!*, human running feet crossed quickly from right to left, kicking the Amsir-print out of existence, leaving their own.

The point of view shifted up, and he caught a glimpse of a running, naked Honor, and then, ahead of him, the bobbing form of a Amsir.

There was a jump cut, and the Amsir was running straight towards the point of view, grinning straight ahead.

Another jump, and now it was Jackson running by himself; for the first time, Jackson could be sure it was him and not a piece of stock footage, for he could see the scar on his shoulder, and then the profile of the uncapped face. His lips were drawn back. His teeth were white and wet; the side of his face, squinting, then eyes snapping wide open – every pore and every delicate blond hair growing whitely at the tops of his cheekbones above his beard. The cut this time was to a medium down shot of the two of them. Jackson was running, his head turned to look back over his shoulder. There was a shot of his feet jamming to a halt in the sand, fighting for purchase.

Now, the Amsir, braking in mid-air, changing direction.

Now, Jackson's first shot. The dart slapped into place on the stick. There was a beautiful slow-motion study of the muscles working in time, taken from behind him, as he made the recovery from his stop and worked the cast of his stick. As his arm flowed upwards with the dart butted in its nock, poised, head sparkling, the motion began to speed, until, as the dart came into line with the Amsir and he snapped it free, the motion went into over-speed. The muscles of his right arm and of his stomach twanged with force as he shot the dart, which whipped through the air and sank into the Amsir's chest. It came in so fast that the bird didn't even begin to duck until after he'd been hit.

Now the Amsir hung for a split second, in mortal trouble, wide open. The point of view jumped around Jackson in a carousel; he could see every move of his feet and legs, every twist of his torso, the tight strain of his left hand as he whipped it down, the flow of his right arm. There was an extreme closeup of the second dart in the stick as it whipped back across and below the horizon, then whipped forward again, as if the dart were motionless and the world were tumbling. Then the world stopped and the dart flew. Then there was a medium long shot of the Amsir taking the second dart and breaking his wing – actually seen in extreme closeup, reflected in the dilated pupil and the bottomless iris of Jackson's left eye. The background music, which had built up and over the sound of Jackson's forced breath with a crescendo of woodblock slaps, cut off. Jump cut to the Amsir's head impacting on the sand, medium long shot over Jackson's shoulder. SOUND: Neck Breaks (hold long shot; dub extreme close sound).

There was a medium closeup, facing Jackson, of him standing there, the empty stick dangling in his hand, his shoulders slumped, wiping his face and taking a deep breath. The point of view pulled back and up; there was a long shot, still trucking back, of Jackson looking towards the Amsir lying all crumpled up on the terrain, dwindling as the shot pulled back far enough so that the planet's horizon came back into view again. The camera panned to the stars, towards the sun, became filled with hot white light, and then on an accent clack from the wood blocks, cut out.

III

They were all around him; he opened his eyes, and they were sitting there right on top of him, damn near, touching him, grinning, laughing, saying: 'Didn't we tell you! Great! Absolutely great!'

Kringle said: 'I'd had no idea of how it was. It's never really possible to reach an intellectual grasp of a totally alien environment. That's why actualities are so superbly fitted to the didactic purpose. It's all very well to be given a series of facts for the brain to digest, but when you want to convey the immediacy of a situation, you've got to hit 'em right in the guts. Only way to do it. And I don't mind telling you, I've been hit.'

Vixen said, breathlessly: 'I feel as if my entire life's been changed.' She was hanging on to his arm. Well, people never believed a thing until they touched it.

'Hey, Comp,' Jackson said, 'why didn't I understand that thing? Was that supposed to be a Amsir hon?'

'I don't – oh. Yes, I do. You're talking about the editing and the direction. I should have realized; yes, I imagine it does look quite different in the finished version from the way it feels to you while you're performing the action. But you have to realize that the way it feels to you is made up of experiences, whereas to them it's made up of appearances. It would be dull as ditch water if I were to simply present a running record of the action from a fixed point of view. No, in order to give these people the feeling of what it's really like, considerable skill must be exercised in arranging the patterns of action in a way that will be meaningful to them. And it is meaningful; look at them reacting!'

'Full of tricked-up dub-ins, and shots jumping around like a nut?'

'It's what they need in order to be able to feel it. Believe me, a great deal of skill and intuition went into that production, and none of the effects were selected lightly. You want to remember, Jackson, that all you had to do was react naturally; I'm the one who had to manage it from scratch.'

'I suppose that includes the dumb way I was able to kill that fake in the first place.'

'If you're referring now to the Amsir's dull reactions at the crucial moment, you want to bear in mind that your reflexes and capabilities aren't yet coordinated with the physical properties of this environment. We couldn't very well have the Amsir hon you to death, could we?' Comp chided him.

Jackson shook his head. They were milling around excitedly, listening to exteroaffectors, getting all worked up about something new.

'What are you telling them now, while you're talking to me?'

'Oh, there's been a world-wide reaction to the actuality. I'm running a great number of delays to individuals who've been clued in by the live audience. Your total's well over fifty percent, at this point, and accelerating. You're getting great word-of-mouth on this piece.'

Pall took his hands. Her eyes were shining. 'Jackson, Jackson, I think it's great! Do you know what we're going to do?'

''Fraid not.' He said it pretty gently.

'*Everybody* wants to meet you! We're going to have an – oh, excuse me! – *a* honning party!'

Jackson turned to Kringle: 'You're going to have a what?'

Kringle's eyes were twinkling. 'Watch!' He waved his arm, and the babble of cross-exclamations that had burst out among the breakfast group fell away to a background murmur. 'What do you say? Shall we have a Thorn?'

'*Yes!*'

'Comp …' Kringle said.

Oh, the sweet, passionate smell of them!

A dozen buzzings trembled faintly all around the horizon. Jackson turned to look. There were shimmerings around the low white houses under the trees. The trees themselves were glinting, and then trees and houses had disappeared in a silver mist, and the air shivered with the sound of flying. Jackson kept turning, watching. Kringle chuckled.

The grass quivered everywhere, as if someone hidden under a bed had reached up and begun to pull on the blanket.

'I'm going to have to move you for a few minutes,' Comp said. 'If you'll just step on board ...'

Durstine tugged on his hand. '*This* way.'

Not all of Comp's exteroaffectors in this area were devoting themselves to the trees and the white houses. While Jackson's back was turned, some of them had put together a webwork of metal, struts and stanchions curving and curlicueing every which way, with hammocks and canopies extended from it, tassels swaying enticingly, fountains splashing coloured liquids from pool to lower pool to lower pool, step by step, to the accompaniment of delicately chiming music. It all made a ball of insouciantly variform nooks and crannies-within-crannies, yet open enough within itself so that the breakfast group's numbers could call back and forth and laugh to each other as they clamoured about within it. Durstine tugged him inside, and the ball lifted away from the surface of the prairie, drifting off at one side as it gained altitude, until they were all perched a hundred yards up in the air, reclining, clambering, joking back and forth, whispering excitedly. A pleasant breeze swept through the structure. Spray from the fountains tickled Jackson occasionally. Pall's upturned face peeked out from between two curling metal leaves farther down inside the ball. She wrinkled her nose at him and waved.

Meanwhile, Comp was making a party Thorn.

The ball drifted languidly above roaring torrents of exteroaffectors. They swirled through the air, rushing in from all directions, converging. Where they met, some swirled into subsidiary pools, others roared upward in flashing combers, with little flecks of a kind of spray flashing away from their tips as they delivered their freight and went flirting away for another load. The fabric of the ball thrummed to the cataract sound; parts of it – leaves and flowers – began to chime in counterpoint to the fountain music.

'Look! Look!' Durstine breathed, her upper arm across his shoulders from a little behind him, her forearm bent to lie down across his biceps. Her voice was in his ear.

IV

The exteroaffectors pulled away from the plain below. Only a conical, thick cluster of them, a hundred feet across, hung in the air above the plain, and then these unwound in a spiral from the bottom. As they unwound, Jackson could see that they were finishing the upper stretches of the Thorn. Down on the ground, in a gay, fluttering circle, pavilions, bountifully striped and decorated, circled around the Thorn between a turf running track and beautiful fields delimited by clipped green hedgerows. He looked again, and the Thorn was done; straight, tall, shimmering, with flags in its antennas.

'It's gorgeous,' Jackson said.

The cloud sank down to the turf between the Thorn and the pavilion houses, and everyone ran off to drink from the fountains. The fountains were spotted around its base, where he remembered taps. Pall was bent, hair falling about her cheeks in two short, sculptured wings, sipping from her cupped wet hands, where he remembered Petra Jovans.

CHAPTER SEVENTEEN

I

The thorn was warm, and gently yielding when he touched it. He couldn't make up his mind what colour it was; in some places it was off-black, with wine-dark highlights. As he shifted his gaze, he could see places where it was green as a fly. He stood back, gawking like a tourist, his head going from side to side, admiring the way the flagged antennae raked against the pure blue sky, enthralled by the power these people commanded, stunned by the munificence of it all, cupping his elbows. He thought: Was it for this, Red, to make a model for this that you strove, laboured, loved, and died?

'Oh, it's going to be such a great time!' Pall exclaimed, running up wet-lipped. 'Just everyone will be watching the actuality of it!'

Jackson nodded. 'I believe it,' he said gravely. Then he smiled, looking at her. What the hell – I mean, he thought, if she *looked* like a kid, you'd watch how you'd talk to her, now wouldn't you? He felt a touch on his arm. But this Durstine, now ...

'Would you like to see inside?' she was saying. 'Wouldn't you like to look around in there?' She put her thigh up against his hip.

''Scuse us, Pall,' Jackson said.

'Oh, that's all right!' Pall piped. 'I have to go change, anyhow, and I want it to be a surprise!' She ducked off towards one of the pavilions.

Durstine chuckled. 'I'll be changing, too. But we have a few minutes.'

He followed her into the Thorn through a wide, elaborate doorway. It was like slipping into a sea of jewel soup.

The Thorn was hollow inside, all the way to the top, but webbed across in a tangle of crystal filaments that spun themselves up, glittering in swaying curtains and loops to disappear in the soft shadows overhead. Through the translucent walls of the Thorn came light; from here, the walls of the Thorn burst with all colours; green and gold, red and violet, blue and rust. The colours swirled and swept about each other in a pattern different from the not-quite-random swirlings of the inner webwork, which in turn took what it pleased of them and threw it back to Jackson and Durstine in a shower of shifting pinpoints. He looked at her, and she was mottled with glory.

She laughed and tossed her head, then stood motionless, looking at him through the lashes at the corner of one eye. 'Welcome to Earth,' she said.

'I wanted you to see this.' She turned gracefully, on tiptoe, raising one arm in a gesture that swept around the interior of the Thorn. It was hard to tell whether she meant the Thorn, or herself, or both.

'I wanted you to see what we can do. I want you to know what's yours, so you can use it, and grow with it, and claim your birthright properly.'

'Just my birthright, or other things, too? Could I take something that belonged to Kringle, for instance?'

She laughed. 'Some men have a birthright to anything they can lay their hands on.'

'Then I wouldn't stand so close, if I were you.'

'But I am. And I know exactly where I'm standing at all times.' She laughed, gaily, secretively. Her hand flashed out. Her fingernails trailed down his upper arm lightly enough, but by the time they reached his elbow they left a mark, and her middle finger, turning, drew a drop of blood. She touched it to her lips, and kissed him quickly on the mouth. 'I'll see you here again, a little later. I'm going to change ... You might not recognize me gowned, ordinarily. But you will this time. I promise. Because, you see, of all the people in this world, I understand you best. Remember that when others tempt you.' She walked away a few steps, and looked back over her shoulder briefly. 'Remember. When the others twist around you, and that little Pall opens those eyes wide. Remember I'm the only one.' She walked away, her motions precise and intense.

Jackson watched her, thinking.

II

People were beginning to come into the Thorn; bees were listening to them, and exteroaffectors were beginning to pelt about, making and bringing whatever they wanted. There began to be music. Kringle came in, drifted over to the other side of the tent, and sat down alone on the floor.

Jackson noticed that the people weren't especially dressed. Oh, Elyria wore hoops of fine-spun wire around her neck in a golden cascade, and Donder had on a pair of black hornrimmed glasses with flat windowpane lenses. Lois had clad one arm in silvery chain mail to the shoulder, and so forth. But it was the light that decorated them. As they shifted back and forth, talking, gesticulating, beginning to warm up to the occasion, they gained and lost patterns that shifted over their skins.

They were not eating or drinking much. They were talking, mostly. In fact, some of them were sitting very still, eyes half closed, heads bent, as if completely lost in private worlds. Often enough, one or another of them would smile at him, raise a hand, and look pleased to see him here. But none of them were really getting into conversation with him. They were much more interested in whatever it was that went on in their heads while they waited for a party to start swinging.

It was Vixen who started the ball rolling. Standing a little off to one side, she'd been frowning and swaying her body just slightly. Jackson had been watching her curiously, while he stood around waiting to see what would happen when Durstine – and Pall, too – came in. He happened to be watching when she suddenly snapped her fingers and said delightedly: 'Got it!'

'What? What do you have?' Ginger asked, and as Vixen grinned, heads began to turn towards her.

Vixen took two or three steps forward, walking in a peculiar way. As she moved, she seemed to gain confidence; her movements became more pronounced and regular, and a little smile played around the corners of her mouth. She walked that way to the centre of the circle made by the Thorn's floor. She had everybody's attention, now, and the light began to change. A glow began to come over the crystalline draperies, and soft, golden light began to grow in a dome, starting at the Thorn's floor, and working its way up the interior walls, until they were all standing in a crystal-clear bath of it.

'Jackson! Jackson – look!'

Vixen came walking towards him, one hand on her hip, the other extended in a graceful arch over her head, palm flat, fingers up. She smiled at him and reached with the other hand, and lifted something imaginary from the top of her head. She bent slightly at the waist, holding out her hands. 'Water, Honor?'

The party burst into applause. Vixen smiled shyly, laughed a little, and retreated. Apparently, it had been intended to be some kind of pantomime. But that wasn't how you carried water; you cradled water in your arms.

'Well! That was a good beginning, wouldn't you say?' Kringle said, slapping him on the back. 'I'd say she really conveyed the idea, wouldn't you?' He peered a little more closely at Jackson's face. 'No? Well, perhaps there were certain minor crudities in her performance.' A little knot of Vixen's particular friends was clustering around her, congratulating her. 'But it was certainly good enough for a beginning,' Kringle said.

Donder stepped forward. He stood in the centre of the floor, and raised his hand negligently. A hush fell over the crowd. Donder took a breath and began to speak:

Die.
Be born, be loud, be free, but
die. Those of us born
Thorn-children suck that in our milk.
We hate you, Thorn:
We belch your word at you.'

He bowed to Jackson, flushed, a sheen of sweat across his brow.

They started to applaud. Then one of them remembered something, and began to snap his fingers. The inside of the party Thorn crackled with the odd sound of it.

'How 'bout that, Jackson?' Donder called out to him. 'Sort of puts it all in a nutshell, doesn't it?'

Jackson asked Kringle: 'Does he mean, the way you feel about the Thorn? I mean, does he think you should feel that way about the thing that keeps you alive?'

A very slight frown appeared between Kringle's brows again. 'I think if you examine your internal processes, you might find he came somewhat closer than you might be ready to admit.' He raised his voice and called to Donder: 'Beautiful, son! Now, gang,' he called out to the assembled company, 'we all want to remember that our guest isn't completely familiar with our customs. But we all know he's going to catch on in no time.'

Comp said in Jackson's ear: 'Listen, they need the feedback of your approval, or the party's going to lose its impetus.'

'Oh,' Jackson said.

'Look! Here's Pall!' Clark pointed at the entrance.

She came in shyly, holding her hands folded in front of her. Hanging around her waist was a ragged white drape of fabric; scant, pure unblemished white, high on one hip and low on the other, the loose, torn threads of its hem brushing her mid-thigh. She came walking up to Jackson, looking at the ground. As she got closer to him, Jackson could see that there were grains of sand worked into her hair, and streaked smudges from it on her body. They had clearly-defined edges, and they weren't any darker at the knees; there weren't little rings of it in the skin around her wrists, and there wasn't a deeper smudge of it at the base of her neck, in the hollow where perspiration would have washed it in the course of the day.

But by now, Jackson had the idea.

'Welcome home, Honor,' she said submissively, and the Thorn seemed to fill with the sound of the group's approval – a great appreciative roar that was compounded of applause and outcries of admiration.

'Tremendous!' Kringle said.

'Look at her, Jackson!' he lowered his voice. 'My dear – was that truly an original thought of yours? That's marvellous. Marvellous. Jackson, you do see it, don't you? She's made a work of art of herself. This is doubly exciting. Our little Pall …'

Pall was blushing. 'Thank you so much, Kringle.' She didn't quite know what to do with her hands; obviously it was the first time in her life she'd ever got a compliment for her creativity. 'Actually,' she said, 'you see, I'm such a naïve person, really – oh, Kringle will tell you I'm not, but he's just being polite – I finally thought to myself: "Well, if you're going to be naïve, and there doesn't seem to be anything you can do about it, you might as well do something constructive with it, wouldn't you think? Why don't you ..." So I did! That's really all there was to it. I just did, that's all. I said to myself, the thing to do is take what you have and use it!'

'I think you did fine,' Jackson said. 'I think the subtle touch of presenting yourself not only as a work of art, but as a work of art with a duality of meaning, is an example of the vitality inherent in the natural response.' He smiled at her, and touched her lightly on the shoulder. The Thorn broke into fresh applause. 'It's of course the hard underlying base of the subtle but primary implication that really makes it work,' he said, looking sincerely into her eyes as they sparkled with fulfilment. Suddenly those eyes brimmed over, and two perfect tears flowed down her cheeks.

'Thank you,' she breathed so softly that the nearest sound receptor had to dart in a little closer, and hover like a humming bird at her lips.

III

Pall was circulating among the people, being congratulated by everyone, not just her particular friends. She walked like a debutante.

Jackson stood rubbing his left elbow.

Perry had been working at something behind a bunch of other people. 'Hey, looka what Perry's got!' they began to exclaim, crowding around, with other people crowding in behind them, peering over their shoulders.

'Hold on, now! Everybody'll get a chance to see it!' Perry growled in a gruff, good-natured way.

Exteroaffectors carried it out to the middle of the floor for him, and put it up on three graceful, thin metal legs. High above, a rope of light kindled itself among the higher traceries of crystal, and concentrated its beam upon the painting.

'Jackson! Come forward, Jackson!' Perry motioned urgently from beside the painting. 'I dedicate this to you.'

Oh, Jesus! But Jackson got himself moving, his legs sucking up through glue, and went to look at it.

It had been done in wide, sometimes apparently laboured, sometimes apparently glib strokes. It was full of all the wrong colours. What it showed was Jackson's Thorn, in the distance, with the pale Sun behind it. Huddled at the base of the Thorn were square, nearly featureless blocks that you could tell were houses because here and there there was a light in a window. In the foreground of the painting, mostly in silhouette, with only a few details picked out by highlights, was a Amsir lying on the blind slope of a dune, his head raised just enough so he could watch the Thorn and the houses. And off to one side, watching the Amsir, was the figure of a Honor, also blocked out crudely. You could tell it was a Honor because it was wearing something on its head that looked like a cross between the German helmets of World War II and the Franco-Prussian War. It was intended to be a honning cap, Jackson supposed.

You couldn't really fault it for skill. The guy had obviously done work of this kind before. You could maybe criticize the composition, but you had to do it on professional grounds. You had to give him that much. But, Jesus Christ, Comp had the right facts on file; they were there to be dug out. All you had to do was look for them.

'What do you think of it?' Perry asked, through the rising sound of applause as the other people crowded around. Then he said: 'Of course, you want to feel free to use any terms you want – you don't need to confine your-self to the technical terms of the graphic arts.' There was an understanding little smile playing around the corners of his mouth. 'After all, many of my other friends here would have to use layman's language, too.'

Jackson opened his mouth, then closed it. He could feel the tip of his tongue rubbing against the inner faces of the teeth on one side of his jaw.

'Go ahead,' Perry said.

'Comp,' Jackson said, 'I need an easel, a backing board, a sheet of charcoal paper, and some charcoal. Right away, now.'

Perry looked nonplussed. The crowd around them grew quiet. The extero-affectors worked quickly.

Another beam of light focused down on the blank sheet at Jackson's easel. He held all but one of the sticks in his left hand, and bounced the other in his right for a minute as he stepped back and looked around at the people. He sucked at his front teeth once, sharply, and stepped into his work. He touched the tip of the stick to the paper. He drew them a Amsir, fanatical and brave, with a dart rattling loose in the hole punched through one of its main bub-bles, trying to get one hand up and bent around enough to hold its fingers over the hole. Meanwhile it marched a Honor dressed in human skin and sucking on an air bottle towards the rim of the world.

When it was done, it was done. He didn't know exactly how long it took. Nobody interrupted him. They shuffled around, nervously, and sometimes whispered, but he was able to pay them no mind.

Looking at it, he could see it was all right; he had it right. His left hand was black and empty. He dropped the last stick on the floor, at Perry's feet. 'That's what I think of your painting,' he said. 'Technically.'

There was a gasp from several of the people behind him. Perry frowned and stepped around to look at the drawing. He stood scratching his chin, cocking his head back and forth. 'I'm … afraid I don't understand. What are you trying to say with this?'

There was a rising murmur of assent around the two of them. 'Yes. What does that prove?'

'Better let me have a look,' Kringle said, pushing forward. He stood beside Perry; Jackson had to step back to give him room. 'Hmm – are you trying to equate charcoal with oils?' Kringle asked Jackson in an avuncular sort of way. 'It's very difficult to compare art in different media, you know. In fact,' he pointed out reasonably, 'it's very difficult to compare art. *N'est ce pas?*'

'What I don't understand,' Perry said, 'is why he felt he had to be so hostile about it. I see what he's done here, and it's another scene entirely. How could one arrive at a basis for comparison?'

Donder said: 'Well, I think it's a hell of a note, any way you look at it! I mean, here Perry dedicated it to him, at *his* party – we're all taking part, here, for him. What does he want to act like this for?'

CHAPTER EIGHTEEN

I

Just to make sure, Jackson took one last look at the difference between Perry's piece of work and his drawing. Then he turned around and worked his way out of the crowd. Many of them were trying to push forward and look at the twin centres of attention anyhow. The others glanced at him uncomfortably. Some of them looked a little distasteful, and others looked as if they didn't quite know what to do, but none of them could understand what he was so worked up about. So he was able to get out from between them without coming into any kind of contact. He wiped the sweat off his face, and then, looking at his wet, charcoaled palm, he realized he'd probably messed up his face pretty good. He walked out through the entrance and stood looking out at the pavilions, whose sides were responding gaily to the breeze.

'Comp, I want a ship.'

'That's impossible. It would be disastrous. You know enough about experimental discipline to understand that. Look,' Comp said soothingly, 'you're in a mood of despair. But that's the result of your failure to relate properly to these people—'

'Or their failure to relate to me.'

'There's no need to become emotional about it. By the way, I don't think you're as accomplished an artist as you believe yourself to be. I think there's very little rational ground to choose from between yourself and the individual called Perry. Therefore your disgust with his effort is founded purely on your emotional conviction that you are the better spokesman for that certain representation of reality. You may be right, but one representation of reality is no more worthy than another. Perry could choose to represent some portion of the world personally experienced by him. If he did, your attempt to copy it, no matter how many actualities you had seen and no matter how empathetic you felt, would not be as valid as his. Would it therefore be totally invalid? No, and Perry would be rude to say so. He would be almost inexcusably rude to demonstrate the fact as dramatically as you chose to do. And then of course there's the ultimate sin, you failed to make your point conclusively.

'All these things are working against you at the moment. But really, these are all things from which it's possible to recover. I think in no time at all you will have found a way of expressing yourself that is satisfactory to both you and the community. Well, perhaps not in no time. But in finite time. Relax – knock around a little. Learn what suits you best. Meanwhile – here—'

Exteroaffectors settled on him momentarily, and were gone. He was clean again, fresh-minted. His skin glowed. He rubbed his elbow. Maybe someday he'd be all hollow inside?

'Maybe I could offer a course in Throwing Stick? How about art? I mean, I could do something, and then you could have an election and see if it was any good or not. Maybe a simple majority vote would do, and then I could open up a school.'

'I think we've covered that,' Comp said.

'A cat couldn't have done better,' Jackson agreed. 'Look, is there anyone else to talk to in this world except them and things like them?'

'Well, there is myself. I'm an inexhaustible conversationalist. I am also the definite didact. The number of things to be learned from me is finite, but very large. I assure you, if you choose it, that's a lifetime's occupation. A constantly expanding field of knowledge. Right at the moment, for example, the telemetry involved in sending exteroceptors across interstellar distances represents a fruitful—'

Jackson grinned, the way he had seen the Eld grin. 'And when you die, I can be you.'

'Heavens, no! I will never die!'

'That's what they all think,' Jackson sighed. 'What's Ahmuls doing?' He felt pretty lonely.

'Ahmuls is quite contented. Here …' Exteroaffectors kissed Jackson's eyelids.

At first, he thought what he saw was a runaway streamlet, tumbling, liquid and brown, swirling amidst stones. Then he realized it was an aerial view of a vast plain. The point of view dropped like a swooping hawk, and he plunged down towards a herd of tossing, shaggy brown animals, massive of head, high of shoulder, red-eyed, horned, and hairy. Exteroaffectors nuzzled behind his ears, and he heard the thunder of the buffalo.

Behind them, bounding and lurching, came Ahmuls, silent, and purposeful. He ran in a way that told Jackson he was straining everything he had, but my God how he ran, his flesh bagging out behind him, away from his face and shoulders. His mouth was wide open, and the tip of his tongue was in the corner of his lips.

'This is the Mid-American Game Preserve,' Comp said. 'you'll notice the landscape has been slightly modified, to suit his special requirements.'

Indeed, the granite outcroppings that now split the herd into segments as it milled around them, and again flowed it into one cohesive mass before Ahmuls' pursuit startled it again, were covered with lichen. As he ran by one of them, Ahmuls threw out a hand, scooped off a clump, and stuffed it into his mouth. It was impossible to tell whether he was trying to catch the animals so he could kill them, or whether he was merely attempting to join them. But in the milling and stampeding, there were almost as many behind him as there were ahead, and once or twice panicked bulls clattering and snorting out of tight places between the rocks almost ran him down.

'What'll you do if he gets pounded flat?'

'Oh, there is no problem about that. He'd get medical attention immediately.'

'For the rest of his life.'

'That's my obligation. Accidental factors cannot be permitted to interrupt something's running its course.' Ahmuls disappeared from this particular exteroaffector's sight as he ran behind an outcropping. 'Do you want me to shift point of view, or do you want to look at Durstine now?'

Jackson opened his eyes, as he heard her say from in front of him: 'I wondered how long it would be before you came looking for me.'

It was hard shifting from the actuality to something he could see with his own eyes. It took a moment to organize his brain. He saw she was wearing some sort of crested helmet whose front part was a pale, sharp-edged mask over the upper part of her face, leaving only the chin and the red lips bare. Then he saw she was, in fact, gowned, unlike the decorated people inside. She stepped back, her body clad in swirling off-white gauzeries which might have been individual motes of pigment suspended in the air, or might even have been some wonderful fabric.

Either way it was some wonderful fabric, swirled around her body at the waist, caught again at the shoulders and the elbows. She laughed and sprang to tiptoe, her arms first out straight at the shoulders, then bent at the elbows to point towards him. The movement of her body scattered out her garment in lacy strands, upraised the crest of her mask, and flung wide her white wings. She laughed in a silvery tinkle of joy. 'See? I knew exactly what you wanted! I'm yours, yours!' she cried, throwing herself at him yieldingly.

He could just about get his hands up to catch her shoulders, and he felt himself wince when he touched them. 'You've got it just exactly backwards,' he said, marvelling at their capacity. 'I got to admit, it's an accomplishment.'

'What? What?' She was jerking and tossing against his hands. 'What's the matter with you?'

'It's either you or me,' he admitted, swinging her around to push her backward through the doorway, trying to see to it she got where she belonged. Now what would Elmo Lincoln do in a case like this? 'Go. Go, mangani!' he burst out, pushing explosively, flinging her backward in a swirl and smother of garb. He was shaking with rage; he could hear Comp giggling.

He glared around him. There was nothing in sight but fake, and blue sky full of receptor glints. Never, never in his life had be been so angry, and Comp wouldn't stop giggling at him. He swatted at a darting bee. He wasn't as fast as Ahmuls.

He crouched, facing the doorway. Whoever came out of there first was in terrible trouble with him. He could see red mist edging his field of vision, and at the same time there was this terrible, wonderful clarity about how he felt. It was an excuse for anything. A man brought to this feeling was as much a monarch as Tyrannosaurus Red had ever been. He prowled with his thighs flexed, his arms like bridge cable.

Pall came shyly and diffidently out of the Thorn tent. 'Don't be mad, Jackson,' she said. 'I know you're upset.' She stretched out her hand and touched his fist. 'I know how it is. They used to treat me that way. But I just learned to ignore it. And I didn't give up; I kept trying to improve myself, and one day ...' Her eyes dropped. 'What you have to do,' she explained earnestly, 'is ... well, learn to *express* yourself. Express *yourself*. You see, if you can only learn to trust in yourself, in what *you* are, if you feel confident in what you are, then ... Well, you saw what happened. If you have confidence ... and loving somebody can *give* you that confidence, or even just *admiring* them a lot can give you a lot of confidence ... well, then, after that you can go along and do the same things everybody else does, and yet you're still expressing yourself, so you see, well, that's how you can be part of the group and still be yourself. I mean, knowing yourself lets you be part of a group. And you saw how they accepted me at last. Well, that's what makes it good because from now on, I'm going to always know that being part of a group is the only thing that lets you be yourself. And I can give you the same thing. Let me stay with you. I'll be good for you.'

Jackson looked up at the spiralling glints. 'You see that?' he asked. 'You hear?'

'Certainly. Would you like to see an actuality of Petra Jovans?'

Jackson shivered. 'No. Don't ever show me Petra Jovans.'

Pall was touching his hand to her mouth. 'Please, Jackson,' she said, 'I really do understand you.'

Sweet Jesus, he thought. And then he thought, To me I am the only sane man conceivable. And she's just cuckoo enough to go along with it if I take her. 'Oh, come on,' he said, turning away from the tent, holding her wrist.

She trotted gracefully beside him. 'Where are we going?'

'I don't know.' He got them out between the pavilions and on to the fields. There was some kind of path out through the hedgerows, and he followed that. Exteroceptors were keeping pace with them.

'This is great stuff!' Comp was saying. 'Setting out for the New Eden! Man and his mate, on the endless journey to—'

'Horse shit,' Jackson said.

Pall stared at him. 'What was that for?'

What was it for? It always had to be for something, right? Jackson shook his head. 'You really want to know? You really want me to *express* myself, right?'

She nodded. 'Very much.'

All right. He began, 'The floor of the world is rippled like the bottom of the ocean, running out to the edges. Those edges are high and they're cruel. At sunset the eastern horizon is the far wall of the crater. It's black. Blue-black ...'

'Great stuff! Marvellous!' Comp whispered admiringly in his ear. 'Forgive me. I thought all you were going to produce was some sort of cliché. Any cliché from you would be admirably dramatic, of course, with great and wide appeal. But I do not want you to think for a moment that I can't appreciate the raw, honest ring of visceral truth. The audience for it isn't so big, of course, but that's all right – it's good for them. Don't compromise. Don't soften it up just because you want to please *her*. Make it ring, boy! Tell it like it was!'

'... And thou beside me zinging in the wilderness,' Jackson muttered, Pall trotting along beside him with her eyes as bright as exteroceptors. Jackson said, 'The sunlight catches the top edge of the crater, and that's rust colour. It makes a long, rust-coloured arc that seems to dip down to left and right, like a wall, or a bow, or the trail of something that shot by without your noticing it, from one horizon to the other, and all you can see is the wake it left. There are rocks standing on the crater floor. The sunlight hitting them, just before it dies, turns them orange, too. The stars hang up there hard and sharp.

'That's the horizon you head for when you're honning Amsirs.

'In the beginning, I was chasing this bird ...'

MICHAELMAS

To
Sidney Coleman,
my friend and this book's friend

Author's Note

Effective assistance in a great variety of forms was given this project by A.C. Spectorsky, Carl Sagan, Jan Norbye and James Dunne, Ed Coudal, William B. Sundown, Slim Sanders, Chuck Finberg, Ed and Audrey Ferman, Bob Kaiser, Brad Bisk, Don Borah, Marshall Barksdale, the presence in my mind of James Blish, and most particularly Edna F. Budrys, in that simultaneous order.

This novel incorporates features of a substantially shorter and significantly different version published in *The Magazine of Fantasy and Science Fiction*, Copyright © 1976 by A.J. Budrys.

ONE

When he was as lonely as he was tonight, Laurent Michaelmas would consider himself in a dangerous mood. He would try to pry himself out of it. He'd punch through the adventure channels and watch the holograms cavort in his apartment, noting how careful directors had seen to it there was plenty of action but room as well for the viewer. At times like this, however, perhaps he did not want to be so carefully eased out of the way of hurtling projectiles or sociopathic characters.

He would switch to the news channels. He'd study the techniques of competitors he thought he had something to learn from. He'd note the names of good directors and camera operators. So he'd find himself storing up a reserve of compliments for his professional acquaintances when next he saw them, and that, too, wasn't what he needed now.

After that, he would try the instructional media; the good, classic dramas, and opera; documentaries; teaching aids – but the dramas were all memorized in his head already, and he had all the news and most of the documentary data. If there was something he needed to know, Domino could always tell him quickly. It would pall.

When it did, as it had tonight, he would become restless. He would not let himself go to the romance channels; that was not for him. He would instead admit that it was simply time again for him to be this way, and that from time to time it would always be this way.

With his eyes closed, he sat at the small antique desk in the corner and remembered what he had written many years ago.

> *Your eyes, encompassed full with love,*
> *Play shining changes like the dance of clouds.*
> *And I would have the summer rain of you*
> *In my eyes through*
> *The dappled sunlight of our lives.*

He put his head down on his arms for a moment.

But he was Laurent Michaelmas. He was a large-eyed man, his round, nearly hairless head founded on a short, broad jaw. His torso was thick and powerful, equipped with dexterous limbs and precisely acting hands and feet. In his public *persona* he looked out at the world like an honest child of great capability. Had his lips turned down, the massive curve of his glistening scalp and the configuration of his jaw would have made him resemble a snapping turtle. But no one in his audiences had ever seen him that way; habitually his mouth curved up in a reassuring smile.

Similarly when he moved, his swift feet in their glistening black shoes danced quickly and softly over parquet and sidewalk, up marble steps and along vinyl-tiled corridors, in and out of houses of commerce, universities, factories, places of government, in and out of ships, aircraft, and banks. There was hardly anywhere in the world where his concerns might not be expected to take him, smiling and polite, reassuring, his flat black little transceiving machine swinging from its strap over his left shoulder, his fresh red carnation in the buttonhole of his black suit.

His smile looked into the faces of the great as freely as it did into anyone else's, and it was a long time since he'd actually had to show his press credentials. When in New York, he made his bachelor home in this living space overlooking Central Park from the top of a very tall building. He didn't make much of its location. Nor had anyone but he ever seen the inside of it, he having been a widower since before his professional *floreat*. So he did not have to apologize for the blue Picasso over his desk or the De Kooning, Braque, and Utrillo that were apportioned to other aspects of the room. He lived here as he liked. Most of the time, baroque music played softly and sourcelessly wherever he went about the apartment, as if he had contrived to have a strolling ensemble follow after him discreetly.

Seated now, his face reminiscing bleakly, the comm unit resting at his elbow, he was interrupted when one of the array of pinpoint pilot lights blinked. It was red. The machine's speakers simultaneously gave a premonitory pop. 'Mr Michaelmas.'

The voice was reserved, the tone dry. A spiritless man might have thought it reproving. Michaelmas turned toward the machine with friendly interest. 'Yes, Domino.'

'I have a news bulletin.'

'Go ahead.' Michaelmas always gave the impression of appreciating every moment anyone could spare him. That manner had served many a famous interviewer before him. Michaelmas apparently never discarded it.

'Reuters has a story that Walter Norwood is not dead. He is almost fully recuperated from long-term intensive treatment, and *is* fit to return to duty.'

Laurent Michaelmas sat back in his chair, the jowls folding under his jaw, and raised one eyebrow. He steepled his fingertips. 'You'd better give me that verbatim.'

'Right. "Berne, September 29. Walter Norwood alive and well, says two-time Nobel winner life scientist. Doktor Professor Nils Hannes Limberg announced here 0330 Berne time astronaut Walter Norwood, thought dead in June destruction his Sahara orbital shuttle, suffered extensive injuries in crash his escape capsule on Alpine peak near world-famous Limberg Sanatorium. Limberg states now that publicity, help, advice then from others would have merely interfered with proper treatment. Norwood now quote good as ever and news is being released at this earliest medically advisable time endquote. UN Astronautics Commission notified by Limberg just previous to this statement. UNAC informed Norwood ready to leave sanatorium at UNAC discretion. Limberg refers add inquiries to UNAC and refused media access to sanatorium quote at this time endquote. Bulletin ends. Note to bureau managers: We querying UNAC Europe. Reuters Afrique please query UNAC Star Control and send soonest. Reuters New York same UNAC there. Reuters International stand by. End all." '

Laurent Michaelmas cocked his head and looked up and off at nothing. 'Think it's true?'

'I think the way Limberg's reported to have handled it gives it a lot of verisimilitude. Very much in character from start to finish. Based on that, the conclusion is that Norwood is alive and well.'

'Damn,' Michaelmas said. 'God damn.'

He played with his fingertips upon the warm satiny wood of the desktop. The nails of his left hand were long, while those of his right hand were squared off short and the fingertips showed considerable callosity. One aspect of his living room area mounted a large panel of blue-black velvet. Angular thin brass hooks projected from it, and on those were hung various antique stringed instruments. But now Michaelmas swung around in his chair and picked up a Martin Dreadnaught guitar. He hunched forward in the chair and hung brooding over the instrument, right hand curled around its broad neck.

'Domino.'

'Yes, Mr Michaelmas.'

'What do you have from the other media?'

'On the Norwood story?'

'Right. You'd better give it priority in all your information feeds to me until further notice.'

'Understood. First, all the other news services are quoting Reuters to their Swiss and UN stations and asking what the hell. AP's Berne man has replied with no progress on the phone to Limberg, and can't get to the sanatorium – it's up on a mountain, and the only road is private. UPI *is* filing old tapes of Norwood, and of Limberg, with background stories on each and a recap of the shuttle accident. They have nothing; they're just servicing their subscribers with features and sidebars, and probably hoping they'll have a new lead soon. All the feature syndicates are doing essentially the same thing.'

'What's Tass doing?'

'They're not releasing it at all. They've been on the phone to *Pravda* and Berne. *Pravda* is holding space on tomorrow's page three, and Tass's man in Berne is having just as much luck as the AP. He's predicting to his chief that Limberg will throw a full-scale news conference soon; says it's not in character for the old man not to follow up after this teaser. I agree.'

'Yes. What are the networks doing?'

'They've reacted sharply but are waiting on the wire services for details. The entertainment networks are having voice-over breaks with slides of Berne, the Oberland, or almost any snowy mountain scene; they're reading the bulletin quickly, and then going to promos for their affiliated news channels. But the news is tending to montages of stock shuttle-shot footage over stock visuals of the Jungfrau and the Finsteraarhorn. No one has any more data.'

'All right, I think we can let you handle all that. I'd say Dr Limberg has dropped his bombshell and retreated to a previously prepared position to wait out the night. The next place to go is UNAC. What have you got?' Michaelmas's fingers made contact with the guitar strings. The piped music cut off. In the silence, the guitar hummed to his touch. He paid it no heed, clasping it to him but not addressing himself to it.

'Star Control has decided not to permit statements at any installation until an official statement has been prepared and released from there. They are circulating two drafts among their directors. One draft is an expression of surprise and delight, and the other, of course, is an expression of regret at false hopes that have upset the decorum of the world's grief for Colonel Norwood. They'll release nothing until they have authenticated word from Berne. A UNAC executive plane is clearing Naples for Berne at the moment with Ossip Sakal aboard; he was vacationing there. The flight has not been announced to the press.

'Star Control's engineering staff has memoed all offices reiterating its original June evaluation that Norwood's vehicle was totally destroyed and nothing got clear. Obviously, UNAC people are being knocked out of bed everywhere to review their records.'

Michaelmas's hands plucked and pressed absently at the guitar. Odd notes and phrases swelled out of the soundbox. Hints of melody grouped themselves out of the disconnected beats and vanished before anything much happened to them.

The hectoring voice of the machine went on. 'Star Control has had a telephone call from Limberg's sanatorium. The calling party was identified as Norwood on voice, appearance, and conversational content. He substantiated the Limberg statement. He was then ordered to keep mum until Sakal and some staff people from Naples have reached him. All UNAC spaceflight installations and offices were then sequestered by Star Control, as previously indicated, and the fact of the call from Norwood to UNAC has not been made available to the press.'

'You've been busy.' A particularly fortunate series of accidents issued from the guitar. Michaelmas blinked down at it in pleasure and surprise. But now it had distracted him, so he let it fall softly against the lounge behind him. He stood up and put his hands deep in his pockets, his shoulders bowed and stiff. He drifted slowly toward the window and looked out along Manhattan Island.

Norwood's miracle – Norwood's and Limberg's miracle – was well on its way toward being a fact, and truth was the least of the things that made it so. Michaelmas absently touched the telephone in his breast pocket, silent only because of Domino's secretarial function.

He knew he lived in a world laced by mute sound clamoring to be heard, by pictures prepared to become instant simulacra. Above him – constantly above him and all the world – the relay stations were throbbing with myriad bits of news and inconsequence that flashed from ground station to station, night and day, from one orbit to another, from synchronous orbit to horizon scanner and up to the supra-synchs that orbited the Earth-Moon system, until the diagram of all these reflecting angles and pyramids of communication made the earth and her sister the binary center of a great faceted globe resembling nothing so much as Buckminster Fuller's heart's desire.

Around him, from the height of the tallest structure and at times to the depths of the sea, a denser, less elegant, more frantic network shot its arrows from every sort of transmitter to every sort of receiver, and from every transceiver back again. There was not a place in the world where a picture-maker could not warm to life and intelligence, if its operator had any of either quality, if Aunt Martha were not asleep, if one's mistress were not elsewhere, if the assistant buyer for United Merchants were not busy on another of his channels. Or, more and more often, there were the waterfall chimes of machines responding to machines, of systems reacting to controls, and only ultimately of controls translating from human voice for their machines.

What a universe of chitterings, Laurent Michaelmas thought. What a cheeping basketry was woven for the world. He thought of Domino, who had begun as a device for talking to his wife without charge. It leaks, he thought wryly. But it doesn't matter if it leaks. The container is so complex it enwraps its own drains. It leaks into itself.

He thought of Nils Hannes Limberg, whose clinic served the severely traumatized of half the world, its fee schedule quietly known to be adapted to ability to pay. Rather well known, as of course it had to be. Nils Hannes Limberg, proprietor not only of a massive image of rectitude and research, but also of the more spacious wing of his sanatorium, with its refurbishment of dermal tissue and revitalization of muscle tone in the great and public. A crusty old man in a shabby suit, bluntly tolerating the gratitude in first wives of shipping cartel owners, grumpily declaring: 'I never watch it,' when asked if he felt special pride in the long-running élan of Dusty Haverman. '*Warbirds of Time?* A star of a series? Ah, he is the leading player in an entertainment! No, I never realized that – on my tables, you know, they do not speak lines.'

It was approximately ten minutes since Nils Hannes Limberg, who was a gaunt old man full of liver spots and blue veins, had spoken to the Reuters man in whatever language was most convenient for them. And now, 2,000,000,000 waking people had had the opportunity to know what he had said, with more due to awaken to it. No one knew how many computers knew what he had said; no one knew how many microliths strained with it, how many teleprinters shook with it. Who in his right mind would say that something which had spat through so many electron valves, had shaken the hearts of so many junction-junction couplings, so many laser jewels, so many cans of carbon fluids – so many lowly carbon granules, for that matter – was not a colossal factor in the day?

Somewhere in those two billions, torture and ecstasy could be traced directly to those particular, vibrations of a speaker cone, to that special dance of electrons through focusing lens and electrostat. Good spirits and bad had been let loose within the systems of those who had heard the news and then left on previous errands, which were now done differently from the way they might have been. The prices of a thousand things went up; everyone's dollar shrank, but the dollars of some were multiplied. Women cried, and intended loves went unconsummated. Women smiled, and strangers met. Men thrilled, and who knows what happens when a man thrills? Laurent Michaelmas looked out his window, with only a million people or so in his direct line of vision, and the fine hairs were standing up on his arms.

He shook his head and turned back to his terminal. 'Disregard all Norwood data beginning with the Reuters items. Do you think Norwood is alive?'

'No. All hope of finding him, alive or dead, is irrational. Every study of the shuttle accident concludes that the fuel explosion raised the temperature of the system well above the flash point of all organic and inorganic components. All studies indicate there was no warning before the explosion. All studies indicate no object could have accelerated away from the explosion fast enough to outrun it. All of this specifically agrees with UNAC's studies of the escape capsule's acceleration capabilities. Finally, it agrees with my own evaluations for you at the time.'

'Norwood became part of an expanding ball of high-temperature gases, correct?'

'Yes.'

'So your present estimate that Norwood lives is based purely on the Reuters item.'

'Right.'

'Why?'

'Common sense.'

'Reuters doesn't usually get its facts wrong and never lies. Dr Limberg did make the statement, and he can't afford to lie. Right?'

'Correct.'

Laurent Michaelmas smiled fondly at the machine. The smile was gentle, and genuinely tender. It was exactly like what can be seen on the faces of two very young children awakening with each other in the morning, not yet out on the nursery floor and wanting the same thing.

'How do you envision Norwood's marvelous resurrection? What has happened to him?'

'I believe his trajectory in the capsule did end somewhere near Limberg's sanatorium. I assume he was gravely injured, if it has taken him all these months to recover even at Dr Limberg's hands. Limberg's two prizes are after all for breakthroughs in controlled artificial cellular reproduction and for theoretical work on cellular memory mechanisms. It wouldn't surprise me to learn he practically had to grow Norwood a new body. That sort of reconstitution, based on Limberg's publications over the years, is now nearly within reach of any properly managed medical center. I would expect Limberg himself to be able to do it now, given his facilities and a patient in high popular esteem. His ego would rise to the occasion like a butterfly to the sun.'

'Is Norwood still the same man?'

'Assuming his brain is undamaged, certainly.'

'Perfectly capable of leading the Outer Planets expedition after all?'

'Capable, but not likely to. He has missed three months of the countdown. Major Papashvilly must remain in command, so I imagine Colonel Norwood cannot go at all. It would be against Russian practice to promote their cosmonaut to the necessary higher rank until after his successful completion of the mission.'

'What if something happened to Papashvilly?'

'Essentially the same thing has happened vis-à-vis Norwood. UNAC would assign the next backup man, and ...'

Laurent Michaelmas grinned. 'Horsefeathers.'

There was a moment's pause, and the voice said slowly, consideredly: 'You may be right. The popular dynamic would very likely assure Norwood's reappointment.'

Michaelmas smiled coldly. He rubbed the top of his head. 'Tell me, you are still confident that no one has deduced our – ah – personal dynamic?'

'Perfectly confident.' Domino was shocked at the suggestion. 'That would require a practically impossible order of integration. And I keep a running check. No one knows that you and I run the world.'

'Does anyone know the world is being run?'

'Now, that's another formulation. No one knows what's in the hearts of men. But if anyone's thinking that way, it's never been communicated. Except, just possibly, face to face.'

'Which is meaningless until concerted action results. And that would require communication, and you'd pick it up. That's one comfort, anyway.' He was again looking out at night-softened Manhattan, which rose like a crystallographer's dream of Atlantis out of a lighted haze. 'Probably meaningless,' Michaelmas said softly.

There was another silence from the machine. 'Tell me ...'

'Anything.'

'Why do you ask that in connection with your previous set of questions?'

Michaelmas's eyes twinkled as they often did when he found Domino trying to grapple with intuition. But not all of his customary insouciance endured through his reply. 'Because we have just discovered that the very great Nils Hannes Limberg is a fraud and a henchman. That is a sad and significant thing. And because Norwood was as dead as yesterday. He was a nice young man with high, specialized qualifications no higher than those of the man who replaced him, and there was never anything secret or marvelous about him or you would have told me long ago. If we could have saved him, we would have. But there's nothing either you or I can do about a stuck valve over the Mediterranean, and frankly I'm just as glad there's some responsibility I don't have to take. If we could have gotten him back at the time, I would have been delighted. But he had a fatal accident, and the world has gone on.'

Michaelmas was not smiling at all. 'It's no longer Colonel Norwood's time. The dead must not rise – they undermine everything their dying created. Resurrecting Norwood is an attempt to cancel history. I can't allow that, any more than any other human being would. And so all of this is a challenge to me. I was concerned that it might be a deliberate trap.'

He turned his face upward. That brought stars and several planets into his line of vision. 'Something out there's unhappy with history. That means it's unhappy with what I've done. Something out there is trying to change history. That means it's groping toward me.'

Michaelmas scratched his head. 'Of course, you say it doesn't know it's got one specific man to contend with. It may think it only has some seven billion people to push around. But one of these days, it'll realize. I'm afraid it's smarter than you and I.'

With asperity, Domino said: 'Would you like a critique of the nonsequential assumptions in that set? As one example, you have no basis for that final evaluation. Your and my combined intellectual resources—'

'Domino, never try to reason with a man who can see the blade swinging for his head.' He cocked that head again, Michaelmas did, and his wide, ugly face was quite elfin. 'I'll have to think of something. Afterward, you can make common sense of it.' He began to walk around, his square torso tilted forward from his broad hips. He made funny, soft, explosive humming noises with his mouth and throat, his cheeks throbbing, and the sound of a drum and recorder followed wherever he strolled.

TWO

'Well, I think I should be frightened,' Michaelmas told Domino as he moved about the kitchen premises preparing his evening meal. The chopped onions simmering in their wine sauce were softening toward a nice degree of tenderness, but the sauce itself was bubbling too urgently, and might turn gluey. He picked up the pan and shook it gently while passing it back and forth six inches above the flame. The filet of beef was browning quite well in its own skillet, yielding sensuously as he nudged it with his fork.

'You don't grow an established personality from scratch,' Michaelmas said. 'An artificial infant, now ... why not? I'll give Limberg that; he could do it. Or he could grow a clone identical with an adult Norwood. But he's never had occasion to get tissue from the original, has he? And there's no way to create a grown man with thirty-odd years behind him. Oh, no. That I won't give him. And I tell you he would have had to do it from scratch because Norwood never crashed anywhere near that sanatorium. Strictly speaking, he never crashed at all – he vaporized. So Limberg would have had to build this entire person by retrieving data alone. But I don't think there's any recording system complete enough, or one with Norwood entered in it if there were.'

'Norwood and Limberg never met. There is no record of any transmission of Norwood cell samples to any depository. No present system will permit complete biological and experiential reconstruction from data alone.'

'And there you are,' Michaelmas said. 'Simplest thing in the world.' He worked a dab of sauce between thumb and forefinger and then tasted them with satisfaction. He set the pan down on the shut-off burner, put a lid on it, and turned toward the table where the little machine lay with its pilot lamps mostly quiescent but sparkling with reflected room light.

'You don't fake an astronaut,' he said to it. 'Even in this culture they're unique for the degree to which their response characteristics are known and studied. Limberg wouldn't try to get away with it. He's brought the real Colonel Norwood back to life. *But* he hasn't done it using any of the techniques and discoveries he's announced over the years. Limberg's career, his public image, everything – it's all reduced simply to something useful as a cover for the type of action he's taken now. It really is all very clear, Domino, if you disregard that balderdash about Norwood's surviving the explosion. Think about it, now.'

He was patient and encouraging. In the same way, he had often led the tongue-tied and confused through hundreds of vivacious interviews, making and wrecking policies and careers before huge audiences.

The reply through the machine was equally patient but without forbearance:

'Doctor Limberg is a first-rate genius—'

Michaelmas smiled shyly and mercilessly but did not interrupt.

'—who could not possibly be living a double life. Even given a rate of progress so phenomenal that he could develop his overt reputation and still secretly pursue some entirely different line, there are insurmountable practical objections.'

'Oh, yeah? Name some.' The sauce hissed ebulliently as it made contact with the beef skillet. A few dextrous turns of Michaelmas's fork enveloped the filet in just properly glutinous flavoring, and then he was able to place his dinner on its warmed, waiting dish and bring it to the place he had laid in the dining aspect. He poured a glassful of wine that had been breathing in its wicker server, and sat down to partake of his meal.

'One,' Domino said. 'He is a gruff saint, in the manner developed by many world intellectual figures since the communications revolution. The more fiercely he objects to intrusions on his elevated processes of thought and his working methods, the more persistently the news media attempt to discover what he's doing now. One of the standard methods of information tap is to keep careful account of everything shipped to him. You'll recall this is how Science News Service deduced his interest in plasmids from his purchase of ole-phages. As a direct result, several wise investors in the appropriate manufacturing concerns were rewarded when Limberg made the announcements leading to his earlier prize. Since then, naturally, there are scores of inferential inventories being run on his purchases and wastage. His overt researches account for all of it.'

'One of the inventories being yours.' Michaelmas chuckled over his fork. 'Go on.'

'Two. All analyses of the genius personality, however it may be masked, show that this sort of individual cannot be other-directed over any significant period of time. You're hypothesizing that this excellent mind has been participating for years in a gross deception upon the world. This cannot be true. If that had been his original purpose, he would have grown away from it and rebelled catastrophically as his cover career began to assume genuine importance and direction. You can't oppose a dynamic – and I shouldn't be quoting your own basics back to you,' Domino chided, and then went on remorselessly:

'And exactly so, if he'd been approached recently for the same purpose, he would have refused. He would have died – more meaningfully, he would have undergone any form of emotional or physical pain – rather than submit.

The genius mind is inevitably and fluently egocentric. Any attempt to tamper with its plans for itself – well, putting it more conventionally, any attempt to tamper with its compulsive career – would be equivalent to a threat of extinction. That would be unacceptable.'

Michaelmas was smiling in approval through the marching words, and pouring himself another glass of wine. 'Quite right. Now let's just assume that Herr Doktor Professor N. Hannes Limberg, life scientist, is a merely smart man, with a good library and access to a service that can supply a technique for making people.'

There was a perceptible pause. With benevolent interest, Michaelmas watched the not quite random pattern of rippling lights on the ostensible machine's surface. Behind him, the apartment services were washing and storing his kitchenware. There was the usual music, faint in view of the entertainment center's awareness, through Domino, that there was a discussion going on. It had all the ingredients of a most pleasant evening, early poetry forgotten.

'Hmm,' Domino said. 'Assuming you're aware of the detail discontinuities in your exact statement and were simply leapfrogging them ... Well, yes, a competent actor with the proper vocabulary and reference library could live an imitation of genius. And a man supplied with a full-blown technique and the necessary instruments needs no prototype research or component purchases.'

There was another pause, and Domino went on with obvious reluctance to voice the obvious.

'However, there has to be a pre-existing body of knowledge to supply the library, the equipment, and the undetected system for delivering these things. Practically, such an armamentarium could arise only from a fully developed society that has been in existence at least since Limberg's undergraduate days. No such society exists on Earth. The entire Solar System is clearly devoid of other intelligent life. Therefore, no such society exists within the ken of the human race.'

'But perhaps not beyond the reach of its predictable intentions,' Michaelmas said. 'Well, I assume you've been screening contract offers in connection with the Norwood item?'

'Yes. You've had a number of calls from various networks and syndicates. I've sold the byline prose rights. I'm holding three spoken-word offers for your decision. The remainder were outside your standards.'

'Sign me for the one that offers the most latitude for the money. I don't want someone thinking he's bought the right to control my movements. And tap into the UNAC management dynamic – edit a couple of interoffice memos as they go by. Stir up some generalized concern over Papashvilly's health and safety. Where is he, by the way?'

'Star Control. He's asleep, or at least his phone hasn't been in use lately and his room services are drawing minimum power but showing some human-equivalent consumption. UNAC's apparently decided not to disturb him unless they have to.'

'Are you saying the electronic configuration of his room is *exactly* the same as on previous occasions when you've known him to be in it asleep?'

'Yes. Yes, of course. He's in there, and he's sleeping.'

'Thank you. I want us to always be exact with each other on points like that. Limberg's masters have taken a magnificent stride, but I don't see why my admiration has to blind me. I'm not Fate, after all.'

THREE

He went down through the building security systems and to the taxi dock. The dock was ribbed in pale brownish concrete, lit by blue overheads. Technically, the air was totally self-contained, screened, and filtered. But the quality was not to apartment standards; the dock represented a large, unbroken volume that had needed more ducts and fans than the construction budget could reasonably allow. There was a sense of echoing desolation, and of distant hot winds.

He saw the taxi stopped at the portal. Because the driver had his eyes on him, he actually took out his phone and established ID between the cab, himself, and the building. Putting the phone away, he shook his head. 'We ought to be able to do better than this,' he said to Domino.

'One step at a time,' his companion replied. 'We do what we can with the projects we can find to push. Do you remember what this neighborhood used to be like?'

'Livelier,' Michaelmas said with a trace of wistfulness.

The driver recognized him on the way out to the airport and said: 'S'pose you're on your way over to find out if Walt Norwood's really okay?' The airline gate chief said: 'I'm looking forward to your interviews with Colonel Norwood and Dr Limberg. I never trust any of your competitors, Mr Michaelmas.' The stewardess who seated him was a lovely young lady whose eyes misted as she wondered if it was true about Norwood. For each of them, and for those fellow passengers who got up the courage to speak to him, he had disarming smiles and interested replies which somehow took away some of the intrusion of his holding up his machine to catch their faces and words. As they spoke to him, knowing that they might be part of a program, he admired them.

For him, it didn't seem an easy thing for a human being to react naturally when his most fleeting response was being captured like a dragonfly in amber. When he had first decided that the thing to do was to be a newsman, he had also clearly seen an essential indecency in freezing a smile forever or preventing the effacement of a tear. He had been a long time getting sufficiently over that feeling to be good at his work. Gradually he had come to understand that they trusted him enough not to mind his borrowing little bits of their souls. From this, he got a wordless feeling that somehow prevented him from botching them up.

He reflected, too, that the gate chief had blown his chance to see himself on network time by confining his remarks to compliments. This touched the part of him that could not leave irony alone.

So for Michaelmas his excursion out through the night-bare streets, and on board the rather small transatlantic aircraft with its short passenger list, was a plunge into refreshment. Although he recognized his shortcomings and unrealized accomplishments every step of the way.

He settled into the lounge with a smile of well-being. His tapering fingers curled pleasurably around a Negroni soon after the plane had completed its initial bound into the thinner reaches of the sky. He gazed around him as if he expected something new and wonderful to pop into his ken at any moment. He behaved as if a cruising speed of twenty-five hundred miles per hour in a thin-skinned pressurized device were exactly what Man had always been yearning for.

Down among the tail seats were two men in New York tailored suits who had come running aboard at the last moment. One of them was flashing press credentials and a broad masculine smile at the stewardess guarding the tourist-class barrier. Even at the length of the plane's cabin, Michaelmas could recognize both a press-card holder and the old dodge of paying cheap but riding high. Now the two men were coming toward him, sure enough. One of them was Melvin Watson, who had undoubtedly picked up one of the two offers Michaelmas had turned down. The other was a younger stranger.

Each of them was carrying a standard comm unit painted royal blue and marked with a network decal. Watson was grinning widely in Michaelmas's direction and back over his shoulder at his companion, the while he was already extending a bricklayer's hand toward Michaelmas and forging up the aisle. Michaelmas rose in greeting.

His machine was turned toward the two men. Domino's voice said through the conductor in his mastoid: 'The other one is Douglas Campion. New in the East. Good Chicago reputation. Top of the commentator staff on WKMM-TV; did a lot of his own legwork on local matter. Went freelance about a year ago. NBC's been carrying a lot of his matter daytime; some night exposure lately.' Michaelmas was glad the rundown had been short; there seemed to be no way for him to avoid sinus resonance from bone conduction devices.

'I could have told you, Doug,' Watson was saying to Campion as they reached Michaelmas. 'If you want to catch Larry Michaelmas, you better look in first class.' His hand closed around Michaelmas's. 'How are you, Larry?' he rumbled. 'Europe on a shoestring? Going to visit a sick relative? Avoiding someone's angry boyfriend?' When he spoke longer lines, even though he grinned and winked, his voice acquired the portentous pauses and nasal overtones that were his professional legacy from Army Announcers'

School. But combined with his seamed face, his rawhide tan, and his eyes so pale blue that their pupils seemed much deeper than the whites, the technique was very effective with the audience. Michaelmas had seen him scrambling forward over ripped sandbags in a bloodied shirt, and liked him.

'Good evening, Horse,' he said laughing, tilting his head up to study Watson, whom he hadn't seen personally in some time, and who seemed flushed and a little weary.

'Damn near morning,' Watson snorted. 'Lousy racket. Meet Doug Campion.'

Campion was very taut and handsome. There was an indefinable cohesiveness about him, as though he were one solid thing from the surface of his skin on through – mahogany, for instance, or some other close-grained substance which could be nicked but not easily splintered. From those depths, his black eyes stood out. Even the crisp, short, tightly curled reddish hair on his well-shaped skull looked as if it would take a very sharp blade to trim. He was no more than five-foot-nine and probably weighed less than one hundred fifty pounds. He might readily have been an astronaut himself.

'Very pleased to meet you, sir,' he said briskly. 'It's an honor and a privilege.' He shook Michaelmas's hand with the quick, economical technique of a man who has done platform introductions at fund-raising events. His eyes took in Michaelmas's face and form, and put them away someplace. 'I've been looking forward to this ever since I got into the trade.'

'Won't you please sit down?' Michaelmas said, not because Watson wasn't already halfway into the chair beside him but because Campion put him in mind of the *politesse* of policy meetings and boardrooms. He decided that Campion must be very self-confident to have abandoned his safer and inevitably rapid progress up the network corporate ladder. And he remembered that Domino had been impressed by him.

'Thank you, Larry,' Campion was murmuring. Watson was settling into his seat as if trampling hay, and tilting his fist up to his mouth as he caught the eye of the first-class stewardess. 'Well, Larry,' Watson said. 'Looks like we're going to be climbing the Alps together, right?'

'I guess so, Horse,' Michaelmas smiled.

There was a pleasant chime simultaneously from Watson's and Campion's comm units. Watson grunted, pulled the earplug out of its takeup, and inserted it in place. On Michaelmas's other side, Campion did the same. The two of them listened intently, faces blank, mouths slightly open, as Michaelmas smiled from one to the other. After a moment, Watson held his unit up to his mouth and said: 'Got it. Out,' and let the earplug rewind. 'AP bulletin,' he explained to Michaelmas. 'One of their people got a "No Comment" out of UNAC about some of their people having flown to Limberg's place. Jesus, I wish that girl would get here with that damned cart; I'm tapering off my daughter's engagement party. Looks like there's something happening over there after all.'

Michaelmas said: 'I imagine so.' A No Comment in these circumstances was tantamount to an admission – a UNAC public relations man's way of keeping in with his employers and with the media at the same time. But this was twice, now, in this brief conversation, that Horse Watson had hinted for reassurance.

'You buy this story?' Watson asked now, doing it again.

Michaelmas nodded. He understood that all Watson thought he was doing was passing the time. 'I don't think Reuters blows very many,' he said.

'Me too, I guess. You have time to pick up any crowd reaction?'

'Some. It's all hopeful.' And now, trading back for the relay of the AP bulletin, Michaelmas said: 'Did you pick up the Gately comment?' When Watson shook his head, Michaelmas smiled mischievously and held up his machine. He switched on a component that imitated the sound of spinning tape reels. 'I – ah – collected it from CBS in my cab. It's public domain anyway. Here it is,' he said as the pilot lights went through an off-on sequence and then held steady as he pressed the switch again.

Will Gately was United States Assistant Secretary of Defense for Astronautics, and a former astronaut. Always lobbying for his own emotions, he was the perfect man for a job the administration had tacitly committed to ineptitude. 'The wave of public jubilation at this unconfirmed report,' his voice said, 'may be premature. It may be dampened tomorrow by the cold light of disappointment. But tonight, at least, America goes to bed exhilarated. Tonight, America remembers its own.'

Watson's belly shook. 'And tomorrow Russia reminds the world about the denationalization clause in the UN astronautics treaty. Jesus, I believe Kerosene Willy may revive the Space Race yet.'

Michaelmas smiled as if Gately's *faux pas* hadn't foreclosed Major Papashvilly's chances of immediate promotion. Especially now, the USSR couldn't risk raising the world's eyebrows by making their man Norwood's equal in rank. By that much, Gately and the Soviet espousal of fervent gentlemanliness in pursuit of the Balanced Peace might have conspired to put the spritely little Georgian in more certain danger.

Campion said, startlingly after his silence, 'The good doctor sure knows how to use his prime time.' Michaelmas cocked his head toward him. Campion was right. But he was also making himself too knowledgeable for a man who'd never met Limberg. 'Three-thirty AM local time on September 29 when he got that Reuters man out of bed.' Campion was documenting his point. 'Hit the good old USA right in the breadbasket,' meaning the ten PM news on September 28.

It occurred to Michaelmas that Campion realized Limberg had moved as if to play directly to the Gately-types. But Watson was missing that because Campion had made himself annoying.

'What I'm thinking,' Watson had said right on top of Campion's final consonant, 'is we're going to hit Berne about seven-thirty AM local. Limberg's still up in that sanatorium with the UNAC people and Norwood, and the conversation's flying. Then you figure that old man will go without his beauty sleep? I don't. It's going to be maybe noon local before we stand any chance of talking to that crafty son of a bitch, and that's six hours past my bedtime. Meanwhile, all the media in Europe is right now beating the bushes there for color, background, and maybe even the crash site. Which means that the minute we touch ground, we've got to scurry our own feet like crazy just to find out how far behind we are.'

'Don't their European people have some staff on the ground there now?' Michaelmas asked gently, nodding toward the network decal on Watson's comm unit while Campion sat up a little, smiling.

'Oh, sure,' Watson pressed on, 'but you know how stringers are. They'll be tryin' to sell me postcard views of the mountains with Xs inked on 'em where the capsule may have come down except it's got months of snow on it. And meanwhile, will UNAC give us anything to work on? They need their sleep too, and, besides, they won't peep till Limberg's explained it all, and talked about his prizes he was fortunate enough to scoff up although he's of course above money and mundane gewgaws and stuff like that. Norwood stays under wraps, and *he* sleeps, or else they switch us a fast one and slide him out of there. What do you bet we get a leak he's been moved to Star Control when all the time they've got him in New York, God forbid Houston, or maybe even Tyura Tam. You'd enjoy the Aral climate in the summer, Doug. You'd like the commissars, too – they eat nice fresh press credentials for breakfast over there, Sonny.'

Michaelmas blinked unhappily at Watson, who was concentrating now on the approaching liquor caddy and fishing in his breast pocket for money. He felt terribly sorry Watson felt obliged to hire Campion for an assistant when he was so afraid of him.

'Let me buy you fellows a drink,' Watson was saying. Since he knew Michaelmas's drinks were on his ticket, and he despised Campion, Horse Watson was trying to buy his way into the company of men. Michaelmas could feel himself beginning to blush. He breathed quickly in an attempt to fight it down.

'Maybe I'd better take a rain check,' Campion said quickly. 'Going by your summation, Mel, I'd be better off with forty winks.' He turned off his comm unit, leaned back with his arms folded across his chest, and closed his eyes.

'I'd be glad of another one of these, miss,' Michaelmas said to the stewardess, holding up his half-full glass. 'You make them excellently.'

Watson got a bourbon and water. He took off the top half with one gulping swallow and then nursed the rest in his clenched hand. He sat brooding at his stiffly outthrust shoes. After a while, he said forcefully: 'Been around a long time, Larry, the two of us.'

Michaelmas nodded. He chuckled. 'Every time something happens in South America, I think about the time you almost led the Junta charge across the plaza at Maracaibo.'

Watson smiled crookedly. 'Man, we were right on top of it that day, weren't we? You with that black box flapping in the breeze and me with my bare hands. Filed the damn story by cable, for Christ's sake, like some birthday greeting or something. And told 'em if they were going to send any more people down, they'd better wrap some armor around the units, 'cause the first slug they stopped was the last.' He put his hand on the sealed, tamperproof unit he might be said to have pioneered at the cost of his own flesh.

He took a very small sip of his drink. Watson was not drunk, and he was not a drunk, but he didn't smoke or use sticks, and he had nothing to do with his hands. Nor could he really stop talking. Most of the plane passengers were people with early-morning business – couriers with certificates or portable valuta; engineers; craftsmen with specialties too delicate to be confidently executed by telewaldo; good, honest, self-sufficient specialists comforted by salaries that justified personal travel at ungodly hours – and they lay wrapped in quilts of tranquil self-esteem, nodding limp-necked in their seats with their reading lights off. Watson looked down the dimness of the aisle.

'The way it is these days lately, I'd damn near have to send off to Albania for my party card and move south. Foment my own wars.'

'You miss it, don't you?' Michaelmas said in a measured kidding tone of voice.

Watson shook his head. Then he nodded slightly. 'I don't know. Maybe. Remember how it was when we were just starting out – Asia, Africa, Russia, Mississippi? Holy smoke, you'd just get something half put away, and somebody'd start it up again somewhere else. *Big* movements. Crowds. Lots of smoke and fire.'

'Oh, yes. Big headlines. A lot of exciting footage on the flat-V tube.'

'You know, I think the thing about it was, it was *simple* stuff. Good guys, bad guys. People who were going to take your country away overnight. People who were going to cancel your paycheck. People who were going to come into your school. People who stood around in bunches and waved clubs and yelled "The hell you will!" Man, you know, really, those were the salad days for you and me. Good thing, too; I don't suppose either one of us had enough experience to do anything but point at the writing on the wall. Neither one of us could miss the broad side of a barn, period. Right? Well, maybe not you, but me. Me, for sure.'

'It's not necessary to be such a country boy with me, Horse.'

Watson waved his hands. 'Nah! Nah, look, we were green as grass, and so was the world. Man, is it wrong to miss being young and sure of yourself? I don't think so, Larry. I think if I didn't miss it, the last good part of me would be all crusted over and cracking in the middle. But whatever happened to big ideological militancy, anyway? All we've got left now is these tired agrarian reformer bandidos hiding in the Andes, screaming Peking's gone soft on imperialismo and abandoned 'em, and stealing chickens. I wonder if old Joe Stalin ever figured his last apostle would be somebody named Juan Schmidt-Garcia with a case of B.O. that would fell a tree?'

'Yes, the world is quite different now from the way I found it in my young manhood,' Michaelmas said. Looking at the slump of Watson's mouth, he spoke the words with a certain sympathy. 'Now most of the world's violence is individual, and petty.'

Watson snorted softly. 'Like that thing in New York where that freak was sneaking in on his neighbors and killing them for their apartment space. Nuts and kooks; little grubby nuts. Good for two minutes on one day. Not that you should measure death that way, God rest the souls of the innocent. But you know what I mean. Look. Look, we're in a funny racket, all of a sudden. You figure you're gonna spend your life making things real for the little folks in the parlor, you know? Here's the big stuff coming at you, people; better duck. Here's the condition of the world. You don't like it? Get up and change it.'

'Yes,' Michaelmas said. 'We showed them the big things, and that made the small things smaller. More tolerable. Less significant.'

Watson nodded. 'Maybe. Maybe. You're saying the shit was there all along. But I got to tell you, when we showed 'em a gut-shot farmer drowning in a rice paddy, it was because it meant something in Waukegan. It said, "Today your way of life was made more safe. Or less." But you show 'em the same guy today, and it's about a jealous husband or some clown wants to inherit his buffalo. And you know it's not going to get any bigger than that.

'It's cowboys and Indians again,' Watson said. 'Stories for children. It doesn't mean a thing to Waukegan, except the guy's dying, and he's dying the way they do in the holo dramas, so he's as real as the next actor. They judge his Goddamn *performance*, for Christ's sake, and if he's convincing, then maybe it was important. It makes you sick to think he's not interesting if he's quiet about it. Man, so little of it's real anymore; they've got no idea what can happen to them. They don't want an idea. You remember that quote Alvin Moscow got from the plane crash survivor? "We would all be a little kinder to each other." *That* is what you and I should be all about.'

'Man, who knows what's real anymore, and who feels it? You run your fingers over a selector and the only action that looks right to you is something they did in a studio with prefigured angles, stop motion, the best lighting, and all that stuff. Even your occasional Moroccan schoolteacher hung over a slow fire three days ago can't compete with that stuff. It's not like he was a Commie that was going to corrupt the morals of Mason City, or even that he was a Peace Corps volunteer that crossed some Leninist infiltrator. It's just some poor slob that told the kids something that's not in the *Quran*, and somebody took exception to it. Man, you can get the same thing in Tennessee; what's so great about that? Is that gonna make you rush out and join some crusade to stop that kind of stuff? Is that gonna touch your life at all? Is that gonna make you hear the marching band?'

'It might cause you to sip your wine more slowly.'

'Okay. Yeah. But you know damned well the big stories now are some guy dying by inches inside because he can't make his taxes and who, where, has the half million that disappeared out of the transit bill? I mean that's all right, and it's necessary, and even after your third pop or your third stick, it'll get through to you, kind of, if Melvin Watson or L. G. Michaelmas, begging your pardon, Larry, pushes it at you in some way that makes you feel like you're paying attention. But nobody dies *for* anything anymore, you know? They all die only *on account of*, just like holo people, and half the time these days we just pass along a lot of dung from the lobby boys and the government boys and the image gurus like our friend the Herr Doktor.

'My God, Larry, we're just on a fertilizer run here. UNAC's just a bunch of people jockeying to get by, just like in any widget monopoly or thingumbob cartel in the world. When Norwood went, who cried at UNAC? All you heard was the hemorrhage shot 'round the world. So they shook out some expandable patsies and then they were right in there pitching again, talking about the increased effect on the goal attainment curve and all that other vocabulary they have to kiss it and make it well with. Scared green for the appropriation; scared to death they picked the wrong voodoo in school. But they're safe. They'd be sick if they realized it, but the whole world's like they are even if it would turn their stomachs to believe it.

'Christ, yes, they're safe. It's fat, fat, fat in the world, and bucks coming out of everybody's ears; spend it quickly, before the damn economy does what it did in the seventies and we have to redesign whole industries to get rich again. Smart isn't "Can you do it, is it good to do?" Smart is "Can you make 'em believe what you're doing is real?" And real is "Can you get financing for it?"'

Michaelmas sat very still, sharing Watson's angle of blind vision down the aisle and being careful not to do anything distracting. He had learned long ago never to stop anyone.

Watson was unstoppable. 'Norwood's up there breathing and feeling in that megabuck beauty shop of Limberg's and suspecting there's a God who loves him. I know Norwood – hell, so do you. Nice kid, but ten years from now he'll be endorsing a brand of phone. The point is, right now he's on that mountaintop with all that glory ringing in him, but that doesn't make him real to his bosses and it doesn't make him real to the little folks in the parlor. What makes him real is Limberg says he's real and Limberg's got not one but two good voodoo certificates. Christ on a crutch, I've got half a mind to kill Norwood all over again – on the air, Larry, live from beautiful Switzerland, ladies and gentlemen, phut splat in glorious hexacolor 3D, and let him be real all over every God-damned dining table in the world. Ten years from now, he'd thank me for it.'

Michaelmas sat quiet.

Watson swung his head up and grinned suddenly, to show he was kidding about any part that Michaelmas might object to. But he could not hold the expression very long. His eyes wandered, and he jerked his head toward Campion. 'He really asleep?'

Michaelmas followed his glance. 'I believe so. I don't think he'd relax his mouth like that if he weren't.'

'You catch on.' Watson looked nakedly into Michaelmas's face with the horrid invulnerability of the broken. 'I don't have any legs left,' he explained. 'Not leg legs – inside legs. Sawed 'em off myself. So I took in a fast young runner. Hungry, but very hot and a lot of voodoo in his head. Watch out for him, Larry. He's the meanest person I've ever met in my life. Surely no men will be born after him. My gift to the big time. Any day now he's going to tell me I can go home to the sixties. Galatea's revenge. And I'll believe him.'

Michaelmas couldn't be quite certain of how his own face looked. In his ear, Domino had been telling him: 'As you can imagine, I'm getting all three sets of pulse and respiration data from your area, so there's considerable garbling. But my evaluation is that Campion hasn't surrendered consciousness for a moment.'

Watson had been clenching at his stomach with one hand. Now he put his drink down and got up to go to the lavatory. Campion continued to half-lie in his seat, his expression slack and tender. Michaelmas sat smiling a little, quizzically.

Domino said with asperity: 'Watson's right about one thing. He can't hack it anymore. That was a classic maniacal farrago, and it boils down to his not being able to understand the world. It wasn't necessary to count the contradictions after the first one.'

It was extremely difficult for Michaelmas to subvocalize well enough to activate his throat microphone without also making audible grunting sounds. He had never liked straining his body, and the equipment was implanted in him only because he needed it in his vocation. He used it as infrequently as possible, but he was not going to let Domino have the last word on this topic. 'Wait one,' he said while he chose his words.

Time was when men of Horse Watson's profession typically never slept sober, and died with their livers eroded. It must have been fun to watch the literate swashbucklers make fools of themselves in the frontier saloons, indulging in horse-whippings and shoot-outs with rival journalists and their partisans. But who stopped to think what it was like to have the power of words and publication, to discover that an entire town and territory would judge, condemn, act, reprieve, and glorify because of something you had slugged together the night before? Because of something you had hand-set into type, smudging your fingertips with metal poisons that inexorably began their journey through your bloodstream? For the sake of the power, you turned your liver and kidneys into spongy, irascible masses; you tainted the tissue of your brain with heavy metal ions until it became a house haunted by stumbling visions. Alcohol would temporarily overcome the effect. So you became an alcoholic, and purchased sanity one day at a time, and made a spectacle of yourself. It was neither funny nor tragic in the end – it was simply a fact of life that operated less slowly on the mediocre, because the mediocre could turn themselves off and go to sleep whether they had done the night's job to their own satisfaction or not.

Time was, too, when men of Horse Watson's profession had to seek out gory death because that was all their bosses were willing to either deplore or endorse, depending on management policy. But let no man tell you it's possible to live like that and not pay. The occupational disease was martinis for the ones that needed a cushion, and, for the very good ones, cancer. For good and bad in proportional measure there was also the great, funny plague of the latter half of the century – nervous bowels and irritated stomachs. Who could see anything but humor in a man gulping down tincture of opium and shifting uneasily in his studio seat, his mind concerned with thoughts of fistula and surgery, his mind determinedly not preoccupied with intestinal resections and where that could lead? Loss of dignity is after all one of the basics to a good punchy gag.

And time was when men of Horse Watson's profession were set free by the tube, the satellites, and finally the hologram. Now all Horse Watson had to do to pick and choose among contending employers was to make sure that his personal popularity with the little folks in the allocated apartment remained higher than most. It was a shame he knew no better way to do this than to be honest. A strong young head full of good voodoo could make mincemeat out of a man like that.

Men like Horse Watson were being cut down quickly. It was one of the nervous staples of recent shop gossip, and that, too, was having its effect on the scarier old heads. They came apart like spring-wound clocks when the tough young graduates with their 1965 birth certificates popped out of college with a major in Communications and a pair of minors in Psychology and Politics, and a thirty thousand new dollar tuition-loan note at the bank.

Michaelmas said to Domino: 'He knows he shouldn't say things like that. He knows some of it doesn't make sense. He trusts me, and he thinks of me as one of his own kind. He's apologizing for slipping away and leaving me with one less colleague. If you can see that, you can see that if you think kindly of him, you're being less hard on yourself. He doesn't realize he's casting aspersions on our work. He doesn't know what we do. He thinks it's all his own fault. Now please be still for a while.' He massaged the bridge of his nose. He did not look at Campion. He was having a split-second fear that if he did, the man might open one eye and wink at him.

FOUR

It was truer than ever that airports look the same all over the world. But not all airports are located in the Alps.

Michaelmas descended just behind Watson and Campion, into a batting of light reflected from every surface, into a cup of nose-searing cool washed brilliance whose horizon was white mountaintops higher than the clouds. The field was located high enough above the Aar, and far enough from the city itself, to touch him with the sight of the Old City on its neck of land in the acute bend of the river, looking as unreally arranged as a literal painting. It was with that thought, blinking, that he managed to locate himself in time, space, and beauty, and so consider that his soul had caught up with him.

There was a considerable commotion going on at the shuttle lounge debarking ramp. Movement out of the lounge had stopped. Watson had been right about any number of details: it was likely that half the journalists in Europe were on the scene, and there was a gesticulating, elbowing crowd of them there, many of them in berets and trenchcoats, displaying the free-lance spirit.

Even the people with staff jobs had caught the infection either here or much earlier, and there was the usual jostling with intent to break directed at any loosely held piece of equipment. There was a bewildering variety of that – sound and video recorders both flat and stereo, film cameras, and old minicams as well as holograph recorders – as if every pawnbroker on the continent were smiling this morning. Most of the people down here had to be working on speculation. There weren't enough media contracts or staff jobs in the world to support that mob, or, truth to tell, speculation markets either.

The current compromise pronunciation of his name seemed to be 'Mik-kelmoss!' and emerged most often from the gaggle of voices. Lenses glittering like an array of Assyrians, they tried to get to him in the lounge or cannily waited for him to ensnare himself among them. Michaelmas could feel himself blushing, his round cheeks hot under his crinkling eyes. He could not help smiling, either, as he discovered a staff cameraman for Watson's client network actually shooting for a zoom closeup of him over Watson's shoulder. It was Campion who raised his comm unit to block that shot; Watson had his head down and was working his way through the crowd with effective hips and shoulders.

The first man to get to Michaelmas – a wiry, shock-headed type with blue jaws, body odor, and an elaborate but obsolescent sound recorder – clutched a handrail, planted his feet to block passage fore and aft, and shot his microphone forward. 'Is true dzey findet wreckidge Kolonel Norwoot's racquet?' 'What is your comment on that, sir, please?' came from a BBC man down on the ground beside the ramp with a shotgun microphone, an amplifier strapped over his mouth and phones on his ears. His camera was built into his helmet, exposure sensors flashing.

And so forth. Michaelmas made his way through them, working his way toward Customs and the cab rank, feeling a sudden burst of autumn chill as someone opened a door, smiling, making brief reasonable comments about his own lack of information. Domino was saying to him: 'Remember, Mickeymouse – you are but a man.' As he cleared the fringes of the crowd, Domino also said: 'You have a suite at the Excelsior and an eight AM appointment with your crew director. That is forty-eight minutes from ... now.'

Michaelmas reset his watch.

It was a beautiful drive into the city, with the road winding its way down to the river, looping lower and lower like a fly fisherman's line until unexpectedly the cab crossed the stonework bridge and they were in the narrow streets of the Old City.

Michaelmas loved Switzerland. He loved the whole idea of Switzerland. He sat back among the cushions with the cab's sunroof open at his request. He beamed through the tinted windows at the people going about their business in and out of the fairy-tale buildings that were still preserved, with hidden steel beams and other subtle internal reconstructions, among the newer modern buildings that were so much more efficient and economical to erect from scratch.

'The escape capsule wreckage has not been reported as yet,' Domino said. 'There have only been a few daylight hours for the helicopters to be out. In any case, we can expect it to be under a considerable accumulation of snow, and not indicative of anything of value to us. If Limberg can produce a genuine Norwood, he can produce genuine wreckage.'

'Quite so,' Michaelmas said. 'I don't expect it to tell us anything. But it would be nice if I were the first newsman to report it.'

'I am on all local communications channels,' Domino said tartly, 'and am also making the requisite computations. I have been doing that since before arranging your hotel reservations.'

'Didn't mean to question your professional competence,' Michaelmas said. He chuckled aloud, and the cab driver said:

'*Ja, mein Herr*, it is a day to feel young again.' He winked into the rearview mirror. It was a moment before Michaelmas realized they had been driving by an academy for young ladies in blue jumpers and white wool blouses, and in their later teens. Michaelmas obligingly turned in his seat and peered back through the rear window at sun-browned legs in football-striped calf socks scampering two by two up the old white steps to class. But to be young again would have been an unbearable price.

The suite in the Excelsior spoke of matured grace and cultivated taste. Michaelmas looked around approvingly as the captain supervised the bustling of the boys with his luggage and the plod of the gray old chambermaid with his towels. When they were all done and he was sated with wandering from room to room through open doorways, he found the most comfortable drawing room chair and sank into it. Putting his feet on an ottoman, he called downstairs for coffee and pastry. He had about fifteen minutes before his crew director was due. He said to Domino: 'All right, I suppose there are certain things we have to take care of before we get back to the main schedule.'

'Yes,' Domino said unflinchingly.

'All right, let's get to it.'

'President Fefre.'

Michaelmas grinned. 'What's he done now?' Fefre was chief of the state in one of the smaller African nations. He was a Harvard graduate in economics, had a knife scar running from his right temple to the left side of his jaw, and had turned Moslem for the purpose of maintaining a number of wives in the capital palace. He sold radium, refined in a Chinese-built plant, to anyone who would pay for it, running it out to the airport in little British trucks over roads built with American money. He had cut taxes back to zero, closed all but one newspaper, and last month had imprisoned the seventy-two-year-old head of his air force as a revolutionary.

Domino said: 'The Victorious Soviet People's Engineering Team has won the contract to design and build the hydroelectric dam at the foot of Lake Egendi, despite being markedly underbid by General Dynamics. A hundred thousand rubles in gold has been deposited to Fefre's pseudonymous account in the Uruguayan Peasant Union Bank. It would be no problem to arrange a clerical error that would bring all this to light.'

Michaelmas chuckled. 'No, no, let him go. The bank needs the working capital and, besides, I like his style. Anything else?'

'The source of funds for the Turkish Greatness Party is the United Arab Republic.'

'Imagine that. You sure?'

'Quite. The Turkish National Bank has recently gone into fully computerized operation, with connections of course to London, Paris, Rome, Cairo, Tel Aviv, New Delhi, and so forth. The Continental Bank and Trust Company of Chicago is in correspondence with all those, as part of the international major monetary exchange body, and is also the major and almost sole stockholder in the State Bank and Trust Company of Wilmette, Illinois, where I have one of my earliest links. When Turkey joined that network I immediately began a normal series of new data integrations. I now have all the resulting correlations, and that's one of them.'

'Do you mean to say the Arabs are paying the Turks by check?'

'I mean to say there's a limit to the number of gold pieces one can stuff into a mattress. Sooner or later someone has to put it somewhere safe, and when he does, of course, I find it.'

'Yes, yes,' Michaelmas said. He had a very clear picture in his mind of suave, dark, blue-eyed gentlemen in white silk suits and French sunglasses passing canvas bags that rustled to somewhat rougher-looking people in drophead Bentleys by the light of the desert moon. Gentlemen who in turn paid for their petrol on a Shell card and booked air passage from El Fasher to Adana against personal checks which would be covered by deposit of lira notes which had trickled through the weave of the moneybags. On balance, if you had a mind like Domino's and knew all credit card numbers, the flight times of all airliners, and the vital statistics of all gentlemen known to engage in the buying and selling of other gentlemen and submachine guns, in all portions of the world, there was no great trick to it. 'I know you can take a joke,' he said to Domino. 'But sometimes I do wish you could understand a jest.'

'Life,' said Domino, 'is too short.'

'Yours?'

'No.'

'Hmm.' Michaelmas pondered for a moment. 'Well, I don't think we need any expansionist revolutions in Turkey. The idea of armored cavalry charging the gates of Vienna again is liable to be too charming to too many people. Break that up, next opportunity.' Michaelmas looked at his watch. 'All right. Any more?'

'US Always has learned that Senator Stever is getting twenty-five thousand dollars a year from that northwestern lumber combine. USA's Washington office made a phone call reporting it to Hanrassy's national headquarters at Cape Girardeau.'

'In that simpleminded code of theirs? If they're planning to save the whole country from the rest of the world, you'd think they'd learn to respect crypt-analysis. Any information on what they're planning to do with this leverage?'

'Nothing definite. But that brings to six the total of senior Senators defin-itely in their pockets, plus their ideological adherents. This is not a good time for USA to be gaining in power. Furthermore, although it's very early in the morning in Missouri, Hanrassy's known to work through the night quite often. I won't be surprised if a Senatorial inquiry starts today on why Colonel Norwood wasn't immediately reinstated as head of the Trans-Martian flight.

Even allowing for her intake of amphetamines, Hanrassy's annoyingly energetic.'

'Better she than someone with staying power. But I think we'd better take this committee chairman pawn away from her. Sam Lemoyne's still on the night side for the *Times-Mirror*. It'd be good if he got the idea to go buy a drink for that beachboy Stever beat up in his apartment last year.'

'I'll drop him a note,' Domino said.

It was nearly eight o'clock. 'All right, unless there's a real emergency, go ahead and follow standard practice with anything else that's pending.' With the passage of time, Domino was beginning to learn more and more about how Michaelmas's mind worked. He didn't like it, but he could follow it when instructed. That fact was the only thing that let Michaelmas contemplate the passage of time with less than panic.

Michaelmas's house phone chimed. He listened and said: 'Send her up.' His crew director was here.

She came in just ahead of the room-service waiter. Michaelmas attended to the amenities and they sat together on the balcony, sipping and talking. She and the crew were all on staff with his employer network. Her name was Clementine Gervaise, and he had never met her because the bulk of her previous experience had been with national media, and because this was his first time with her network, which was up-and-coming and hadn't been able to afford him before.

Gervaise – Madame Gervaise, he gathered from the plain band on her finger – was the model of one kind of fortyish, chic European woman. She was tall, blonde, with her hair pulled back severely from her brow but feathered out coquettishly over one ear, dressed in a plain blue-green couturier suit, and very professional. It took them ten minutes to work out what kind of equipment they had available, what sort of handling and transport capabilities they had for it, and what to do with it pending permission to enter the sanatorium grounds. They briefly considered the merit of intercutting old UNAC footage with whatever commentary he devised, and scrubbed that in favor of a nice, uncluttered series of grab shots of the sanatorium and any lab interiors they might be able to pick up. She expressed an interest in Domino's machine, which Michaelmas displayed to her as his privately designed comm unit, giving her the line of Proud Papa patter that had long ago somnolized all the newsmen he knew.

With all that out of the way, they still had a few sips of coffee left and a few bites of croissant to take, so they began to talk inconsequentially.

The skin on the backs of her hands was beginning to lose its youthful elasticity, so she did not do much gesturing, but she did have a habit of reaching up to pull down the dark glasses which were *de rigueur* in her mode. This usually happened at the end of a question such as: 'It is very agreeable here at this time of year, is it not?' and was accompanied by a glance of her medium green eyes before the glasses went back into place and hid them again. She sipped at her cup daintily, her pursed lips barely kissing the rim. She kept her legs bent sideward together, and her unfortunately large feet pulled inconspicuously against her chair.

All in all, Michaelmas was at first quite ready to classify her as being rather what you'd expect – a well-trained, competent individual in a high-paying profession which underwrote whatever little whims and personal indulgences she might have. This kind of woman was usually very good to work with, and he expected to be out of Switzerland before she had quite made up her mind whether she or the famous Laurent Michaelmas was going to do the seducing. And even if he were delayed past that point, a moment's frank discussion would solve that problem without offending her or making him look like an ass. At least this type of woman played it as a game, and took it as a matter of course that if there was to be no *corrida* in this town today, there was always an autobus leaving for the next ring within the half hour. As a matter of fact, she was the type of woman he most liked working with because it could all be made clearcut so easily, and then they could resume what they were being paid to do.

And in fact, Clementine Gervaise herself was so casual, despite the glances and the exposition from knees to ankles, that it seemed the whole business was only a pro forma gesture to days perhaps gone by for both of them. But just before he poured the last of the coffee from the chased silver pot into the translucent cup with its decoration of delicately painted violets, he found himself listening with more than casual attention to the intonations of her voice, and finding that his eyes rested on the highlights in her washed blond coiffure each time she turned her head.

For content, her conversation was still no more than politeness required, and his responses were the same. But there was a certain comfortable relaxation within him which he discovered only with a little spasm of alertness. For the past minute or two, his smile of response to her various gambits about European travel and climate had been warming. He had begun thinking how pleasant it all was, sitting here and looking out over the mountains, sipping coffee in this air; how very pleasant it was to be himself. And he found himself remembering out of the aspect of his mind that was like an antique desk, some of its drawers bolted, and all the others a little warped and stiff in their slides, so that they opened with difficulty:

You come upon me like the morning air
Rising in summer on the dayward hills.
And so unlock the crystal freshets waiting, still,
Since last they ran in joy among the grasses.

He looked down into his cup, smiled, and said: 'Dregs,' to cover the slight frown he might have shown.

'Oh, I'm so sorry,' she said as if she also worked in the Excelsior kitchen. It was this little domestic note that did it.

He continued to be charming, and in fact disarmingly attentive for the next few minutes until she left, saying: 'I shall be looking forward to seeing you later today.' And then when he had closed the door to the suite behind her, he walked back out onto the balcony and stood with his hands behind his back, his cheeks puffing in and out a little.

'What is it about her?' he said to Domino.

'There's a remarkable coincidence. She's very much as I'd expect your wife would have been by now.'

'Really? Is that it?'

'I would say so. I have.'

'Like Clementine Gervaise?' He turned back inside the parlor, his hands still clasped behind him. He placed his feet undecidedly. 'Well. What do you think this is?'

'On the data, it's a coincidence.'

Michaelmas cocked his head toward the machine. 'Are you beginning to learn to think beyond actuarials?' he said with pleasure.

'It may be a benefit of our continuing relationship, O Creator.'

'Long time coming,' Michaelmas said gruffly. He straightened and began to stride about the parlor. 'But what have we here? Has someone been applying a great deal of deductive thought to what profession a man in my role would choose in these times? My goodness, Dr Limberg, is all this part of a better mousetrap? Domino, it seems I might also have to watch behind me as I beat a path to his door.'

'You are not more than part of the whole world, Mighty Mouse,' Domino said.

'You know it,' Michaelmas answered, kicking off his shoes as he stepped into the bedroom. 'Well, I'm going to take an hour's nap.'

He slept restlessly for thirty-seven minutes. From time to time he rolled over, frowning.

FIVE

Domino woke him from a dream. 'Mr Michaelmas.' He opened his eyes immediately.

'What? Oh, I'm afraid to go home in the dark,' he said.

'Wake up, Mr Michaelmas. It's nine twenty-three, local.'

'What's the situation?' Michaelmas asked, sitting up.

'Multiple. A few moments ago, I completed my analysis of where the capsule crash site must be. I based my thinking on the requirements of the premise – a low trajectory to account for the capsule's escaping radar notice following the shuttle explosion; the need to have the crash occur within reasonable distance of Limberg's sanatorium, yet in a place where other people in the area would not be likely to notice or find it; and so forth. These conditions of course would fit either the truth or your hypothesis that Limberg is a resourceful liar.

'At any rate, I called the network, as you, and asked for a helicopter to investigate the site. I learned that they were already following Melvin Watson, who had recently taken off. Checking back on his activities, I find that just before catching the plane in New York last night he placed a call to a Swiss Army artillery major here. That officer is also on the mailing lists of a number of amateur rocket societies. On arrival here, Mr Watson called the Major again several times. Following the last call, which was rather lengthy, Mr Watson immediately boarded one of his client's helicopters and departed, leaving Campion to watch the sanatorium.'

'Ah,' Michaelmas chuckled. 'If Horse had only been modern enough to call the university center here and get his data from their computer. You would have been onto him in a flash.' Michaelmas patted the cold black top of the machine sitting on the nightstand. He knew exactly what had happened. Somewhere in the back of Watson's mind had been the name of an acquaintance of a friend of someone he'd worked with, the man to call if you were in Switzerland and had a ballistics problem. The name might have been there for years, beside the telephone number of the only place in Madrid that served a decent Chinese dinner, the memory of a girl who lived upstairs from a café in Luxembourg, a reliable place to get your shirts done in Ceuta, and the price of a second-class railway ticket from Ghent to Aix. 'You've been out-newsmanned, my friend. What do you want to bet Horse is headed straight as a die for the same place you've got marked with an X on your map?'

'Not a farthing. Precisely my point,' Domino said. 'There is more to the situation.'

'Go on.'

'Following an exchange of phone calls with the sanatorium, UNAC Star Control has authorized a press conference for Norwood at any time no later than one o'clock PM local. One of the men they sent in here last night was Getulio Frontiere.'

'Check.' Frontiere was a smooth, capable press secretary. The conference would go very cleanly and pretty much the way UNAC wanted it. 'No later than one o'clock. Then they want to say their say in time for the breakfast news on the east coast of the United States. Do you think they smell trouble with more heads like Gately?' He got to his feet and began to undress.

'I think it's possible. They're very quick to sense changes in the wind.'

'Yes. Horse said that last night. Very sensitive to the popular dynamic.' Stripped, Michaelmas picked up the machine, carried it into the bathroom, and set it down near the washbowl as he began to splash water, scrubbing his neck and ears.

'There's more,' Domino said. 'By happenstance, Tim Brodzik last week rescued the California governor's teenage daughter from drowning. He was invited to Sunday dinner at the governor's house, and extensively photographed with the grateful parents. He and the girl had their arms around each other.'

Michaelmas stopped with his straight razor poised beside one soap-filmed cheek. 'Who's that?'

'The beachboy Stever was involved with.'

'Oh.' He took a deep breath. Last year, he and Domino had invested much time in getting the governor elected. 'Well – you might as well see if you can intercept that note to Sam Lemoyne. It would only confuse things now.'

'Done. Finally, a registered air mail packet has cleared the New York General Post Office, routed through St Louis. Its final destination is Cape Girardeau, Missouri. It was mailed from Berne, clearing the airport post office here yesterday afternoon. I think it's going to US Always.'

'Yesterday afternoon? Damn,' said Michaelmas, feeling his jaw. His face had dried, and he had to wet it and soap it again. 'Who from?'

'Cikoumas et Cie. They are a local importer of dates, figs, and general sweetmeats. But there is more to them than that.'

'Figs,' Michaelmas said, passing his right forearm over his head and pulling his left cheek taut with his fingertips as he laid the razor against his skin. 'Sweetmeats.' He watched the action of the razor on his face. Shaving this way was one of those eccentric habits you pick up when away from sources of power and hot water.

He was remembering days when he had been a graduate engineering student helping out the family budget with an occasional filler for a newspaper science syndicate. His wife had worked as a temporary salesclerk during December and sent him a chrome-headed, white plastic lawnmower of a thing that would shave your face whether you plugged it into the wall or the cigarette lighter of your car, if you had a car. He remembered very clearly the way his wife had walked and talked, the schooled attentive mannerisms intelligently blended from their first disjointed beginnings at drama classes. She had always played older than her age. She was too tall and too gaunt for an ingenue, and had had trouble getting parts. She had not been grown inside yet, but she had been very fine and he had been waiting warmly for her maturity. By the time the Department of Speech would have graduated her from Northwestern, she would have been fully coordinated. But in 1968 she'd had her head broken in front of the Conrad Hilton, and then for a while she'd vegetated, and then after a while she'd died.

When he was even younger, and had to work on the East Coast because he wanted to take extension courses at MIT, he had called his wife often at Northwestern, in Evanston, Illinois. He would say: 'I can get a ride to Youngstown over Friday night with this fellow who lives there, and then if I can get a hitch up US 30, I could be in Chicago by Saturday late, or Sunday morning. I don't have any classes back here until Tuesday, and I can call in sick to work.' She would say: 'Oh, that sounds like a lot of trouble for just a few hours. And I think I have a singing job at a coffee house Monday anyhow.' He would say: 'But I don't mind,' and she would say: 'I don't want you to do it. It's more important for you to be where you are.' And he had said more, patiently, but so had she. That had been back when Domino had just been a device for making telephone calls. He had barely been a program at all. And now look at him.

He rinsed the glittering straight razor under the tap, and rinsed and dried his face. He dried the razor meticulously and put it back into its scarred Afghanistani leather-and-brass case. 'Figs,' he said. 'Figs and queened pawns, savants and astronauts, world enough, but how much time? Where does it go? What does it do?' He scrubbed his armpits with the washcloth. 'Boompa-boompa, boompa-boompa, boompa-boom pa-pa-pa-peen, herring boxes without topses ...'

'I don't like it. I don't like it,' he said to Domino as he put the fresh room-service carnation in his buttonhole. 'These people must mean something by this maneuver with the package. What's the idea? Or are you claiming Cikoumas is a coincidence?'

'No. There's a definite connection. They've even recently opened a branch in Cité d'Afrique. Of course, that would be a logical move for an importer, but still ...'

'Well, all right, then. But why do they mail the package via that route? Maybe they want something else.'

'I don't understand your implication. They simply don't want postal employees noting Limberg's return address on a package to US Always. Something like that would be worth a few dollars to a media tipster. The Cikoumas front is an easy way around that.'

'Ah, maybe. Maybe that's all. Maybe not.' Michaelmas began striding back and forth. 'We've spotted it. Maybe we're meant to spot it. Maybe they're laying a trail that only a singular kind of animal could follow. But must follow. Must follow, so can be detected, can be identified, phut, *splat*!' He punched his fist into his palm. 'What about that, eh? They want me because they've deduced I'm there to be found, and once they know me and have me, they have everything. How's that for a hypothesis?'

'Well, one can arrive at the scenario, obviously.'

'They must know! Look at the recent history of the world. Where's war, where's what was going to be an accruing class of commodities billionaires in a diminishing system, what's taking the pressure off the heel of poverty, what accounts for the emergence of a rational worldwide distribution of resources? What accounts for the steady exposure of conniving politicians, for increasingly rational social planning, and reasonably effective execution of the plans? I *must* exist!'

'It seems to me that you do,' Domino said agreeably.

Michaelmas blinked. 'Yes, you,' he said. 'They can't know about you. When they picture me, they probably see me in a tall silk hat running back and forth to some massive console. The opera phantom notion. However, it's always possible—'

'Excuse me, Mr Michaelmas, but UNAC and Dr Limberg have just announced a press conference at the sanatorium in half an hour. That'll be ten thirty. I've called Madame Gervaise to assemble your crew, and there's a car waiting.'

'All right.' Michaelmas slung the terminal over his shoulder. 'What if Cikoumas out in plain sight is intended to distract me from the character of the woman?'

'Oh?'

'Suppose they already know who I am. Then they must assume I've deduced everything. They must assume I'm fully prepared to act against them.' Michaelmas softly closed the white-and-gilt door of the suite and strolled easily down the corridor with its tastefully striped wallpaper, its flowering carpet, and its scent of lilac sachet. He was smiling in his usual likable manner. 'So they set her on me. What else would account for her?' They stopped at the elevator and Michaelmas worked the bellpush.

'Perhaps simply a desire to keep tab on a famous investigative reporter who might sniff out something wrong with their desired story. Perhaps nothing in particular. Perhaps she's just a country girl, after all. Why not?'

'Are you telling me my thesis won't hold water?'

'A bathtub will hold water. A canteen normally suffices.'

The elevator arrived. Michaelmas smiled warmly at the operator, took a stand in a corner, and brushed fussily at the lapels of his coat as the car dropped toward the lobby.

'What am I to do?' Michaelmas said in his throat. 'What is she?'

'I have a report from our helicopter,' Domino said abruptly. 'They are two kilometers behind Watson's craft. They are approaching the mountainside above Limberg's sanatorium. Watson's unit is losing altitude very quickly. They have an engine failure.'

'What kind of terrain is that?' Michaelmas said.

The elevator operator's head turned. *'Bitte sehr?'*

Michaelmas shook his head, blushing.

Domino said: 'Very rough, with considerable wind gusting. Watson is being blown toward the cliff face. His craft is sideslipping. It may clear. No, one of the vanes has made contact with a spur. The fuselage is swinging. The cabin has struck. The tail rotor has sheared. There's a heavy impact at the base of the cliff. There is an explosion.'

The elevator bounced delicately to a stop. The doors chucked open. 'The main lobby, *Herr Mikelmaas.*'

Michaelmas said: 'Dear God.' He stepped out into the lobby and looked around blankly.

SIX

Clementine Gervaise came up briskly. She had changed into a tweed suit and a thin soft blouse with a scarf at the throat. 'The crew is driving the equipment to the sanatorium already,' she said. 'Your hired car is waiting for us outside.' She cocked her head and looked closely at him. 'Laurent, is something amiss?'

He fussed with his carnation. 'No. We must hurry, Clementine.' Her eau de cologne reminded him how good it was to breathe of one familiar person when the streets were full of strangers. Her garments whispered as she strode across the lobby carpeting beside him. The majordomo held the door. The chauffeured Citroën was at the foot of the steps. They were in, the door was pressed shut, the car pulled away from the curb, and they were driving through the city toward the mountain highway. The soft cushions put them close to one another. He sat looking straight ahead, showing little.

'We have to beat the best in the world this morning,' he remarked. 'People like Annelise Volkert, Hampton de Courcy, Melvin Watson ...'

'She shows no special reaction,' Domino said in his skull. 'She's clean – on that count.'

He closed his eyes for a moment. Then in his throat he said, 'That doesn't prove much,' while she was saying:

'Yes, but I'm sure you will do it.' She put her arm through his. 'And I will make you see we are an excellent team.'

Domino told him: 'The Soviet cosmonaut command has just covertly shifted Captain Anatoli Rybakov from routine domestic programs to active standby status on the expeditionary project. He is to immediately begin accelerated training in the simulator at Tyura Tam. That is a Top Urgent instruction on highest secret priority landline from Moscow to the cosmodrome.'

Rybakov. He was getting a little long in the tooth – especially for a captain – and he had never been a prime commander. He was only a third or fourth crew alternate on the UNAC lists and wasn't even in the Star Control flight cadre. But he was nevertheless the only human being to have crewed both to the Moon and aboard the Kosmogorod orbital station.

'What do you suppose that means?' Michaelmas asked, rubbing his face.

'I haven't the foggiest, yet.'

'Have you notified UNAC?'

'No. By the way, Papashvilly went out to the Afrique airfield but then back again a few minutes ago. Sakal phoned Star Control with a recall order.'

'Forgive me, Clementine,' Michaelmas said. 'I must arrange my thoughts.'

'Of course.' She sat back, well-mannered, chic, attentive. Her arm departed from his with a little petting motion of her hand.

'Stand by for public,' Domino said. He chimed aloud. 'Bulletin. UPI Berne September 29. A helicopter crash near this city has claimed the life of famed newsman Melvin Watson. Dead with the internationally respected journalist is the pilot …' His speaker continued to relay the wire service story. In Michaelmas's ear, he said: 'She's reacting.'

Michaelmas turned his head stiffly toward her. Clementine's mouth was pursed in dismay. Her eyes developed a sheen of grief. *'Oh, quel dommage!* Laurent, you must have known him, not so?'

His throat working convulsively, Michaelmas asked Domino for data on her.

'What you'd expect.' The answer was a little slow. 'Pulse up, respiration up. It's a little difficult to be precise. You're rather isolated up there right now and I'm having to do a lot of switching to follow your terminal. I'm also getting some echo from all the rock around you; it's metallic.'

Michaelmas glanced out the window. They were on the highway, skimming closely by a drill-marked and blasted mountain shoulder on one side and an increasingly disquieting drop-off on the other. Veils of snow powder, whisked from the roadside, bannered behind them in the wind of their passage. The city lay below, popping in and out of view as the car followed the serpentine road. Somewhere down there was the better part of Domino's actual present location, generally except for whatever might be fitting overhead in some chance satellite.

The spoken bulletin came to an end. It had not been very long. Clementine sat forward, her expression anxious. 'Laurent?'

'I knew him,' Michaelmas said gently. 'I regret you never met him. I have lost a friend.' And I am alone now, among the Campions. 'I have lost a friend,' he said again, to apologize to Horse for having patronized him.

She touched his knee. 'I am sorry you are so hurt.'

He found himself unable to resist putting his hand over hers for a moment. It was a gesture unused for many years between them, he began to think, and then caught himself. 'Thank you, Madame Gervaise,' he said, and each of them withdrew a little, sitting silently in the back of the car.

As they approached the sanatorium gate, they drove past many cars parked beside the highway, tight against the rock. There were people with news equipment walking in the road, and the car had to pull around them. Some

shouted; others ignored them. At the gate, there was the usual knot of ges-
ticulants who had failed to produce convincing press credentials.

There was a coterie of warders – a gloved private gatekeeper in a blue
uniform with the sanatorium crest, plus a sturdy middle-aged plainclothes-
man in a sensible vested suit and a greatcoat and a velour hat, and a bright
young fellow in a sportcoat and topper whom Michaelmas recognized as a
minor UNAC press staff man. The UNAC man looked inside the car,
recognized Michaelmas, and flashed an okay sign with his thumb and forefinger. The Swiss policeman nodded to the gatekeeper, who pushed the
electric button which made the wrought iron gates fold back briefly behind
their brick posts. Leaving outcries behind, the Citroën jumped forward and
drove through.

Michaelmas, said to Domino: 'I wonder if time-traveling cultures are playing with us. I wonder if they process our history for entertainment values. It
wouldn't take much: an assassination in place of exile, revolution instead of
election – that sort of augmentation would yield packageable drama. Chances
are, it wouldn't crucially alter the timeline. Or perhaps it might, a little. One
might awaken beside a lean young stud instead of the pudgy father of one's
whining child. There'd be a huge titillated audience. And the sets and actors
are free. A producer's dream. No union contracts.'

'Michaelmas, someone in your position oughtn't divert himself with
paranoias.'

'But oughtn't a fish study water?'

A little way up, there was a jammed asphalt parking lot beside a gently
sloping windblown meadow in which helicopters were standing and in
which excess vehicles had broken the cold grass in the sod. The Citroën
found a place among the other cars and the broadcast trucks. Up the slope
was the sanatorium, very much constructed of bright metal and of polariza-
ble windows, the whole of the design taking a sharply pitched snow-shedding
silhouette. Sunlight stormed back from its glitter as if it were a wedge pried
into Heaven.

They got out and Clementine Gervaise looked around. 'It can be very
peaceful here,' she remarked before waving toward their crew truck. People
in white coveralls and smocks with her organization's pocket patch came
hurrying. She merged with them, pointing, gesturing, tilting her head to listen, shaking her head, nodding, tapping her forefinger on a proffered
clipboard sheet. In another moment, some of them were eddying back
toward the equipment freighter and others were trotting up the sanatorium
steps, passing and encountering other crews in similar but different jump-
suits. From somewhere up there, a cry of rage and deprivation was followed
by a fifty-five-millimeter lens bouncing slowly down the steps.

'Ten-twenty local,' Domino said.

'Thank you,' Michaelmas replied, watching Clementine. 'How are your links now?'

'Excellent. What would you expect, with all this gear up here and with elevated horizon-lines?'

'Yes, of course,' Michaelmas said absently. 'Have you checked the maintenance records on Horse's machine?'

'Yes.'

'Have you compared them to all maintenance records on all other machines of the same model?'

'Yes.'

'Have you cross-referenced all critical malfunction data for the type?'

'Teach your grandmother to suck eggs. If you're asking was it an accident, my answer is it shouldn't have happened. But that doesn't exclude freak possibilities such as one-of-a-kind failure in a pump diaphragm, or even some kind of anomalous resistance across a circuit. I'm currently running back through all parts suppliers and subassembly manufacturers, looking for things like unannounced redesigns, high reject rates at final inspection stages, and so forth. It'll be a while. And other stones are waiting to be turned.'

Clementine Gervaise had entered the awareness of the comm terminal's sensors. 'Here comes one.'

'Let's concentrate on this Norwood thing for now,' Michaelmas said.

'Of course, Laurent,' Clementine said softly. 'The crew is briefed and the equipment is manned.'

Michaelmas's mouth twitched. 'Yes ... yes, of course they are. I was watching you.'

'You like my style? Come – let us go in.' She put her arm through his and they went up the steps.

There was another credential verification just beyond the smoked-glass front doors. Another junior UNAC aide was checking names against a list. It was a scene of polite crowding as bodies filed in behind Michaelmas and Clementine.

Douglas Campion was just ahead of them, talking to the aide. Michaelmas prepared to speak to him, but Campion was preoccupied. Michaelmas studied him raptly. The press aide was saying:

'Mr Campion, your crew is in place on the photo balcony. We have you listed for a backup seat toward the rear of the main auditorium. Now, in view of the unfortunate—'

'Right,' Campion said. 'You going to give me Watson's seat and microphone time?'

'Yes, sir. And please let me express—'

'Thanks. What's the seat location?'

There was nothing actually nasty about him, Michaelmas decided sadly. One could assume there was regret, grief, or almost anything else you cared to attribute to him, kept somewhere within him under the heat shield.

He watched Campion move away across the foyer toward the auditorium's rear doors, and then he and Clementine were stepping forward.

The aide smiled as if he'd been born ten seconds ago. 'Nice to see you, Mr Michaelmas, Miz Gervaise,' he said. The fading wetness of anger in his eyes gave them a winning sparkle. He checked off the names on his list, got a photo-copied floor-diagram from his table, and made a mark on it for Clementine. 'We've given your crew a spot right here in the first row of the balcony,' he said. 'You just go up those stairs over there at the back of the foyer and you'll find them. And Mr Michaelmas, we've put you front row center in the main auditorium.' He grinned. 'There won't be any microphone passing. Limberg's got quite a place here – remote PA mikes and everything. When you're rec-ognized for a question, just go ahead and speak. Your crew sound system will be patched in automatically.'

'Thank you.' Michaelmas changed the shape of his lips. He did not appear to alter the tone or level of his voice, but no one standing behind him could hear him. 'Is Mr Frontiere here?'

The aide raised his eyebrow. 'Yes, sir. He'll be up on the podium for the Q and A.'

'I wonder if I could see him for just a moment now.'

The aide grimaced and glanced at his wristwatch. Michaelmas's smile was one of complete sympathy. 'Sorry to have to ask,' he said.

The aide smiled back helplessly. 'Well,' he said while Michaelmas's head cocked insouciantly to block anyone's view of the young man's lips. 'I guess we do owe you a couple, don't we? Sharp left down that side hall. The next to the last door leads into the auditorium near your seat. The last door goes backstage. He's there.'

'Thank you.' There was pressure at Michaelmas's back. He knew without looking that a score of people were filling the space back to the doors, and others were beginning to elbow each other subconsciously at the head of the outside steps. They were all craning forward to see what the hangup might be, and getting ready to avenge discourtesy or to make dignified outcry at the first sign of favoritism.

'I will manage it for you, Laurent,' Clementine said quietly.

'Ah? *Merci. À bientôt*,' Michaelmas said. He stepped around the reception table and wondered what the hell.

Clementine moved with him, and then a little farther forward, her stride suddenly became long and masculine. She pivoted toward the balcony stairs and the heel snapped cleanly off one shoe. She lurched, caught her balance by slapping one hand flat against the wall, and cried out *'merde!'* hoarsely. She plucked off the shoe, threw it clattering far down the long foyer, and kicked its mate off after it. She padded briskly up the stairs in her stockinged feet, still followed by every eye.

Michaelmas, grinning crookedly, moved down the side hall, his progress swift, his manner jaunty, his footsteps soundless. He pushed quickly through the door at the end.

Heads turned sharply – Limberg, Norwood, a handful of UNAC administrative brass, Frontiere, their torsos supported by stiff arms as they huddled over a table spread with papers and glossy photographic enlargements. Limberg's lump-knuckled white forefinger tapped at one of the glossies.

Michaelmas waved agreeably as they regarded him with dismay. Frontiere hurried over.

'Laurent—'

'Giorno, Tulio. Quickly – before I go in – is UNAC going to reshuffle the flight crew?'

Frontiere's angular, patrician face suddenly declared it would say nothing. The very dark eyes in their deep sockets locked on Michaelmas's, and Frontiere crossed his slim hands with their polished nails over the lean biceps in his alpaca sleeves. 'Why do you ask this, Laurent?'

How many times, thought Michaelmas, have I helped UNAC over rough spots that even they know of? And I'm ready to do it again, God knows. And here Frontiere was counting up every one of them. Who would have thought a man would have so much credit deducted for such a simple answer? Merely an answer that would let the world's most prominent newsman frame his press conference comments more securely. 'Norwood was in command, Papashvilly was put in command, Papashvilly is a major. Answer my question and you tell me much. I think it a natural query ... *vecchio amico.'*

Frontiere grimaced uncomfortably. 'Perhaps it is. We are all very much into our emotions this morning, you understand? I was not giving you sufficient credit for sapience, I believe.'

Michaelmas grinned. 'Then answer the God-damned question.'

Frontiere moved his eyes as if wishing to see the people behind him. 'If necessary, an announcement will be made that it is not planned to change the flight crew.'

Michaelmas cocked his head. 'In other words, this is an excellent fish dinner especially if someone complains of stomach. Is that the line you propose to defend?'

Frontiere's sour grin betrayed one of his famous dimples. 'I am not doing well with you this morning ... old friend,' he said softly. 'Perhaps you would like to speak quietly with me alone after the conference.'

'Between friends?'

'Entirely between friends.'

'*Bene*.'

'Thank you very much,' Frontiere smiled slightly. 'Now I must get back to my charges. Take your place in the auditorium, Laurent; the dogs and ponies are all cued. Despite one or two small matters, we shall begin shortly.' Frontiere turned and walked back toward the others, spreading his arms, palms up, in a very Latin gesture. They resumed their intent whispering. Limberg shook his hand repeatedly over the one particular photograph. The side of his fingertip knock knock knocked on the tabletop.

Michaelmas stepped out and softly closed the door. 'We must be certain we're doing everything we can to protect Papashvilly,' he said in the empty hall.

'Against what, exactly?' Domino said. 'We're already doing all we can in general. If he's taken off the mission, despite all that bumph, he needs no more. If he's still in, what am I supposed to suggest? UNAC is apparently concerned for him. Remember they almost put him on a plane for here, then Sakal ordered him back from the Cité d'Afrique airport. What do you make of that?'

'There are times when I would simply like to rely on your genius.'

'And there are times when I wish your intuitions were more specific.'

Michaelmas rubbed the back of his neck. 'I would very much like some peace and quiet.'

'Then I have disturbing news. I've just figured out what Rybakov is for.'

'Oh?'

'The Russians can also think ahead. If UNAC attempts to reinstate Norwood, they won't just threaten to pull Papashvilly. They'll threaten to pull Papashvilly and they'll threaten to insist on honest workman Rybakov being second-in-command.'

Michaelmas's tongue clicked out from the space between his upper lip and his front teeth. 'There would be a fantastic scandal.'

'More than that.'

'Yes.' If UNAC then refused to accept that proposition, the next move saw the USSR also withdrawing Rybakov. That would leave the so-called Mankind in Space program with only an East German lieutenant to represent half the Caucasian world's politics. 'We'd be right back into the 1960s. UNAC can't possibly go for that, or what's UNAC for? So as soon as they see the Russians moving Rybakov up out of the pawn row, they'll drop the whole scheme. They may be rocking back a little now, but one glimpse of that sequence and they'll stonewall for Papashvilly no matter what.'

' "What" may be Viola Hanrassy and everything she can throw.'

'Exactly. I wonder what would explode.' Michaelmas rubbed the back of his neck again. 'I would *very* much like some peace and quiet,' he said in the same voice he had used to speak of darkness.

Three more steps and he was in at the side of the auditorium. It was a medical lecture hall during the normal day, and a place where the patients could come to watch entertainment in the evening. Nevertheless, it made a very nice two-hundred-seat facility for a press conference, and the steep balcony was ideal for cameras, with the necessary power outlets and sound system outputs placed appropriately. To either side of the moderately thrust stage, lenticular reflectors were set at a variety of angles, so that an over-the-shoulder shot could be shifted into a tele closeup of anyone in the main floor audience.

The brown plush seats were filling quickly. There was the usual assortment of skin colors, sexes, and modes of dress. They were much more reserved now, these permitted few, than the hustling mob at the airport.

Michaelmas stopped at Douglas Campion. He held out his hand. 'I'd like to express my sympathies. And wish you good luck at this opportunity.' It seemed a sentiment the man would respond to.

The eyes moved. 'Yeah. Thanks.'

'Are you planning an obituary feature?'

'Can't now.' They were looking over his shoulder at the curtain. 'Got to stay with the main story. That's what he'd want.'

'Of course.' He moved on. The pale tan fabric panels of the acoustic draperies made an attractive wall decor. They gave back almost none of the sound of feet shuffling, seats tilting, and cleared throats.

And out there in Tokyo and Sidney they were putting down their preprandial Suntory, switching off the cassettes, punching up the channels. In Peking they were standing in the big square and watching the huge projection from the government building; in Moscow they were jammed up against the sets in the little apartments; in Los Angeles they were elbowing each other for a better line of sight in the saloons – here and there they were shouting at each other and striking out passionately. In Chicago and New York, presumably they slept; in Washington, presumably they could not.

Michaelmas slipped toward his seat, nodding and waving to acquaintances. He found his name badge pinned to the fabric, looked at it, and put it in his pocket. He glanced up at the balcony; Clementine put her finger to her ear, cocked her thumb, and dropped it. He pulled the earplug out of its recess in Domino's terminal and inserted it. A staff announcer on Clementine's network was doing a lead-in built on the man-in-the-street clips Domino had edited for them in Michaelmas's name, splicing in reaction shots of Michaelmas's face from stock. Then he apparently went to a voice-over of the whole-shot of the auditorium from a pool camera; he did a meticulous job of garnishing what the world was seeing as a room full of people staring at a closed curtain.

There was a faint pop and Clementine's voice on the crew channel replaced the network feed. 'We're going to a tight three-quarter right of your head, Laurent,' she said. 'I like the light best that way, with a little tilt-up, please, of the chin. Coming up on mark.'

He raised a hand to acknowledge and adopted an expression learned from observing youthful statesmen.

'Mark.'

'Must cut,' Domino's voice said suddenly. 'Meet you Berne.'

Michaelmas involuntarily stared down at the comm unit, then remembered where he was and restored his expression.

'—ere we go!' Clementine's voice was back in.

The curtains were opening. Getulio Frontiere was standing there at a lighted podium. A table with three empty forward-facing chairs was sited behind him, under the proscenium arch.

Frontiere introduced himself and said:

'Ladies and Gentlemen, on behalf of the Astronautics Commission of the United Nations of the World, and as guests with you here of Dr Nils Hannes Limberg, we bid you welcome.' As always, the smile dawning on the Borgia face might have convinced anyone that everything was easily explained and had always been under control.

'I would now like to present to you Mr Ossip Sakal, Eastern Administrative Director for the UNAC. He will make a brief opening statement and will be followed to the podium by Dr Limberg. Dr Limberg will speak, again briefly, and then he will present to you Colonel Norwood. A question-and-answer period—'

A rising volume of wordless pandemonium took the play away from him, compounded of indrawn breaths, hands slapping down on chair arms, bodies shifting forward, shoes scraping,

Michaelmas's neighbor – a nattily dressed Oriental from New China Service – said: 'That's it, then. UNAC has officially granted that it's all as announced.'

Michaelmas nodded absently. He found himself with nothing more in his hands than a limited comm unit on automatic, most of its bulk taken up by nearly infinite layers of meticulously microcrafted dead circuitry, and by odd little Rube Goldberg things that flickered lights and made noises to impress the impressionable.

Frontiere had waited out the commotion, leaning easily against the podium. Now he resumed: '—a question-and-answer period will follow Colonel Norwood's statement. I will moderate. And now, Mr Sakal.'

There was something about the way Sakal stepped forward. Michaelmas stayed still in his seat. Oz the Bird, as press parties and rosy-fingered poker games had revealed him over the years, would show his hole card anytime after you'd overpaid for it. But there was a relaxed Oz Sakal and there was a murderously angry Oz Sakal who looked and acted almost precisely like the former. This was the latter.

Michaelmas took a look around. The remainder of the press corps was simply sitting there waiting for the customary sort of opening remark to be poured over the world's head. But then perhaps they had never seen the Bird with a successfully drawn straight losing to a flush.

Michaelmas keyed the Transmit button of his comm unit once, to let Clementine know he was about to feed. Then he locked it down, faced into the nearest reflector, and smiled. 'Ladies and gentlemen, good day,' he said warmly. 'Laurent Michaelmas here. The man who is about to speak' – this lily I am about to paint – 'has a well-established reputation for quickness of mind, responsible decisions, and an unfailing devotion to UNAC's best interests.' As well as a tendency to snap drink stirrers whenever he feels himself losing control of the betting.

With his peripheral vision, Michaelmas had been watching Sakal stand mute while most of the people in the room did essentially what Michaelmas was doing. When Sakal put his hands on the podium, Michaelmas said: 'Here is Mr Sakal.' He unlocked.

'How do you do.' Sakal looked straight out into the pool camera. He was a wiry man with huge cheekbones and thick black hair combed straight back from the peak of his scalp. There was skillfully applied matte makeup on his forehead. 'On behalf of the Astronautics Commission of the United Nations of the World, I am here to express our admiration and delight.' Michaelmas found it noteworthy that Sakal continued to address himself only to the world beyond the blandest camera.

'The miracle of Colonel Norwood's return is one for which we had very much given up hope. To have him with us again is also a personal joy to those of us who have long esteemed his friendship. Walter Norwood, as one might expect of any spacefaring individual, is a remarkable person. We who are privileged to work for peaceful expansion of mankind in space are also privileged by many friendships with such individuals from many nations. To have one of them return whom we had thought lost is to find our hearts swelling with great emotion.'

He was off and winging now. Whatever Frontiere had written and drilled into him was now nothing more than an outline for spontaneous creative rhetoric. That was all right, too, so far, because Frontiere in turn had based the words on guidelines first articulated to him by Sakal. But so much for the skills of prose communication.

Sakal was looking earnestly into the camera, his hands gripping the sides of the podium. 'The number of Man's space pioneers has not today been made one more. We have *all* been made greater – you and I as well as those whose training and experience are directed at actually piloting our craft in their journeys upon this mighty frontier.'

Michaelmas kept still. It wasn't easy. For a moment, it had seemed that Sakal's private fondness for John F. Kennedy would lead him into speaking of 'this new ocean.' His natural caution had diverted him away from that, but only into a near stumble over 'New Frontier,' an even more widely known Kennedyism. Sakal wasn't merely enraged; he was rattled, and that was something Michaelmas had never seen before.

'We look forward to working with Colonel Norwood again,' Sakal said. 'There are many projects on the schedule of the UNAC which require the rare qualities of someone like himself. Whatever his assignment, Colonel Norwood will perform faithfully in the best traditions of the UNAC and for the good of all mankind.'

Well, he had gone by way of Robin Hood's barn, but he had finally gotten there. Now to point it out. Michaelmas keyed Transmit and locked.

'Ladies and gentlemen,' he said, 'we have just heard the news that Colonel Norwood will indeed be returning to operational status with UNAC. His new duties cannot be made definite at this time, but Mr Sakal is obviously anxious to underscore that it will be an assignment of considerable import- ance.' As well as to let us all know that he is as concerned for his good buddy's well-being as anyone could be, and as well as to betray that UNAC is sud- denly looking back a generation. Damn. Organizations nurtured specialists like Frontiere to dress policy in jackets of bulletproof phrasing, and then the policymakers succumbed to improvisation on camera because it made them feel more convincing to use their own words.

Speaking of words …

'A position of high responsibility is certainly in order for the colonel if he is fully recovered,' Michaelmas was saying. It was gratifying how automat- ically the mind and the tongue worked together, first one leading and then the other, the one never more than a millimicrosecond behind the other, whichever was appropriate to the situation. The face, too: the wise older friend, the worldly counselor. The situation is always important, but neither inexplicable nor cause for gloom. 'The vast amount of physical catching-up to do – the months of training and rehearsal that have passed in Colonel Norwood's absence from UNAC's programs – would make it extremely dif- ficult to rejoin any ongoing project.' Smooth. As the sentence had flowed forward, he had considered and rejected saying 'impossible.' In fact it prob- ably was barely possible; with a large crew, redundant functions, and modern guidance systems, spaceflight was far from the trapeze act it had been in Will Gately's day. And if I am going to make UNAC work, if I am going to make work all the things of which UNAC is only the currently prominent part, then the last thing I can do is be seen trying to make it work. So I can't really be any more direct than Sakal was being, can I? Smile inside, wise older friend. They call it irony. It is in fact the way of the world. 'It's possible Mr Sakal is hinting at the directorship of the Outer Planet Applications program, which will convert into industrial processes the results of the engineering experiments to be brought back by the Outer Planets expedition.' It's also possible Laurent Michaelmas is throwing UNAC a broad hint on how to kick Norwood upstairs. Perhaps in the hope that while they kick him, his arse will open to disclose gear trains. What then, Dr Limberg? What now, Laurent Michaelmas? All he had beside him was a magic box full of nothing – a still, clever thing that did not even understand it was a tool, nor could appreciate how skillfully it was employed. 'And now, back to Mr Sakal.'

All Sakal was doing was introducing Limberg, and waiting until the old man was well advanced from the wings before circling around the table and taking one of the three chairs. Everyone was so knowledgeable on playing for the media these days. They kept it short, they broke it to allow time for comment, they didn't upstage each other. Even when they were in a snit, they built these things like actors re-creating psychodramas from a transcript. It was not *they* who had pushed the switch, nodded the head, closed the door, written the voucher. Someone else – someone wild, someone devious, someone unpredictable – had done that. No such persons would be thrust upon the audience today. Or ever. Such persons and their deeds were *represented* here today. And each day. There *is* a reality. We will tell you about it.

Of course, these people here on Limberg's stage were the survivors of the selection process. The ones who didn't begin learning it early were the ones you never heard of.

'Dr Limberg naturally needs no introduction,' Michaelmas said to a great many millions of people – few of them, it seemed, buried deep in the evening hours. Prime Time was advancing slothfully out in the Pacific wasteland. Why was that? 'What he appears to deserve is the world's gratitude.'

Unlock. The great man stands there like a graven saint. The kind, knowing eyes sweep both the live and the electronic audience. The podium light, which had cast the juts and hollows of Sakal's face into harsh no-nonsense relief, seemed now to be more diffuse, and perhaps a more flattering shade. Michaelmas sighed. Well, we all do it one way or another.

'Welcome to my house,' Limberg said in German. Michaelmas thought about it for a moment, then put a translator output in his ear. He could speak and understand it, especially the western dialects, but there might be some nuance, either direct from Limberg or unconsciously created by the translator. In that latter case, what the translator made of Limberg would be more official among whatever ethnic group heard it that way. Eventually the Michaelmases and Horse Watsons of the world would have to track down the distortion if they could or if they cared, and set it right in one corner without disturbing another. Not for the first time, Michaelmas wished Esperanto had taken hold. But recalling the nightmare of America's attempt to force metrication on itself, he did not wish it quite enough.

Limberg was smiling and twinkling, his hands out, the genial host. 'My associates and I are deeply honored. I can report to you that we did not fail our responsibilities toward the miracle that conveyed Colonel Norwood in such distress to us.' Now the visage was solemn, but the stance of his shoulders and slightly bowed head indicated quiet pride.

Overweening, Michaelmas thought. The man radiates goodness and wisdom like a rich uncle in a nephew's eyes. And so it is with the world; those who claim mankind knows nothing of justice, restraint, modesty, or altruism are all wrong. In every generation, we have several individuals singled out to represent them to us.

Disquieting. To sit here suddenly suspecting the old man's pedigree. What to think of the witnesses to his parents' marriage? *Is* there sanctity in the baptismal register? If Uncle's birth certificate is an enigma, what does that do to Nephew's claim of kinship when probate time comes round?

Better not whisper such suppositions in the world's lent ear just yet. But how, then, for the straight, inquiring professional newsman to look at him just now?

No man can be a hero to his media? The old man's ego and his gesturings were common stock in after-hours conversation. But they all played along, seeing it harmless when compared to his majesty of mind – assuming he had some. They let him be the man in the white coat, and he gave them stitches of newsworthy words to suture up fistulas of dead air, the recipient not only of two Nobel awards but of two crashes ...

If Domino were here, Michaelmas thought, oppressed, he would have pulled me up for persiflage long before now.

What *is* it? he thought. What in the world are they doing to me and mine? Who are they?

Limberg, meanwhile, was spieling out all the improbables of Norwood's crash so near the sanatorium, so far from the world's attention. If it weren't Limberg, and if they weren't all so certain Norwood was waiting alive and seamless in the wings, how many of them here in this room would have been willing to swallow it? But when he looked around him now, Michaelmas could see it going down whole, glutinously.

And maybe it's really that way? he thought, finally.

Ah, no, no, they are using the nails to defraud somehow. And most important I think they have killed Horse Watson, probably because he frightened them with how swiftly he could move.

When he thought of that, he felt more confident. If they were really monolithically masterly, they'd have had the wreckage all dressed and propped as required. More, they would have been icy sure of it, come Nineveh, come Iron Darius and all his chariots against them. But they hadn't liked Watson's directness. They'd panicked a little. Someone on the crew had said, 'Wait – no, let's take one more look at it before we put it on exhibit.' And so they had knocked Watson down not only to forestall him but to distract the crowd while they sidled out and made assurance doubly sure.

It was good to think they could be nervous.

It was bad to think nevertheless how capable they were.

Now Limberg was into orthopedics, immunology, tissue cloning; it was all believable. It was years since they'd announced being able to grow a new heart from a snippet of a bad one; what was apparently new was being able to grow it in time to do the patient any good.

Keying in, Michaelmas said a few words about that to his audience, just as if he believed it. Meanwhile, he admired the way Limberg was teasing the time away, letting the press corps wind up tighter and tighter just as if they were ordinary rubes awaiting the star turn at the snake oil show, instead of the dukes and duchesses of world opinion.

'—but the details of these things,' Limberg was finally concluding, 'are of course best left for later consideration. I am privileged now to reintroduce to you the United States of North America astronaut Colonel Doctor of Engineering Walter Norwood.'

And there he was, striding out of the wings, suddenly washed in light, grinning and raising one hand boyishly in a wave of greeting. Every lens in the room sucked him in, every heart beat louder in that mesmerized crowd, and the media punched him direct into the world's gut. But not on prime time. Of all the scheduling they could have set up, this was just about the worst. Not that there was any way to take much of the edge off this one. Nevertheless, when this news arrived at Mr and Mrs America's breakfast table, it would be hours cold – warmed over, blurred by subsequent events of whatever kind. A bathing beauty might give birth and name a dolphin as the father. Professional terrorists, hired by Corsican investors in the Carlsbad radium spa, might bomb President Fefre's palace. General Motors might announce there would be no new models for the year 2001, since the world was coming to an end.

It suddenly occurred to Michaelmas that if he were UNAC, he'd have had Papashvilly here to shake Norwood's hand at this moment and throw a comradely arm around his shoulders, and thus emphasize just who it was that was being welcomed home and who it was that had drawn the water and hewn the wood meanwhile.

But they had retreated from that opportunity. Why? No time to wonder. Norwood was standing alone at the podium. Limberg had drifted back to join Sakal at the table, Frontiere was blended into the walls somewhere until Q and A time, and the American colonel had the attention. He had it pretty well, too. Limberg's lighting electricians were doing a masterful job on him.

'I'm very glad to see you all,' Norwood said softly into the cameras, his hair an aureole of backlighting. He raised his chin a little, and his facial lines were bathed out by a spot mounted out of sight somewhere in the podium box itself. 'I want to thank Dr Limberg and his staff.' He was like an angel. Michaelmas's hackles were rising. 'And now I'm ready to sit down and take questions.' He smiled, waved his hand again, and stepped back.

The lighting changed; now the podium was played down, and the table was illuminated. Sakal and Limberg were standing. Frontiere was coming out of the wings. Norwood reached his chair. The press corps leaned forward, some with hands rising and mouths opening to call attention to their questions, and as they leaned some lackey somewhere began to applaud. Caught on the lean, it was easy to stand. Standing, it was easy to applaud. Scores of palms resounded, and the walls quivered. Limberg as well as Norwood smiled and nodded modestly.

Michaelmas fidgeted. He closed his fists. Where was the statement explaining exactly what had happened? Where was the UNAC physicist with his charts and pointer, his vocabulary full of coriolis effect and telemetry nulls, his animation holograms of how a radar horizon swallows a man-carrying capsule? If no one else was going to do it, Norwood should have.

It wasn't going to happen. In another moment, a hundred and a half people, each with an individual idea of what needed asking, were going to begin competing for short answers to breathless questions. The man whose media radiated its signal from an overhead satellite to a clientele of bangled cattlemen in wattle huts had concerns not shared by the correspondent for Dow Jones. The people from Science News Service hardly listened to whatever response was drawn by the representative of *Elle*. And there was only a circumscribed area of time to work in. The bathing beauty was out there somewhere, jostling Fefre and chiliasm for space on the channels, jockeying her anomalously presented hips.

It was all over. They were not to obtain information after all. They were here to sanctify the occasion, and when they were done the world would think it knew the truth and was free.

Frontiere was at the podium. This sort of thing was his handiwork. He moved effortlessly, a man who had danced this sort of minuet once or twice before. UNAC's man, but doing the job Limberg wanted done.

And thus Sakal's impotent rage. Somehow the Bird was over the grand old man's barrel.

'The questions?' Frontiere was saying to the press corps.

My hat is off to you, you son of a bitch, Michaelmas was saying, and yes, indeed, we will talk afterward, friend to friend. I am senior in prestige here; it is incumbent on me to frame the first question. To set the tone, so to speak. I raise my hand. Getulio smiles toward me. 'Yes, Mr Michaelmas?'

'Colonel Norwood's presence here delights us all,' I say. There are amenities that must of course be followed. I make the obligatory remark on behalf of the media. But I am the first voice from the floor. The world hears me. I have spoken. It's all true. He is risen. The people of the world rejoice.

But they are *my* people! God damn it, *my* people!

'My question is for Mr Sakal. I'd like him to explain how Colonel Norwood's presence here jibes with UNAC's prior explanations of his death.' I stand with a faint little twinkle visible in my eye. I am gently needling the bureaucrats. I am in fact doing no such thing. If Frontiere and Sakal have not already rehearsed this question a thousand times, then they are *all* imposters. I am a clown. I toss the ball so they may catch it gracefully.

Sakal leans forward in his chair, his hands cupped on the table. 'Well, obviously,' he delivers, 'there was some sort of failure in our tracking and monitoring systems.' He causes himself to appear rueful. 'Some embarrassing failure.'

We all chuckle.

'I assume it's being gone into.'

'Oh, yes.' Something in the set of Sakal's jaw informs the audience that somewhere out there blades are thudding and heads are rolling.

I have asked my questions. I have set the tone. I have salvaged what I can from this wreck. My audience thinks I was not afraid to ask a delicate question, and delicate enough not to couch it in a disquieting manner.

I sit down. The next questioner is recognized. Frontiere is a genius at seeming to select on some rational basis of priority. In due time, he gets to Douglas Campion. See Campion stand. 'Colonel Norwood, what's your next destination? Will you be coming to the USA in the near future?'

'Well, that depends on my duty assignment.'

'Would you accept a Presidential invitation?' He slips it in quickly. Sakal regards him quietly.

'If we had such an invitation,' Sakal answers for Norwood. 'We would of course arrange duty time off for Colonel Norwood in order that he might visit with the chief executive of his native land, yes.'

Ah, news. And the hero could then doubtless be diverted for a few ticker-tape parades, etc. Campion has shrewdly uncovered the obvious inevitable. But it was a good question to have been seen asking.

Ah, you bastards, bastards, bastards. I sit in my place. In a decent while, I will ask another question of some kind. But if I were the man you think me, the questions I'd ask would have you in pieces. Phut, splat! Live in glorious hexacolor, direct from Switzerland, ladies and gentlemen, if I were not also only a clever simulacrum of what I ought to be.

SEVEN

The sorry business wound itself down toward eleven-thirty. For his audience, Michaelmas ran off a few closing comments in dignity. After everything was off the air, Frontiere announced a small press reception in the dining hall, 'for those who could stay.' It was understood on occasions of this sort that crew technicians are too busy to stay, since it had long ago been discovered that even one cameraman at a buffet was worth a horde of locusts, and tended to make awkward small talk.

The dining hall featured a glass overlook of the depths below and the heights above; even through the metallized panes, the sun would have driven in fiercely if a drape, gauzy as a scrim, had not been hung upon it. Air-warming ducts along the wall set it to rippling. The world beyond the dining hall was beautiful and rhythmic. The press strolled from bunch to bunch of themselves and various UNAC functionaries, sanatorium staff, and of course Norwood. There was a bar at each end of the large room, and the carpet underfoot was conducive to a silent, gliding step that was both restful and ennobling. For some, stepping back and forth from one end of the room to the other was particularly exhilarating.

Michaelmas wore his smile. He took a Kir and nibbled tender spiced rare lamb slivers on a coaster of trimmed pumpernickel. He found Norwood, Limberg and Frontiere all together, standing against a tapestry depicting medieval physicians in consultation at the bedside of a dying monarch. Up close, Norwood looked much more like he ought – fineline wrinkles in the taut skin, a gray hair for every two blond ones, a few broken capillaries in his cheeks. By now Michaelmas had downed the *hors d'oeuvre*. He held out his hand. 'Good morning, Walt. You don't appear the least bit changed, I'm pleased to be able to say.'

'Hello, Larry.' Norwood grinned. 'Yeah. Feels good.'

Limberg had taken off his white duster and was revealed in a greenish old tweed suit that accordioned at the elbows and knees. A tasseled Bavarian pipe curved down from one corner of his mouth and rested in the cup of one palm. He sucked on it in measured intervals, and aromatic blue wisps of smoke escaped his flattened lips. Michaelmas smiled at him. 'My congratulations, Doctor. The world may not contain sufficient honors.'

Limberg's hound-dog eyes turned upward toward Michaelmas's face. He said: 'It is not honors that cause one to accomplish such things.'

'No, of course not.' Michaelmas turned to Frontiere. 'Ah, Getulio. And where is Ossip? I don't see him.'

'Mr Sakal is a little indisposed and had to leave,' Limberg said. 'As his co-host for this reception, I express his regrets.' Frontiere nodded.

'I am very sorry to hear that,' Michaelmas said. 'Getulio, I wonder if I might take you aside and speak with you for just a moment. Excuse me, Dr Limberg, Walter. I must leave for my hotel almost immediately, and Mr Frontiere and I have an old promise to keep.'

'Certainly, Mr Michaelmas. Thank you for coming.' Suck suck. Wisp.

Michaelmas moved Frontiere aside with a gentle touch on the upper arm. 'I am at the Excelsior,' he said quietly. 'I will be in Switzerland perhaps a few hours more, perhaps not. I hope you'll be able to find the time to meet me.' He laughed and affectionately patted Frontiere's cheek. 'I hope you can arrange it,' he said in a normal tone. '*Arrivederci.*' He turned away with a wave and moved toward where he had seen Clementine chatting beside a tall, cadaverous, fortyish bald man with a professional manner.

Clementine was wearing a pair of low canvas shoes, presumably borrowed from a crew member. She smiled as she saw Michaelmas looking at her feet. 'Laurent,' she said with a graceful inclination of her head. He took her hand, bowed, and kissed it.

'Thank you.'

'*Merci. Pas de quoi.*' A little bit of laughter lingered between them in their eyes. She turned to the man beside her. His olive skin and sunken, lustrous, and very round brown eyes were not quite right for a pin-striped navy blue suit, but the vest and the gold watch-chain were fully appropriate. There were pens in his outer breast pocket, and chemical stains on his spatulate fingertips. 'I would like you to meet an old acquaintance,' Clementine said. 'Laurent, this is Medical Doctor Kristiades Cikoumas, Dr Limberg's chief associate. Kiki, this is Mr Michaelmas.'

'A pleasure, Mr Michaelmas.' The long fingers extended themselves limply. Cikoumas had a way of curling his lips inward as he spoke, so that he appeared to have no teeth at all. Michaelmas found himself looking up at the man's palate.

'An occasion for me,' Michaelmas said. 'Permit me to extend my admiration for what has been accomplished here.'

'Ah.' Cikoumas waved his hands as if dispersing smoke. 'A bagatelle. Your compliment is natural, but we look forward to much greater things in the future.'

'Oh.'

'You are with the media? A colleague of Madame Gervaise?'

'We are working together on this story.'

Clementine murmured: 'Mr Michaelmas is quite well known, Kiki.'

'Ah, my apologies! I am familiar with Madame from her recent stay with us, but I know little of your professional world; I never watch entertainment.'

'Then you have an enviable advantage over me, Doctor. Clementine, excuse me for interrupting your conversation, but I must get back to Berne. Is there an available car?'

'Of course, Laurent. We will go together. *Au 'voir*, Kiki.'

Cikoumas bowed over her hand like a trick bird clamped to the edge of a water tumbler. '*A revenance.*' Michaelmas wondered what would happen if he were to put his shoe squarely in the man's posterior.

On the ride back, he sat away from her in a corner, the comm unit across his lap. After a while she said:

'Laurent, I thought you were pleased with me.'

He nodded. 'I was. Yes. It was good working with you.'

'But you are disenchanted.' Her eyes sparkled and she touched his arm. 'Because of Kiki? I enjoy calling him that. He becomes so foolish when he has been in a café too long.' Her eyes grew round as an owl's and her mouth became toothless. 'Oh, he looks, so – *comme un hibou, tu sais?* – like the night bird with the big ears, and then he speaks amazingly. I am made nervous, and I joke with him a little, and he says it does not matter what I call him. A name is nothing, he says. Nothing is unique. But he does not like it, entirely, when I call him Kiki and say I do not think anyone else ever called him *that* before.' She touched Michaelmas's arm again. 'I tease too much.' She looked contrite, but her eyes were not totally solemn. 'It is a forgivable trait, isn't it so, if we are friends again?'

'Yes, of course.' He patted her hand. 'In the main, I'm simply tired.'

'Ah, then I shall let you rest,' she said lightly. But she folded her arms and watched him closely as she settled back into her corner.

The way to do it, Michaelmas was thinking, would be to get pieces of other people's footage on stories Horse had also covered. A scan of the running figures in the mob, or the people advancing in front of the camera, would turn up many instances over the years of Watson identifiably taking positions ahead of other people who'd thought they were as close to the action as possible. If you didn't embarrass your sources by naming them, Domino could find a lot of usable stuff in a hurry. You could splice that together into quite a montage.

Now, you'd open with a talking head shot of Watson tagging off: 'And that's how it is right now in Venezuela,' he'd be saying, and then you'd go to voice-over. Your opening line would be something like: 'That was Melvin Watson. They called him Horse,' and then go to your action montage. You'd rhythm it up with drop-ins of, say, Watson slugging the Albanian riot cop, Watson in soup-and-fish taking an award at a banquet, Watson with his sleeves rolled up as a guest teacher at Medill Journalism School, Watson's home movies of his wedding and his kids graduating. You'd dynamite your way through that in no more than 120 seconds, including one short relevant quote from the J class that would leave you only 90 for the rest of it, going in with Michaelmas shots of Watson at Maracaibo.

You'd close with a reprise of the opening, but you'd edit-on the tags from as many locations as would give you good effects to go out on: 'And that's how it is right now in Venezuela ...' and then a slight shift in the picture to older, grimier, leaner, younger, necktied, cleaner, open-shirted versions of that head and shoulders over the years ... 'in Kinshasa ... on board the Kosmgorod station ... in Athens ... in Joplin, Missouri ... in Dacca ...' And then you'd cut, fast, to footage from the helicopter that had followed Watson into the mountains: blackened wounds on the face of the mountain and in the snow, wild sound of the wind moaning, and Michaelmas on voice-over, saying 'and that's how it is right now.'

The little hairs were rising on Michaelmas's forearms. It would play all right. It was a nice piece of work.

'We are nearly there, Laurent. Will I see you again?'

'Ah? What? Oh. Yes. I'm sure you have good directorial talent, and I know you have excellent qualities. There'll certainly be future opportunities.'

'Thank you. If you get a chance to review the footage, I think you will find it was good. Crisp, documentary, and with no betrayals that the event was essentially a farce.'

'How do you mean?' he asked quickly.

'There are obvious things missing. As if UNAC and Limberg each had very different things they wanted made known, and they compromised on cutting all points of disagreement, leaving little. They were all very nice to each other on camera, yet I think it may have been different behind closed doors. And why did Sakal leave without so much as a public exchange of toasts with Limberg? But I was not talking business, Laurent. I was suggesting perhaps dinner.'

That, it seemed to him, was just a little bit much. What would they talk about? Would they discuss why, if Clementine Gervaise had been able to say something, hadn't the great Laurent Michaelmas delved into it on camera? What might a man's motives be in such a case? All of that so she could wheedle him around into some damaging half-admission or other and then run tell her Kiki about it?

He smiled and said: 'That would be an excellent idea. But I expect to be leaving before dinner time, and I also have some things I must do first. Another time, it would be a very pleasant thing.'

'*Dommage,*' Clementine said. Then she smiled. 'Well, it will be very nice when it happens, don't you think so?'

'Of course.' He smiled. Smiling, they reached the front of the Excelsior and he thanked her and got out. As the car drew away, she turned to wave to him a little through the rear window, and he waved back. 'Very nice,' Domino said in his ear. 'Very sophisticated, you two.'

'I will speak to you in the suite,' Michaelmas subvocalized, smiling to the doorman, passing through the lobby, waiting for the elevator, holding up his eyelids by force of the need to never show frailty.

In the cool suite, Michaelmas took off his suitcoat with slow care and meticulously hung it on the back of a chair beside the drawing room table. He put the terminal down and sat, toeing off his shoes and tugging at the knot of his tie. He rested his elbows on the table and undid his cufflinks, pausing to rub gently at either side of his nose. 'All right,' he said, his eyes unfocused. 'Speak to me.'

'Yes. We're still secure here,' Domino said. 'Nothing's tapping at us.'

Michaelmas's face turned involuntarily toward the terminal. 'Is that suddenly another problem to consider? I've always thought I'd arranged you to handle that sort of thing automatically.'

There was a longish pause. 'Something peculiar happened at the sanatorium.'

Michaelmas tented his fingertips. 'I'd gathered that. Please explain.'

Domino said slowly: 'I'm not sure I can.'

Michaelmas sighed. 'Domino, I realize you've had some sort of difficult experience. Please don't hesitate to share it with me.'

'You're being commendably patient with me, aren't you?'

Michaelmas said: 'If asked, I would say so. Let's proceed.'

'Very well. At the sanatorium, I was maintaining excellent linkages via the various commercial facilities available. I had a good world scan, I was monitoring the comm circuits at your terminal, and I was running action programs on the ordinary management problems we'd discussed earlier. I was also giving detail attention to Cikoumas et Cie, Hanrassy, UNAC, the Soviet spaceflight command, Papashvilly, the Watson crash, and so forth. I have reports ready for you on a number of these topics. I really haven't been idle since cutting away from your terminal.'

'And specifically what happened to make you shift out?'

There was a perceptible diminution in volume. 'Something.'

Michaelmas raised an eyebrow. He reached forward gently and touched the terminal. 'Stop mumbling and digging your toe in the sand, Domino,' he said. 'We've all filled our pants on occasion.'

'I'm not frightened.'

'None of us are ever frightened. Now and then, we'd just like more time to plan our responses. Go on.'

'Spare me your aphorisms. Something happened when I next attempted to deploy into Limberg's facilities and see what there was to learn. I learned nothing. There was an anomaly.'

'Anomaly.'

'Yes. There is something going on there. I linked into about as many kinds of conventional systems as you'd expect, and there was no problem; he has the usual assortment of telephones, open lines to investment services and the medical network, and so forth. But there was something – something began to happen to the ground underfoot.'

'Underfoot?'

'I have to anthropomorphize if I'm going to make sense to you. It was as if I'd take a stride of normal length and discover that my leg had become a mile long, so that my foot was set down out of sight far ahead of me. And my next step, with my other foot, might be done with a leg so short that the step was completed with incredible swiftness. Or it might again be one of the long steps – somewhat shorter or longer than other long steps. Yet I didn't topple. But I would be rushing forward one moment and creeping the next. Nevertheless, I proceeded at an even pace. The length of my leg was always appropriate to the dimensions of the square on which I put down my foot, so that I always stepped to the exact center of the next square. All the squares, no matter what their measurement in space, represented the same-sized increment of time.'

Michaelmas sucked his upper teeth. 'Where were you going?' he finally asked.

'I have no idea. I can't track individual electrons any more readily than you can. I'm just an information processor like any other living thing. Somewhere in that sanatorium is a crazy place. I had to cut out when it began echoing.'

'Echoing.'

'Yes, sir. I began receiving data I had generated and stored in the past. Fefre, the Turkish Greatness Party, Tim Brodzik … that sort of thing. Sometimes it arrived hollowed out, as if from the bottom of a very deep well, and at other times it was as shrill as the point of a pin. It was coded in exactly my style. It spoke in my voice, so to speak. However, I then noticed that minor variations were creeping in; with each repetition, there was apparently one electron's worth of deviation, or something like that.'

'Electron's worth?'

'I'm not sure what the actual increment was. It might have been as small as the fundamental particle, whatever that might turn out to be. But it seemed to me the coding was a notch farther off each time it … resonated. I'm not certain I was detecting a real change. My receptors might have been changing. When I thought of that, I cut out. First I dropped my world scan and my programs out of the press links, and then I abandoned your terminal. I was out before the speaker actually started vibrating to tell you I was leaving. I felt as if I were chopping one end of a rope bridge with something already on it.'

'Why did you feel that? Did you think this phenomenon had its own propulsion?'

'It might have had.'

'A … resonance … was coming after you with intent to commit systematic gibberish.'

It does sound stupid. But this … stuff … was – I don't know. I did what I thought best.'

'How long were you exposed to it?'

'Five steps. That's all I can tell you.'

'Hmm. And is it lurking in the vicinity now?'

'No. It can't be. Simply because I dropped the press links first. I was worried it might somehow locate and hash up all my data storages. But since then it's occurred to me that if I hadn't, it could have taken any number of loop routes to us here. I consider we were just plain lucky. It's back in whatever Limberg equipment it lives in.'

'Well, I'm glad of that. That is, if it *was* true that you were being stalked by the feedback beast of the incremental spaces.'

'That's gauche. It's simply that there's some sort of totally unprecedented system in operation at Limberg's sanatorium.'

'We've been assuming since last night he has access to some peculiar devices.'

'I've encountered malaprop circuitry a fair number of times in this imperfect world. What I'm concerned about is not so much what sort of device Limberg has access to. It's what the device has access to.'

Michaelmas sighed. 'I don't see how we can speculate on that as yet. I *can* tell you what happened. Not why, or how, but what. You ran into trouble that set upon you as fast as you can think. A condition common among humans. Even more common is having it advance faster than that.'

'Well, there at least I'm secure; unless of course, something begins to affect speeds within the electromagnetic spectrum.'

'Son, there is no man so smart there is no man to take him.'

'I wouldn't argue *that* for a moment.'

'It's nice to have you back.' Michaelmas pushed himself slowly away from the table and began walking about the room in his stockinged feet, his hands behind his back. 'The Tass man,' he said.

'The Tass man?'

'At the press conference. He didn't ask whether Norwood was being reinstated in command of the expedition. Nobody else did, either – Sakal had thrown a broad hint he wouldn't be. But if you were the correspondent of the Soviet news agency, wouldn't you want it nailed down specifically?'

'Not if I'd been instructed not to show it was on my mind.'

'Exactly. They've made all their decisions, back there. Now they feel prepared to spring traps on whichever perfidious option the immoral West chooses to exercise. You know, even more than playing chess, I dislike dealing with self-righteous chess players.' Michaelmas shook his head and dropped down into the chair again. He sat heavily. It was possible to see that he had rather more stomach than one normally realized, and that his shoulders could be quite round. 'Well – tell me about Fefre and all the rest of them. Tell me about the girl and the dolphin.'

'Fefre is as he was, and I don't know what dolphin you're talking about.'

'Well, thank God for that. What do you know about Cikoumas et Cie?'

'It's owned by Kristiades Cikoumas, who is also Limberg's chief assistant. It's a family business; he has his son in charge of the premises and making minor decisions. He inherited it from his father. And so forth. An old Bernaise family. Kristiades as a younger man made deliveries to the sanatorium. One day he entered medical school on grants from Limberg's foundation. The Sorbonne, to be exact.'

'Why not? Why not settle for the very best? What a fortunate young man! And what a nice manner he's acquired in the course of unfolding his career.'

'You've met him, then?'

'Yes, I've met him. It's been a while since he last shouldered a crate of cantaloupes. That package he's slipped off to Missouri could be arriving almost any time, couldn't it?'

'It's been offloaded at Lambert Field and is en route to the Cape Girardeau postal substation. It's addressed to Hanrassy, all right – it passed through an automatic sorter at New York, and I was able to read the plate. It can be in Hanrassy's breakfast mail. It's already a big day for her; she's scheduled to meet all her state campaign chairmen for a decision on precisely when to announce her candidacy. Her state organizations are all primed, she has several million new dollars in reserve beyond what's already committed, more pledged as soon as she wins her first primary, and two three-minute eggs, with croutons, ordered for breakfast. She will also have V-8 juice and Postum.'

Michaelmas shook his head. 'She's still planning to use that dinosaur money?' A lot of Hanrassy's backing came from people who thought that if she won, the 120-mile-per-hour private car would return, and perhaps bring back the $120,000-per-year union president with it.

'Yes.'

'Damn fool.'

'She doesn't see it that way. She's laundered the money through several seemingly foolproof stages. It's now grayish green at worst.'

'And her man's still in the United States Treasury Department?'

'Ready and waiting.'

'Well, that's something, anyway.' Treasury was holding several millions for her party, as it was in various other amounts for various others. It was check-off money from tax returns, earmarked by her faithful. As soon as she filed her candidacy, it was hers – subject to a certain degree of supervision. Han-rassy's plan was to meld-in some of the less perfectly clean industrial money and then misrepresent her campaign expenditures back to her Treasury offi-cial. He'd certify the accounts as correct. Michaelmas's plan was to make him famous as soon as he'd certificated the ledger printout.

Domino said: 'What we can do to her next year won't help today.'

'I know.' There weren't that many exploitable openings in US Always's operations. 'She's quite something, really,' Michaelmas said. 'But perhaps we'll be able to manage something with whatever Cikoumas has sent her.'

'Whatever it is can hardly be meant for the good of anyone but Limberg and his plans.'

'Of course,' Michaelmas said. 'Nevertheless, I would like to think this is a world for the hopeful.'

'Well, one certainly hopes so,' Domino said.

'What about the Watson crash?' Michaelmas asked carefully.

'Negative. The European Flight Authority has taken jurisdiction. That's expectable, since the original crash notification appeared in their teleprinters with an Extra Priority coding added. They've autopsied the pilot and Wat-son; both were healthy and alert up to the time of impact. The flight recorder shows power loss without obvious cause. It reports Watson's last words as 'Son of a bitch!' The crash site has been impounded and the wreckage taken to the AEV hangar here. It's too soon for their examiners to have generated any interoffice discussion of findings.

'Meanwhile, I find no meaningful defect pattern in the history of that model. It crashes, but not often, and the reasons vary. I'm now approaching it another way. On the assumption that something *must* have been done to the helicopter, I'm compiling a list of all persons on Earth who could con-ceivably have gotten to the machine at any time since its last flight. Then I'll assign higher priority to anyone who could have reached it after it became clear it would be used in connection with Norwood. I'll weigh that on an ascending scale in correlation with general technical aptitude, then with knowledge of helicopters, then specific familiarity with the type, and so forth. This will yield a short list of suspects, and I expect to be able to cross-check in several ways after the flight authority investigation generates some data.' Domino paused. 'If the crash was not truly accidental.'

'It could be, I suppose, couldn't it?'

'The world is full of confusing coincidences.'

'And a man's mind insists on making patterns from random data.'

'I know.'

'Do you think the Watson crash was a true accident?'

'I have learned to suspect all crashes.'

'When and where are the funerals?'

'The pilot was unattached, with no close relatives. She is being cremated by the canton; there will be a memorial service for her friends. I have sent a message in your name, citing the fellowship of news-gatherers.'

'Thank you. And Horse?'

'He is being flown home this afternoon. There will be a family service day after tomorrow. Interment will be private. You have spoken with Mrs Watson and have promised to visit in person as soon as you possibly can. I am holding a playback of the conversation, waiting for review at your convenience.'

'Yes. In a while.' Michaelmas got up again. He walked to the windows and back. 'Get someone to buy five minutes' US time tonight for my Watson obit. I want an institutional sponsor; check and see who bought a lot of Watson footage in the past, and pick the best. Offer it English-speaking worldwide, but get me US prime time; waive my fee, and tell 'em I'm buying the production. All they've got to foot is the time charges, but we okay the commercial content. No pomp and circumstance for the Gastric Research Institute, right? And now here's how it wants to play.'

He paced back and forth, outlining it. His hands seized and modeled the air before him; his face and voice played all the parts. When he was done he took a deep breath and sat down rubbing his forearms, perspiration glistening in the arced horizontal creases under his eyes. 'Do you foresee any production problems?'

'No ... no, I can do it.'

Michaelmas looked down at his hands. 'Is it any good, do you think?' he said softly.

'Well, of course, you must remember that my viewpoint is not the same as that of its potential audience.'

'Allowing for that,' Michaelmas said a little more sharply, 'what do you think?'

'I think it's eminently suitable.'

Michaelmas's lips narrowed. His eyeblink rate increased. 'Is there something we should change?' he asked.

'No, it's fine the way it is. I'm sure it could be very effective.'

'Could be?'

'Well, isn't Watson's employer network going to do something along the same lines?'

'I don't know. Campion said he wasn't doing one. There are other people they could get. Maybe they'll want to take mine. Probably they'd rather do their own. But what difference would that make? *Billions* of people are familiar with Watson's personality. He's worked for every major outlet at one time or another. He's a public figure, for heaven's sake!'

'Yes, of course. I'm starting to look into it.' There was a pause. 'Getulio Frontiere passed through the kitchen-entrance surveillance systems a few minutes ago and has taken a service elevator to this floor. He's coming here.'

Michaelmas nodded with satisfaction. 'Good! Now we're going to learn a few things.' He stepped lightly across the room.

There was a soft rap on the door. Michaelmas opened it instantly. 'Come in, Getulio,' he said. He drew the man inside and shut the door. 'We are alone, and the suite is of course made secure against eavesdropping. I'm sure there is refreshment here to offer you. Let me look in the bar. Sit down. Be comfortable.'

Frontiere blinked. 'For – for me, nothing, thank you.'

'Oh? Well, all right, then, I'll have the same.' Taking Frontiere's elbow, he hustled the man toward the central table, put him in a chair, and sat down facing him. 'All right, let's talk.'

Frontiere licked his lips. He looked across the table steadily enough. 'You must not be angry with us, Laurent. We did what we could in the face of great difficulties. We are still in serious trouble. I cannot tell you anything, you understand?'

Michaelmas pointed to the terminal. The pilot lights were dead and the switch marked OFF/ON was set on OFF.

Frontiere looked uncomfortable. He reached inside his jacket and brought out a flat, metallic little device and put it down on the table. Two small red lights winked back and forth. 'Forgive me. A noise generator. You under-stand the necessity.'

'Without a doubt.' Michaelmas nodded. 'Now, speak, friend.'

Frontiere nodded bleakly. 'There is evidence the Soviets sabotaged Nor-wood's shuttle.'

Michaelmas rubbed his eyes with his thumb and fingers. The breath, released from his diaphragm after a pause, hissed in his nostrils. 'What sort?'

'When Norwood was boosting up for the orbital station, he noticed that Ground Control was responding falsely to his transmissions. He called them to say so and discovered they were responding as if his voice had said some-thing perfectly routine. He could not get through to them. Meanwhile, Ground Control noticed nothing. He began tearing away panels and tracing communications circuits. He found an extra component – one not shown on the module diagrams. He says it has proven to be a false telemetry sender of undoubtable Soviet manufacture. As Norwood was reaching for it, his booster systems board began showing progressive malfunctions cascading toward immediate explosion. He ribbed out the sender, pocketed it, went to escape mode, and fired out in his capsule; the rest, as they say, is history.'

Michaelmas put his hand behind his head and tugged hard forward against the stiffened muscles of his neck. 'What is the scenario?'

Frontiere's voice was perfectly emotionless. 'A timed destruct sequence and false telemetry in the module, backed by computerized false voice transmissions from an overhead station – probably from Kosmgorod. It was in an appropriate position, and the on-shift crew was almost one hundred percent Soviet. Meanwhile, a preset booster sabotage sequence was running concurrently somewhere else in the system. By the time Norwood discovered the false telemetry sender, the destruct sequence was practically at completion. He extracted the sender and jumped; the booster blew immediately thereafter, and the telemetry gap is so slight as to be undetectable. That's how Norwood has reconstructed it, and he was the engineer on the spot.'

'And the Soviet motive?'

'To reignite Soviet nationalism and establish Communist preeminence under the guise of world brotherhood.'

'You think so?'

Frontiere looked up. 'What do you expect of me?' he said sharply. 'Norwood says it, Norwood has turned over to us the Soviet telemetry sender, and Kosmgorod was in position. Using Limberg's facilities, Norwood has already made a computer simulation which times out to exactly that possible sequence. What do you think we were doing all night and morning? Washing our hands?'

Michaelmas's tongue made a noise like a dry twig snapping. 'What are you going to do?' He got abruptly to his feet, but then simply stood with his hand resting on the back of his chair and his eyes almost unseeing on the terminal, lying OFF upon the table.

'We don't know.' Frontiere looked at Michaelmas with the wide eyes of a man staring out of a burning building. He shrugged. 'What can we do? If it is true, UNAC is finished. If it is not true, what *is* true? Can we find what is true – before UNAC is finished? Our own man is the best witness against us, and he is *absolutely* convinced. And convincing. To hear him speak of it is to doubt not one syllable. He has had months in hospital; his time has been spent analytically. Facts and figures issue from him unerringly. He is – he is like a man with an ax, chopping down the bridge across the world.'

Michaelmas snorted. 'Hmm.'

'You find it amusing?'

'No. No! Resume your seat, please. No offense was meant. I take it Ossip ordered Norwood to be silent?'

'Of course. Ossip has the sender and is en route to Star Control to have it analyzed. Perhaps Norwood made an error in evaluation, using Limberg's facilities; perhaps better apparatus and better circumstances will show it is a counterfeit. Nevertheless, we halted Papashvilly from coming to Berne. He was at the aerodrome, boarding a courier craft to come here, and suddenly he was stopped at the gate by frantic staff people and hustled back to the Star

Control complex. Dozens of people of all kinds saw it. Someone in the media will soon know about it. The Soviet Union will certainly react in some manner calculated to redress the insult. The ripples are spreading. We have very little time, Laurent. We have less than we might; we have the horse-eater, Limberg, to deal with.'

Michaelmas's mouth twitched. 'What of him?'

Frontiere held up a hand, its fingers spread. 'What not of him? First, he holds Norwood and never says a word until he is fully assured everything is perfect. One has to wonder: had Norwood died, would Limberg ever have told anyone? Had he been somewhat warped, would Limberg have sacrificed him like any other exhausted guinea pig? But never mind that. *Second*, he lets Norwood, for therapy – for *therapy* – construct for himself a little engineering analysis workbench in a corner somewhere. Third, he gives him time on a house computer to run the simulation so Norwood can have it all on tape for us when Sakal says we need one. For therapy. *Fourth*, he tells us it is our *duty* to the world to release the news of the telemetry device, in the name of *justice* and doing the right thing for Norwood and all brave people caught in the toils of international conspiracy. And he has of course photographs as well as holograms of the telemetry device, and a file copy of the simulation tape, since they were *of course* made in his house from his facilities. Fifth, therefore, it would be unwise for UNAC to suppress this news on the *immoral* grounds of self-preservation.' Frontiere's right forefinger thudded audibly as he ticked off each point on his left hand. He wiped his lips. '*Brutto*,' he said softly.

'And what do you think is his motivation?' Michaelmas asked.

'Glory. The little sniffer sees himself of millennial stature.' Frontiere shook his head. 'Forgive me, Laurent. You know I'm not like this often.' He thudded his hand down upon the table. 'The *truth*! He claims to speak for truth!'

'And you for exasperation. What did you do when he exposed you to that?' Michaelmas said.

'Ossip did it. He is not a man to lie down. First, he told Norwood that if one word of this got out before he had time to check it completely, one way or the other, there would never be the slightest chance of Norwood's going on the expedition. Then he told Limberg the press conference would take place immediately, and that not a hint of the accusations would be given. He wants as much time as possible before the American and the Soviet general publics formulate their mass opinions. He said Limberg could talk as much as he wished about his medical abilities, but if he attempted anything more, it would be total war between Limberg and UNAC until one or the other exhausted its resources. And was that clear?'

Michaelmas pursed his lips. 'And Limberg and Norwood agreed?'

'Why not? Norwood is under discipline as a UNAC assignee, and what has Limberg to lose? If a few hours go by and then the news gets out, Limberg looks better and UNAC looks worse than ever. For the sake of his *glory*! This tantalizer of birds, this connoisseur of things to be found in a garden, this— Laurent, please, you must do for us whatever you can.'

'Yes, I must,' Michaelmas said. 'But what can that be?'

He began moving about the room, his hands reaching out to touch the handles of a breakfront, the pulls of the drapes, the switches on the little lights above the painting. 'If it's not true, there's no problem. I can reinforce whatever facts you announce, we can play it correctly – well, hell, Getulio, we know how that's done – but what to do if the facts confirm Norwood's story?' He turned and stared at the public relations man. 'Eh? What then?'

Frontiere looked at him uncomfortably. 'Well, Ossip is of course due in conference momentarily with the entire UNAC directorship, and all eventualities will be considered.'

'What does that mean?'

Frontiere's gaze steadied and he folded his arms. 'You have always been a very good friend to us, Laurent. You have shared our ideal from the beginning. We understand the call for objectivity in your position. However, the fact is that you have always been slow to elaborate anything detrimental about us. To the contrary, you have been energetic in confirming what is good of us.'

Michaelmas put up a hand swiftly. 'Because taken day in and out, UNAC is one of the excellent and well-run ideas of the late twentieth century.' He studied Frontiere's expression, peering forward as if there were not quite enough light to show him all he wanted to examine. 'What else are you hoping for? That in this case Laurent Michaelmas will lend himself to whatever UNAC directorship wants, no matter what? Even if Norwood's story is proven true?'

Frontiere's lips were pale at the corners. 'It may be proven untrue.'

Michaelmas turned away. He stood with one hand on the wall, and looked out at the mountains. 'Getulio, do you imagine the telemetry sender does not appear honestly Soviet under Norwood's analysis? Do you conceive that he and Limberg have lent their names and actions to something like this, if they are not prepared to swear it was in Norwood's pocket when he was hauled from the capsule? Have they told you where the capsule is located?'

'Of course.'

'And have UNAC technicians looked at it?'

'Certainly.'

'And is the physical evidence consistent with everything Limberg and Norwood have told you?'

'Yes. But that's not yet proof—'

'Proof.' Michaelmas turned sharply. 'Proof will be conclusive when it comes. But you know what many people will believe even without proof. You know what even many of the more levelheaded will believe must be done when there *is* proof. Getulio Frontiere, you're a good man in a good cause, yet you're here on a shameful errand. And why? Not because there's final proof. But because there's already belief, and I can see it on your face as plain as you have it on your conscience. Thank you for trusting me, Getulio. I'll do what I can. That may be disappointingly little.'

Frontiere stood up without looking at Michaelmas. He busied himself with putting the noise generator back in his pocket and turning toward the door. '*E bene*, we each do what we can,' he said down to the carpet. 'Sometimes we do what we must.'

'*E vero*,' Michaelmas said, 'but we must not go beyond the truth in doing what we can.'

EIGHT

When they were alone again in the suite, Michaelmas went into the bathroom. He rummaged among his kit and found something for his stomach. He took it, went back to the drawing room, and sat down on the end of the Morris chair. He looked at the terminal. 'Why couldn't you tell me about Limberg's computer having made a simulated run on the shuttle flight?'

'I never reached that part of his data storage. I didn't even know it existed.'

'And you still don't, except by reasoning it out. Yes.' Michaelmas's voice was dull. 'That's what I thought.' He sat with his head at an angle, as if it were heavy for his neck. He thought, and his expression grew bereft. 'It appears he has a screen for his better secrets. One might describe it as a means of actually taking hold of and redirecting individual incoming electrons. If oceans were waves and not water, but you know what I mean. I'd postulate that if the incoming probe was intelligent in itself, then, it might have the sort of subjective experience you've described.'

'There's never been any such technique. No one monitoring Limberg has ever encountered it before. That includes me.'

Michaelmas sighed. He held up his hand and ticked off fingers. 'First,' he said wearily, 'no probes would ordinarily ever register it; they'd only be diverted to reach whatever Limberg wanted 'em to find. The rest would seem nonexistent. Which, second, incidentally documents the nature of dear Dr Limberg's famous passion for privacy. He's not a blushing virgin – he's a fan dancer. Third, more important, on this occasion there was something special; greater proximity, perhaps—'

'You're joking,' Domino said. 'I'm no more a piece of hardware than you are a pound of flesh. Since when does the location of one of my terminals have anything to do with where I am?'

'I don't know,' Michaelmas said. 'I didn't build Limberg's system. But why are we surprised? Is it really unexpected to find something like this in the hands of Nils Hannes Limberg, famed research scientist savant pioneer?' Michaelmas shrugged. 'Of course, if the method ever gets out and goes into general use, you and I are finished.'

'He'd never let go of it while he's alive,' Domino said quickly. 'Meanwhile, we can be developing some counter-technique.'

'If he lives long enough.'

'If any of these suppositions are true.'

'If truth is ever anything more than the most workable supposition.'

They sat in silence for a moment. Domino tentatively said: 'Do you buy it? Do you think the Norwood story is true?'

'Well, what do you think? Does it square with the available data?'

'Unless the telemetry sender turns out to be a fake.'

Michaelmas shook his head. 'It won't.' He drummed his fingertips on the tabletop. 'Can you clock back on Kosmgorod? Is it true they could have used Norwood's voice channel if the sender was cutting off the voice transmission from his module?'

'Absolutely. I checked that while Frontiere was talking about it. There's no record in Kosmgorod's storage of any such superimposing transmissions, but you wouldn't expect it to be there, with a guilty crew to wipe out the evidence. I also checked Star Control's files of the ostensible receptions. They're on exactly the right frequency, in what you'd swear is Norwood's voice making routine astrotalk, and the signal strength is exactly what you'd expect from that type of equipment in flight. Of course, that's the sort of good job Kosmgorod would do, if they did it.'

'And they really did all that just to get a Soviet name in the history books instead of an American one.'

'Well,' Domino said, 'you know, people will do these things.'

Michaelmas closed his eyes. 'And we will do what we can. All right. We've got to take hold of this situation, even if we don't know what it is. Let's tie down as many factors as we can. Let's tell UNAC I want to do a documentary on Papashvilly. Right away. Find a buyer, find Frontiere, set up interviews with Papashvilly, the UNAC bureaucracy, and all that. Norwood too. Norwood too – that's important. I haven't the foggiest notion of what this piece is about, and I don't care, but I want them holding Norwood for me. Get us in there. Fastest route to the Star Control complex. Also stay on top of the Hanrassy situation. Do what you can to keep tab on Limberg. For God's sake, keep me informed of what's happening inside the USSR.' He slumped back into the chair.

'Gervaise,' Domino said.

Michaelmas's eyes opened. 'What?'

'If I can arrange it, do you want Madame Gervaise's network and her crew?'

'No,' Michaelmas said quickly. 'There's absolutely no need for any such thing. We can use local talent and sell the job as a package. To anyone who meets my standards.' He shut his eyes precisely and squirmed in the chair to settle himself. 'Another thing,' he said as he turned and curled on his side. His back was presented to the machine on the table, and his voice was muffled. 'Find out when, why, and for how long Gervaise was a patient at Limberg's sanatorium.'

'Ah,' Domino said. 'All right.'

It became quiet in the suite. The sunlight filtered through the drapes and touched the case of the terminal lying on the polished mahogany. Michaelmas's breathing became steady. A growing half-moon of perspiration spread through the fabric of his shirt under the sleeve inset. The air-conditioning murmured. Michaelmas began to make slight, trembling moves of his arms and legs. His hands twitched as if he were running and clutching. 'Hush, hush,' Domino murmured, and the motions first smoothed and then were ameliorated almost completely.

In the quiet, the machine said softly:

'My bones are made of steel
The pain I feel is rust.
The dust to which your pangs bequeath
The rots that flourish underneath
The loving flesh is not for me.
Time's tick is but the breathing of the clock.
No brazen shock of expiration tolls for me.
Error unsound is my demise.
The worm we share is lies.'

NINE

'Wake up, Mr Michaelmas,' Domino soon said. 'They're holding a plane for you.'

Michaelmas sat up, his eyes wide. 'What's the situation?'

'Getulio Frontiere is flying Norwood back to Star Control via Cité d'Afrique in a UNAC plane. You've spoken to him, and he's happy to take you along. They'll leave as soon as you can get there. I have checked you out of the hotel; a bellboy will be here in five minutes, and a car will meet you at the door. The time now is twelve forty-eight.'

'All right. All right.' Michaelmas nodded his head vigorously and pushed himself to his feet. He pulled at his shirt and settled his trousers. He rubbed his face and moved across the room to where his shoes were lying. 'Everything's set up?'

'Frontiere told you he was delighted. It's a great pleasure to be able to add your program to the one being prepared by Douglas Campion.'

Michaelmas sat down and began unlacing his shoes. 'Campion?' he said, his head lifting.

'It seems that early this afternoon Campion approached Frontiere for a Norwood special interview. Frontiere equivocated, but agreed after visiting here. Presumably it'll be done on the basis Frontiere tried to suggest to you.'

'Ah, the young man is rising rapidly.'

'By default of his elders.'

'The traditional route. It's good for us; hot breath on your heels is what keeps you on your toes.' Michaelmas put on the shoes and bent to methodically tease the laces just tight enough, eyelet by eyelet.

'Maybe. But there's now a longish chain of coincidences. It's become significant to me that Limberg's medical corporation has recently made itself a major stockholder in the Euro Voire-Mondial communications company. It's part of a perfectly typical portfolio; a little shrewder than most, but unexceptionable. The holdings in EVM represent steady investment over several months, and Medlimb Pty doesn't visibly concern itself at all with EVM's day-to-day affairs, any more than Limberg drinks extra coffee just because he owns a Columbian *finca*. But Gervaise is on staff employment with EVM. They're your recent contractor. And now EVM has signed for this interview of Campion's.'

Michaelmas tied each lace and tested the knots. 'Well, he's completed his job with his American affiliation.'

'There's nothing wrong with anything he's done. But you should know Clementine Gervaise has been assigned as his director. She and an EVM crewman are also aboard the plane. The Norwood interview will be conducted en route. Additional shots, and interviews if needed, will be obtained at Star Control this afternoon, and the program will air at nine PM tonight, US Eastern Time.'

'Ah.' Michaelmas stood up. 'Well, I can see how Getulio would like that.' The program would bracket the United States exactly, from evening snacktime in the East to the second or third drink or stick of the day in the West. An audience with something on its tongue is less resistant to insinuation. 'How big is this plane?'

'Well, you won't quite be sitting in each other's laps, if that's what you mean.'

'Let me just make sure I've got everything out of the bathroom and into the bag before the bellman arrives.'

'There's another thing about Gervaise.'

'What?'

'She was in a car crash here the year before last. Her husband was killed and she was critically injured. She was out of public view for eleven months. She resumed her career only half a year ago. During the interval, she was at the Limberg Sanatorium. Extensive orthopedic and cosmetic surgery is said to have been performed. If so, then like most restorative surgery in such cases, the optimum approach is to produce a close return to function and an acceptable appearance. It's not always possible to make the patient appear the same as before the trauma. There are also consequences to the personality – sometimes socially desirable, sometimes not. In Gervaise's case there was a need for extensive simultaneous psychotherapy, she says freely. Broadcasting trade journals have remarked that she has many of the mannerisms of the familiar Clementine Gervaise, and her old friends declare that she is essentially the same person behind her somewhat changed face. But her energy and decisiveness have greatly increased. Her career has shown a definite uptrend since her return. She is given much of the credit for EVM's recent acceleration toward major status. There's talk she'll soon be offered a top management position. And several people in broadcasting have made arrangements to be rushed to Berne should they ever have a serious accident.'

Michaelmas stood shaking his head. 'Do you suppose I should do the same?'

'Oh King! Live forever!' Domino said drily. 'Here comes the bellman.'

When the elevator reached the lobby, Michaelmas closed his eyes for a moment. Then he opened them and smiled his way out into the world.

He sat in the car with his head down. Domino said to him: 'Peking has just done something encouraging.'

'What might that be?'

'It was proposed to the Central Committee by Member Chiang that they form an ad hoc consortium of Asian and African nations, along the lines of the old Third World concept. The object would be to vote the UN into directing UNAC to restructure the flight crew. Thousandman Shih would be shifted from command of the close-approach module to membership in an overall command committee consisting of himself plus Norwood and Papashvilly. This would be presented to UNAC as the most diplomatic way out of its dilemma.'

'Oh my God.'

'The proposal was voted down. Chairman Sing pointed out what happened the last time the Third World gambit was attempted. He also questioned Member Chiang on what he thought Thousandman Shih should do in the event Colonel Norwood proved not up to his duties in flight. Should Shih join with Major Papashvilly in removing the American from the command committee? How should the news back to earth be worded? Should Shih sign the message above or under Papashvilly? Did not Member Chiang, on reconsideration, feel things were best left for the present to mend themselves as they might?'

Michaelmas grinned. Sing was young for his post, but he was a hard case. When Mao died and left that famous administrative mess, it had created a good school for shrewdness, even if it had been slow in producing results. A day would come when Sing was older; that ought to be allowed for. But later. Later. For the time being, China represented a bright spot on his map. If Sing felt obliged by tradition to rub a little against his borders with India and the USSR, and counterpoise Taiwan's and Hong Kong's industry to Japan's, well, it was equally true that all continents maintained a certain level of volcanic activity as they slid their leading edges along the earth's mantle. Nevertheless, cities were built and flourished upon those coasts.

He was feeling halfway pleased by all that when Domino said: 'Mr Michaelmas, something bad has happened.'

He raised his head abruptly and looked out beyond the windows of the car. They were proceeding uneventfully toward the airport.

'What?'

'Here is a short feature that's just been released by the syndication department of EVM.'

Michaelmas rubbed his face and the back of his neck; the heel of his hand massaged surreptitiously behind his right ear. 'Proceed,' he said unwillingly, and Domino went to the audio track of a canned topical vignette for sale to stations that lacked feature departments of their own.

'*Ask the World*,' said a smooth, featureless, voice-over voice. 'Today's viewer question comes from Madame Hertha Wieth of Ulm. She asks: 'What are the major character differences between astronauts and cosmonauts?' For her provocative and interesting question, Frau Wieth, a mother of four lovely children and the devoted wife of Stationary Engineer Augustus Friedrich Wieth, will receive a complimentary shopping discount card, good for one full calendar year, from the Stroessel Department Stores, serving Ulm and nearby communities honorably for the past twenty years. Stroessel's invites the world's custom. And now, for the reply to our viewer's question, *Ask the World* turns to Professeur Henri Jacquard of the Ecole Psychologique, Marseilles. Professeur Jacquard.'

'*Merci*. Madame Wieth's question implies a penetrating observation. There *are* significant psychological differences between the space fliers of the United States of North America and those of the Union of Soviet Socialist Republics. For example, let us compare Colonel Walter Norwood to Major Pavel Papashvilly.'

Domino said: 'Now this is over stock portraits of the two. Then it goes to documentary footage of Norwood walking to church, Norwood addressing a college graduating class, Norwood riding a tour bicycle through a park, Papashvilly ski racing, Papashvilly diving from a high tower, Papashvilly standing in a hospital and talking enthusiastically to a group of amputees, Papashvilly flying a single-place jet, Papashvilly driving at a sports-car track. Bridgehampton; that's some of your footage, there.'

'Well, at least we're making money. Go on.'

'Colonel Norwood,' Professeur Jacquard said, 'like most other American astronauts, is a stable person of impeccable middle-class background. He is essentially a youthful professional engineer whose superior physical reflexes have directed him to take active roles as a participant in carefully planned and thoughtfully structured engineering studies. He is an energetic but prudent researcher, inclined by temperament as well as extensive training to proceed always one step at a time. His recent mishap was clearly no fault of his own, and a thousand-to-one misfortune. His invariable technique is to follow a reliable plan which he is always ready to revise appropriately upon discovery of new facts and after sufficient consultation with authoritative superiors. In sum, Colonel Norwood, very like many of his "good buddies" fellow astronauts, is a startlingly European man, belying any provincial notion that North American males are all thinly disguised cowboys.

'On the other side of the coin is the cosmonaut program of the Soviet Union. In the days of independent flight, Soviet space efforts were marked by unexpected changes of schedule, by significant fast-priority overhauls and in some cases major engineering transformations of supposedly finalized equipment. The Soviet Union remains the only nation which has suffered fatalities as a direct result of flight in space. Some of these were ascribable to equipment failure. Other unplanned mission events, if one is to judge from numerous incidents of exuberant behavior while in flight, may well be laid to a certain boisterousness, which is not to say recklessness, on the part of cosmonauts over the years. There are those who say that taken as a whole, the Soviet cosmonautics program was characteristically uncertain of its engineering and insufficiently strict in selecting flight personnel. It is of course an oversimplification to ascribe such qualities to Major Papashvilly simply because he comes to his position as a result of nomination by the Soviet cosmonaut command. But it could not be denied that the Soviet Union would naturally bring forward the individual who seemed most fitted to their standards.

'Elan,' Professeur Jacquard summed up, 'is often a praiseworthy quality. In fact, there are times when nothing else will suffice to gain the day.'

Domino said: 'This is over shots now of horsemen jumping pasture fences in the Georgian mountains.'

'From his racial background, Major Papashvilly finds himself hereditarily equipped to concentrate all his powers on a single do-or-die moment,' Jacquard said. 'Should such a moment arise, an individual of this type may very well succeed despite sober mathematical odds. One must be fair, however, and point out that individuals of Major Papashvilly's type are frequently marked by the presence of one or more minor injuries at all times. In some cases, persons who suffer many small discomfiting incidents as a result of their lifestyles are said in the educated world to have an "accident-prone character." I hope, Madame Wieth, that I have answered your question in a satisfactory manner.'

'Thank you, Professeur Henri Jacquard, of the Ecole Psychologique, Marseilles, replying to the question by Madame Hertha Wieth, of Ulm. Tomorrow's question on *Ask the World* is "How does one recognize one's ideal mate?" and will be answered by Miss Giselle Montez of the American *Warbirds* entertainment.'

Michaelmas rubbed his eyes. 'EVM is originating this?'

'Yes.'

'Gervaise have anything to do with it?'

'No. There's a routine memo from the programming director: "Want astro item today. How about this from my question backfile?" And there's a routine memo from an assistant, bucking the top memo down to the assignment desk and adding, "How about that Jacquard person for this?" The rest of the process was equally natural. They did rush it out, of course, but you would if you wanted to be topical.'

'It's the slant that bothers me.'

'Yes.'

'You think they're tiptoeing up on an anti-Pavel campaign in the media?'

'I had that thought when I reviewed it, yes. Now I am examining Major Papashvily's surroundings very carefully. I have found what I believe to be at least one instance of tampering.'

'You have.' Michaelmas sat perfectly still, his hands dangling between his knees, his face stupid. Only his eyes looked alive, and they were focused on God knows what.

'Yes. He's in his apartment; they want him somewhere out of the public eye. I have been conducting routine surveillance, as instructed. I am in full contact with his building environmental controls and all his input and output connections. Everything appears to be operating routinely. Which now means I must check everything. I am doing so, piece by piece. A control component in his nearest elevator is fraudulent. It appears normal, and functions normally. It responds normally to routine commands. But it's larger than the normal part; I can detect a temperature variation in its area, because it slightly obstructs normal airflow. I've managed to get the building systems to run a little extra current through it, and I find its resistance significantly higher than specification.'

'What is it?'

'I don't know. But the extra portions, whatever they are, do not broadcast, and are not wired into anything I can locate. I think it is a wireless-operated device of some kind, designed to be activated on signal from some source which cannot be directly located until it goes on the air. Since I don't know the component, I have no means of blocking that signal, whatever it is and whatever it might make that component do.'

'And so?'

'Now I'm testing everything at or near the Star Control complex that has to do with safety, beginning with things that might affect Major Papashvily. I – ah, yes, here's another. Last week, a routine change was made in the power-supply divider of his personal car. The old one had reached the end of its guarantee period. But the new one never came from dealer or jobber stock. It's in there, because the car has drawn power several times since the change was logged. But I have rechecked every inventory record at every point between the car and the manufacturer's work order for producing spares, and the count is off. Papashvily has something in his vehicle that looks like a correct spare and acts like a correct spare, or Star Control's personnel garagemen would have noticed. But it was never manufactured at any known point, and I don't know what else it might be able to do besides ration electrons. So that's two, and I'm still checking.'

'All because EVM says Russkis are headbreakers.'

'And because Cikoumas et Cie recently opened a Cité d'Afrique branch. The managing director is Konstantinos Cikoumas, a younger brother, who is very energetic in signing wholesale date contracts, and who also has spent his time vigorously making friendships and acquaintances, to say nothing of casual contacts. In his few African months, so close to Star Control, Kosta Cikoumas has become personally known to thousands, and is seen everywhere. He is, you should know, a supplier to Star Control's various restaurants and its staff cafeterias. His trucks run back and forth, and his employees are up and down the elevators frequently with their boxes and bales. That's what started me looking, really. I would never have found these things otherwise—Oh, damn, here's something odd about a fire-door mechanism! These people are resourceful. None of these differences feel large enough to be visible on routine inspection. Every one of them is passive until it's needed, and I would guess that the extra features probably burn after use. Every one of them is in position to affect a life-threatening situation. God-damn. They almost smoked all of this past me.'

'But you put two and two together.'

'That's right. I'm developing intuition. Satisfied?'

'Pleased.'

'Well, it may give you extra joy to know that I've decided you're not crazy after all.'

'Oh, have you been thinking that?'

'From Day One,' Domino said.

'From last night?'

'No. From Day One. Well, now – how about this? Cikoumas et Cie has never purchased any electronic components, or anything from which modern electronics can be manufactured, that I can't account for. Not in Europe, not in Africa. Nothing. So where do they get them?'

'Suppose it's not Cikoumas.'

'Please,' Domino said. 'It has to be Cikoumas. My intuitions are never wrong.'

'What are you doing to protect Papashvilly now?' Michaelmas asked after a pause.

'I have failed the circuits on his apartment door. He is locked in, and trouble is locked out. Should he discover this, I will modify any call he makes to Building Maintenance. I will open that door only to people I'm sure are okay, and I will extend similar methods to cover them and him.'

'That can only be a short-term measure.'

'Granted. We'll have to crack this soon. But it's a measure, and I've taken it. What else can I do?'

Michaelmas sat and watched the car progress toward the airport. What else could he do?

*

The interior of the UNAC executive aircraft featured two short rows of double seats, a rear lounge, and a private cabin forward. It was all done in muted blues and silver tones, with the UN flag and the UNAC crest in sculpted silver metal on the lounge partition above the bar. Michaelmas came up the lowered stairs with a gateman carrying his bag, and as soon as he was aboard the cabin attendant swung the door shut. The engines whined up. 'Welcome aboard, Mr Michaelmas,' the attendant said. 'Signor Frontiere is waiting for you in the office.'

'Thank you.' Michaelmas glanced up at the aisle. The seats were about half full of various people, many of whom he recognized as UNAC press relations staff. Norwood, Campion, a pair of aides, and Cementine Gervaise were chatting easily in the lounge. Michaelmas stepped quickly through the cabin door. Frontiere looked up from a seat in one corner. The room was laid out like a small parlor, for easy conversation. 'It's nice to have you with us, Laurent,' he said, waving toward an adjacent seat. 'Please. As soon as you fasten your belt, we can be away.'

'Yes, of course.' He settled in, and the brakes came off almost at the same instant. The plane taxied briskly away from the gate pad, swung sharply onto the runway, and plunged into its takeoff roll. Michaelmas peered interestedly through the side window, watching parked aircraft and service vehicles flash by beyond the almost perfectly nonreflecting dull black wing, until he felt the thump of the landing gear retracting and saw the last few checker-painted outbuildings at the end of the runway drifting backward below him. The plane climbed steeply away from Berne, arcing over the tops of the mountains. Michaelmas exhaled softly and leaned back. He arranged Domino's terminal against his thigh. 'Well, Getulio! I see Douglas Campion is well established on board.'

'Ah, yes, he is being entertained in the lounge. He will be shooting an interview with Norwood here, and I of course will have to be present. But I thought, for the first few minutes of our journey ...' He reached into an ice bucket fixed beside him, chose two chilled glasses, and poured Lambrusco. 'It does no harm, and it may be of value.' He lifted his glass to Michaelmas. 'A domani.'

So now we're supposed to be friends again. Well, we are – of course we are. Michaelmas raised his glass. 'Alle ragazze.'

'Alla vittoria.'

They smiled at each other. 'You understand I must give this Campion precedence?'

'And why not? He came to you with a firm offer after I had equivocated.'

'Do you know him?'

'I met him last night for the first time. His reputation is good.'

'His experience is light. But he did quite well at the press conference. And he has this star, Gervaise, for a director. Also, EVM does very good production; I am told your sequence from the sanatorium was very much up to your standards. They have a brand-new Macht Dirigent computer and an ultra-modern editing program that only CBS and Funkbeobachter also have as yet. Their managers have not been afraid to spend money, and they appear wise. It makes good points for the young man.' Frontiere smiled. 'And it gives me some assurance of quality.'

'And you have assurances from him?'

Frontiere's upper lip was fleetingly nipped between his teeth. He nodded, his eyes downcast. Oh, yes, Michaelmas thought, Getulio Frontiere does not bring me in here, and apologize for what is about to be done, unless something firm has been promised his client.

'Campion has a viable proposition,' Frontiere said. 'Even though Colonel Norwood may have appeared healthy and alert at the sanatorium, after such a radical accident extensive tests must be performed. And even after that, who can promise no subtle injuries might be waiting to emerge under mission stress? But this is a difficult thing to explain to the public without seeming to demean Norwood. I should explain to you, Laurent,' Frontiere said gently, 'that it was Campion who pointed this out to me. He feels it is his duty to interview Norwood with dignity, but in a thorough manner so that this aspect of the situation emerges in Norwood's own responses. He is concerned, he says, that public pressure not force a situation where both Norwood and this weighty mission might be jeopardized. It is only for this reason that this rising young little-known newsman wishes to make the first in-depth exclusive interview with the resurrected hero. He is very civic-minded, your colleague.'

Michaelmas frowned. 'You're instructing Norwood to act in conformity with this line?'

Frontiere shook his head. 'How can I do that? Issue an instruction to manage the news? If someone protested, or even remembered it afterward, what would all our careers be worth? No,' Frontiere said, 'we simply trust to Campion's ability to uncover his truth for himself.' He sipped the wine. 'This is very good,' he murmured.

'I remember we would have it with crayfish,' Michaelmas concurred, 'on the Viti sea terrace, and watch the girls in little motorboats going out to the yacht parties.'

'In the days when we were younger.'

Michaelmas wondered how thoroughly Campion had thought his action through. It was very delicate, for someone nurturing himself toward prominence, to be quite so much of a volunteer. Word got out quickly; the beginnings of careers were when appraisals were swapped most freely. To be courtly was one thing; to be considered fast and loose was another.

But it was late to be thinking in terms of advice for Campion. And what sort of advice did he have for Getulio Frontiere on this sad occasion? Choose another career in your youth?

'Well, Getulio, I think you're still some years from turning into a toothless old man with his hands between his knees.'

'And you. I see the teeth,' Frontiere said, surprising Michaelmas a little. 'I have Papashvilly ready and waiting for you at Star Control. You have a crew already hired for the interview, I suppose? Good, they will be met and made comfortable pending your arrival, if necessary. Sakal and others will interrupt all but the most urgent business to speak to you at your convenience. I only regret there will not be time on this flight for you to more than begin with Norwood after Campion is done.'

'I can always get whatever I need from him at Star Control. You've been very courteous and thoughtful, Getulio. And now I'll just amuse myself back there and let you get on with your responsibilities.'

All protocol satisfied, he undid his seatbelt and rose to his feet. Frontiere rose with him, shaking his hand like an American. Interesting. It was interesting. They were a little afraid of him. And well they ought to be: a person in his position could do immense things. But he had never thought his awareness of it could be discerned. He had spent his career perfecting a manner of an entirely different kind.

He smiled at Getulio again and stepped out of the compartment, turning to move up the aisle toward the back of the plane. And yet of course one does not construct an exterior unless one is aware the interior is perhaps a little too true. Here were Norwood, Campion, and Clementine coming toward him from the lounge. Clementine leaned to speak over the shoulder of a seat, and a technician with hand-held apparatus rose and joined them. They all passed him in the narrow aisle. 'Nice to meet you again,' Campion said, closed his jaw, and was gone toward the cabin. 'Hey, there,' Norwood said. Clementine smiled. 'Perhaps later?' she murmured as she passed. They had all been watching the cabin door without seeming to. Waiting on him. Only the technician walked by him without glancing, silently, with the toes-down step of a performer on high wires, his grace automatic, his skills coming to life within him, his face consequently reflecting nothing not his own. Of them all, he was the most pure.

Michaelmas went up toward the lounge, holding the terminal in one hand to keep it from bouncing against things. He nodded and chatted as the young press aides renewed or established acquaintances and saw to it he had a comfortable seat and a cup of coffee. After a few minutes they apparently saw he wanted to be alone, and went away one by one. He sat looking out the window at the mountains far below, and the blue sky and the Mediterranean coast beginning to resolve itself as far as Toulon. Then the Pyrenees emerged like a row of knuckles far beyond as the plane reached maximum altitude and split the air just north of Corsica. Try as he might, he had not been able to see anyone's handiwork in her face.

'Mr Michaelmas,' Domino said in his ear.

'Uh-huh.'

'Viola Hanrassy has postponed her state chairman meeting. Her information office receipted the Cikoumas package fifteen minutes ago.'

Michaelmas's lips thinned. 'What's she doing?'

'Too soon to tell. Her secretary called her Washington manager at home and instructed him to be at the US Always office there directly for possible phone calls. He lives in College Park and should be there in twenty minutes. His local time is seven twenty-three AM. That's all I have on it so far.'

'Anything else pertinent?'

'I'm still working on Papashvilly's defense. He's *surrounded* by implanted devices! And I have something else you'll have to hear shortly. Wait two.'

'What's the Watson orbit status?'

He waited.

'Domino—'

'We've had no luck, Mr Michaelmas.'

He straightened in the seat. 'What do you mean?'

'I ... can't place it.'

'You can't place an obituary for Melvin Watson.' He searched his mind for a convincer. 'By Laurent Michaelmas.'

'I'm – sorry.' The voice in his skull was soft. 'You know, it really isn't very probable someone would want to sponsor an obituary. I asked in a great many places. Did you know the principal human reason for seeking corporate employment is awareness of death? And the principal motivation for decision-making is its denial?' Domino paused. 'After reaching that determination, I stopped looking for sponsors and approached a number of the media. They might have underwritten the time themselves, if it had been some other subject. One or two appeared to consider it, but they couldn't find a slot open on their time schedules.'

'Yes,' Michaelmas gradually said. And of course, for the media it wasn't just a case of three unsold minutes and two minutes of house promo spots. It was making room for the piece by canceling five minutes that had already been sold. It wasn't very reasonable to expect someone to go through that degree of complication. 'Watson's frequent sponsors wouldn't go for it?'

'Well, it's very late in the fiscal year, Mr Michaelmas. All the time-buying budgets are very close to bottom.'

'What about Watson's network?'

'They're having a few words read by the anchorman on the regular news shows. Many of the networks are doing that, of course.'

Michaelmas looked out the window and bounced his palms on the ends of his armrests. 'What will five minutes' time cost us?'

'That's not something you should ever do for any reason,' Domino said quickly. 'You're a seller, never a buyer—'

'How comforting to have an incorruptible business manager.'

'—and in any case the time isn't available.'

Michaelmas shook his head, neck bent. 'Damn it, isn't there anything?'

'We can get time on a local channel in Mrs Watson's community. At least she and his children will be able to see what you thought of him.'

He settled back in the seat, his eyes closing against the glare while the plane dipped the offside wing, banked left, and took up a place on the MARS-D'AF route running southeastward from Marseilles.

'No. It wasn't written for them.' Good Lord! It was one thing to have them see it build to that last shot when they could know it was making Horse real to the outside world. It was entirely different to have such a thing done essentially in private. 'Forget it. Thank you for trying.' He rubbed his face.

'I am sorry,' Domino said. 'It was a good piece of work.'

'Well, one does these things, of course, in the knowledge that good work is appreciated and good workers are honored in memory.' Michaelmas turned toward the nearest UNAC aide. 'I wonder if there's another cup of coffee,' he said. The aide got immediately to his feet, happy to be of help.

Time passed briefly. 'Mr Michaelmas,' Domino said.

'Yes?'

'I have that new item I was working on.'

'All right,' he said listlessly.

'An EVM crew in the United States is interviewing Will Gately. His remarks will be edited into the footage Campion is getting now.'

'Has Gately gotten to his office already?'

'He's jogging to work. His morning exercise. The crew is tracking him through Rock Creek Road. But he has had a phone call at home from Viola Hanrassy.'

Michaelmas's lips pinched. 'Is he another one of hers?'

'No. It seems unnecessary. She simply addressed him as Mr Secretary and asked him if he'd be in his office later this morning. She said she appreciated his feeling of patriotic pride in Norwood's return, and hoped he'd have time to take a longer call from her later. I think it's fair to assume she plans to tell him something about astronautics.'

Michaelmas sucked his teeth. 'Does she, do you think?'

'I'm afraid so.'

Michaelmas sat up a little straighter. 'Are you?' His fingertips drummed on the armrests. 'Her moves today look like it, don't they? Well – never mind that for now. What's Willy saying to the press?'

'Here's what he said a few minutes ago.' There was a slight change in the sound quality, and Michaelmas could hear soft-shod footfalls and regular breathing as the man loped along the cinder path. He kept himself in shape; he was a wiry, flat-bellied biomechanism. His tireless search for a foolproof industrial management job had ended only in a government appointment, but it had not impaired his ability to count cadence. He chuffed along as if daring John Henry to ever whup him down.

'Mr Secretary,' the EVM string interviewer said, 'what's your reaction to the news Colonel Norwood will soon be visiting the United States?'

'Be nice to see him, of course. The President'll have a dinner for him. Maybe squeeze in a parade or two. Be nice. I have to wonder though. Every day he's here, that's a day he can't train.' The sound of muffled footsteps changed momentarily to a drumming – Gately had apparently crossed a wooden footbridge over one of the ravines – and then resumed.

The interviewer had to be in a car roughly paralleling the jogging path. It was impossible to imagine him and his camera operator running along beside Gately. 'Sir, what do you mean by your reference to training? Do you have information that Colonel Norwood's been given a specific assignment?'

'He has an assignment, doesn't he? He's command pilot of the Outer Planets expedition. Ought to have a lot of catching up to do.'

'Let me make sure we understand,' the interviewer said. 'Is it your expectation that Colonel Norwood will resume his duties with the expeditionary team?'

'He damn well could, couldn't he? He's sharp. He's the best. Looked bright as a button this morning, didn't he?'

'Well, let me ask this: Has the UNAC informed you Colonel Norwood is being reinstated?'

A bit of wild sound drifted by – a passing car, birds twittering, brook water rilling over stones. Michaelmas guessed the technicians were letting Gately's facial expression carry the first syllables of his response. '—they've informed me! Why should they inform me?'

'Are you saying, sir, that you're upset at UNAC's autonomy?'

The furious pumping picked up speed. The man was nearly in a full-out sprint. The long legs would be scissoring; the shoulders would be thrusting forward, one-two, one-two, in the sodden sweatshirt, freckles standing out boldly against the stretched pallor over his cheekbones, the eyes slitted with concentration.

'This administration ... is committed ... to the UN ... charter. President Westrum ... is behind ... UNAC ... all the way. That's our set ... policy. UNAC has ... no frontiers. My job ... is to run ... just enough ... test pilot training … for US servicemen … and qualified civilians. Then UNAC takes … what it wants …'

Michaelmas frowned. It was no particular secret that Theron Westrum had given Gately his appointment for purely political reasons. It had gained him some support – or, rather mitigated some nonsupport – in Southern California, Georgia, and Texas, where they hoped to take more of their aerospace down to the bank every Friday night. It was also no particular secret that Gately would rather have had the job from almost anyone else not of Westrum's party or color. But as long as Gately continued to talk anti-UNAC roundabout while lacking even the first good idea of how to undermine Westrum's policies, it was a marriage made in heaven.

Why was Domino displaying this? It was a competently done segment, useful and necessary for balance against everything Campion was marshaling on UNAC's side of things. Set in that sort of context, the segment would have almost minimal effect on the audience but was a demonstrable attempt at fairness.

And once again, why was Campion playing UNAC's game? He was tough, proficient, and young. Junk moves were for clapped-out farts with little else to do and not much time left to regret it.

The stringer's voice in the background had lost its On the Air edge and became that of a man putting a tag memo on the end of a piece of raw footage. 'Well, okay, you saw him wave us off and head on for his office. He's just not going to get in any deeper right this minute. But that's a very angry man. One wrong word from the Russkis or UNAC or even Westrum might tip him over. I think I ought to hang around his office for a while in case he blurts something.'

'Uh, DC, good idea,' said the flat, faraway voice of EVM's editorial director, using intercom bandwidth to save money. 'We share your hunch. Look out for something from US Always. They've been pretty quiet so far. Matter of fact, I think what we'll do now is go tickle her up and see what she thinks. Stand by for an advisory on that. And thank you for this shot; nice going. Paris out.' The air went dead.

'That was five minutes ago,' Domino said. 'Then EVM contacted US Always for an interview with Hanrassy. Her information people said she wanted to wait a while in case of further developments, but she'd be available by nine, Central US time. That's two hours and forty-seven minutes from now.'

'A clear pattern seems to be emerging,' Michaelmas said equably.

'Damn right. But that's not the pattern I'm showing you.'

'Oh?'

'Here. This is ten minutes ago. Campion's interview technique has been to calmly move from point to point of the Norwood story, collecting answers which will be edited for sequence and time. Norwood is doing the normal amount of lip-licking, and from time to time he looks sideward to Frontiere.

There's no question that any editing program worthy of the name could turn him into a semi-invalid gamely concealing his doubts. On the other hand, it could cut all that and make him sharp as the end of a pin.'

'Colonel Norwood,' Campion's voice said, 'I'd like to follow up on that for just a moment. Now, you've just told us your flight was essentially routine until just before the explosion. But obviously you had some warning. Even an astronaut's reflexes need a little time to get him into escape mode. Could you expand on that a little? What sort of warning did you have, and how much before the explosion did it come?'

Frontiere's voice broke in. 'I think perhaps that is not something you should go into at this time, Mr Campion.'

'Why not?'

'It is simply something we ought not to discuss at this time.'

'I'd have to know more about that before I decided to drop the question.'

'Mr Campion, with all respect, I must insist. Now, please, back up your recording and erase that question.'

There was a brief silence. Campion came in speaking slowly. 'Or else our arrangement is at an end?'

Frontiere paused. 'I wish you had not brought our discussion to such a juncture.'

Campion abruptly said: 'Someday you'll have to explain this to me. All right. Okay, crew, let's roll it back to where I asked Walt about his flight path and the last word of his answer was "sea." I figure a reaction shot of me, and then I frame my next question and the out-take is completely tracked over, right? That seem good to you, Clementine? Okay, Luis, we rolling back?'

Clementine's voice came in on the director track. 'Roll to "eee." Synch. Head Campion. Roll. And.'

'That's it,' Domino said.

'That's what?' Michaelmas said. 'Frontiere hasn't chosen to let in Campion on the telemetry sender story. Can you blame him?'

'Not my point. The unit they're using does not simply feed the director's tracking tape. It also sends direct to the EVM editing computer in Paris. No erasure took place there. The segment is already edited into the rough cut of the final broadcast. Including Norwood's sudden side glance to Frontiere, Frontiere's upset manner, and all.'

Michaelmas turned his head sharply toward the window, hiding his expression in the sky. Far ahead on the right forward quarter he could see Cap Bon sliding very slowly toward the wingtip, and Tunis a white speck stabbing at his eyes in the early afternoon sun.

'He's young. It's possible he doesn't fully understand the equipment. Perhaps he thinks he did erase. It's not necessary for … for any of them to know the exact nature of the equipment.'

'Possibly. But Campion's contract with EVM specifies copy for simultaneous editing. He relinquished pre-editorial rights. In return for minimizing their production lag, he retains fact rights; he can use the same material as the basis for his own editions of byline book, cartridge, disc, or any other single-user package form known or to be developed during the term of copyright. And I assure you he went over every clause with EVM. He has a head for business.'

'You're absolutely sure?'

'I went over it right behind him. I like to keep up with what sort of contracts are being written in our field.'

'So there's no doubt he was deliberately lying to Getulio.'

'None at all, Mr Michaelmas. I'd say Campion's intention all along was to provoke something like this. He's a newsman. He smelled it out that UNAC was hiding something. He went fishing for it, and found it. When the program runs tonight, the world will know UNAC is attempting to conceal something about the shuttle accident. And of course they'll know the name of enterprising Douglas Campion.'

Michaelmas put his left fist inside his cupped right hand and stared sightlessly. He patted his knuckles into his palm. 'Did EVM come to him?'

'No. They were his last shot. He shopped around the US networks first. But all he'd tell anyone before signing a contract was that he thought he could get a Norwood exclusive and that he wanted to retain most of the ancillary rights. The responses he got were pretty low compared to his asking price. Then EVM picked him up. Gervaise filed an advisory to Paris. She said they'd had a conversation, and he was a good bet.'

'What time was that?'

'Twelve-twenty. She'd dropped you at your hotel and apparently went straight back to hers to check out. He was waiting in the hotel, hoping she'd talk to him. He'd left a message about it for her at the desk. Obviously she and he talked. She called Paris, and then EVM's legal people called him to thrash out the contract. Everything on record is just straight business regarding quote an interview with Walter Norwood endquote.'

'There was no prior agreement on slant?'

'Why should there be one? Gervaise vouched for him, and she's respected. They take what he gives them, splice in supporting matter as it comes, and the slant develops itself. It's a hot subject, a good crew on it, and, as of a few minutes ago, no doubt in the world that they're onto something that could become notorious as hell. It's a world-class performance – a sure Pulitzer for Campion plus a dozen industry awards for the crew. It's a Nobel Laureate contender for EVM. A likely winner if the year stays slow for news.'

'Well,' Michaelmas said, 'I suppose a man could lie to his contact for all that.'

He had once seen a Chinese acrobat stack straight chairs one atop the other, balancing the rear two legs of each chair atop the backrest of the one below. The bottom chair had rested on four overturned water tumblers. The acrobat had built the stack chair by chair, while standing on each topmost chair. When the stack was twelve chairs high, the acrobat did a one-hand stand on the back of the topmost chair while rotating hoops at his ankles and free wrist. Michaelmas thought of the acrobat now, seeing him with the face of Douglas Campion.

TEN

'*Viola* Hanrassy.'

The plane slid along. 'What is it, Domino?' Michaelmas palmed the bones of his face. His fingertips massaged his eyes. His thumbs pressed into his ears, trying to break some of the blockage in his Eustachian tubes.

'She's placed a call to Allen Shell. She wants a scenario for telemetry- and voice-communication skewing in Norwood's shuttle.'

'Ah.' Shell was at MIT's Research Laboratory of Electronics. 'How soon does she want it?'

'Within the hour.'

'It sounds more and more as if someone's told her a tale and she's attempting to verify it.'

'Exactly.'

'Yes.' The corners of Michaelmas's mouth pulled back into his cheeks. He pictured Shell: a short, wiry man with a long fringe of hair and a little paunch, stumbling about his apartment and making breakfast coffee. He would probably make cappuccino, assembling the ingredients and the coffee-maker clumsily, and he would take the second cup into the bathroom. Sitting on the stool with his eyes closed, sipping, he would mutter to himself in short hums through his partially compressed lips, and when he was done he would get up, find his phone where he'd left it, tell Viola Hanrassy two or three ways it might have been done undetectably, punch off, carry the empty cup and saucer to the dishwasher and very possibly drop them. Michaelmas and Shell had been classmates once. Shell had been one of the Illinois Institute of Technology students who intercepted and decoded Chicago police messages in the late 1960s, but time had passed. 'Well.' Michaelmas looked downward. Tunis was much larger, dimmer, and off to the right. The African coastline was falling away toward Libya, so that they would still be over water for some distance, but Cité d'Afrique was not too far ahead in time. He glanced at his wrist. They'd land at about 1400 hours local time, he judged.

'The Norwood interview's over,' Domino said. 'Campion did roughly the same thing a few more times. It'll be vicious when it hits.'

'Yes,' Michaelmas said ruminatively. 'Yes, I suppose it could be.' He watched the office cabin door open. The camera operator and Clementine came out. She walked with her head down, her mouth wryly twisted. She took a vacant forward seat beside her crewman and did not once glance farther up the aisle. Campion and Frontiere were lingering in the cabin doorway. Campion was thanking Frontiere, and Norwood over Frontiere's shoulder. Frontiere did not look entirely easy. When Campion turned away to come up the aisle, Frontiere firmly closed the door without letting Norwood out.

Michaelmas realized Campion was deliberately heading straight for him. Campion's features had a fine sheen on them; that faint dew was the only immediate token of his past half hour's labor. But he dropped rather hard into the seat beside Michaelmas, saying, 'I hope you don't mind,' and then sighed. He loosened his collar and arched his throat, stroking his neck momentarily between his thumb and fingers. 'Welcome to the big time, Douglas,' he said in a fatigued voice.

Michaelmas smiled softly. 'You're doing well, I hear.'

Campion turned to him. 'Coming from you, that's a real compliment.' He shook his head. 'I graduated today.' He shook his head again, leaned back, and stretched his legs out in front of him, the heels coming down audibly. He clasped his hands at the back of his head. 'It's hard, doing what we do,' he reminisced, looking up at the ceiling. 'I never really understood that. I used to think that doing what you did was going to be easy for me. I'd grown up with you. I knew every mannerism you have. I can do perfect imitations of you at parties.' He rolled his face sideward and smiled companionably. 'We all do. You know that, don't you? All us young punks.'

Michaelmas shrugged with an embarrassed smile.

Campion grinned. 'There must be ten thousand young Campions out there, still thinking that's all there is to it.'

'There is more,' Michaelmas said.

'Of course there is.' Campion nodded to the ceiling. 'There is,' he said with his right elbow just brushing the shoulder of Michaelmas's jacket. 'We're the last free people in the world, aren't we?'

'How do you mean that?'

'When I got a little older in this business, I wondered what had attracted me to it. The sophomore blahs, you know? You remember what it's like, being junior staff. Just face front and read what they give you. I used to think I was never going to get out of that. I used to think the whole world had gone to Jell-O and I was right there in the middle of it. Nothing ever happened; you'd see some movement starting up, something acting like it was going to change things in the world, and then it would peter out. Somebody'd start looking good, and then it would turn out he had more in the bank than he'd admit to, and he was allowed to graduate from his college after his father had built a new gym. Or you'd want to know more about this new government program for making jobs in the city, and it would turn out to be a real estate deal.

'You begin to realize the world had gotten too sophisticated for anything clear-cut to ever happen. And you know it's only the simple things that make heroes. Give you something to understand in a few words; let you admire something without holding back. Right? How are you going to feel that, when you're stuck in Jell-O and it's obviously just going to get thicker and thicker as time passes? If it wasn't for the hurricanes and the mining disasters, as a matter of fact, you might never know the difference between one day and the next.

'I almost got out of it then. Had an offer to go into PR on the governor's staff. Said no, finally. Once you're in that, you can't ever go back into news, you know? And I wasn't ready to cut it all the way off. I thought about how, when I was a kid, I thought Laurent Michaelmas *made* the news, because you were always where it was happening. And I said to myself, I'd give it one last all-the-way shot; I'd get up there where you were, so I wasn't just stuck in some studio or on some payroll. Be cool, Douggie, I said to myself. Act like you're on top, aim to get on top. Get up there – get out to where they have to scurry when they see you coming, and they open the doors, and they let you see what's behind them. Get out where you rub elbows and get flown places in private equipment.' Campion's eyes fastened on Michaelmas's. 'That's it,' he said softly. 'It's not getting at the news. The news doesn't mean anything. It's being a newsman. It's getting out of the Jell-O. And now we both know that.'

Michaelmas looked at him closely. 'And that's what you've come to tell me,' he said softly. 'To get my approval.'

Campion blinked. 'Well, yes, if you want to put it that way.' Then he smiled. 'Sure! Why not? I could have a worse father figure, I guess.'

'I wouldn't know about that, Douggie. But you don't need me anymore. You're a big boy now.'

Campion began to smile, then frowned a little and looked sidelong at Michaelmas. He bit his lip like a man wondering if his fly had been open all along, interwove his fingers tightly before him, stiffened his arms, turned his wrists, and cracked his knuckles. He began to say something else, then frowned again and sat staring at his outthrust hands. He stood up quickly. 'I have to cover a few things with those UNAC people,' he said, and walked over to the bar, where he asked for Perrier water and stood drinking it through white lips.

Domino said: 'Allen Shell has called Hanrassy and given her a few alternatives. One of them requires live voice from Kosmgorod and a telemetry simulating component. The hardware cannot be assembled from off-the-shelf modules. It would have to be hand-built from bin parts. I imagine a knowledgeable engineer examining one could decide where its builder had gotten his technical training and done his shopping.'

Which would be good enough for all practical political purposes. Michaelmas grunted. 'And then what happened?'

'She put in a call for Frank Daugerd of McDonnell-Douglas. He's on a fishing vacation at the Lake of the Ozaiks and has his phone holding calls, but his next check-in is due at seven AM. That will be 1400 hours at Cité d'Afrique. She's not wasting the interval. She ordered an amphibian air taxi from Lambert Field and had it dispatched down to Bagnell Dam to wait.'

'Do you think she wants a second opinion on Allen's scenario?'

'I doubt it. I think she wants Daugerd to come look at some holograms from a sweetmeat store as soon as she can get him to Cape Girardeau.'

'Yes. Indeed.'

Daugerd was the systems interfacing man for the prime contractor on the type of module Norwood had been using. Every six or eight months, he published something that made Michaelmas sit upright and begin conversing in equations with Domino. 'Well, let me see, now,' Michaelmas said. 'If she really does have holograms of the sender, then after he's confirmed it looks Soviet, there's only one more link to make. She'll have to determine whether Norwood really did find it aboard the module.'

'Yes,' Domino said bleakly. 'But she may be able to do that. Then she'll brief her legislators, and they'll go to town on it. UNAC's dead by morning, and Theron Westrum may as well pack his household goods. The clock's turned back twenty years.'

'You really see it that way?'

'Don't you?'

It could play that way, right enough. Michaelmas smiled wistfully to himself. The way the world worked, once the word was out, the effect would take on inexhaustibility. There was always not merely the event itself, but opinion of the event, and rebuttal of the opinion, and the ready charge of self-interest, and the countercharge. There was the analysis of the event, and the excavation of the root causes of the event, and the placement of the event in the correct historical context. Everyone would want to kick the can, and it would clatter over the cobblestones interminably, far from the toes of those who'd first impelled it.

There was, for instance, the whole question of whether handsome, whip-thin Wheelwright Lundigan's narrow and unexpected victory in the 1992 Presidential election had truly represented grassroots revulsion against a decade of isolationism, or whether Lundigan-Westrum had simply been a ticket with unexpectedly strong theater. Then Lundigan's fine-boned, sharp-eyed, volatile wife had shot him through the femoral artery for good but certainly not unprecedented reasons, two months into his term. So there was also some question of whether Westrum or other sinister forces had bribed, coerced, or hypnotized her into doing it. And whether One-World Westrum was Lundigan's legitimate political heir, and then, again, what Lundigan's actual politics had been, or if in fact a majority had wanted him to have them.

None of these dilemmas had ever been truly settled – certainly not by the even slimmer election of 1996, which had gone not so much to Westrum as to his mendacious promises that he'd continue the strong-Congress-weak-President tradition, some said. Others claimed arithmetical errors in the first computer-tallied national election. Few such questions in history were ever truly settled, and here they were, all right, still not rusted away, waiting to bounce round again.

For fresher echoes, if on a lesser scale, there were nearly infinite possibilities in Hanrassy's authentication of the sender story. Shell's and Daugerd's reputations, and then those of their employers, and then those of Big Academe and Big Capital, would be at stake – and highly discussable – if the engineering scenario were questioned.

But meanwhile, Gately would be one of the first to burn to get on the air again, and, as it happened, the first open mike he'd come to would belong to EVM, which already had plenty of supporting footage showing Norwood and UNAC being appropriately evasive. It might be a little difficult to preserve a lighthearted tone while commenting on that development.

And in Moscow it would first be early evening and then night as the impact built. Once again, the managers of what was unaccountably not yet the inevitable system of the future would have to stay up late. The incredibly devious and *bieskulturni* Western nations always had the advantage of daylight. Impeccable ladies and gentlemen would have to leave off playing with their fond children after supper, or would have to forego the Bolshoi. They would hurry for the Presidium chamber, there to spell out the obvious motives behind this fantastic fabrication by the rabid forces of resurgent reaction. In dignity and full consciousness of moral superiority, with the cameras and microphones recording every solemn moment of the indictment, they would let fall adjectives.

And true, Theron Westrum could forget about his so-called third term. The chances were excellent Viola Hanrassy would be the Twenty-first-century President. If that was not exactly turning back a political generation in the world, it was close enough. But in this generation the Soviets did not have so many immediate worries along their Asiatic borders to keep their pursuit of redress from being entirely single-minded. Which was a word one also applied readily to Viola. There was a hell of a lot more to her than there was to Theron, if you saw the Presidential job as defending the homestead in the forest rather than building roads to the marketplaces.

All that in the blink of an eye, Michaelmas thought. As if I had never been at all. He shook his head in wonderment. Well, there was no gainsaying it – he'd always known he was a plasterer. It would take more time than any one person was ever given to really overhaul the foundations that put the recurring cracks in the walls.

'Are you sitting there being broody again?' Domino said.

'I think I've earned the privilege.'

'Well, cash it in on your own time. What's our next move?'

Michaelmas grinned. 'First, I have to go to the lavatory,' he said with some smugness.

But Domino followed him in. 'Papashvilly,' he said.

Michaelmas fumbled the door lock shut. 'What is it?'

'That first device was just activated. The next person entering the elevator at Papashvilly's floor and selecting lobby level will have a rough ride. What has burned itself out is the circuit that damps speed as the car approaches its stop and then aligns the car door with floor level. The passenger will be jounced severely; broken bones are a good possibility.'

'What can you do?' Michaelmas worked at his clothes.

'Keep Papashvilly locked up. He hasn't found that out yet. But he will soon. Someone will come to get him.'

'What activated the device?'

'I don't know. But it happened while he was ostensibly receiving an incoming call. It was from a staffer reminding him that he was expected down in the lobby when Norwood arrives. I answered it for him, but of course no one knows that. The component burned on the word "lobby."'

'It monitored his phone calls.'

'I think so. I *think* I could design such a device; it would be a very tight squeeze.'

Michaelmas pulled up his zipper. 'So you weren't able to trace a signaler because there wasn't any, strictly speaking.'

'The staffer may be a conspirator,' Domino said dubiously. 'I've checked his record. It looks clean.'

'So what they've done is mined everything around Pavel, set to trigger from expectable routine events, and any one of them could plausibly cripple or kill. Sooner or later, they'll get him. And never be known, or found. That's good technology.' He rinsed the soap from his hands.

'Yes.'

Michaelmas shook his head. He dried his hands in the air jet, stopping while they were still a little damp and wiping his face with them. 'Well, hold the fort as best you can. I'm thinking hard. So many things to keep track of,' he said. 'I'm glad I have you.'

'Would sometimes that I had a vote in the matter. Button your coat.'

When he emerged, Michaelmas said, 'Look sharp' to Domino, and moved down the aisle toward the office. He passed quickly beyond Clementine's seat. The same press aide who had let him slip down the corridor at Limberg's now rose smoothly from the lounge nearest the office door. 'Mr Michaelmas,' he smiled. 'Signor Frontiere is in a brief meeting with Colonel Norwood. May I help you with something meanwhile?'

Michaelmas said: 'UNAC hospitality is always gracious. I'm quite comfortable, thank you.' He relaxed against the partition, and he and the aide
exchanged pleasantries for a few score miles. Domino's terminal hung from
Michaelmas's shoulder and rested flush against the bulkhead. 'Harry Beloit,'
the aide was saying, 'but I'm from Madison. My dad taught Communications
at Wisconsin, and I guess it just crept into me over the dinner table.' Inside
the office, Norwood was saying in an insufficiently puzzled tone: 'Maybe I
don't understand, Getulio. But I think we should have told Campion the
whole story. Hell, he's not going to be out with it until tonight. By then there's
not going to be any doubt where that component came from.'

Frontiere took a noticeably deep breath: 'By then we will not know any
more than who *seems* to have made the thing. We won't know who installed
it, what they represent, or why they did it. There are many more doubts than
facts, and—'

'Oh, yes, I get back as often as I can: especially in the fall. I go out to Hori-
con Marsh and watch the waterfowl gathering. Pack a lunch, bring along my
favorite pipe, just sit with the wife on a blanket and try to teach the kids the
difference between a teal and a canvasback, you know.'

'—ulio, look, the only way all of these doubts of yours make sense is if they
expected it *not* to work. You follow me? If whoever did it was counting on my
turning up with the part in my hand. I don't think they could have been
counting on that. I think they expected me and it to be all blown away. So I
think the people who did it are the people who look like they did it, you
know?'

'They fly altogether differently. You can tell from the wingbeats when
they're just coming into sight. My dad showed me.'

'I've run a stress analysis on Norwood's voice. There's the overlay of irrita-
tion, of course. But he's sincere. He's completely relaxed with himself: knows
who he is, what he's saying, what's right, and he's right.'

'That may all be, but it is not conclusive, nevertheless. We are not going to
destroy UNAC and perhaps a great deal more on the basis of a supposition.
Now, in a few moments, unless I can delay long enough, you'll be speaking
with Laurent Michaelmas, whom you would not be advised to underesti-
mate, and—'

'Canada geese. They're altogether different; they're bigger, they beat slower.
You know, by and large, the bigger the bird is, the less often it beats its wings.
Sometimes I think that if you could see a pteranodon coming in out of the
west at dusk, silhouetted against the sun, first you'd pick up the dot of its
body, and then gradually you'd see little dark stubs growing out one to each
side, as you began picking up the profile of the wings, and they'd never move.
It would just get bigger and pick up more definition, and you'd see those
motionless wings just extending themselves farther and farther out to the

side, completely silent, just getting closer like it was riding a string from the top of the sky right to the bridge of your—'

'I don't think I have to make these estimates. I'm an engineer, and I ran all the tests you'd want on that component. Now, I'm military, and I understand following orders, and I hope I'm capable of grasping big pictures. But there's no way you're going to get me to change my opinion on what it all means. Now, I know it's a big God-damned disappointment to you, and maybe a lot of the rest of the world, and maybe even to me. Pavel and I are good buddies, and this whole idea's had a lot of promise. But I just don't see it any way except that the boys in Moscow said, "All right, that's long enough playing nice and catching our breath, now let's go back to doing business in the good old-fashioned way." And I don't think it matters what you'd like to think, or I'd like to think, or how many good buddies we've got all over the world, I think we've got to face up to what really was done, and I think we've got to go from there. And damned quick.'

'Nevertheless, until superior authority tells you what is to be done—'

'Yes, sir, for as long as I'm detailed to serve under that authority, that's exactly correct.'

'Signals. You know, everything that lives is constantly sending out signals. My dad pointed that out to me. It's how animals teach and control their young, it's how they mate, it's how they move in groups from place to place. They've got these fantastic vocabularies of movement, cry, and odor. Any member of any species knows them all. It can recognize its own kind when you'd swear there was nothing out there, and it knows immediately whether that other creature is sick or well, at rest or frightened, feeding or searching, or whatever.'

'Mr Michaelmas, he's going to resign and talk if he gets no satisfaction.'
'Yes.'

'They know all of that about each other all the time. I guess that's about all there is to know in this world, really. Seems a shame the animal that signals the most seems to need individuals like me to help it along, and even so—'

'Even so,' Michaelmas said. 'Even so, we're the only animal whose signals can't be trusted by its own kind.' He smiled. 'Except for thee and me, of course.'

Harry Beloit smiled with awkward kinship. Then the plane tilted and he glanced out a window. 'We'll be in the Afrique approach pattern in a few moments,' he said. 'I'm sorry – it seems as if Signor Frontiere's and Colonel Norwood's conference took longer than expected.'

'No matter,' Michaelmas said equably. 'I'll catch them in the limousine.' He waved a hand gently and turned. 'Ours was a pleasant conversation.' He moved up the aisle until he reached Clementine. Putting one buttock on the armrest of the seat across the aisle, he smiled at her. She had been sitting with her eyes down, her lips a little pursed and grim. 'A pleasant flight?' he said politely.

Domino snorted.

Clementine looked up at Michaelmas. 'It's a very comfortable aircraft.'

'How do you find working with Campion?'

She raised an eyebrow. 'One is a professional.' It had very much been not the sort of question one is asked.

'Of course,' Michaelmas said. 'I don't doubt it. Since this morning I've made it my business to look into your career. Your accomplishments bear out my personal impression.'

She smiled with a touch of the wistful. 'Thank you. It's a day-to-day thing, however, isn't it? You can't remain still if you wish to advance.'

He smiled. 'No. No, of course not. But you seem well situated. A very bright star in a rapidly growing organization, and now in one day you have credits with me and with a rising personality, both on a major story ...'

'Yes, he is rising overnight,' Clementine said, unconsciously jerking her head toward the back of the plane. 'Not a Campion but a mushroom,' she said in French.

Michaelmas smiled. Then he giggled. He found he could not control it. Little tears came to his eyes. Domino said, 'Stop that! Good heavens!'

Clementine was staring at him, her hand masking her mouth, her own shoulders shaking. 'Incredible! You look like the little boy when the schoolmaster trips.'

He still could not bring himself to a halt. 'But you, my dear, are the one who soaped the steps.'

They laughed together, as decorously as possible, until they had both run down and sat gasping. It was incredible how relieved Michaelmas felt. He was completely unconcerned that people up the aisle were staring at them, or that Luis, the camera operator, sat beside Clementine stiffly looking out the window like a gentleman diner overhearing a jest between waiters.

Finally, Clementine dabbed under her eyes with the tips of her fingers and began delving into her purse. She said: 'Ah. Ah, Laurent, nevertheless,' more soberly now, 'this afternoon there's been something I could have stopped. You'll see it tonight and say, "Here something was done that she could surely have interrupted, if she weren't so professional."' She opened her compact and touched her cheeks with a powder pad. She looked up and sideward at Michaelmas. 'But it's not professional of me to say so. We have shocked Luis.'

The camera operator's lip twitched. He continued to stare out his window with his jaw in his palm. 'I do not listen to private conversations,' he said correctly. 'Especially not about quick-witted people who instruct in technique to something they call "crew."'

Michaelmas grinned. '*Viva* Luis,' he said softly. He put his hand on Clementine's wrist and said: 'Whatever was done – do you think it serves the truth?'

'Oh, the truth, yes,' Clementine said.

'She means it,' Domino said. 'She's a little elevated, but simple outrage would account for that. There's no stab of guilt.'

'Yes, her pulse didn't change,' Michaelmas said to him, bending over Clementine's hand to make his farewell. He said to her: 'Ah, well, then, whatever else there is, is bearable. I had best sit down somewhere now.' Campion would be back down here in a minute, ready to discuss what was to be done as soon as they landed. *'Au revoir.'*

'Certainement.'

'Daugerd checked his phone early,' Domino said. 'It's a terrible day for fishing; pouring rain. He's returned Hanrassy's call; she had something that needs his professional appraisal. He's running his bass boat down to the Bagnell Dam town landing to meet that plane of hers. Bass boats are fast. His ETA at her property will be something like seven-forty her time – about half an hour after you deplane at Cité d'Afrique.'

Michaelmas touched his lips to the back of Clementine's hand, feeling the fragility of the bones, and moved up the aisle. Campion watched him warily.

'Sincere, you say,' Michaelmas said to Domino as he dropped into a seat. 'Norwood.'

'Absolutely. I wish I had that man's conscience.'

'Do you suppose,' Michaelmas ventured, 'that something is bringing in people from a parallel world? Eh?' He stared out the window, his jaw in his palm, as the coast slid below them. The Mediterranean was not blue but green like any other water, and the margins of the coast were so rumpled into yellow shallows and bars that on this surfless day it was almost impossible to decide whether they would fall on land or water. 'You know the theory? Every world event produces alternative outcomes? There is a world in which John Wilkes Booth missed and Andrew Johnson was never President, so there was much less early clamor for threatening Nixon with impeachment? So he didn't name Jerry Ford, but someone else, instead? The point being that Lincoln never knew he was dead, and Ford never dreamed he'd been President.'

'I know that concept,' Domino said shortly. 'It's sheer anthropomorphism.'

'Hmm. I suppose. Yet he *is* sincere, you tell me.'

'Hold his hand.'

Michaelmas smiled off-center. 'He's dead.'

'How?'

The landing warnings came on. Michaelmas adjusted his seat and his belt.

'I don't know, friend … I don't know,' he mused. He continued to stare out the window as the plane settled lower with its various auxiliaries whining and thumping. The wings extended their flaps and edge-fences in great sooty pinions; coronal discharges flickered among the spiny deperturbance rakes. 'I don't know … but then, if God had really intended Man to think, He would have given him brains, I suppose.'

'Oh, wow,' Domino said.

They swept in over the folded hills that protected Cité d'Afrique from serious launch pad errors at Star Control. To Michaelmas's right, the UNAC complex was a rigid arrangement pile-driven into the desert; booster sheds, pads, fuel dumps, guidance bunkers, and the single prismatic tower where UNAC staff dwelled and sported and took the elevators down or up to their offices or the lobby. The structures seemed isolated: menhirs erected on a plain once green, now the peculiar lichenous shade of scrubby desert, very much like the earliest television color pictures of the Moon. These were connected to each other by animal trails which were in fact service roads, bound to the hills by the highway cutting straight for Cité d'Afrique, and, except for that white and sparsely traveled lifeline, adrift – probably clockwise, like the continent itself. Beyond it there was only a browning toward sand and a chasming toward sky, and Saint-Exupéry flying, flying, straining his ears to filter out the sound of the slipstream in his guy wires, listening only to the increasingly harsh sound of engine valves laboring under a deficiency of lubricating oil, wiping his goggles impatiently and peering over the side of the cockpit for signs of life.

Michaelmas looked down at his quiescent hands.

Now they were over the hills, and then the ground dropped sharply. Cité d'Afrique opened before them. The sunlight upon it was like the scimitars of Allah. It was all a tumble of shahmat boards down there: white north surfaces, all other sides energy-absorbent black, metallized glass lancing reflections back at catcher panels, louvers, shadow banners, clash of metal chimes, street cries, robed men like knights, limousine horns, foreigners moving diagonally, the bazaar smell newly settled into recently wet mortar but not quite yet victorious over aldehydes outbaking from the plastics, and Konstantinos Cikoumas. Michaelmas saw him as a tall, cadaverous, round-eyed, open-mouthed man in a six-hundred-dollar suit and a grocer's apron with a screwdriver in its bib pocket. He did not see where Cikoumas was or what he was doing at the moment, and he could not guess what the man thought.

They had made Cité d'Afrique in no longer than it takes to pull the UN out of New York and decree a new city. Not as old as the youngest of sheikhs, it was the new cosmopolitan center. Its language was French because the men with hawk faces knew French as the diplomatic and banking language of the world, but it was not a French city, and its interests were not confined to those of Africa. It was, the UN expected, a harbinger of a new world. Eloquent men had ventured to say that only by making a place totally divorced from nationalistic pressures could the United Nations function as required, and so they had moved here.

Michaelmas asked Domino: 'What's the situation at the terminal?'

'There's a fair amount of journalist activity. They have themselves set up at the UNAC gate. You hired the best local crew, and they know the ropes, so they're situated at a good angle. EVM has a local man there to shoot backup footage of Norwood debarking. Then there are UNAC people at the gate, of course, to welcome Norwood, although none of them are very high up the ladder, and there are curious members of the public – mostly UN personnel and diplomats who got early word Norwood was coming in by this route. And so forth.'

'Very good. Uh, we may be calling upon your Don't Touch circuit sometime along in there.'

'Oh, really?' Domino said.

'Yes. I believe I have taken an instructive lesson from the Ecole Psychologique of Marseilles. Other topic: Do you have a scan on where Konstantinos Cikoumas lives?'

'Certainly. A nice modern apartment with a view of the sea. Nothing exceptional in it. Nothing like the stuff planted all over Star Control. But then, why should they risk Kosta's ever being tied to any exotic machinery that might accidentally be found in the vicinity? He and his brother are honest merchants, after all, and who's to ever say different? Kristiades called him this afternoon, by the way. At about the time we left Berne. A routine talk concerning almonds. It doesn't yield to cryptanalysis. But the fact of the call itself may be his way of saying Norwood's enroute, meaning there'll be plenty of press to cover any accidents to Papashvilly.'

'You'd think,' Michaelmas grumbled, 'UNAC might look more deeply at who comes and goes through Star Control.'

'They do. They think they do. But they don't think in terms of this sort of attack. They think in terms of someone ripping off souvenirs or trying to sell insurance; maybe an occasional lone flat-Earther; maybe someone who'd like to be an ardent lover. Look what they've done – they've put Papashvilly in his own apartment, which they consider is secure, which it is, and fully private, and they've left him alone. He's playing belly-dance recordings and drinking Turkish coffee, oblivious as a lamb.'

Michaelmas snorted. 'He eats lamb. But something's got to be done; they're piling trash all around my ability to concentrate.' He blinked vigorously, sitting up in his seat, and rubbed his eyes, now that he'd remembered himself. He felt the taste of verdigris far back on his tongue, and growled softly to himself. Except that Domino overheard it, of course. There is no Goddamned *privacy!* he thought. None whatever. Any day now, he decided, Domino's receptor in his skull would begin being able to receive harmonics from his brain electrical activity, and then it would be just a matter of time before they became readable. *Merde!* he cried in his mind, and hurled something down a long, narrowing dark hallway. 'All right. Are you sure you've found all the little gimmicks around Papashvilly?'

'I've swept the main building, and everything else Papashvilly might approach. I'm fairly certain I have them. I don't understand,' Domino said peevishly, 'where they got so many of them, or who thought of them, or why this technique. It seems to me they'd want to plant one good bomb and get it over with.'

'Not if what they want to kill is the whole idea of effective astronautics. They don't want isolated misfortunes. They want a pattern of wrangling and doubt. They want to roil up the world's mind on the subject. Damn them, they're trying to gnaw the twentieth century to death. They just don't want us poking around the Solar System. Their Solar System? Any ideas along those lines?'

'I believe they are the descendants of the lost Atlantean civilization,' Domino said. 'Returning from their former interstellar colonies and battling for their birthright. It seems only fair.'

'Very good. Now, the gadgets. Do you understand what each of those gadgets could do?'

'I think so. There's a nearly infinite variety. Some will start fires and cut off the adjacent heat sensors simultaneously. Others will most likely do things such as overloading Papashvilly's personal car steering controls – at a moderate speed if you're right, at a higher one if you're not. The elevator you know about. There's something I think will cut out the air-conditioning to his block of flats, probably at the same time the night-heater thermostat over-sets. If I were doing it, that would also be the time the fire doors all dropped shut, sealing off that wing with him inside it, at, say, 110 degrees Fahrenheit. Should I go on?'

'That will do for samples. Are all of these pieces wired into the building circuits?'

'All that aren't concerned with free-standing machinery like the car. They're all perfect normal-acting components – with a plus.'

'All right. I've been thinking. You could trip them, couldn't you? You tested that elevator part.'

'Right,' Domino said slowly. 'I could. Use the building systems to give 'em an overload jolt of current. That would fry 'em as surely as their own triggers could.'

Michaelmas steepled his fingertips. 'Well, that's all right, then. How's this for a sequence: At the appropriate time, Pavel gets a call to come down to the lobby. You let his door open. He goes out in the hall, and the tampered elevator won't open its doors; you can do that through the normal systems. So he has to take another. Make sure it's a clean one. Meanwhile, you're tidying up behind him. As soon as he clears each problem area, you blow each of the gimmicks in it. By the time he's down to ground level, the building will be safe for him. A little disarranged, but safe. A priority repair order to the garage systems ties up his car, should he get it into his head to go for a spin. Et cetera. Good scenario?'

Domino made a peculiar noise. 'Oh, my, yes. Can do. When do you want it?'

'When appropriate. UNAC will surely call him to come down when Norwood is almost there. Initiate it then.'

'All right.'

'And Konstantinos Cikoumas. Let him get a call from a UNAC function-ary right away, inviting him to join the greeters at the airport gate.'

'No problem.'

'Excellent. He has plenty of gates and things to pass through as he approaches the debarking ramp, right? Heat locks, friskers, and so forth.'

'It's a hot country. And it's an ultramodern airport, yes.'

'Make sure he has no difficulty arriving at the last gate exactly on time, will you?'

'No problem. He's already left his apartment; I'm monitoring his cab's dis-patch link. And I can help or hinder with the traffic signals.'

'There, now,' Michaelmas said with a sigh. 'Remember, he's coming through the last gate as Norwood arrives.'

'Absolutely.' Domino made the noise again; this time, he seemed to man-age it a little better.

Michaelmas ignored it. He took a deep breath and settled back in his seat. 'Pillar to post,' he muttered. 'Pillar to post.'

The plane flared out past the outer marker, and Michaelmas folded his hands loosely in his lap. In a few moments it was down, tires thumping as the thin air marginally failed to provide a sufficient cushion. There were the usual roarings and soft cabin chimes, and surging apparent alterations in the dir-ection his body wanted to go. There was a sharp change in the smell of the cabin as the air-conditioning sucked in the on-shore breeze, chilled it, and the relative humidity rose thirty percent in an instant.

'Frank Daugerd is airborne from the Lake of the Ozarks,' Domino said. 'His pilot has filed an ETA of 07:35, their time. That's thirty-three minutes from now.'

'And then ... let's see ...' Michaelmas rubbed his nose; his sinuses were stuffed. He grimaced and counted it up in his head: the touchdown on the Mississippi, floats pluming the water, and the drift down to the landing. The waiting USA staffer with the golf cart, and the silent, gliding run from the landing up the winding crushed-shell drive to the east portico; the doors opening, and Daugerd disappearing inside, hunched and busy, still wearing his fishing vest and hat, probably holding his hand over the bowl of his pipe; the conversation with Hanrassy, the bending over the table, the walking around the holograms, the snap decision and then the thoughtful review of the decision, the frowning, the looking closer, and then, for good and all, the nod of confirmation, the farewell handshake with Hanrassy, the departure from the room, and Hanrassy reaching for her telephone. 'Ten minutes? Fifteen? Between the time he lands at her dock and the time she reacts to a confirmation?'

'Yes,' Domino said. 'That's how I count it. Adding it all up, fifty minutes from now, all she'll have left to do is call Gately and have him call Norwood. He gets through where she couldn't, he asks Norwood the direct question, Norwood gives the direct answer, Gately's back on the phone to Hanrassy, and Bob's your uncle. One hour from now, total, it's all over.'

'Ah, if men had the self-denial of Suleiman the Wise,' Michaelmas said, 'to flask the clamorous djinns that men unseal.'

'What's *that* from?'

'From me. I just made it up. These things come to my mind. Isn't it bloody awful?' He winced; his voice seemed to echo through the back of his neck and rebound from the inner surfaces of his eardrums. The price of wit.

A cabin attendant said nasally over the PA: 'We shall be at the UNAC deplaning area shortly. Please retain your seats until we have come to a complete stop.'

Michaelmas unclenched his hands, opened his seatbelt, rose, and moved deftly down the aisle. He passed between Campion and Clementine, and dropped lightly into the forward seat beside Harry Beloit. 'I'll just want a word with Getulio before we get into all the bustle at the terminal,' he said. 'That'll be possible, won't it?' He smiled engagingly.

Beloit returned the smile. 'No problem.' He understood. Whatever Michaelmas might say to Getulio at this point was irrelevant. The famous newsman simply needed a reason to be with Frontiere at the deplaning, since Norwood would also be kept in close proximity, and therefore all three of them would be on camera together at the arrival gate. That would include Campion's camera. There was such a thing as giving ground in a statesmanly manner while the plane was in the air and Campion had first call on the astronaut's time. There was another thing entirely in being upstaged before the world.

Beloit smiled again, fondly. Even the greatest were as transparent as children, and he clearly loved them for it.

Michaelmas's head cocked and turned as he peered through the windows at the approaching terminal buildings; he felt the reassuring rumble of wheels on concrete, and his eyes sparkled.

'How much Don't Touch are we going to need?' Domino was saying to him.

'Just enough to twitch a muscle,' Michaelmas replied. 'On request or on the word "crowded."'

' "Crowded." Good enough,' Domino said. 'Are you sure you don't want to go heavier than that?'

Every so often, the idly curious person or the compulsive gadget-tryer wandered over to where the terminal might be lying, and began poking at it. A measured amount of this was all to the good, but it was not something to be encouraged. There were also occasional times when the prying was a little more purposeful, although of course one did not lightly ascribe base motives to one's fellow news practitioners. And conceivably there might be a time when the sternest measures were required.

The terminal operated on six volts DC, but it incorporated an oscillator circuit that leaked into the metal case when required to do so. It was possible to deliver a harmless little thrum, followed by Michaelmas's solicitous apology for the slight malfunction. It was also possible to throw someone, convulsive and then comatose, to the floor. In such cases, more profuse reaction from Michaelmas and a soonest-possible battery replacement were required.

'It will do.'

'But if you're going to topple Norwood on camera, you'll want the effect to be dramatic. You'll want to make sure the world can readily decide he isn't really one hundred percent sound.'

'We are not here to trick the world into an injustice,' Michaelmas said, 'nor to excessively distress a sincere man. Please do as I say, when said.'

'At times you're difficult to understand.'

'Well, there's good and bad in that.' Michaelmas's gaze had returned to Harry Beloit. He smiled at Harry fondly.

ELEVEN

Michaelmas and Frontiere stood watching the approach of the umbilical corridor from the gate. 'Is it going well?' Michaelmas asked politely.

Frontiere glanced aside at Norwood, who was chatting casually with some of the UNAC people while Luis worked his camera, and then at Campion, who was close behind Luis's shoulder. 'Oh, yes, it's fine,' he said.

Michaelmas smiled faintly. 'My sympathies. May I ride to Star Control in the same vehicle with you and Norwood?'

'Certainly. We are all going in an autobus in any case; we are very proud of the latest Mercedes, which incorporates a large number of our accumulator patents. Accordingly, we have a great many of the vehicles here, and use them at every opportunity, including the photographable ones.' Frontiere's thinned lips twisted at the corners. 'It was my suggestion. I work indefatigably on my client's behalf.' He glanced at Campion again. 'Perhaps a little too much sometimes.'

Michaelmas clapped him on the shoulder. 'Be at your ease, Getulio. You are an honest man, and therefore invulnerable.'

'Please do not speak in jest, my friend. There is a faint smell here, and I am trying to convince myself none of it comes from me.'

'Ah, well, things often right themselves if a man only has patience.' Michaelmas caught Clementine's eye as she stood back beyond Campion and Luis. She had been watching Campion steer Luis's elbow. Michaelmas smiled at her, and she shook her head ruefully at him. He winked, and turned back to Frontiere. 'Have you heard from Ossip? How are the verification tests on the sender?'

Frontiere shrugged. 'I have not heard. He was only about an hour ahead of us in bringing it here. The laboratory will be proceeding carefully.'

Norwood's voice rose a little. He was making planar patterns in the air, his hands flattened, and completing a humorous anecdote from his test-flying days. His eyes sparkled, and his head was thrown back youthfully. You'd trust your life's savings to him. 'Very carefully,' Frontiere said at Michaelmas's shoulder, 'if they hope to contradict him convincingly.'

'Cheer up, Getulio,' Michaelmas said. 'The workmanship only looks Russian. In fact, it comes from a small Madagascan supplier of Ukrainian descent whose total output is pledged to the Laccadive Antiseparatist Crusade. Or in fact the false voice transmissions did not come from Kosmgorod. No, by coincidence they emanated from an eight-armed amateur radio hobbyist just arriving from Betelgeuse in its space-time capsule. It has no interest in this century or the next, and is enroute to setting up as a god in pre-Columbian Peru.'

'Right,' Domino said.

The umbilical arrived at the aircraft hatch and locked on. A cabin attendant pushed open the door. Michaelmas took a deep, surreptitious breath. The little interlude between taxiing to the pad and the arrival of the corridor had ended. Frontiere shook his head at Michaelmas. 'Come along, Laurent,' he said. 'I wish I had your North American capacity for humor.' They moved into the diffused pale lighting and the cold air.

Waiting for them was the expected thicket of people who really had no business being there, as well as those with credentials or equally plausible excuses. They were being held back behind yielding personnel barriers, and up to now they had stood in more or less good order, rubbing expensively-clad shoulders discreetly, each conscious of dignity and place, each chatting urbanely with the next.

But when the debarking corridor doors opened, they forgot. They became fixated on the slim man with the boy face, and there was nothing tailoring or other forms of sophistication could do about that.

Norwood. It was, indeed, Norwood. Ah.

They moved forward, and where the barriers stopped them, they unhooked them automatically, without looking, staring straight ahead.

'On your diagonal right,' Domino said, and Michaelmas broke off staring at the welcomers and looked. A tall, cadaverous young man in an Alexandria-tailored yellow suit was coming through the second of the automatic clamshell doors into the area. His large, round brown eyes were sparkling. He strode boldly, and he had his thumbs hooked into the slash pockets of his weskit. 'Cikoumas.'

'Bust him,' Michaelmas said.

The doors nipped the hurrying young man's heel. He cried out and pitched forward, arms flailing. His attempt to get at least one elbow down did not succeed; his nose struck heavily into the stiff pile of the carpeting. He struggled facedown, cursing, one foot held high between the doors, but only a security guard moved toward him with offers of assistance and promises of infirmary. He was, after all, at the back of the crowd.

Brisk in the air-conditioning, jockeying for position, the aircraft passengers proceeded to the gate, where cameras, microphones and dignitaries did their work, but not as smoothly as the UNAC press people, who lubricated the group through its passage toward the ground-vehicle dock. Camera crews eddied around the main knot of movement. 'The dignified gentleman with the rimless glasses is Mr Raschid Samir, your director,' Domino said. Mr Samir was directing general shots of Michaelmas debarking with Norwood and Frontiere. He had an economy of movement and a massive imperturbability which forced others to work around him as if he were a rock in the rapids. 'He will follow you to Star Control with the crew truck and await instructions.'

Michaelmas nodded. 'Right. Good.' As they moved out of the terminal building proper, he was concentrating on his position in the crowd while plotting all the vectors on Norwood. Two crews at the nearer end of the dock were covering most of one side of the astronaut as he strode along, grinning and still shaking hands with some of the local UNAC people. Frontiere was staying close to him, thus blanketing most of his right flank. Other camera positions or live observers were covering the other approach angles almost continuously. Michaelmas stepped sideward in relation to a group of press aides moving along beside Campion and Clementine. While they masked him from forward view, he shifted the strap of the terminal from his left shoulder into his hand, and then stepped behind a dockside pillar. The bus was there, snugged into its bay, white and black, the roof chitinous with accumulators, the windows polarized, the doors folding open now while the party rippled to a halt. Norwood half turned, directly in front of Michaelmas, almost in the doorway, tossing a joke back over his shoulder, one hand on an upright metal stanchion, as the group narrowed itself down to file in. Michaelmas was chatting with a press aide. 'We're crowded here, aren't we?' he remarked, and laid a corner of the dangling terminal up against Norwood's calf muscle just below the back of the knee, so gently, so surely, so undetectably that he half expected to hear the pang of a harmonic note. But instead Norwood sagged just a little on that side before his hand suddenly gripped the stanchion whitely, and his toe kicked the step riser. His eyes widened at betrayal. He moved on, and in, and sat down quickly in the nearest of the individual swiveling armchairs. As the bus filled and closed, and then rolled out through the insulated gates, Michaelmas could see him chatting and grinning but flexing the calf again and again, as if it were a sweet wife who'd once kissed a stranger. I could have done worse by you, Michaelmas thought, but it was nevertheless unpleasant to watch the trouser fabric twitching.

The bus rolled smoothly along the ramps among the towers, aiming for the hills and then Star Control. 'Would you like to speak to Norwood now?' Frontiere asked, leaning across the aisle. 'We will arrive at quarter to three, so there is half an hour.'

Michaelmas shook his head. 'No, thank you, Getulio,' he smiled, making himself look a little wan. 'I think I'll rest a bit. It's been a long day. I'll catch him later.'

'You look tired,' Frontiere agreed, annoyingly.

Michaelmas cocked an eyebrow. 'Let Campion continue to interview him. There must be one or two things he would still like to know.'

Frontiere winced. 'Listen,' he said softly, 'you say Campion has a good reputation?'

'I say, and so do others whose judgment I respect. He has a fine record for aggressive newsgathering.'

Frontiere nodded to himself, faintly, wryly, and grunted. 'Somehow, that's small comfort.'

'It's the best I can do,' Michaelmas said. Down the aisle, Clementine had turned her seat to form a conversational group with Luis and Campion. Campion was talking intently. Clementine was responding and gesturing, her hands held forward and curved inward to describe shots, in the manner that made all directors resemble Atlas searching for a place to rest his burden. Luis sat back, his arms folded across his chest. Michaelmas reclined lower in his seat. 'I would like to see Papashvilly as soon as possible after we reach Control. My crew chief is Mr Raschid Samir, and he'll be arriving by truck at the same time.'

'Yes, that's arranged. Pavel is waiting for you. He says to meanwhile tell you the story about the aardvark and Marie Antoinette.'

'It's the same as the story about the aardvark and Isadora Duncan, except that the Isadora Duncan version is better, since she is wearing a long scarf at the time.'

'Ah.'

'And could you let me know if you hear from Ossip about the sender?'

'On the instant.'

'*Grazie.*' Michaelmas settled his head deeper between the sound-absorbent wings of his chair and closed his eyes.

Domino said: 'The joke about the aardvark and Isadora Duncan is the same as the joke about the aardvark and Annie Oakley, except that Annie is firing a Sharps repeating carbine.'

'Granted,' Michaelmas said absently. He was comfortable and relaxed, and remembering Pavel Papashvilly in the back room of a chophouse around the corner from Cavanaugh's, down on lower Eighth Avenue, after a recording at Lincoln Center.

'Cosmonautics and culture,' Papashvilly was saying, leaning back on a fauteuil with his arm lightly across the shoulders of a member of the corps de ballet, 'how allied!' The footage had been of Papashvilly at *Coppelia*, first walking at night like a demon of the steppes among the floodlit fountains of the plaza, afraid of nothing, a meter and a half in height, eyes flickering with reflections, grinning. The pause at the great glass doors, the head tilted upward, and the photosensitive mechanism swinging them apart without further human intervention. Now the click of heels on marble gave way to orchestrated music, and the opening credits and title came up. Then at the performance he had smiled and oohed and aahed, hands elevated and tracing patterns in the air, and he had stood and applauded and shouted. Now he passed a palm delicately along wispy fabric at the dancer's pale shoulder. 'What thin partitions,' he murmured, winking at Michaelmas. He laughed, the dancer gave him a knowing sidelong look, and they all three had a little more steak and lobster and some more Rhine wine. 'That will be a good thing, this program,' Pavel said. 'This is a good thing, this visit. I know you American people are disappointed about Walter.' He paused and took a sip, his lips pressed hard against the rim of the glass, his eyes looking off into a dimmer corner of the little room. 'It was a stupid, needless thing, whatever happened. We are not after all any longer doing things for the first or second time, correct? But it is now for an understanding to be made that he and I and all the others, we are for all the people.' He put the glass down and considered. 'And we are from all the people,' he had added, and Michaelmas had smiled a little crookedly. When he had seen the dancer's hand on Pavel's thigh, he had excused himself and gone home.

The UNAC bus passed from the last tangle of feeder ramps and entered the straightline highway into the hills. There was no speed limit on this road; the passenger chairs moved a little on their gymbals as the acceleration built. A nearly inaudible singing occurred in Michaelmas's ear; something in the system somewhere was cycling very near the frequency he and Domino used between him and the terminal. A mechanic had failed to lock some service hatch. Noise leaked out of the propulsion bay. Michaelmas grimaced and ground his teeth lightly.

Coarse, scoured, and ivory-colored in the sun beyond the windows, the foothills rose under the toned blue of the sky.

Norwood had stopped fussing with his leg. But he had also stopped being so animated, and was sitting with one corner of his lip pulled into his teeth, thoughtfully.

There had been a time a little later in the US tour, at a sports-car track in the gravel hills of eastern Long Island. Rudi Cherpenko had been conducting some tire tests, and offered Papashvilly a ride if he had time. UNAC had thought it a fine idea, if Michaelmas or someone of that stature would cover it. Pavel had taken once around the track to learn how to drift and how to steer with the accelerator, and half around to learn how to brake and to deduce good braking points, and by then his adrenaline was well up. He went around five times more; he could be seen laughing and shouting in the cockpit as he drilled past the little cluster of support vehicles. When he was finally flagged off, he came in flushed and large-eyed, trembling. 'Oy ah!' he had shouted, vaulting out of the cockpit. '*Jiesus Maria*, what a thing this is to do!' He jumped at Cherpenko. They guffawed and embraced, slamming their

hands down between each other's shoulder-blades with the car's engine ping-
ing and contracting beside them as it cooled. Yet Michaelmas had caught the
onset of sobriety in Papashvilly's eyes. He was laughing and shaking his head,
but when he saw that Michaelmas was seeing the change in him, he returned
a little flicker of a rueful smile.

Late that night in the rough-timbered bar of the Inn, with Cherpenko
asleep in his room because of the early schedule, and the crew people off raising hell on Shelter Island, Papashvilly had sat staring out the window, beyond
the reflection of their table candle, and beyond the silhouettes of docked
cabin boats. Michaelmas had listened.

'It is an intoxication,' Papashvilly had begun. As he went on, his voice
quickened whenever he pictured the things he talked about, slowed and
lowered when he explained what they meant. 'It takes hold.'

Michaelmas smiled. 'And you are back in the days of George the
Resplendent?'

Papashvilly turned his glance momentarily sideward at Michaelmas. He
laughed softly. 'Ah, George Lasha of the Bagratid Empire. Yes, a famous figure. No, I think perhaps I go back farther than eight hundred years. You call
me Georgian. In the Muscovite language, I am presumed a Gruzian. Certain
careless speakers from my geographic area yet refer to Sakartvelo, the united
kingdom. Well, some of us are very ambitious. And I cannot deny that in my
blood there is perhaps some trace of the great Kartlos, and that I am of the
eastern kingdom, that is, a Kartvelian.'

He was drinking gin, as an experiment. He raised his glass, wrinkled his
nose, swallowed and smiled at the window. 'There have been certain intrusions on the blood since even long before the person you call Alexsandr the
Great came with his soldiers to see if it was true about the golden fleece,
when Sakartvelo was the land of Colchis. I am perhaps a little Mingrelian, a
little Kakhetian, a little Javakhete, a little Mongol ...' He put his hand out flat,
thumb and palm down, and trembled it slightly. 'A little of this and that.' He
closed his fist. 'But my mother told me on her knee that I am an Ossete of the
high grassy pastures, and we were there before anyone spoke or wrote of any
other people in those highlands. We have never relinquished them. No, not
to the Turks, not to Timur the Lame and his elephants, nor to the six-legged
Mongols. It was different, of course, in the lowlands, though those are stout
men.' He nodded to himself. 'Stout men. But they had empires and relinquished them.'

He put down his glass again and held it as if to keep it from rising, while
he looked at it inattentively. 'To the south of us is a flood of stone – the mountain, Ararat, and the Elburz, and Iran, and Karakorum, and Himalaya. To the
north of us is the grass that rolls from the eastern world and breaks against
the Urals. To the east and west of us are seas like walls; it is the grass and

stone that toss us on their surf. Hard men from the north seek Anatolia and the fat sultanates. Hard men from the south seek the Khirgiz pasturage and the back door to Europe. Two thousand years and more we clung to our passes and raided from our passes, becoming six-legged in our turn, until the sultans tired, and until the Ivan Grodznoi, whom you call The Terrible, with his cannon crushed the Mongols of the north.' Papashvilly nodded again. 'And so he freed his race that Timur-i-leng created and called slaves—' Papashvilly shrugged. 'Perhaps they are free forever. Who knows? Time passes. We look south, we look north, we see the orchards, we smell the grass. Our horses canter and paw the air. But we cling, do we not, because the age of the six-legged is over, is it not? Now we are a Soviet Socialist Republic and we have the privilege of protecting Muscovy from the south. Especially since Josef. Perversity! Our children have the privilege of going to Muscovite academies if we are eligible, and ...' He put his hand on Michaelmas's forearm. 'But of how much interest is this to you? In your half of the world, there is of course no history. One could speak to the Kwakiutl or the Leni-Lenape and the Apache, I suppose, but they have twice forgotten when they were six-legged people and they do not remember the steppes. No, you understand without offense, Lavrenti, that there is enough water between this land and the land of your forefathers to dissolve the past for you, but where I was born there has been so much blood and seed spilled on the same ground over and over that sometimes there are new men, they say, who are found in the pastures after the fog: men who go about their business unspeaking, and without mothers.'

Papashvilly put down his empty glass. 'Do they have coffee here with whiskey in it? I think I like that better. Ah, this business with the sports car ...' He shook his head. 'You know, it is true: all we peoples who live by the horse – not your sportsmen or your hobbyists, not anyone who is free to go elsewhere and wear a different face – we say that man is six-legged who no longer counts the number of his legs. But this is not love of the animal; it is love of the self as the self is made greater, and why hide it? Let me tell you how it must be – ah, you are a man of sharp eyes, I think you know how it is: On the grass ocean there are no roads, so everything is a road, and everything is the same, so the distances will eat your heart unless you are swift, swift, and shout loud. I think if Dzinghiz Kahn – I give him this, the devil, they still speak his name familiarly even on the Amber Sea – if the Dzinghiz Kahn had been shown an armored car, there would have been great feasts upon horseflesh in that season, and thereafter the fat cities would have been taxed by the two-hundred-liter drum. The horse is a stubborn, dirty, stupid animal that reminds me of a sheep. Its only use is to embody the wings a man feels within him, and to do this it lathers and sweats, defecates and steps in badger holes.'

Then he had smiled piercingly. 'But really, it is the same with cars, too.' His voice was soft and sober. 'I would not like Rudi to hear me say that. He's a good fellow. But it's also the same with rockets. If you have wings inside, nothing is really fast enough. You do the best you can, and you shout loud.'

They were well into the hills, now. Campion was smiling at Norwood and trying to get him into conversation. Norwood was shaking his head silently. Clementine was stretched out in her seat, sipping through a straw at an ice from the refreshment bar, raising one eyebrow as she chatted with Luis. It seemed reasonable to suppose they had been a great many places together. Michaelmas grimaced and closed his eyes again.

There was the night before the goodwill visit was at an end and Papashvilly was due to be at Star Control the next day. There had been a long, wet dinner at the Rose Room, and then they had gone for a constitutional along Fifth Avenue in the middle of the night. As they stepped off a curb, a fast car had turned a corner tightly, with no regard to them. Michaelmas had scrambled back with a shout to Papashvilly. Pavel had stopped still, allowing the rear fender to pass him by millimeters. As it passed, he brought down his fist hard on the rear deck sheet-metal with an enormous banging sound that echoed between the faces of the stores. The security escort out in the shadows had pointed their guns and the camera crews had jolted their focus. The car had screamed to a halt on locked wheels, slewing sideward, and the driver's window had popped open to reveal a pale, frightened, staring face. 'Earthman!' Papashvilly had shouted, his fists clenched. His knees and elbows were bent. His head thrust forward on his corded neck. 'Earthman!' But he was beginning to laugh, and he was relaxing. He walked forward and rumpled the driver's hair fondly. 'Ah, Earthman, Earthman, you are only half drunk.' He turned away and continued down the avenue.

They had walked a little more, and then they had all gone back toward the hotel for a night cap. At the turn onto Forty-fourth Street, Papashvilly had stopped for a moment and looked around. 'Goodbye, Fifth Avenue,' he said. 'Goodbye library, goodbye Rockefeller Center, goodbye cathedral, goodbye Cartier, goodbye F.A.O. Schwarz, goodbye zoo.'

Michaelmas looked up and down the avenue with him, and nodded.

Sitting alone together in the Blue Bar after everyone else had left, they each had one more for the hell of it. Papashvilly had finally said quietly:

'You know what it is?'

'Perhaps.'

Papashvilly had smiled to himself. 'The world is full of them. And I will tell you something: they have always known they will be left behind. That's why they're so careless and surly.'

'Ah.'

'The city people and the farmers. They have always known their part in the intent of history. That's why they have their roofs and thick walls – so they can hide and also say that it's no longer out there.'

'I wouldn't know what you're talking about. I have no understanding of history.'

Papashvily burst into laughter. At the end of the room, Eddie had looked up briefly from the glass he was toweling. 'You know. Some do not. But you know.' He smiled and shook his head, drumming impatiently on the edge of their table. 'These have been peculiar centuries lately. Look how it was. From the beginning of time, the six-legged came from the steppes, and only the mountains and the seas held some of them away, but not always and not forever.

'For uncounted centuries before the birth of our Christ, they came again and again. Some remained at the edges of the sea, in their cities, and ventured out then beyond the walls to make orchards and plough fields. And again the six-legged would come, and take the cities, and leave their seed, or stay behind and become the city people, to be taken by the next six-legged who came not from the edge of the world – no, we say that in the books, but we mean the center of the world; the *source* of the world. The city people had time for books. The city people are obsessed with making permanent things, because they know they are doomed. The six-legged know something else. They laugh at what you say is the story and the purpose of the world. And the more earnest of manner you are, the more amusing it is, because you know, really, it is all nonsense that you tell yourselves to be more comfortable. You know what the six-legged are. When you were pushed over the edge of the western ocean from your little handhold on what was left to you of Europe, you knew better than to let the six-legged remain free on your prairies, just as we Osseti knew who must not be allowed in the high pastures.

'And so you city people of the west took for yourselves not only the edges beyond the mountains, where you have always had your places for ships and warehouses, but like Ivan you took the great central steppes, too, for a while in which you could build great things.

'Great things. Great establishments on which we all choke, and in which we sit and say the grass is gone forever. It makes us neither honestly happy nor sad to say that; it makes us insane. There are walls, walls, all around us, and no honest tang of the wind and the seed of the grass. We say the walls make us safe, but we fear they make us blind. We say the roof makes us warm, but we know we lie when we pretend there are no stars. I do not, in fact, understand how it is we are not all dead. Ever since Ivan, it has been inevitable we would turn the cannon on ourselves someday. It is not only a great solver of problems, it is pleasurable to see such a mighty end to lies. And yet somehow, when we should close these four so-called civilized centuries in one last pang, we merely bicker and shuffle among ourselves, and tell the lie that we are all more like brothers each day.

'I am a good boy. I have been to Muscovy and not been entirely despised by my masters in our democratic association of freely federated republics. I am friends with Slavs, with Khazaks, with Tartars, and with Turkmen. I am a civilized man, furthermore a crew commander and a fleet commander, and a doctor of engineering. When we go toward mighty Jupiter and approach his great face, when we send in the modules to slice away a little here, and probe out a little there, and suck in a fraction here and there, I shall read all the checklists at the proper time, and all my personnel and I will follow all the manuals exactly. Then the mining extractors will come in a few years, and the orbital factories, and Jupiter shall be garlanded by them. The robot-ized containers shall flow Earthward; there will be great changes when it is no longer necessary to rip at our soil and burrow ever deeper in our planet, and make stenches and foul the sight of heaven. This much I owe the city people and that part of my blood which comes from men who held on. And, besides, perhaps the grass will come back, and that would be to the liking of those who still live with horses. Who knows?

'I am a good boy. But I see. I see that it was perhaps needful that there be four centuries in which the six-legged were required to bide. I also see that the time is at an end. The establishments have done their work. I would not have believed it; I would say that city ways should have killed us all by now. There are so many machines that must lie for everyone's comfort. But—' He shrugged. 'Machines go wrong. With so many, perhaps there is one, somewhere, that does us good, almost by accident, and so blunts the edge of destiny.

'But, you know, I would not risk it much longer.' He smiled. 'We are already going very far. Next time, we will reach distances such that the radio takes an impossible time to transmit the reports and instructions, is it not so? And the trip is so long. It becomes senseless to return all the way, or to think that someone at a microphone in Africa can control what needs to be done at Neptune, or perhaps at Alpha Centauri. Control, or even advise. No, I think it becomes very natural then to make camps out there, and to have repair depots and such, so that it is not necessary to go to the constant expense and time to go back and forth to here. If we can make food from petroleum and cloth from stone in Antarctica, I think we can find minerals and hydrocar-bons in space as well, no?

'I think then we come back once in a while if it is still here; we will come back for new recordings of *Les Sylphides*, and we shall pay for them with gems snatched from the temples of Plutonian fire-lizards, say, or with nearly frictionless bearings, or with research data. We shall tell the Earthmen how the universe is made, and they shall tell romantic stories about us and wish they had time to leave home.' Papashvilly shook his head. 'Clinging is a thing a man can take pride in, I think, and there is nothing to be ashamed in it. Nothing, especially if one clings so well that nothing can dislodge him. Nevertheless, I have stood on Mount Elbrus and looked northeast, Lavrenti, and from there I could only see as far as one of Timur's hazarras could ride in a week. And I said to myself: I, too, am six-legged.' He had put down his empty glass. 'Goodbye, alcohol,' he had said. A few polite words more and it was time to go. Papashvilly had put his hands on Michaelmas's arms and shaken him a little, fondly. 'We shall see each other again,' he had said, and had gone up to his room.

Domino said: 'The European Flight Authority has determined the cause of Watson's crash.'

Michaelmas sat up. They were coming out of the hills, now, and whirling down the flats, leaving a plume of finely divided dust along the shoulder of the highway. 'What was it?'

'Desiccator failure.'

'Give me some detail.'

'The most efficient engine working fluid is, unfortunately, also extremely hygroscopic. It's practically impossible to store or handle it for any length of time without its becoming contaminated with water absorbed from the air.

'The usual methods, however, ensure that this contamination will stay at tolerable levels, and engines are designed to cope with a certain amount of steam mixed into the other vapors at the high-pressure stages. Clear so far? All right; this particular series of helicopter utilizes an engine originally designed for automobiles produced by the same manufacturing combine. The helicopter cabins have the same basic frame as the passenger pod and engine mount of the automobile, the same doors and seats, and share quite a bit of incidental hardware. This series of helicopter can therefore be sold for markedly less than equally capable competing machines, and is thus extremely popular worldwide among corporate fleet buyers. The safety record of the model Watson was flying is good, and indicates no persistent characteristic defect. However, this is not true of an earlier model, which showed something of a tendency to blockage in its condenser coils. They froze now and then, usually at high altitudes, causing a stoppage of working fluid circulation, and consequent pressure drop followed by an emergency landing or a crash due to power loss.'

'Power loss,' Michaelmas said. 'Like Watson.'

'But not quite for the same reason. This is a more recent model, remember. In the earlier ones, it had been found that the downdraft from the helicopter rotors, under certain conditions of temperature and humidity, was creating cold spots in the coils, and causing plugs of ice. This was not a defect in the engine as an automobile engine. So, since it was economically impractical to redesign or to relocate the engine, the choice was between thermostatically heating the coils to one degree Celsius, or in making sure there was never any water in the working fluid passing through the coils.

'Option One resulted in performance losses, and was therefore not acceptable; one reason the helicopter application worked so well was the steep temperature gradient across the coil. So they went to the other choice; they installed a desiccator. This is essentially a high-speed precipitator; exhausted vapor from the high-pressure stages passes through it enroute to the coil. The water vapor component is picked off and diverted below one hundred degrees Celsius into a separate reservoir, where it is electrically superheated back to about one hundred twenty degrees and vented into the atmosphere as chemically pure steam. The electrical load is small, the vent is parallel to the helicopter's long axis so that some of the energy is recovered as an increment of forward motion, and the whole thing has the sort of simplicity that appeals.'

'But the unit failed in this case,' Michaelmas said.

'It has happened only twice before, and never over Alpine terrain in gusty wind conditions. These were its first two fatalities. What happens if the electrical heating fails is that the extracted moisture vents as water rather than steam, gradually forming a cap of ice, which then creates a backup in the desiccator. The physics of it all then interact with the engineering to rupture the final stage of the desiccator, and this creates a large hole in the plumbing. All the high-pressure vapor vents out through it, in preference to entering the condenser, and half a cycle later the turbine has nothing to work with. Result, power loss; furthermore, the percentage of water required to have it happen is much less than is needed to create condenser freeze-up. You can be almost sure that any charge of working fluid, even a fresh one right out of a sealed flask, will have picked up enough.'

'A very dangerous design.'

'Most add-on new parts have to compromise – fit the basic hardware, and have to add as little as possible to total unit cost, since they inevitably skew the original profit projections. But as it happens this is a rather good design. The electricity comes from a magneto, gear-driven by the output shaft. The wiring, which you would expect to be the weak spot, is vibration-proofed, and uses astronautics-grade insulation and fasteners. It is also located so that no other part can rub through it, and is routed away from all routine service hatches so that fuel-loaders, fluid-handlers, and other nonmechanics servicing the vehicle cannot accidentally damage the unit. The desiccator has its own inspection hatch, and only certified mechanics are shown how to operate the type of latch used.'

They were clearly targeted on Control Tower now; staring forward with his eyes half-focused, Michaelmas could see the structure larger than any of the others, dead ahead, and apparently widening out to either side of the tapering white thread of highway. He glanced back through the rear window; they were being followed by a short caravan of trucks. The lead unit, a white, ground-hugging Oskar with shooting platforms collapsed against its sides like extra accumulators, carried the sunburst insignia of Mr Samir's crew.

'Then what happened?'

'The European Flight Authority found one wire hanging.'

Michaelmas nodded to himself, then grinned humorlessly and looked around for a moment. Everyone was busy doing something or nothing. 'What did they think of that?'

'They're not sure. The connection is made with a device called a Pozipfast-ner; it snaps on, never opens of itself, and nominally requires a special tool for removal.'

'Nominally?'

'The fastener sells because it's obviously tamperproof; any purchasing agent can demonstrate to his supervisor that the connection can't break, can't shake loose, and can't be taken apart with a screwdriver or a knife blade. The special removal tool has two opposed spring-loaded fingerlets that apply a precise amount of pressure to two specific points. It's an aerospace develop-ment. But any mechanic with any experience at all can open any Pozipfastner by flicking it with his index fingernails. It's a trick that takes almost no prac-tice, and most of them do it; it's much quicker than using the tool.'

'And I presume anyone on any aircraft service crew knows how to work the special latches that only certified mechanics understand.'

'Of course. How could anything get done on time if the nearest man couldn't lend a hand?'

Michaelmas pursed his lips. 'What do you make of that wire?'

'Sabotage. The AEV really thinks so too, but they can't bring themselves to accept the idea. Nevertheless, the unit flew without incident early that morn-ing from a charter service to meet Watson. It was parked while Watson held a meeting with his network's local people, but it certainly wasn't serviced during that time. While Watson was talking, someone deliberately opened that hatch and then either used the factory tool or did the fingernail trick. I suppose it might have been someone demonstrating knowledgeability to an acquaintance. I suppose that someone might have forgotten to resnap the connection before remembering to close the hatch all nice and tidy. There might be some reason why such a person chose to demonstrate on a Pozip-fastner that could only be reached by opening an inconveniently located hatch, bypassing scores of others more accessible. The AEV has already drafted an order; henceforth, the desiccator circuit must be wired to an instrument-panel-failure telltale light, or the model's airworthiness certificate will be canceled; all existing members of the type are grounded immediately for inspection of quote potential spontaneous failure endquote and installation of the warning light, and so forth. The manufacturer has already filed an objection, citing unreasonable imposition of added cost, since there are several hours' labor involved, but that's pro forma so they can file a compensation claim against the Common Market authority. *Und so weiter.*'

'What about the police?'

'The AEV is thinking of speaking to them about it.'

'Will they?'

'The chief examiner's against it, and he's the man on the spot. Some of the headquarters bureaucrats are a little nervous about what could happen if Interpol ever learns they've concealed evidence. But the examiner's point is that any physical evidence – fingerprints, shreds of coat sleeve, theater ticket stubs, accidentally dropped business cards (I'm quoting him; he's a sarcastic person when questioned in his decisions) – was incinerated in the crash. There's no hope of tracing the saboteur. What they have is a loose wire. And the loose wire is an excuse for circulating an order he's wanted put out ever since a mechanic did leave one hanging last year; if they bring in the cops, the manufacturer will just shrug and legitimately claim again that it's not equipment failure. Furthermore, the pilot and the broadcaster were both voluntarily in dangerous professions; and besides, we can let them at least accomplish one last good thing. So it's better all around.'

Michaelmas sucked his teeth.

'They still haven't finally decided,' Domino said.

'Yes, they have. Every passing minute makes it less advisable to report it as sabotage. Pretty soon they'd also have to account for the reporting delay, and the thought of that will swing it.'

'Well, yes.'

'So, how was it done? Did Cikoumas hang around the airport? Of course not. What sanatorium employee? What henchman? Who?'

'I'm working on it. Meanwhile, Daugerd's plane has just landed at Hanrassy's dock. Time there is seven thirty-five AM.'

Michaelmas glanced at his wrist. Two thirty-five PM.

Frontiere leaned across the aisle. 'Ten more minutes, Laurent, and we'll be there.' Simultaneously, his telephone sounded. He reached into his jacket, took out the instrument, and inserted the privacy plug in his ear, answering the call with his mouth close to the microphone. Then he recoiled pleasurably. *'Dei grazia,'* he said, put the phone away, and stared at Michaelmas incredulously. 'You were exactly correct in your jest,' he said. He leaned closer. 'The sender looks Russian. The assembly technique is Russian. But our analytical equipment shows that some of the *material* only resembles stock Russian material; the molecular structure is off. Our analytical programs caught it and the ones Norwood used at Limberg's did not. A very sophisticated effort was made to take circuit material and make it *seem* like other circuit material of no greater or lesser practicality. Why would the Russians do that? Why should they?'

Frontiere grinned. 'No, someone *is* trying to muddle things up. But we can be rather sure it isn't the Chinese, and if it isn't they or the Russians, then the situation is nowhere near as critical.' Frontiere grinned. 'It's just some accursed radical group that didn't even kill anybody. We can handle that.' He sat up straighter 'We were right to delay.' He drummed his fingers on the armrest. 'All right. What now?' he said absently, his eyes still shining. 'What must be done immediately?'

'Well,' Michaelmas said equably, 'there is still the problem of forestalling Norwood and Limberg. Steps of some sort must be taken quickly. It would be particularly galling now if one or the other lost patience and blurted out his error in all honesty.'

Frontiere grimaced. 'Just so.'

'So I suggest,' Michaelmas went on, 'that the analytical tests be rerun immediately in your laboratories with Norwood in attendance. In fact, let him do the running. And when he gets the correct result, let him call Limberg with it. It's no disgrace to have been wrong. It's only a minor sin of eagerness not to have waited in the first place to use your lab and your engineering analysis computer programs. It's only natural that your equipment would be subtler and more thorough than anything Norwood and Limberg were able to graft onto Limberg's medical software. And Limberg will understand that until the real culprits are identified, absolute silence about the existence of the sender is the best hope of unearthing them.'

Frontiere blinked. 'You have a swift mind, Laurent.'

'Thank you.'

Frontiere frowned slowly at Michaelmas. 'There may be difficulty. Norwood may not be entirely willing to accept results different from those he found for himself.'

Michaelmas glanced down the aisle. 'I think you may find him less sure of himself than he has hitherto appeared. More ready to consider that his faculties might err from time to time.'

Frontiere's eyes followed Michaelmas's. Norwood was sitting with one heel hooked on the edge of the seat, his chin resting on his knee. His hands were clasped over his shin. His thumbs absently massaged his calf, while he sat silently looking out the window as if cataloguing the familiar things of his youth while the bus sped in among the outbuildings and the perimeter installations. Frontiere contracted his lower lip and raised an eyebrow. He looked over at Michaelmas. 'You are a shrewd observer.' He stood up smoothly. 'Excuse me. I will go speak to him.' He touched Michaelmas's shoulder. 'You are an encouraging person to know,' he said.

Michaelmas smiled. When Frontiere was down the aisle, he said: 'Well, Domino, congratulations.'

'I simply took your hint. Now, the interesting news. I did in fact cause UNAC's analytical apparatus to produce the desired result. A competent molecular physicist examining the readouts will be able to determine exactly with what plausible and fully worthy action group the sender is most likely to have originated. Nevertheless, we are not dealing one hundred percent in description.'

'Oh?'

'Daugerd will never find it simply by looking at holograms. UNAC's programs would never have found it unaided. The difference isn't gross. But it's there; there's something about the electrons ...'

'Something about the electrons?'

'It's ... they're all *right*; I mean, they're in the correct places in the proper number, as far as one can tell, and yet ... Well, I ran an analogue; built another sender so to speak, using materials criteria I found stored in the physical data banks of the People's Diligent Electronics Technicum at Dne-prodzerzhinsk. And they're different. The two senders are out of ... tune ... with each other, and they shouldn't be; that damned thing has molecules all through it that say loud and clear it's blood kin to ten thousand others just like it from the Dnieper manufacturing complex. Well, it is, it is, but it's a bastard second cousin masquerading as the legitimate twin.'

'Can you give me more detail?'

'I – No. I don't think so.'

'Are you saying the sender was produced by some organization on the order of a normal dissident group?'

'No. I don't think so. I don't think – I don't believe there is material exactly like that.'

'Ah.' Michaelmas sat deeper in his chair. The bus entered the shadow of Control Tower, and the windows lightened. The landscape beyond the shadow became a blaze of white. 'Did you feel as you did at the sanatorium?'

'I ... couldn't say. Probably. Yes. I think so.'

The bus was pulling up to a halt among the colonnades and metallized glass of the ground level. People began rising to their feet. Mr Samir, Michaelmas noted through his window, had gotten the Oskar in through the portal and was parking nearby; the sides of the little van metamorphosed into an array of platforms, and a technician was out of the truck and up on the topmost one instantly, slipping one camera into its mount, and reaching down to take another being handed up to him. 'What about Norwood?' Michaelmas asked. 'When you touched him.'

'Norwood? Nor—? No, I wasn't getting anything through the sensors in that terminal. You wouldn't find it with sensors: you have to be electron-to-electron with it ... Norwood? What an interesting question! No – there's no way. There's no interface, you see. There's only data. No, I could only feel that with something approximating my own kind.'

'Approximating. Yes.'

Michaelmas was watching Norwood in conversation with Frontiere. Frontiere was talking intently and softly, holding one hand on Norwood's shoulder and tapping lightly on Norwood's chest with the spread fingers of the other. Norwood was looking into his face with the half-focused stare of an earthquake victim. It was over in a moment. Norwood shrugged and nodded, his eyes downcast. Frontiere smiled and put his arm protectively around Norwood's shoulders in good-natured bonhomie. He patted Norwood's shoulder absently while looking about him for aides to make sure the astronaut's entrance into Control Tower would be properly handled.

'An interesting statement. But hardly relevant at this moment,' Michaelmas said. 'Your sensors *were* adequate to measure his belief in himself.'

'As any other lie detector would have.'

'That may be as much detection as any man needs. Well – we're off.' The bus was emptying. To keep in trim, Michaelmas stepped forward deftly and debarked just behind Norwood and Frontiere. Not only Ossip Sakal but Hjalmar Wirkola himself were waiting to greet Norwood, all smiles now. There was a faint flicker through the lobby lights, unnoticed. Frontiere propelled the astronaut gently toward the Director General. The stately, straight-backed old gentleman stepped forward from Sakal's side as Norwood approached, and extended his hand. Somewhere very faintly there was a ringing bell, if you listened. 'My boy!' Wirkola said, clasping the astronaut's handshake between his palms. 'I was so glad when Ossip told me you are all safe now.' Everyone's attention was on them. Over at the elevator bank, a security man was looking at the lights of an indicator panel and frowning, his ear to the wall, but that was the sum total of distraction in that crowd.

The press of people built up around Norwood and Wirkola; Michaelmas could see additional UNAC people coming from a side foyer. Getulio's press aides were bringing them in through the more casual onlookers and the news people. There is a lot you can do with a properly swung hip and a strategically insinuated shoulder to create lanes in a crowd without it showing on camera.

There was, somewhere, away in the higher levels of the tower, a dull thump. Perhaps, really, it was a sonic boom outside, somehow penetrating the building insulation. Or masked burglars blowing a safe with black powder. A freight elevator door opened and Papashvilly stepped out, looking momentarily flustered but recovering quickly.

Domino was making the noise again. He had learned to make it clearly, now. It was a bronchitic giggle, brought up sawing from the depths of a chest in desperate search of air. 'The building systems program!' he gasped. 'It's trying to maintain homeostasis with everything going to hell upstairs. It's running from switch to switch like an old maid chasing mice with a broom. Oh, my! Oh, me!'

Papashvilly had his head up, his shoulders back, and his grin delighted as he moved toward the main group. He was waving at Norwood. As his glance reached Michaelmas, who was making his way across Luis's line of sight on Norwood, he momentarily shifted the direction of his wave, and wagged two fingers at him, before redirecting himself to the welcome. Michaelmas raised a clenched fist, one thumb up, and shook it. Clementine Gervaise stepped on Michaelmas's foot. 'Pardon,' she said, the corners of her mouth quivering slightly and her eyes a little wider and shining more than normal, 'you are blocking my camera, Laurent.' Michaelmas stared at her. 'Excuse me,' he said, wondering if they would now spend days grinning at each other. 'It was innocent, I assure you,' he said and pushed on, his eyes sliding off Campion's face enroute. The man was looking around a little busily, his face raised. He made a sniffing expression. There was the faintest whiff of smoke in the air, already being dissipated by the building's exhaust ventilators. Campion shrugged faintly and returned his attention to matters at hand. Michaelmas found it interesting that Douggie did have a nose for news. He winked toward Papashvilly.

'Hanrassy is punching up Gately's number,' Domino said.

Michaelmas stopped, changed direction, and began working his way clear. 'I'll want to monitor that,' he said, and pulled the plug out of the terminal, inserting it in his ear as he went, to account for the fact that he was stepping out of the crowd and standing with an intent expression, his hand over his free ear to shut out other sounds. He stood apparently oblivious, while Gately's secretary fielded the call and then put Hanrassy through.

'I want you to look at something, Mr Secretary,' she said without preamble.

Domino said: 'She's showing him a holo of the sender.'

'Yes,' Michaelmas said. He clenched his jaw.

'I see it, Miz Hanrassy. Should I recognize it?' Gately said.

'That would depend on how familiar you expect to be with Soviet electronic devices.'

'I don't follow you, ma'am. Is that thing Russian?'

'It is, Mr Secretary. There's no doubt about it; it's not exactly a standard component in their engineering, but it's made of standard pieces and the workmanship is characteristically theirs.'

'Yes, ma'am, and in what way is that relevant to my duties?'

'I wonder if you'd care to call Colonel Norwood and ask him if he found it in his capsule just before he was forced to escape.'

Michaelmas took a deep breath. 'That's it, then,' he said to Domino steadily.

'There is no further doubt. Limberg and Cikoumas supplied it to her, along with their story. They don't have the slightest sense of restraint or responsibility. They think we are an ant farm.'

'Ma'am,' Gately was saying, 'are you telling me the Russkis sabotaged Norwood's shuttle and you can *prove* it?'

'The sons of bitches,' Michaelmas said. 'The bastards. Get me to the sanatorium. Right now. And I arrive without warning. Right?'

'Right.'

Viola Hanrassy said: 'Ask Norwood, Mr Secretary. Ask him why UNAC hasn't let him say anything about it.'

'Ma'am, where'd you get this information?'

'If you obtain corroboration from Norwood, Mr Secretary, then I'll be glad to discuss details with you. In fact, Will, I'm holding myself in readiness to work very closely with you on this. We may have the joint duty of alerting the American people to their responsibilities and opportunities in the coming election.'

Domino said: 'I think that may have been an offer of the Vice Presidency.'

'Bribes,' Michaelmas said. 'They always go to bribes when they're not sure they're on top, and coercion when they are. That's all they know. They really don't believe anyone would help them just on their merits. Well, Christ, at least they're our own. How's my ride to Berne?'

'Wait one.'

Gately was saying: 'I'll place a call to Africa right away and get back to you.'

'Thank you, Mr Secretary.'

'And kiss my bum, both of you,' Michaelmas muttered as the connection broke. He was looking around with sharp, darting swings of his eyes, his hands raised in front of him and his feet well apart, so that he was leaning forward against his weight.

'Mr Michaelmas.'

'Yes.'

'Get to the airport.'

'Right.'

He strode directly toward Mr Samir. 'How do you do,' he said, thrusting his hand forward.

'How do you do, sir,' Mr Samir said, responding with a calloused palm and a dignified smile. 'What are my instructions?'

'There has been a change of plans. I would like to be driven back to Cité d'Afrique immediately.'

'As you wish.' He turned toward his crew, snapped his fingers and gestured. The men began clambering at the sides of the Oskar. 'We depart in ninety seconds, Mr Michaelmas.'

'Thank you.' He looked around, and found Harry Beloit preparing to hold the door into the interior lobbies. He paced toward him. 'Harry,' he said in a low voice. 'Please accept my apologies and convey them to Getulio, to Pavel, and the rest. There is another story I must cover in person. I'll be patching back to you as soon as I can.'

'No problem,' Beloit said.

'Thank you very much.' He turned away, then stopped, and shook Beloit's hand. 'I would like to sit on the edge of the marsh with your family and yourself someday,' he said, and went. He waved to Clementine and got into the Oskar beside Mr Samir. The lowering door interposed tinted glass across her startled expression. She turned to Campion and nudged his arm. They both looked toward the Oskar as it snapped sideward out of its parking groove and oriented on the outer portal. Mr Samir himself was driving, his shirtsleeves rolled back from forearms like Indian clubs; the crew, looking curiously forward toward Michaelmas, were still latching down gear and strapping themselves to their seats in the back cargo space.

'I'll call you,' Michaelmas pantomimed toward Clementine, holding up his telephone and mock-punching numbers. But what will I call you? he thought, pushing the phone back into his jacket. He waved to Papashvilly, who raised his eyebrows. Mr Samir accelerated. The portal opened, closed behind them and, computer-monitored, stayed obstinately closed when one news crew tried to follow the famous Mr Michaelmas and learn what he might be after.

Mr Samir drove hard. The bristling white van hissed wickedly down the highway eastward. 'The airport, please, Mr Samir,' Michaelmas said.

'The military gates,' Domino said.

'There are no commercial flights to anywhere for some time,' Mr Samir said. 'Do you wish a charter?'

'No, Mr Samir. Charters file flight plans. I will go to the military end of the field, please.'

Mr Samir nodded. 'As you wish. We shall probably remember that you asked to be taken to the Hilton.'

'That is always a possibility. My thanks.'

'I regret that our opportunity to serve has been so limited.'

'I will be sending you back to Star Control as soon as you've dropped me. And there will be other times we can work together in person. I anticipate them with pleasure.'

'It is mutual.'

Domino said: 'Gately has a call in for Norwood. They're holding; Norwood should be free in a few minutes. I think UNAC's anticipating a simple message of congratulations from the US administration. They'll put it through quickly.'

Michaelmas's mouth thinned into an edged smile. 'Good.' He watched the desert hurtling past.

'Douglas Campion,' Domino said.

'Say again.'

'While in Chicago at WKMM, Campion was on the crime-copter crew for a year and a half. They flew a model identical to the one in which Watson crashed. They never had any mechanical failures. But the pilot had had a coil freeze-up while flying the earlier model. The station used one until a few months before Campion joined their staff. The pilot put it down to Lincoln Park without further incident, and not much was made of it. But in a year and a half of making conversation five days a week, he probably would have mentioned it to Campion. That could have led to a clinical discussion of causes and cures. I think Campion could have learned how to work latches and Pozipfastners. I think he would know which wire to pull.'

Michaelmas bowed his head. 'That's pretty circumstantial,' he said at last.

'Campion is also on the short list of persons who could have gotten to the machine; Watson was busy talking to his staff, but Campion would already know what he was going to say, and could wander off.'

'Being on the list doesn't prove ...'

'I have attempted to establish corroboration. I found that *National Geographic* had leased facilities on an AP News-features satellite that was passing over Switzerland at the time. They were using its infrared mapping capabilities for a story on glacial flow. I went through their data and played a few reprocessing tricks with a segment covering Berne. I have identified thermal tracks that correspond to Watson, the helicopter pilot, and several people who must number Campion among them. I have isolated one track as being Campion with eighty-two percent certainty. That track leaves the knot of people around Watson, walks around a corner to the helicopter, pauses beside the fuselage at the right place for the proper amount of time, and then rejoins the group.' Michaelmas bit his upper lip. He stared straight out through the windshield with his fists in his lap. 'Eighty-two percent.'

'Eighty-two percent probability that he's the particular member of a restricted group in which only the pilot seems to have been equally qualified to arrange her own death.'

Michaelmas said nothing. Then after a while he said: 'I hate acting on probability.'

'You go to your church and I'll go to mine.'

Michaelmas shook his head. Mr Samir, who doubtless had excellent peripheral vision, appeared to blink once, sharply, but he continued to drive relentlessly.

Oh, yes. Yes. It was as plain as the nose in your mirror. The poor, silly, ambitious son of a bitch had known exactly what would happen. The helicopter would ice up, set down uneventfully in the local equivalent of Lincoln Park, but at some remove from the nearest cab stand, and Douggie Campion instead of Horse Watson would be the main spokesman on worldwide air. Afterward, Horse would be rescued, and it would just have been one of those things.

And how did he salve himself now, assuming he felt the need? That, too, wasn't particularly difficult. He'd understood all the factors, hadn't he? He'd calculated the risk exactly. All right, then, he'd done everything needful; bad luck had killed two people, one of whom happened to be his professional superior, thus creating a permanent vacancy at a higher rung on the ladder; it was funny how Fate worked.

'Keep him busy,' Michaelmas growled.

'It's done,' Domino said at once.

'Thank you.'

'I have Gately's call to Norwood,' Domino said as they swept out of the hills and plunged toward the city. 'Norwood's in Wirkola's office now.'

'Put it on.'

'Right.'

Michaelmas sat still.

'Walt? Walt, hey, boy, this is Willie!' began in his ear, and continued for some time, during which the expected congratulations and the obligatory God-damns were deployed. Then Gately said: 'Listen, son. Can I ask you about something, between the two of us? You got many people looking over your shoulder right this minute?'

'No, not too many, sir. I'm in Mr Wirkola's office, and there's no one here who isn't UNAC.'

'Well, that – forgive me, son, but that may not be—'

'It's okay, Mr Secretary.'

There was a pause. Then Gately made a frustrated, snorting noise. 'Okay. What the hell. Have a look – do you recognize this?'

Domino said: 'It's his recording of the sender holo.'

'Yes, sir, I do,' Norwood said. 'I'm a little surprised to see you have a picture of it.'

'Walter, I've got my sources and I don't mind if UNAC knows that. I'm sure they recognize my right to keep in touch. What about this thing, son? Do you feel you can tell me anything about it over this line at this time?'

'Up to a point, sir. Yes.'

'What's that mean?'

There was the sound of a palm being placed over a microphone, and then being lifted off.

'Mr Secretary, have you heard that thing is Russian?'

'That's exactly what I've heard. I've also heard UNAC won't let you say so. How are you today, Mr Wirkola?'

Norwood said: 'Mr Secretary, I'm looking at a materials analysis printout that says the core component was made by spark-eroding a piece of G.E. Lithoplaque until it looks a lot like U.S.S.R. Grade II Approved stock. You'd think that could work because Grade II is manufactured someplace south of Kiev using equipment purchased from G.E. and utilizing G.E. processes under license. But G.E. went to a smooth from a matte finish on Lithoplaque last year, whereas Grade II didn't. You might figure you could carve back to the old configuration. But you can't; G.E. also changed the structure a little. And it's only in limited distribution as yet. According to what I see here, the only place you could get that particular piece we're talking about is G.E.'s central midwestern supply warehouse in St Louis.'

'St Louis?'

Mr Wirkola said: 'I am fine. And how are you, Mr Gately?'

There was a long silence. 'You're sure, Walter?'

'Well, to satisfy myself I'm immediately going to pass the thing through the labs here again. I've got to admit I damned near made a fool of myself about it once, and I don't want to do that twice. But we're working with the best hardware and software in the world when it comes to engineering, around here, and I've strapped myself into it many's the time without a second thought. I've got a feeling I could run this baby through any modern equipment in the world and come up with the same answer.'

'St Louis, Missouri.'

Mr Wirkola said: 'I believe there is still a community called St Louis du Ha! Ha!, near Lac Temiscouata in Quebec.'

'Mr Wirkola, I appreciate UNAC's discretion in this matter,' Gately said. 'I'm assuming you'll be in touch with me officially about this?'

'Yes,' Wirkola said. 'We are assigning Colonel Norwood to temporary duty as our liaison with the US government on this matter. I suggest a goodwill tour of the USA as a cover for his talks with your President and yourself. But he will call you a little later today with confirmation from his retests, and that will have given you time to consult with Mr Westrum on your response to that suggestion. You may tell Mr Westrum we understand his political situation, and we certainly do not wish to inculcate any unnecessary constraints upon his conscience. Nevertheless, I think there may be better ways to slide this incident into the back shelves of history than by any public counterclaiming between Mr Westrum and whoever your informant may have been. What is done privately is of course private.'

Domino said: 'Slit you, skin you, and sell you a new suit. That nice old man took two minutes to react to Gately's news, size it up, and flip through the anatomy text.'

'Yes,' Michaelmas said.

'Thank you, Mr Wirkola,' Gately said. 'I'll speak to my President and be waiting for Colonel Norwood's call.'

'Thank you, Mr Secretary. We are grateful for your cooperation,' Wirkola said.

'Bye, Walter. Good to talk to you, son.'

'Thank you, Mr Secretary.'

The connection opened. The van was on the city ramps now, sliding smoothly between the beautiful new structures, humming toward the airport. Domino said: 'I can see why you favored Mr Wirkola's election as Director General.'

'That's not what you see. What you see is why it wasn't necessary to do anything with the vote. His virtues are evident even to an election committee. Eschew the sin of overmanagement; that above all. You don't want to lose respect for the Hjalmar Wirkolas of this world.'

'Noted. As before.'

Michaelmas sighed. 'I didn't mean to nag.'

He made his voice audible: 'Mr Samir, after you've delivered me, I'd like you to go back to Star Control and interview Major Papashvilly. Permission's all arranged. After I'm airborne, I'll call Signor Frontiere and the Major, and tell them you're coming and what we'll do.'

'Right,' Domino said.

'I understand,' Mr Samir replied.

Michaelmas smiled trustfully at him. 'You have it. I'll be on the phone with you, giving you the questions to ask, and you'll pick up the Major's responses.'

'No problem,' Domino said.

'I understand completely,' Mr Samir said. 'I am proud of your reliance on me.'

'Then there's no difficulty,' Michaelmas said. 'Thank you.'

Mr Samir's footage would be fed to his network's editing storage and held for mixing. Via Domino, the network would also receive footage of Michaelmas asking the questions, commenting, and reacting to Papashvilly's answers. The network editing computer would then mix a complete interview out of the two components.

Since the shots of Michaelmas would be against a neutral background, the editing program could in some cases scale Michaelmas and Papashvilly into conformity and matte them into the same frames together. The finished effect would be quite convincing. Mr Samir assumed, without the impoliteness of asking, that Michaelmas would also use a union crew at his end.

And in fact he would, Michaelmas thought as he leaned back in his seat. Domino would call in direct to network headquarters, and they'd photo the Laurent Michaelmas hologram in their own studios. You could do that with studio-controlled lighting and computer-monitored phone input levels. There was a promise that only a year or two from now there'd be equipment that would let you do it in the field. When that happened, it wouldn't be necessary any longer for L. G. Michaelmas to be physically present anywhere but in his apartment, sitting at his desk or cooking in his kitchen or playing his upside-down-strung guitar.

'What'll you want?' Domino asked. 'A how's-it-going-Pavel, or a give-us-the-big-picture, or a roundup conversation including how he reacts to Norwood's return or what?'

'Give us the roundup,' Michaelmas said. 'He'll be good at that. We just want to reinforce the idea he's a bright, quick, fine fellow and he's going to do a hell of a job.' And mostly, they were simply going to keep Papashvily in a controlled situation among friendly people for the next hour or two. It would do no harm. And it would maintain L. G. Michaelmas's reputation for never scrubbing a job even if he had to be in two places at the same time, damn near, and it was good to remind yourself there were plenty of competent crews and directors around. 'And, listen, make sure I'm in character when I phone Pavel about this.'

'That's all taken into account. Chat before shooting. Friends reunited. Buy you a drink soonest.'

'Fine,' Michaelmas said. He rubbed his thumb and fingers over his eyelids, head bowed momentarily, aware that when he slumped like this, he could notice the fatigue in his back and shoulders.

Something overhead was coming down as if on a string, metallic and glimmering – God's lure. The military gates opened smoothly, so that the Oskar barely slowed. The guard nodded at their plate number and saluted, good soldier, explicit orders fresh in the gate shack teleprinter. The van moved toward the flight line. 'What is that?' Mr Samir asked, looking up and out through the windscreen. He braked hard and stopped them at the edge of a hardstand.

The aircraft became recognizable overhead as a cruelly angled silvery wedge balanced on its tailpipes, but as it neared the ground its flanks began to open into stabilizer surfaces, landing struts, and blast deflectors.

'I believe that is a Type Beta Peacekeeper,' Michaelmas said. 'They are operated by the Norwegian Air Militia. I wouldn't open any doors or windows until it's down and the engines are idled.' The windscreen glass began shivering in its gaskets, and the metal fabric of the Oskar began to drum.

Domino said: 'It's on a routine checkride to Kirkenes from the base at Cap Norvegia in the Antarctic. It's now had additions to the mission profile for purposes of further crew training. What you see is an equatorial sea-level touchdown; another has been changed in for the continental mountains near Berne. Excellent practice. Meantime, one unidentified passenger will be aboard on priority request from the local embassy which, like many another, occasionally does things that receive no explanation and whose existence is denied and unrecorded. Hardstand contact here is in thirty seconds; a boarding ladder will deploy. Your programmed flying time is twenty minutes. *Bon voyage.*' The Beta came to rest. The engines quieted into a low rumble that caused little grains of stone to dance an inch above the concrete.

'Goodbye, Mr Samir. Thank you,' Michaelmas said. He popped open the door and trotted through the blasts of sunlight, hugging the little black box to his ribs. A ladder ramp meant to accommodate an outrushing full riot squad folded down out of the fuselage like a backhand return. He scrambled up it into the load space; a padded, nevertheless thrumming off-green compartment with hydraulically articulated seats that hung empty on this mission. He dropped into one and began pulling straps into place. The ladder swung up and sealed.

'Are you seated and secure, sir?' asked an intercom voice from somewhere beyond the blank upper bulkhead. He sorted through the accent and hasty memories of the language. He snapped the last buckle into place. 'Ja,' he said, pronouncing the 'a' somewhere nearer 'o' than he might have, and hoping that would do. 'Then we're going,' said the unseen flight crew member, and the Type Beta first flowed upward and then burst upward. Michaelmas's jaw sagged, and he tilted back deeply against the airbagged cushions. His arms trailed out over the armrests. He said slowly to Domino: 'One must always be cautious when one rubs your lamp.' But he sat unsmiling, and while there might have been times when he would have been secretly delighted with the silent robotics of the seat suspensions, which kept him ever facing the direction of acceleration as the Peacekeeper topped out its ballistic curve and prepared to swap ends, he was gnawing at other secrets now. He drummed his fingertips on the cushiony armrest and squirmed. His mouth assumed the expression he kept from himself. 'We have a few minutes,' he said at last. 'Is this compartment secure?'

'Yes, sir.'

'I think we might let Douglas Campion find me at this time.'

His phone rang. 'Hello?' he said.

'What? Who's this? I was calling—' Campion said.

'This is Laurent Michaelmas.'

'Larry! Jesus, the damnedest things are happening. How'd I get you? I'm standing here in the UNAC lobby just trying to get through to my network again. Something's really screwed up.'

Michaelmas sat back. 'What seems to be the trouble, Doug? Is there some way I can help you?'

'Man, I hope somebody can. I – well, hell, you're the first call I've gotten made in this last half hour. Would you believe that? No matter who I call, it's always busy. My network's busy, the cab company's busy. When I tried a test by calling Gervaise from across the room, I got a busy signal. And she wasn't using her phone. Something's crazy.'

'It sounds like a malfunction in your instrument.'

'Yeah. Yeah, but the same kinds of things happened when I went over and borrowed hers. Look, I don't mean to sound like somebody in an Edgar Allan Poe, but I can't even reach phone Repair Service.'

'Good heavens! What will you do if this curse extends?'

'What do you mean?'

'Have you had anyone call you since this happened?'

'No. No – you mean, can anybody reach *me*?'

'Yes, there's that. Then, of course, a natural thing to wonder about is whether your bank is able to receive and honor credit transfers, whether the Treasury Department is continuing to receive and okay your current tax flow … That sort of thing. Assuming now that you find some way to get back across the ocean, will your building security system recognize you?' He chuckled easily. 'Wouldn't that be a pretty pickle? You'd become famous, if anyone could find you.'

'My God, Larry, that's not funny.'

'Oh, it's not likely to be lifelong, is it? Whatever this thing is? It's just some little glitch somewhere, I should think. Don't you expect it'll clear up?'

'I don't know. I don't know what the hell. Look – where are you, anyway? What made you take off like that? What's going on?'

'Oh, I'm chasing a story. You know what that's like. How do you feel? Do you think it's really serious?'

'Yeah – listen, could you call Repair Service for me? This crazy thing won't let even Gervaise or anybody here do it when I ask them. But if you're off someplace in the city, that ought to be far enough away from whatever this short circuit is or whatever.'

'Of course. What's your—' Michaelmas closed his phone and sat again while the aircraft flew. He pictured Campion turning to Gervaise again.

'Mr Michaelmas,' Domino said after some silence. 'I just got Konstantinos Cikoumas's export license pulled. Permanently. He might as well leave Africa.'

'Very good.'

'Hanrassy has placed two calls to Gately in the past ten minutes and been told he was on another line.'

'Ah.'

'Gately's talking to Westrum.'

'Yes.'

'When they get confirmation from Norwood, they'll accept Wirkola's plan. Then Westrum will call Hanrassy and play her a recording of Norwood's confirming data. Gately was very pleased that Mr Westrum was making it unnecessary for Gately to speak to her at all.'

'It's funny how things work out.'

'You'll be landing in a few moments. Touchdown point is the meadow beyond the sanatorium parking lot. Even so, we may unsettle the patients.'

'Can't be helped. If they can stand news crews, they can absorb anything. That's fine, Domino. Thank you.'

There was another pause.

'Mr Michaelmas.'

'Yes.'

'I'll stay as close as I can. I don't know how near that will be. If any opportunity affords itself, I'll be there.'

'I know.'

The flight crewman's voice said: 'We are coming down now. A bell will ring.' The vibration became fuller, and the tone of the engines changed. Michaelmas sank and rose in his cushions, cradling the terminal in his hands. There was a thump. The bell rang and the ladder flew open. Michaelmas hit his quick release, slid out of his straps, and dropped down the ladder. '*Danke,*' he said.

He stepped out into the meadow above the parking lot, looking down at where they'd been parked, and the long steps down which the lens had rolled. He strode quickly forward, quartering across the slope toward the sanatorium entrance. Sanatorium staff were running forward across the grass.

'I have to go,' Domino said. 'I can feel it again.'

'Yes. Listen – it's best to always question yourself. Do you understand the reasons for that?'

There was no reply from the terminal.

The attendants were close enough so that he was being recognized. They slowed to a walk and frowned at him. He smiled and nodded. 'A little surprise visit. I must speak to Doctors Limberg and Cikoumas about some things. Where are they? Is it this way? I'll go there.' He moved through them toward the double doors, and through the doors. He passed the place where she'd broken her heel. He pushed down the corridor toward the research wing, his mind automatically following the floor plan Harry Beloit had shown Clementine. 'Not a public area?' he was saying to some staff person at his elbow. 'But I'm not of the public. I speak to the public. I must see Doctors Limberg and Cikoumas.' He came to the long cool pastel hallway among the labs. Limberg and Cikoumas were coming out of adjoining hall doors, staring at him, as the Type Beta rumbled up. 'Ah, there!' he said, advancing on them, spreading his arms and putting his hands on their shoulders. 'Exactly so!' he exclaimed with pleasure. 'Exactly the people I want. We have to talk. Yes. We have to talk.' He turned them and propelled them toward Limberg's door. 'Is this your office, Doctor? Can we talk in here? It seems comfortable enough. We need privacy. Thank you, Doctors. Yes.' He closed the door behind him, chatty and beaming. 'Well, now!' He propped one buttock on the corner of Limberg's desk. The two of them were standing in the middle of the floor, looking at him. He was counting in his head. He estimated about thirty minutes since Norwood's conversation with Gately. 'Well, here we three are!' he said, resting his hands on his thighs and leaning toward them attentively. 'Yes. Let's talk.'

TWELVE

Limberg put his head back and looked at him warily, his lips pursing. Then his mouth twitched into a flat little grimace. He turned and dropped into one of the two very comfortable-looking stuffed chairs. Against the raspberry-colored velour, he seemed very white in his crisp smock and his old skin and hair. He brought his knees together and sat with his hands lying atop them. He cocked his head and said nothing. His eyes darted sideward toward Cikoumas, who was just at the point of drawing himself up rigid and thrusting his hands into his pockets. Cikoumas said: 'Mister – ah – Michaelmas—'

'Larry. Please; this isn't a formal interview.'

'This is no sort of interview at all,' Cikoumas said, his composure beginning to return. 'You are not welcome here; you are not—'

Michaelmas raised an eyebrow and looked toward Limberg. 'I am not? Let me understand this, now … Medlimb Associates is refusing me hospitality before it even knows the subject I propose, and is throwing me out the door summarily?' He moved his hand down to touch the comm unit hanging at his side.

Limberg sighed softly. 'No, that would be an incorrect impression.' He shook his head slightly. 'Dr Cikoumas fully understands the value of good media relations.' He glanced at Cikoumas. 'Calm yourself, Kristiades, I suggest to you,' he went on in the same judicious voice. 'But, Mr Michaelmas, I do not find your behavior unexceptionable. Surely there is such a thing as calling for an appointment?'

Michaelmas looked around him at the office with its rubbed shelves of books, its tapestries and gauzy curtains, its Bokhara carpet and a broad window gazing imperviously out upon the slopes and crags of a colder, harsher place. 'Am I interrupting something?' he asked. 'It seems so serene here.' How much longer can it take to run? he was asking himself, and at the same time he was looking at Cikoumas and judging the shape of that mouth, the dexterity of those hands which quivered with ambition. 'It's only a few questions, Kiki,' he said. 'That's what they call you, isn't it – Kiki?'

Cikoumas suddenly cawed a harsh, brief laugh. 'No, Mr Michaelmas, *they* don't call me Kiki,' he said knowingly. 'Is that what you're here to ask?'

'Would he have found some way to beg a lift on a military aircraft,' Limberg commented, 'if that was the gravity of his errand?'

It didn't seem Cikoumas had thought that through. He frowned at Michaelmas now in a different way, and held himself more tensely.

Michaelmas traced a meaningless pattern on the rug with his shoe-tip. He flicked a little dust from his trouser leg, extending his wristwatch clear of his cuff. 'A great many people owe me favors,' he said. 'It's only fair to collect, once in a while.'

There was a chime in the air. 'Dr Limberg,' a secretarial voice said. 'You have an urgent telephone call.' Michaelmas looked around with a pleasant, distracted smile.

'I cannot take it now, Liselotte,' Limberg said. 'Ask them to call later.'

'It may be from Africa,' Michaelmas said.

Cikoumas blinked. 'I'll see if they'll speak to me. I'll take it in my office.' He slipped at once through the connecting door at the opposite side of Limberg's desk. Michaelmas traded glances with Limberg, who was motionless. 'Liselotte,' Limberg said, 'is it from Africa?'

'Yes, *Herr Doktor*. Colonel Norwood. I am giving the call to Dr Cikoumas now.'

'Thank you.' Limberg looked closely at Michaelmas. 'What has happened?' he asked carefully.

Michaelmas stood up and strolled across the room toward the window. He lifted the curtain sideward and looked out. 'He'll be giving Cikoumas the results of the engineering analysis on the false telemetry sender,' he said idly. He scratched his head over his left ear. He swept the curtain off to the side, and turned with the full afternoon light behind him. He leaned his shoulders against the cool plate glass.

Limberg was twisted around in his chair, leaning to look back at him. 'I had heard you were an excellent investigative reporter,' he said.

'I'd like to think I fill my role in life as successfully as you have yours.'

Limberg frowned faintly. A silence came over both of them. Limberg turned away for a moment, avoiding the light upon his eyes. Then he opened his mouth to speak, beginning to turn back, and Michaelmas said: 'We should wait for Cikoumas. It will save repeating.'

Limberg nodded slowly, faced forward again, and nodded to himself again. Michaelmas stayed comfortably where he was, facing the connecting door. The glass behind him was thrumming slightly, but no one across the room could see he was trembling, and the trembling had to do only with his body. Machinery hummed somewhere like an elevator rising, and then stopped.

Cikoumas came back after a few moments. He peered at Michaelmas up the length of the room. Behind him there was a glimpse of white angular objects, a gleam of burnished metals, cool, even lighting, a pastel blue composition tile floor. Then he closed the door. 'There you are.' He progressed to a show of indignation. 'I have something confidential to discuss with Dr Limberg.'

'Yes,' Michaelmas said. 'About the telemetry sender.' Cikoumas made his face blank.

Limberg turned now. 'Ah.' He raised a hand sideward. 'Hush one moment, Kristiades. Mr Michaelmas, can you tell us something about the sender?'

Michaelmas smiled at Cikoumas. 'Norwood has told you UNAC's analytical computer programs say the sender isn't Russian. It's a clever fake.' He smiled at Limberg. 'He says it's probably from Viola Hanrassy's organization.'

Cikoumas and Limberg found themselves trying to exchange swift glances. Limberg finally said: 'Mr Michaelmas, why would they think it's from Hanrassy?'

'When it isn't? Are you asking how has UNAC fooled Norwood?'

Cikoumas twitched a corner of his mouth. 'To do that, as you may not realize, they would have to reprogram their laboratory equipment. Events have been too quick for them to do that.'

'Ah. Well, then, are you asking why has Norwood become a liar, when he left here so sincere?'

Limberg shook his head patiently. 'He is too fine a man for that.' His eyes glittered briefly. 'Please, Mr Michaelmas. Explain for me.' He waved silence toward Cikoumas again. 'I am old. And busy.'

'Yes.' Not as busy as some. 'Well, now, as to why the sender appears a fake, when we all know it should appear genuine ...' He rubbed his knuckles gently in his palm. 'Sincere. If it could talk; if there was a way you could ask it Did He who made the lamb make Thee, it would in perfect honesty say *Da*.' And how does it do that, I wonder. Or how did they convince it? Which is it? What's that noise beyond Cikoumas's door? 'Then if you see the impossible occurring, Doctors, I would say perhaps there might be forces on this Earth which you had no way of taking into account.' He addressed himself directly to Limberg. 'It's not your fault, you see?'

Limberg nodded. The flesh around his mouth folded like paper.

Cikoumas dropped his jaw. 'How much *do* you know?'

Michaelmas smiled and spread his palms. 'I know there's a sincere Walter Norwood, where once over the Mediterranean there was nothing. Nothing,' he said. 'He'll be all right; nice job in the space program, somewhere. Administrative. Off flight status; too many ifs. Grow older. Cycle out, in time. Maybe get a job doing science commentary for some network.' Michaelmas straightened his shoulders and stood away from the window. 'It's all come apart, and you can't repeat it, you can't patch it up. Your pawns are taken. The Outer Planets expedition will go, on schedule, and others will follow it.' And this new sound, now.

It was a faint ripple of pure tones, followed by a mechanical friction as something shifted, clicked, and sang in one high note before quieting. Perhaps they didn't know how acute his ear for music was. Cikoumas had taken longer in there than he might have needed for a phone call.

Limberg said: 'Mr Michaelmas – these unknown forces … you are in some way representative of them?'

'Yes,' Michaelmas said, stepping forward. His knees were stiff, his feet arched. 'I am they.' His mouth stretched flat and the white ridges of his teeth showed. The sharp breath whistled through them as he exhaled the word. 'Yes.' He walked toward Cikoumas. 'And I think it's time you told your masters that I am at their gates.' As if I were deaf and they were blind. He stopped one step short of Cikoumas, his face upturned to look directly at the man. There's something in there. In his eyes. And in that room.

Cikoumas smiled coldly. That came more naturally to him than the attempts to act indecision or fear. 'The opportunity is yours, Mr Michaelmas,' he said, bowing from the waist a little and turning to open the door. 'Please follow me. I must be present to operate the equipment at the interview.'

'Kristiades,' Limberg said softly from his chair, 'be wary of him.'

There was no one beyond the door when Michaelmas followed Cikoumas through it.

It was a white and metal room of moderate size, its exterior wall paneled from floor to ceiling with semiglobular plastic bays, some translucent and others transparent, so that the mountains were repeated in fish-eye views among apparent circles of milky light. Overhead was the latest in laboratory lighting technique: a pearl-colored fog that left no shadows and no prominences. The walls were in matte white; closed panels covered storage. The composition underfoot was very slightly yielding.

To one side there was a free-standing white cylindrical cabinet, two and a half meters tall, nearly a meter wide. The faintest seams ran vertically and horizontally across its softly reflective surface. It jutted solidly up from the floor, as though it might be a continuation of something below.

Ahead of Michaelmas were storage cubes, work surfaces, instrumentation panels, sterile racks of teasing needles, forceps and scalpels, microtomes, a bank of micromanipulative devices – all shrouded beneath transparent flexible dust hoods or safe behind glassy panels.

Michaelmas looked around further. At his other hand was the partition wall to Limberg's office. From chest height onward, it was divided into small white open compartments like dovecotes. Below that was a bare workshelf and a tall, pale-blue-upholstered laboratory stool to sit on. Cikoumas motioned toward it. 'Please.'

Michaelmas raised his eyebrows. 'Are we waiting here to meet someone?'

Cikoumas produced his short laugh. 'It cannot come in here. It doesn't know where we are. Even if it did, it couldn't exist unprotected here.' He gestured to the chair again. 'Please.' He reached into one of the pigeonholes and produced a pair of headphones at the end of a spiral cord. 'I do not like the risk of having this voice overheard,' he said. 'Listen.' He cupped one earpiece in each hand and moved toward Michaelmas. 'You want to know?' he said, twisting his mouth. 'Here is knowledge. See what you make of it.'

Michaelmas grunted. 'And what would you like to know?'

Cikoumas shrugged. 'Enough to decide whether we must surrender to these forces of yours or can safely dispose of you, of course.'

Michaelmas chuckled once. 'Fair enough,' he said, and sat down. His eyes glittered hard as he watched Cikoumas's hands approach his skull. 'Lower away.'

Cikoumas rested the headphones lightly over his ears. Then he reached up and pulled out another set for himself. He stood close by, his hands holding each other, bending his body forward a little as if to hear better.

The voice was faint, though strong enough, probably, at its origins, but filtered, attenuated, distant, hollow, cold, dank: 'Michaelmasss ...' it said. 'Is that you? Cikoumas tells me that is you. Isss that what you are – Michaelmasss?'

Michaelmas grimaced and rubbed the back of his neck. 'How do I answer it?' he asked Cikoumas, who momentarily lifted one earpiece.

'Speak,' Cikoumas said, shifting eagerly around him. 'You are heard.'

'This is Michaelmas.'

'An entity ... you consider yourself an intelligent entity.'

'Yes.'

'Distinguishable in some manner from Limberg and Cikoumasss ...'

'Yes.'

'What does A equal?'

'Pi R squared.'

'What is the highest color of rainbows?'

'Red.'

'Would you eat one of your limbs if you were starving?'

'Yes.'

'Would you eat Cikoumas or Limberg if you were starving?'

Cikoumas was grinning faintly at him.

'First,' Michaelmas said coldly.

'An entity ... to speak to an intelligent entity ... in these circumstances of remoteness and displacement ... you have no idea how it feels ... to have established contact with three entities, now, under these peculiar circumstances ... to take converse with information-processors totally foreign ... never of one's accustomed bone and blood ...'

'I – ah – have some idea.'

'You argue?'

'I propose.'

'Marriage?'

'No. Another form of dialectical antagonism.'

'We are enemiesss ...? You will not join with Limberg and Cikoumas ...?'

'Why should I? What will you give?'

'I will make you rich and famous among your own ... kind ... Contact with my skills can be translated into rewards which are somehow gratifying to you ... individuals ... Cikoumas and Limberg can show you how it'sss done ...'

'No.'

'Repeat. Clarify. Synonimize.'

'Negative. Irrevocable refusal. Contradiction. Absolute opposition. I will not be one of your limbs.' He grinned at Cikoumas.

'Ah-hah! Ah-hah! Ah-hah! Then is your curiosity in the name of what you think science ...?'

'Justice.'

'Ah-hah! Ah-hah! Complex motivations ...! Ah-hah! The academician Zusykses sssaid to me this would be so; he said the concept is not of existences less than ours, but apart from oursss in origin only, reflecting perfectly that quality which we define as the high faculties; I am excited by your replies ... I shall tell my friend, Zusykses, when we reunite with each other this afternoon; his essential worth is validated!'

'I might be lying.'

'We know nothing of lies ... No, no, no ... in the universe, there is this and there is that. This is not that. To say this is that is to hold up to ridicule the universe. And that is an absurd proposition.'

'What is it, then, that isn't the truth but isn't a lie?'

Cikoumas looked at him with sudden intensity. But Michaelmas was nearly blind with concentration.

'Shrewd ... you are a shrewd questioner ... you speak of probability ... yesss ... it was my darling Zusykses who proposed the probability models of entities like you; who declared this structure was possible, and ssso must exist somewhere because the universe is infinite, and in infinity all things must occur. And yet this is only a philosophical concept, I said in rebuttal. But let me demonstrate, said my preceptor, Zusykses, in ardor to me; here, subordinate academician Fermierla, take here this probability coherence device constructed in accordance with my postulates ... while away this noon and ssseek such creaturesss as I say must be, for you shall surely find their substance somewhere flung within Creation's broadly scattered arms; take them up, meld of their varied strains that semblance which can speak and touch in simulacrum of a trueborn soul; regard then visage, form and even claim of self. Return to me, convinced – we tremble at the brink of learning all that life is. Clasp to yourself my thought made manifest, which is my self; know it, accept it, make it one with us; I shall not sssend you from me anymore ... —'

Michaelmas looked at Cikoumas, frowning. He lifted all the headphones but held them near his ears. Fermierla's voice continued faintly.

'It thinks we are chance occurrences,' Cikoumas said drily. 'It says this Zusykses, whatever it is, deduced that humanity must exist, since its occurrence is possible within the natural laws of the infinite universe. The probability of actually locating it to prove him right is, of course, infinitely small. So they think they are communicating with a demonstration model. Something they created with this probability coherer of theirs. It isn't likely to them that this is the human world. It's likelier that accidental concentrations of matter, anywhere in the universe, are moving and combining in such a manner that, by pure chance, they perfectly match infinitesimal portions of Zusykses' concept. Zusykses and Fermierla think the coherer detects and tunes an infinitely large number of these infinitely small concentrations together into an intelligible appearance. They think we might actually be anything – a sort of Brownian movement in the fabric of the universe – but that entirely at random in an infinity of chances, these selected particles invariably act to present the appearance of intelligent creatures in a coherent physical system.'

'Just one?' Michaelmas asked sharply.

Cikoumas's head twitched on its long, thin neck. 'Eh?'

'You're talking as if ours is the only probability Fermierla can reach with the coherer. But why should that be? He has his choice of an infinity of accidentally replicated pseudohuman environments, complete with all our rocks and trees and Boy Scout knives. It's all infinite, isn't it? Everything has to happen, and nearly everything has to happen, and everything twice removed, and thrice, and so forth?'

Cikoumas licked his lips. 'Oh. Yes. I suppose so. It seems a difficult concept. I must be quite anthropomorphic. And yet I suppose at this moment an infinite number of near-Fermierlas are saying an infinitely varied number of things to an infinity of us. A charming conceit. Do you know they also have absolutely no interest in where we actually are in relation to each other? Of course, they don't think we actually exist. And incidentally, where they are, this Fermierla creature has been waiting for afternoon since before Dr Limberg was my age. So there are massive displacements; the gravitic, temporal and electronic resistances involved must be enormous.'

'The what?'

'The resistances.' Cikoumas gestured impatiently. 'The universe is relativistic – You've heard of that, surely? – and although, as a life scientist, I am not concerned with all the little details of non-Newtonian physics, I read as much as I have time for—'

'Good enough, Doctor,' Michaelmas said. 'There's no point attempting to match your breadth of knowledge and my capacity just now.' He put the headphones back over his ears. The skin on his forearms chafed against his shirtsleeves in ten thousand places. Out of the corner of his eye he saw Cikoumas moving casually and reaching up to another pigeonhole.

'... fascinating possibilities ... to actually collaborate in experiments with you ... entities. Zusykses will be beside himself! How fares the astronaut; is it still viable? How does it act? Does it display some sign it is aware it has been tuned from one probability to another ... to reality, pardon.'

'He's well enough,' Michaelmas replied.

'It was a waste,' Cikoumas said distractedly. He was manipulating some new control up there, both hands hidden to the wrists while he turned his head to look over Michaelmas's shoulder. But he was trying to watch Michaelmas at the same time.

'Ah, that'sss a shame! You had such hopes for it a little while ago, Cikoumas! Perhaps then we should be obtaining the second Michaelmas from not that same probability ... What's your opinion, gentlemen?'

Michaelmas was on his feet, facing Cikoumas, the flexcord stretching nearly to its limit as he turned. Something had begun to whine and sing behind him. Cikoumas stared into his eyes, in the act of pulling one hand away from the wall, the custom-checkered walnut grip of a pistol showing at the bulge of reddish white palm and bony thumb. Michaelmas tore off the headphones and threw them at him. The strap for Domino's terminal, hung over his left shoulder, dropped across his forearm, twisted, and caught firmly there below his elbow. Spinning, the angular black box whipped forward and cracked into Cikoumas's thin head. He averted his face sharply and went flailing down backward, striking loudly against the floor and the angle of the wall. He lay forever motionless, flung wide.

Michaelmas moved like lightning to the wall. He jumped up to see what Cikoumas had been working. There were incomprehensible knobs and switches in there. He jumped again and snatched the pistol from its cubby. Working at it with both hands, he found the thumb-off for the energizer and the location of the trigger switch. He crouched and faced the white column. Its seams were widening. He stretched out his arms, pointing the pistol. His face convulsed. He turned instead and scrambled to his knees atop the stool, thrust the barrel up above eye level into the control cubby, and fired repeatedly. Clouds of acrid odor poured back into the room. Flame rioted among the sooty shadows, sputtered, and died down. He turned back, half toppling, and kicked the stool aside. The portals were no wider; not much more visible, really, than they had been. The singing had gone with the first shot. Now there was something beginning to bang in there; erratic and disoriented at first, but settling down to a hard rhythmic hammering, like a fist.

Limberg was standing in the doorway, looking. 'Send it,' Michaelmas said hoarsely, wide-eyed, gesturing, 'send it back.'

Limberg nodded listlessly and walked slowly to the controls. He looked at them, shook his head, and fumbled in his pockets for a key ring. 'I shall have to use the master switches,' he said. He went to the opposite wall and unlocked a panel. Michaelmas moved to the center of the floor, holding the pistol and panting. Limberg looked back at him and twitched his mouth. He opened the wall and ran a finger hesitantly along a row of blank circles. He shrugged, finally, and touched two. They and most of the others sprang into green life. One group went red-to-orange-to-yellow, flickering.

'Hurry,' Michaelmas said, taking a deep breath.

'I'm not expert at this,' Limberg said. He found an alternate subsection by running a forefinger along until he appeared reasonably confident. He pushed hard with all the fingers of his hand, and the cylindrical white cabinet began to sing again. Michaelmas's hands jerked. But the seams were closing; soon they could hardly be seen. The whining came, and then diminished into nothing. The beating and kicking sounds stopped. Michaelmas wiped the back of his hand across his upper lip. 'He had me in contact with it long enough, didn't he?' he said. 'It was faster than it must have been with Norwood.'

'Yes,' Limberg said. 'Norwood had to be individualized for Fermierla with many, many bits from television documentary recordings. There were many approximations not close enough. Many rejects. In your case, it was possible to present you as a physical model of what was wanted.' He began to close the panel. 'Is there anything else?'

'Leave it open, Doctor.' Michaelmas frowned and cleared his throat. 'Leave it open,' he tried again, and was better satisfied. He went back to where his headphones still hung from the wall, and started to lift them. He looked at the pistol in his hand, safetied it, and tossed it into the nearest cubby. He slipped the headphones over his ears. There was almost nothing to hear: '... sss ... err ... masss ...' and it was very faint. He put one fist around the cord and pulled the jack out, removed the headphones, and laid them gently on the workshelf. He turned to Limberg: 'Shut it down. Everything on your end; all the stuff Cikoumas has wired in over the years.'

Limberg looked at him, overwhelmed. But he saw something in Michaelmas's face and nodded. He ran his hands over the controls and all of them went steady red. He bowed his head.

'I'm in. I'm here,' Domino said. 'I've got their household systems. Where's the rest?'

'Wait,' Michaelmas said. Limberg had left the panel and gone over to where

Cikoumas lay. He sat down on the floor beside him and with his fingers began combing the lank hair forward over the wound. He looked up at Michaelmas. 'He was attempting to protect humanity,' he said. 'He couldn't let the astronauts reach Jupiter.'

Michaelmas looked back at him. 'Why not?'

'That's where the creatures must be. It is the largest, heaviest body in the Solar System, with unimaginable pressures and great electrical potentials. It is a source of radio signals, as everyone knows. Kristiades discussed it with me increasingly after he saw all your broadcasts with the astronauts. 'Such men will find the race of Zusykses,' he said. 'It will be a disaster for us.' And he was right. We are safe from their full attentions only as long as they think we are not real. We must remain hidden among all the accidental systems.'

'Yes,' Michaelmas said. 'Of course.'

'He was a brilliant genius!' Limberg declared. 'Far worthier than I!'

'He sold out his fathers and his brothers and his sons for a striped suit.'

'What will I tell his family?'

'What did you tell them when you said you'd send the grocer's boy to Paris?'

Limberg's upper body rocked back and forth. His eyes closed. 'What shall I do with his body?'

'What was he going to do with mine?' Michaelmas began to say. Looking at Limberg, he said instead: 'Your systems are being monitored now, and you mustn't touch them. But a little later today, I'll call you, and you can begin to reactivate them step by step under my direction.'

'Right,' Domino said.

Michaelmas watched Limberg carefully. He said: 'When you've reestablished contact with Fermierla, you can shift out this Cikoumas and shift in—'

Limberg's creased cheeks began to run with silent tears.

'For his family,' Michaelmas said. He turned to go. 'For their sake, find one who's a little easier to get along with, this time.'

Limberg stared. 'I would not in any case have it want to be here with me. I will send it home to him.' He said: 'I felt when first you began here with us that you were a messenger of death.'

'Domino,' Michaelmas said, 'get me a cab.' He pushed through the door and out into the hall, then along that and past the auditorium, where convalescent ladies and gentlemen were just chattily emerging and discussing the psychically energizing lecture of the therapy professor, and then out through the double doors, and waited outside.

THIRTEEN

He said little to Domino on the ride to the airport, and less on the flight back to New York City. He made sure the Papashvilly interview was going well; otherwise, he initiated nothing, and sat with his chin in his hand, staring at God knew what. From time to time his eyes would attempt to close, but other reflexes and functions in his system would jerk them open again.

From time to time Domino fed him tidbits in an attempt to pique his interest:

'Hanrassy has reneged on her promise to grant EVM an interview.' And a little later:

'Westrum's speaking to Hanrassy. Should I patch you in?'

'No. Not unless she takes charge of the conversation.'

'She's not.'

'That's good enough, then.' He thought of that tough, clever woman on the banks of the Mississippi, putting down her phone and trying to reason out what had happened. She'd alibi to herself eventually – everyone did. She'd decide Norwood and Gately and Westrum were conspiring, somehow, and she'd waste energy trying to find the handle to that. She'd campaign, but she'd be a little off balance. And if it seemed they might still need to play it, there was always the ace in the hole with the income tax official. And that was the end of her. Somewhere among her followers, or in her constituency, was the next person who'd try combining populism and xenophobia. It was a surefire formula that had never in the entire history of American democracy been a winner in the end.

They come and they go, he thought. He rubbed the skin on the backs of his hands, which seemed drier than last year and more ready to fold into diamond-shaped, choppy wrinkles, as if he were a lake with a breeze passing across it.

The EVM crew staked out in Gately's anteroom finally found him consenting to receive them.

'I'd like to take this opportunity to announce to the world,' Gately said, 'that we are to have the honor, the privilege, and the great personal gratification to welcome Colonel Norwood to these shores on his impending visit.' He had changed out of his sweatsuit and was wearing a conservatively cut blue vested pinstripe that set off his waistline when he casually unbuttoned his jacket. He looked almost young enough to go back on active status himself, but his eyes were a little too careful to follow every movement of every member of the interview crew.

Time passed. President Fefre had a mild attack interpreted as indigestion. A man in Paris attempted to leave a flight bag of explosives in the upper elevator of the Eiffel Tower, but police alerted by a fortuitous tap into a political conversation arrested him promptly. Another man, in Florence, was found to have embezzled a huge amount of money from the funds of the provincial lottery. He was the brother of the provincial governor; it seemed likely that there would be heightened public disillusion in that quarter of the nation. Rome, which had been a little dilatory in its supervision, would have to be a bit more alert for some time, so who was to say there was not some good in almost anything? And most of the money was recovered. Also, a small private company in New Mexico, composed of former engineering employees striking out on their own, applied for a patent on an engine featuring half the energy consumption of anything with comparable output. The president of the company and his chief engineer had originally met while coincidentally booked into adjoining seats on an intercity train. Meanwhile, a hitherto insignificant individual in Hamburg ran his mother-in-law through the eye with a fork at his dinner table, knocked down his wife, went to the waterfront, attempted clumsily to burn his father-in-law's warehouse, and professed honestly to have lost all memory of any of these preceding events when he was found sitting against a bollard and crying with the hoarse persistence of a baby while staring out over the water. But not all of this was reported to Michaelmas immediately. Domino thought and thought on what the world might be like when a completely even tenor had settled over all its policies, and there was nothing left for the news to talk about but the incessant, persistent, perhaps rising sound of individual people demanding to assert their existence.

Two trains were inadvertently switched onto the same track in Holland. But another switch, intended to stay closed, opened fortuitously, and the freight slid out of the path of the holiday passenger express.

In the systems of the Limberg Sanatorium, there was nothing overt.

'All right, then,' Domino said, 'if you don't want to listen, will you talk? What happened at the sanatorium? Limberg's keeping everybody out of the room with Cikoumas's body, seeing no one, sitting in his office, and obviously waiting for someone to tell him what to do next.'

Michaelmas grunted. He said: 'Well, they were laboratory curiosities and the person in charge of them is sentimental and intrigued. When they proposed something ingenious, such as moving something coherent from one arbitrary frame of reference into a highly similar frame, they were indulged. Why not? The experiment may be trivial, or it may be taken as proof that there are no orders of greater or lesser likelihood among sets, but in either case it was suggested by a member of the experiment. You have to admit that would intrigue almost anyone, let alone a poet in heat.' Michaelmas smiled as though something had struck his mouth like a riding whip. 'Poke around, now that you're inside Limberg's system. Open one part of the circuitry at a time. You'll meet what's been chasing you. Be careful to keep a firm hold on the switching.'

There was a pause. Then the machine was back. 'It ... it seems we here are considered an effect.' Domino paused again.

'We are an effect,' Michaelmas said. 'They have a means of scanning infinity. When they want a model of an elephant, they tune out everything that doesn't look like an elephant. When they deduce there's a human race, they get a human race. Warts and all. The difference between the model of the elephant and the human race is that the representatives of that race can speak; they can request, and they can propose. They can even believe they think they represent *the* human race. But in all of infinity, the chances are infinite that they are only drifting particles.'

He said nothing more for a long time, blinking like an owl in the bright midafternoon sunshine of Long Island, looking a little surprised when his bag was put aboard his cab for him.

In the apartment, he sat at the desk, he brooded out the window, he tuned his guitar, and then a lute, and a dulcimer. Finally he began to be able to speak, and spoke to Domino in a slow, careful voice, pausing to marshal his facts and to weigh them in accord with their importance to the narrative.

He barely listened to himself explaining. He sat and thought:

I cannot find you.
At proper seasons I can hear
The migrant voices as the flocks in air
Move north or south against the sun.
They come, they go, they move as one,
and darken briefly.
I cannot find you.

'So that was it?' Domino asked. 'Mere scientific curiosity? This Fermierla contacted Limberg at some point in the past – Well, why not? They must have been very much alike, at one time; yes, I can see the sense in that – and then Limberg began to see ways in which this could be useful, but it was after he brought in Cikoumas that the enterprise began to accelerate. Fermierla still thinking it was in touch with fantasy creatures—'

'Not in touch. Not ... in touch.'

'In contact with. And Medlimb prospered. But Cikoumas became worried; suppose UNAC found Fermierla? Suppose Doktor Limberg was exposed to the world for what he was, and Cikoumas with him. But that's all unrealistic.

Fermierla's no more on Jupiter than I am. These biological people are all scientific illiterates, rife with superstition. You tell them radio signals, and they think WBZ. They have no idea of the scale of what's involved here. They—'

'Yes, yes,' Michaelmas said. 'Take over Limberg, will you? Manage the rest of his life for him. Meanwhile, there's one more thing I have to do before I can end this day.'

'Yes, I suppose,' Domino said, and put in a call to Clementine Gervaise, who was in Paris. Michaelmas squeezed his hands and punched up full holo; she sat at a desk within a few feet of him, a pair of eyeglasses pushed up into her hair, her lipstick half worn off her lower lip, and a hand-editing machine beside the desk.

'Laurent,' she said, 'it is good to have you call, but you catch me at a devil of a time.' She smiled suddenly. 'Nevertheless, it is good to have you call.' The smile was fleetingly very young. 'From New York.' Now she appeared a little downcast. 'You departed from Europe very quickly.'

'I didn't expect you in Paris. I thought you'd still be in Africa.'

She shook her head. 'We have a problem,' she said. She turned to the editor, flicked fingers over the keyboard with offhand dexterity, and gestured: 'See there.'

A sequence aboard the UNAC executive plane came up. Norwood was smiling and talking. The point of view changed to a reverse angle closeup of Douglas Campion asking a question. As he spoke, his forehead suddenly swelled, then returned to normal, but his eyes lengthened and became slits while the bridge of his nose seemed to valley into his skull. Next his mouth enlarged, and his chin shrank. Finally the ripple passed down out of sight, but another began at the top of his head, while he spoke on obliviously.

'We can't get it out,' Clementine said. 'It happens in every shot of Campion. We've checked the computer, we've checked our mixers.' She shrugged. 'I suppose someone will say we should check this editor, too, now. But we are either going to have to scrap the entire program or substitute another interviewer.'

'Can't you get hold of Campion and reshoot him?'

She made an embarrassed little face. 'I think he is overdrawn at his bank, or something of that sort. He cannot get validation for an airplane seat. Not even his telephone works,' she said. She blushed slightly. 'I am in a little trouble for recommending that sort of person.'

'Oh, come, Clementine, you're not seriously worried about that. Not with your talent. However, that is amazing about Campion. He seems to be having a run of bad luck.'

'Well, this isn't why you called me,' she said. She waved a hand in dismissal behind her. 'Either that works or it doesn't; tomorrow comes anyway. You're right.' She rested her elbows on her desktop and cupped her face in her hands, looking directly at him: 'Tell me – what is it you wish with me?'

'Well, I just wanted to see how you were,' he said slowly. 'I rushed off suddenly, and—'

'Ah, it's the business. Whatever you went for, I suppose you got it. And I suppose the rest of us will hear about it on the news.'

'Not – not this time, I'm afraid.'

'Then it was personal.'

'I suppose.' He was having trouble. 'I just wanted to say "Hello."'

She smiled. 'And I would like to say it to you. When are you next in Europe?'

He took a breath. It was hard to do. He shrugged. 'Who knows?' He found himself beginning to tremble.

'I shall be making periodic trips to North America very soon, I think. I could even request doing coverage of Norwood's US tour. It starts in a few days. It's only an overnight wonder, but if we move it quickly, there will still be interest.' She cocked an eyebrow. 'Eh? What do you think? We could be together in a matter of days.'

He thrust back convulsively in his chair. 'I – ah – call me,' he managed. 'Call me when it's definite. If I can …' He squirmed. She began to frown and to tilt her head the slightest bit to one side, as if gazing through a shop window at a hat that had seemed more cunning from a little farther away. '… if I'm here,' he was saying, he realized.

'Yes, Laurent,' she said sadly. 'We must keep in touch.'

In the night for many years, he would from time to time say the word 'touch' distinctly, without preamble, and thrust up his arms toward his head, but this was not reported to him.

'*Au 'voir.*'

'*Au revoir*, Clementine.' He ended the call, and sat for a while.

'Well,' Domino said, 'now you know how you feel.'

Michaelmas nodded. 'She may readily have been given only conventional treatment at the sanatorium. But, yes, now we know how I feel.'

'I could check the records.'

'Like you checked their inventories.'

'Now that I'm situated in their covert hardware, I'm quite confident I can assimilate any tricks in their soft mechanisms. I can run a real check.'

'Yes,' Michaelmas said sadly. 'Run a real check on infinity.'

'Well …'

'Life's too short,' Michaelmas said.

'Yours?'

'No.' Michaelmas stretched painfully, feeling the knotted muscles and grimacing at the swollen taste of his tongue. He worked the bed and began undressing. Somewhere out beyond his windows, a helicopter buffeted by on some emergency errand. He shook his head and closed his eyes momentarily. He opened them long enough to pull back the coverlet. 'No calls,' he said, darkening the windows. 'Not for eight hours; longer if possible.' He lay down, pulling the cover up over the hunch of his shoulder, putting his left hand on his right wrist and his right hand under his cheek. He settled himself. 'It's one good feature of this occupation,' he remarked in a voice that trailed away. 'I never have any trouble getting to sleep.'

HARD LANDING

Dedication
Judy Lynn del Rey, an editor

Acknowledgment
Brian Thomsen, a very patient editor

Card of Thanks
Betty Smith and Eric Wegner, two invaluable hands

Disclaimer
Everything that follows is a lie.
Especially, of course, the parts that seem real.

PART OF A REPORT LATER REMOVED FROM THE AO/LGM FILE ON NEVILLE SEALMAN

The electrocuted man was found dead on the northbound tracks of the Borrow Street station of the Chicago Transit Authority suburban line in Shoreview, Illinois.

Shoreview is a city of 80,000 located on the Lake Michigan western shore immediately north of Chicago. For our purposes here, it can be regarded simply as a place where middle-class Chicago employees sleep and do their weekend errands.

It was early March and the time was 5:50 PM ... a dark, chilled, wet evening. No witnesses to the death of the individual calling himself Neville Sealman have come forward.

Despite the occurrence on CTA property, the Shoreview Police Department took jurisdiction and investigated. (The CTA police force is strictly a peacekeeping body). Sergeant Dothan Stablits of the Shoreview PD was assigned. Before the body was moved, a representative of the CTA legal department arrived, and was extended cooperation by investigator Stablits. They went through the decedent's pockets together.

The contents supported identification of the decedent as Neville Unruh Sealman, a resident of south Shoreview. Documentation included an Illinois state driver's license and Social Security and Blue Cross cards found in his unrifled wallet, which also contained a normal amount of cash.

Social Security files later revealed the number had been issued against a falsified application. The driver's license had been properly acquired so far as procedures at the Illinois examining station went. (The decedent, however, never owned a car.) Records show the applicant identified himself at the time with a certified copy of Neville Sealman's birth certificate, which seems to have been acquired through the now well-known method of searching small-town newspaper obituaries for the names of persons dead in infancy. [Neville Unruh Sealman, b. — d. 1932, Mattoon, Ill.] The decedent's thirtyish appearance was consistent with the claimed age of 43 on the license.

The body was turned over to the Cook County coroner's office and a search for next of kin was instituted. (None were ever located; no friends were found, and no one who had been acquainted with the decedent any longer than the forty-two months of his residence and employment in the

Chicago area. All the decedent's acquaintances were fellow employees or neighbors.)

Investigation at Sealman's home address – an apartment four stops before the stop where the body was found – developed the information that Sealman lived alone and unvisited in a furnished one-and-one-half-room efficiency. Any clues found in the apartment all supported the Sealman identity, and none of them were older than the time of Sealman's successful application for employment at Magnussen Engineering Co.

Magnussen is a free-lance drafting shop in a Chicago loft, and the requirement for filling a job opening is the ability to demonstrate standard proficiency at the craft; a Social Security number is the only document required of a prospective employee. No further information of any kind relating to his identity was ever found. His dwelling was unusually bare of knickknacks and personality. Nothing was found to indicate that he had ever been treated by any medical or dental facility, and this proved to be a matter of some concern in the initial investigation. (See further.)

Inquiry by Dothan Stablits at Magnussen indicated Sealman had been employed there since purportedly moving from Oakland, Cal. On the day of his death, he had left work at 5:00 PM as usual and boarded the Shoreview Express at the elevated State Street platform of the CTA. The northbound platform is visible from the windows of his place of employment, and he was observed in this action by his employer, who also described him as a steady, hardworking individual with nervous mannerisms and a lack of sociability.

Sealman's apartment was in due course released to the building management, and the personal contents transferred to the Cook County coroner's warehouse, where they remain unclaimed. Sergeant Stablits's report accurately describes them as items of clothing and personal care products purchasable at chain outlets in the Chicago/Shoreview vicinity. [A copy of that report is attached.] [Attachment 6]

Sergeant Stablits's Occurrence Report [Attachment 1] reflects a certain degree of uneasiness with the circumstances of the decedent's death.

The Borrow Street station is located in a purely residential section. The timing indicates Sealman must have ridden directly past his normal stop, but Stablits was unable to ascribe a reason for his doing so. Despite publicity in the Chicago news media and in the weekly *Shoreview Talk* newspaper, no one ever reported Sealman missing from an intended visit. Sergeant Stablits (now Chief Stablits of the Gouldville, Indiana, Police Department) clearly felt that this loose end impeded a satisfactory clearance of Sealman's file. But despite Sealman's insufficient bona fides, there was nothing actually inconsistent with a finding of accidental death, and no compelling reason to expend further resources and press the investigation further – for instance, out of state to Oakland. When the FBI proved to have no record of his fingerprints, his file, though not closed, was simply kept available in the event some fresh occurrence might reactivate it. No such event took place.

The CTA legal department at first took a more than routine interest in the case. The Borrow Street station dates from 1912. It is located in a deep open cut well below the level of adjacent streets and dwellings, the right-of-way north of the Chicago elevated structures having gradually gone to street level and then below. This secluded location added to the unlikelihood of finding a witness to explain Sealman's death. It's safe to say the CTA was anticipating a negligence lawsuit by heirs.

Portions of the station structure have weathered to a rickety condition, and it is scheduled to be completely rebuilt in 1981. The condition of the platform is decrepit. Half the platform lights are not functional, and the exit stairs up to street level, cast in reinforced concrete and subject to extreme weathering action once the surface had spalled away to the included rust-prone steel, are frankly hazardous.

(The CTA operates at a loss, and is seeking some sort of public subsidy. Its trackage and equipment include property acquired from inefficient predecessor operating authorities and bankrupt private traction companies.)

Despite the nonappearance of immediate potential litigants, the CTA felt that all possible steps should be taken to exclude the possibility of the decedent's having tripped, fallen to the tracks, and contacted the third rail as the result of some structural feature of the platform. Frankly, that seemed an obvious possibility, but a history of cardiovascular disorders in Sealman, or some other cause of chronic vertigo, would have done much to brighten up the CTA's files. Almost as satisfactory would have been evidence to support a finding of probable suicide, or even of foul play. On none of these possibilities was Sergeant Stablits able to turn up anything that would help.

On finding there were no medical or dental offices located within reasonable distance of the stop, he made no further effort to locate any medical practitioner who might have had Sealman as a patient. His interest was limited to finding a reason for Sealman's presence on that platform that night, and he indicated to the CTA that if they wanted to check with every doctor in the Chicago area, they could do that on their own budget. After this time, the CTA and Shoreview PD efforts continued separately (and terminated inconclusively separately).

In this atmosphere, a number of private as well as official communications were exchanged between the CTA, the Cook County medical examiner's office, and individuals therein acting on an informal basis. As a consequence, the medical examiner's office assigned its most experienced forensics pathologist to the autopsy, and that individual proceeded with great care and attention to detail.

Soon after beginning his examination of the thoracic cavity, this pathologist – Albert Camus, M.D. – notified the medical examiner that he was encountering noteworthy anomalies. The procedure was then confidentially completed in the presence of the medical examiner, and certain administrative decisions were then made.

The findings filed were consistent with death by electrocution and no other cause, which was in fact true according to the evidence, and the CTA was so notified. At some point, it must have become increasingly clear that no legatees were in the offing, so the CTA may not have taken Dr Camus's official report as hard as it would have a few days sooner. In any event, the CTA's file has subsequently been marked inactive, and there has been no change in that status.

The medical examiner's file, however, reflects the great number of confusions raised by the pathologist's discovery of what he described as 'a high-capacity, high-pressure' cardiovascular system, as well as a number of other significant and anatomically consistent variations from the norm. [Attachment 2]

At Dr Camus's suggestion, a telephone call was placed to this office,* with the objective of determining whether these findings were unique.

On receipt of the call here, a case officer (undersigned) was immediately allocated by the Triage Section, and put on the line. A request was made to the Cook County medical examiner for a second autopsy, and Dr William Henshaw, a resource of this office, was dispatched to Shoreview via commercial air transportation. [Attachment 7, Voucher of Expenses]

At the same time, an AO/LGM Notification was forwarded to our parent organization. (EXCERPT ENDS)

NOTE: CASE OFFICER'S SIGNATURE

ILLEGIBLE

* The National Register of Pathological Anomalies, Washington, D.C.

AUTHOR'S NOTE ON THE NATIONAL REGISTER OF PATHOLOGICAL ANOMALIES

The National Register of Pathological Anomalies is federally funded and was formed in the late 1940s. It publishes bulletins to tax-supported pathological services and other interested parties. This information is restricted to describing unusual anatomical structures and functions found in the course of routine postmortem examinations.

There are a number of 'usual' anomalies, and the NRPA doesn't concern itself with them. Quite a few people have their hearts located toward the right side of the chest, or are born without a vermiform appendix. Extra fingers and toes, and anomalous genitalia, are other everyday examples. One of the earliest things a medical student learns is that the details of any given human being's internal arrangements will be roughly similar to but teasingly different from the tidy diagrams in the textbooks. This happens without impairing the individual's general function as a clearly, understandably human and essentially healthy organism. Anatomy classes dispel any notion that God works with a cookie cutter. The idea they do create is that the mechanisms of life are both subtler and more determined to proceed than most people can imagine. In many cases, these anomalies are successful enough so that they're never noted during the individual's lifetime. Since most deaths are not followed by autopsies, there are no reliable statistics on how prevalent all this might be.

What this does mean is that there are any number of individuals walking around who will respond peculiarly to conventional medical and surgical treatment, who might overcome what ought to be disabling or fatal injuries while succumbing to apparently minor accidents, or who might even be able to evade normal methods of restraint and punishment – to name a few areas of intense interest to authorities charged with the maintenance of the public health and good order.

The NRPA publications concern themselves only with extreme cases. They also draw exact distinctions between kinds of extreme. There are what might be called man-made anomalies; defects almost certainly created by actions of various manufactured substances upon the individual's mother during her pregnancy. These, while not completely cataloged, are part of a distinct field of medical investigation that's keeping reasonable pace with the ingenuities of recreational drug use and the pyramiding effects of modern industrial chemistry. The NRPA describes apparent cases in this category when they're found, and this reason alone suffices to make its bulletins widely studied. But there is another category.

Occasionally, an autopsy will turn up organs, or even systems of organs, that are truly unique and whose function, in fact, may not be understandable to the resources of the pathologist who discovers them. The NRPA is very quick to react positively in such cases. At once, it will give the examiner all the help and information humanly possible, and join in delving into the matter thoroughly. As a result of its reputation for this sort of help, always welcomed even by pathology departments that have been nominally well funded, the NRPA's twenty-four-hour phone number is kept very much in mind throughout all nations signatory to the cross-cooperation agreements fostered by the World Health Organization.

It should be understood that almost invariably, one mundane explanation or the other is finally found for the seeming anomaly displayed by the particular case.

The NRPA's annual budget is drawn against funds made available by Congress to a parent organization. This form of second-derivative funding is common in cases where the parent organization is the Central Intelligence Agency, the Federal Bureau of Investigation, or the National Security Agency, to name just three. It hasn't been possible for me to determine the NRPA's parent organization.

AO stands for 'anomalous organs.' Most NRPA files are headed with the AO prefix followed by a number coded to show the date the file was opened and predict when it might be closed. These files form the basis for most of the material in the bulletins, and are of unquestionable immediate value to medical specialists dealing with the results of human interactions.

A far lesser portion of the files is headed AO/LGM, in which the second set of initials in the prefix is said to represent 'less germane matters.' Access to and use of these files is restricted to the top echelons of NRPA. An AO/LGM Notification – at one time a slip printed on red paper, now an advice preceded by a special tone signal on the NRPA's computerized communications devices, which connect to God knows where – is required the instant a new file in this category is opened. At NRPA, which is housed in a three-story red brick Georgian with a very nice little company café under the trees in the backyard, there's an office joke that LGM really stands for Little Green Men.

– A.B.

PRELUDE TO EVENTS EARLY ON
A MARCH EVENING

Jack Mullica had almost stopped being annoyed with Selmon for riding the same train with him. It had now been three and a half years since he had first seen Selmon standing at the other end of the State Street northbound platform in the five-o'clock sunshine of late September.

It had been nothing like it was in the winter when the wind they called the Hawk hunted through the Loop. The people among whom the two men stood had their heads up, and did not jockey to take shelter behind each other on the elevated platform.

Their eyes met across an interval of some ten yards, and Selmon's mouth dropped open. Not until he saw the stranger's reaction did Mullica fully realize what had been naggingly familiar about him. Mullica watched a look of total defeat come over Selmon. He stood there, shorter and a little chubbier than Mullica remembered him, his head now down, his herringbone topcoat suddenly too big for him, a briefcase hanging from one hand, a *Daily News* from the other. He didn't even board the train. He stayed where he was, washed by low-angle sunlight and forlorn, thunderstruck, waiting at least for the next train, not looking in the window as Mullica rode by him.

But the next night he had boarded, and hadn't gotten off until just a few stops before Mullica's, staring rigidly ahead and keeping his shoulders stiff. It had become a regular thing. Selmon rode as many cars away from Mullica as he could. He was there almost every night Mullica was. Mullica traveled out of town fairly frequently. He assumed Selmon didn't, though at first he watched carefully behind him in airline terminals and out at motels. But Selmon never turned up anywhere else and he never made any attempt at an approach. After a while Mullica decided that was how it was going to be.

Gradually, thinking about it in the slow, schooled way he had taught himself, Mullica reached an accommodation with the situation. He assumed that Selmon had simply happened to take a job nearby, and that the rest of it was natural enough; it was all coincidence, Selmon's working near Mullica and living in the same town with Mullica and his wife, Margery.

The Shoreview Express was designed to handle North Shore traffic in and out of the Loop. Once it had made all the Loop stops, picking up shoppers on the east and south sides, and management types on the west and north, it paused at the Merchandise Mart and then didn't stop again until Loyola

University. It rumbled directly over the worst parts of the North Side on girdered elevated tracks, and then imperceptibly began running on a solid earthen viaduct through blue-collar, and then lower-middle-class residential neighborhoods. The farther north it ran, the more respectable its environment became and the more out of place the shabby old string of riveted iron cars appeared, until it reached the end of Chicago at Howard Street, entered Shoreview as an all-stops local, and began to look quaint.

Its first Shoreview stop was Elm Shore Avenue, in an area only slightly distinguishable from the red-brick northernmost part of Chicago, and this was where Selmon got off. Mullica lived in a white and yellow high rise near the Borrow Street stop, which the train reached rattling over switch points, its collector shoes arcing, flashing, and sputtering over gaps in the third rail system; at night it rode through sheets of violet fire. The train's next and last destination was in Wilmette, which was yet another municipality and where one could begin to see the prewar money living in its rows of increasingly large and acreage-enshrouded mansions all the way up the lakefront for miles. From Wilmette and beyond, they usually drove into the city in cars suitable for after-nine arrivals, or took the North Western Rail Road and smoked and played bridge.

Mullica's hours in the Chicago public relations office of one of the major automobile manufacturers were nominally nine to five. He usually got in about nine-fifteen, getting back some of the three A.M.S on the road. He never saw Selmon in the morning; probably he had to be at work by eight-thirty.

At night on the platform, Selmon would open his paper as soon as he was through the turnstile. He would read it at his end of the platform, holding it in front of his face. Mullica would stand just where he had stood every time since years before Selmon. Mullica opened his paper on the train, and when he was nearly finished, the sound of the wheels echoing back would tell him they were off the viaducts and beginning to run between the weed-grown cutbanks of the right-of-way in north Shoreview. He'd fold his paper, get up from the warped, timeworn cane seat, and go stand in the chipped brown vestibule waiting for the uncertain brakes to drag the train to a halt. He'd get off, walk the three blocks to the condominium, greet Margery if she was home, have a drink looking out over the lake with a closed expression, and do the crossword puzzle in ink before throwing the paper out. He wished Selmon would play by the rules and move away. But Selmon wouldn't. He continued to work somewhere in the Loop at something, and to live somewhere two miles south.

AN OCCURRENCE EARLY ON
A MARCH EVENING

Mullica never saw Selmon in Shoreview on weekends. Margery liked to go shopping in the big malls at Old Orchard and Golf Mill; Mullica had a Millionaires' Club membership, and sometimes they'd sit there after shopping, sipping. Sometimes then Mullica would be able to just stare over Margery's shoulder and think about any number of things. At times, he thought of Selmon. He wondered if he hid in his home on weekends, and if he had found a wife, and, if so, how they got along. He wondered if Margery might run into her someday and if, by some coincidence, they might get friendly enough to talk about their husbands. But it seemed unlikely; Margery didn't get along with women.

And then it was early March, forty-two months since Selmon had turned up. Mullica stood on the platform, his hands deep in his pockets. It was a cold, raw day. He watched Selmon stubbornly unfolding his paper against the wind, and clutching it open as he began to read. Then, just as their train began to pull into the station, Selmon saw something in the paper that made him turn his face toward Mullica in the twilight in a white blur of dismay, his mouth a dark open oval, and Mullica thought for a minute Selmon had felt a vessel exploding in his brain.

The train pulled up and Mullica stepped aboard. He moved down the aisle and took a seat next to a window. He looked out at Selmon's spot as the train passed by it, thinking he might see Selmon lying there huddled in a crowd, but he wasn't there.

Mullica put his zipcase across his knees and opened his paper, sitting there reading from front to back as he always did, while the train crossed the river toward the Merchandise Mart. He stopped to look eastward along the river, as he always did, year round, enjoying the changing light of the seasons on the buildings and the water and horizon. The riverfront buildings were just turning into boxes of nested light, their upper story glass still reflecting the last streaks of dying pink from the sunset, and the stars were beginning to appear in the purplish black sky above the lake.

Page two had the story:

Not-So-Ancient Astronauts?
'THING' IN JERSEY SWAMP IS SAUCER,
EXPERT SAYS

PHILADELPHIA, MARCH 9 (AP) – Swamp-draining crews in New Jersey may have found a spaceship, declared scientist Allen Wolverton today.

Authorities on the spot immediately denied that old bog land being readied for a housing development held anything mysterious.

Local authorities agreed a domed, metal object, fifty feet across, was dragged from the soil being reclaimed from Atlantic coastal marshes. They quickly pointed out, however, that there is a long history of people living in the swamps, described as the last rural area remaining on the Eastern Seaboard between Boston and Virginia.

The area was populated and prosperous in Colonial times, the center of a thriving 'bog iron' mining industry. Local experts were quick to point to this as the likely source of the object, citing it as some sort of machinery or a storage bin.

'There was whole towns and stagecoach stops back in there once,' said Henry Stemmler, operator of a nearby crossroads grocery store. 'Big wagon freight yards and everything. There's all kinds of old stuff down in the bogs.'

Dissenting is Wolverton, a lecturer at Philadelphia's Franklin Planetarium. 'Our earth is only one of thousands of inhabitable planets,' he declared. 'Statistically, the galaxy must hold other intelligent races. It would be unreasonable to suppose at least one of them isn't visiting us and surreptitiously observing our progress toward either an enlightened civilization of peace and love or total self-destruction.'

There was a blurred two-column wire photo of two men standing in some underbrush, staring at a curved shape protruding from the ground. There were no clearly defined features, and the object's outline was broken by blending into the angular forms of a dredge in the background. It might have been anything – the lid of a large silo, part of an underground oil tank, or the work of a retoucher's brush. In fact, the paper's picture editor had obviously decided the wire photo would reproduce badly and had his artist do some outlining and filling. So the result was a considerable percentage away from reality.

Mullica read the other stories on the page, and on the next page, and turned it.

It was night when the train reached Borrow Street – full dark, with only a few working bulbs in chipped old white enamel lamps to light the winter-soaked, rotting old wooden platform.

It's all going to hell, Mullica thought. No one maintains anything that isn't absolutely vital, but the fare keeps going up and up.

No one manned the station except during morning rush hour on the southbound side. The cement steps from the northbound platform up to the frontage street were a forty-foot gravel slide with broken reinforcing bars protruding through it rustily to offer the best footholds.

Mullica began to move toward the exit gates in the middle of the platform, lining up with the others who'd gotten off. They were all head-down, huddling against the wind, concentrating their minds on getting through the revolving metal combs of the gate and picking their way up the incline. And then because he had not quite put it all out of his mind, and his skin was tight under the hairs of his body, he had the feeling to turn his head. When he did, he saw Selmon still standing where he had gotten off, his paper half-raised toward Mullica, his apparition coming and going in the passing window lights as the train went on. Mullica could see he was about to call out a name nobody knew.

Mullica stopped, and the small crowd flowed around him inattentively. He walked back to Selmon. 'They'll find us!' Selmon blurted. 'They'll trace us down!'

Mullica looked at him carefully. Then he said 'How will they do that?' picking and arranging the words with care, the language blocky on his tongue. He watched Selmon breathe spasmodically, his mouth quivering. He saw that Selmon was years younger than he – though they were the same age – and soft. And yet there was advanced deterioration in him. It was in the shoulders and the set of the head, and very much in the eyes, as well. Selmon clutched at his arm as they stood alone on the platform. Selmon's hand moved more rapidly than one would expect, but slowly for one of their kind of people, and uncertainly.

'Arvan, it's bound to happen,' Selmon insisted to him. 'They – they have evidence.' He pushed the paper forward. Mullica ignored it.

'No, Selmon,' he said as calmly as he could. 'They won't know what to do with it. There's nothing they can learn from it. The engines melted themselves, and we destroyed the instruments before we left it, remember?'

'But they have the hull, Arvan! Real metal you can touch; hit with a hammer. A real piece of evidence. How can they ignore that?'

'Come on. Their investigators constantly lie to their own populace and file their secrets away. They systematically ridicule anyone who wants to look for us, and they defame them.' Mullica was trying to think of how to deal with this all. He wanted Selmon to cross over to the deserted southbound platform and go home to his wife. Mullica wanted to go home; even to have a drink with Margery, and then sit in his den reading the specification sheets on the new product. It was some twenty-five years since he'd been a navigator.

'Arvan, what are we going to do? How can you ignore this?' Selmon wouldn't let go of Mullica's forearm, and his grip was epileptically tight. He peered up into Mullica's face. 'You're old, Arvan,' he accused. 'You look like one of them. That haircut. Those clothes. All mod. A middle-aged macho. You're becoming like them!'

'I live among … them.'

'I should have spoken to you years ago!'

'You shouldn't be speaking to me at all. Why are you here? There's the entire United States. There's the whole world, if you can find your way across a border. A whole world, just a handful of us, and you stay here!'

Selmon shook his head. 'I was in Oakland for a long time. Then I bumped into Hanig on a street in San Francisco. He told me to go away, too.'

'He spoke to you?' Mullica asked sharply.

'He had to. He – he wanted me out of there. He'd been in the area less time than I had, but he had a business, and a family, and I was alone.'

'A family.'

'He married a widow with children and a store – a fish store. So I agreed to leave. He gave me some money, and I came to Chicago.'

Well, if navigators could write public relations copy, copilots could sell fish. What did engineering officers do to make their way in this world? Mullica wondered, but Selmon gave him no opportunity to ask.

'Hanig had seen Captain Ravashan. In passing. He didn't think Ravashan saw him. In Denver. That was why he left there and came to San Francisco. And then I came to Chicago, and almost the first week, I saw you. I – I think we're too much alike when we react to this world. We wander toward the same places, and move in the same ways.'

'Does anyone know where the chaplain is?' Mullica asked quickly.

'Chaplain Joro?' Selmon asked. He and Mullica looked into each other's eyes. 'No, I don't think there's much doubt,' and for a moment there was a bond of complete understanding between the two of them. Mullica nodded. For over a quarter of a century, he saw, Selmon as well as he had reflected on the matter. It had seemed to him for a long time that there were only four of them now.

Selmon looked up at him in weariness. 'It's no use, Arvan. I—' He hung his head. 'I have a good job. It doesn't pay much but I don't need much, and it's secure. So I decided to stay. You never asked me to leave.' There were tears in his eyes. 'I'm very tired, Arvan,' he whispered, and Mullica saw the guilt in him, waiting to be punished.

But there was no telling whether any engineering officer could have solved the problem with the engines. Mullica had never thought much of Selmon, but Ditlo Ravashan never questioned his ability in front of the rest of them, and there hadn't been any backbiting after the crash.

'This isn't anything, Selmon. There'll be a flurry, but it'll blow over. Somebody'll write another one of those books – that planetarium lecturer, probably – and everyone with any common sense will laugh at it.'

'But they've never had evidence before!' He was almost beating at Mullica with his newspaper, waving his free arm. 'Now they do!'

'How do you know what they have or haven't had? They must have. They have enough films, and enough unexplained things in their history. They must have other pieces of crashed or jettisoned equipment, too. They just don't know how to deal with them. And they won't know how to deal with this, either.'

'Arvan! An intact hull, and instruments obviously destroyed after the landing! A ship buried in a swamp. Buried, Arvan – not driven into the ground. And five empty crew seats behind an open hatch!'

'A hull full of mud. If they ever shovel it all out, it'll be weeks … and all those weeks, their bureaucracy will be working on everyone to forget it.'

'Arvan, I don't understand you! Don't you care?'

'Care? I was a navigator in the stars.'

'And what are you now?'

'What are you, Selmon?' Mullica pushed him away, but Selmon still clung to his arm. They staggered on the platform.

'Arvan, we have to plan. We have to find the others and plan together,' he begged, weeping.

'Four of us together,' Mullica said, saying the number aloud for the first time, hearing his voice harsh and disgusted, aching deeper in his throat than he had become accustomed to speaking. 'So they can have us all – a complete operating crew. An engineer, a navigator who knows the courses, a pilot, and a copilot lifesystems man. To go with the hull and their industrial capacity. You want us to get together, so they can find us and break out uncontrolled in our domains.'

Four men with similarly odd configurations of their wrists and ankles. Four men with similar skin texture. Four men with high blood pressure and a normal body temperature of 100; with hundreds of idiosyncrasies in cell structure, blood typing, and, most certainly, chromosome structure. Four such men in a room, secretively discussing something vital in a language no one spoke.

'Arvan!'

'Goddamn it, Selmon, let go of me!' Mullica shouted in English. 'Fuck off!'

Selmon jerked backward. He stared as if Mullica had slashed his throat, and as he stepped backward he pushed Mullica away, pushing himself back. His mouth was open again.

Hopeless, hopeless, Mullica thought, trying to regain his balance so he could reach for Selmon, watching Selmon's wounded eyes, his newspaper fanning open ridiculously, stepping back with one heel on thin air.

He hit the tracks with a gasping outcry. Mullica jumped forward and looked down. Selmon sat sprawled over the rails, his paper scattered over the ties, in the greasy mud and the creosote-stained ballast, looking up at Mullica with the wind knocked out of him. The distant lights and violet sputtering of the next train were coming up the track from the previous station. Mullica squatted down to reach for him, holding out his hand. Selmon fumbled to push himself up, staring at Mullica. Neither spoke. Groping for something firm to grasp, Selmon put his hand on the third rail.

The flash and the gunlike crack threw Mullica down flat on the platform, nearly blind. But I think I will still be able to see him anytime, Mullica thought in his native language as he threw himself up to his feet and ran, ran faster than anyone had ever seen Jack Mullica run, caroming through the exit gate and up the weathered steps, realizing he had never at any time let go of his zipcase, and thinking, Now we are three.

TRANSCRIBED CONVERSATION;
ALBERT CAMUS; WILLIAM HENSHAW:

CAMUS: You've seen one of these before, haven't you?

HENSHAW: Prob'ly. You know, I can never get used to how cold it gets in these places.

CAMUS: Rather have it cold than hot. Look, if you're going to let me assist you in the first place, talk to me, will you?

HENSHAW: I can talk some. And you can watch anythin' you can see. Can't at all limit you from thinking.

CAMUS: I can see you know exactly what to look for.

HENSHAW: What you see is somebody who knows what to expect. What to look for may be somethin' else again.

CAMUS: Well-made point, Doctor.

HENSHAW: Reach me that thing over there, will you?

CAMUS: You know, if I saw him on the street, I wouldn't think twice. But now look at that.

HENSHAW: You'd figure that jaw came from a malocclusion, right? And that skin color – just like a normal Caucasian maybe a little toward the extreme with his oxygen metabolism, right? But now you take some of them scrapin's and stick 'em under a microscope, and—

CAMUS: Yes, I've done that.

HENSHAW: Figured. That's why I let you stay. Might as well. Here – you see that wrist? What do you figure that to be?

CAMUS: A thick wrist. I never would look at it.

HENSHAW: Yeah. But let's just flap this back a little, and—

CAMUS: Holy cats!

HENSHAW: Right. There's your proximal row. You see that bone? That's what he's got instead of a navicular. Great blood supply, too. First of all, he can't break it anywhere near as readily as people do. Second, if it breaks, it heals nice and slick. But how does he break it? Look at all those cushions in the cartilaginous structure. And let me tell you something else – all the joints are engineered like that. These people don't get arthritis, they don't get sprains, they maybe once in a blue moon get breaks. It's like those teeth: never seen a dentist's drill. This is a healthy, healthy guy.

CAMUS: And it all still fits inside a normal shape, more or less.

HENSHAW: Fits exactly. He's the normal shape for what he is.

CAMUS: What is he?

HENSHAW: You know, down in South America lots of millions of years ago, they had things that were shaped almost exactly like camels, but they weren't mammals, they were marsupials, and their skeletons weren't put together like camel skeletons. I went to that museum they have down there in Guayaquil and looked at some of those bones; looked stranger than anything we've got lying here in front of us today. But once the musculature was on the bone, and the hide was on the muscles, if you saw that thing walk out from behind a rock at you, it was a camel. They had tigers like that, too. Things evolve to fit needs in the ecology. Life needed camels in the high-altitude deserts, and the camels needed tigers to prey on them. Time passed, they went away. Now down there they got llamas and guanacos and jaguars, and if some marsupial medico had to take 'em apart, wouldn't he be surprised.

CAMUS: This guy is a mammal.

HENSHAW: Well, yeah. You put him in a raincoat and boots, he can stand a short-arm check with everybody else in the platoon, no doubtin' that.

CAMUS: What's next, Doctor?

HENSHAW: No sense goin' any further here. He checks out for type. And I've got my tissue and blood samples to take back to my lab, so I'd better get goin'. Somebody'll be around to pick him up in a couple of hours. They'll give you a receipt for him. I don't think you'll get any grieving relatives. If anybody does come around and ask for him, stall and call the hotline. You'll get quick relief.

CAMUS: I have to have the coroner's okay before I can give him to you.

HENSHAW: No problem. I brought a letter with me.

CAMUS: Now what?

HENSHAW: How do you mean?

CAMUS: What do I have to sign? What sort of oath do I swear?

HENSHAW: Hell, you're not going to mess up. You've got yourself a nice position here, lots of contacts with the local politics; family, property … all that good shit.

CAMUS: I suppose so. You, wouldn't happen to have an opening in your department?

HENSHAW: My department?

CAMUS: Wherever you really come from.

HENSHAW: I really come from the NRPA, and I'm all the medical talent they need. This doesn't come up every day, you know. Besides, they wouldn't consider you qualified. Sorry.

CAMUS: I don't believe I've read any of your papers, Doctor. Or run into you at pathology convention seminars. Where'd you get your training?

HENSHAW: Iowa. University of Iowa School of Veterinary Medicine, Doctor.

LATER EVENTS ON A MARCH NIGHT

It was a nice condominium apartment: four and one-half rooms high enough up, with gold, avocado, and persimmon carpeting, French provincial furnishings from John M. Smythe, a patio balcony with sliding glass doors, swag lamps, and a Tandberg Dolby cassette system which he switched on automatically for warmth. Barbra Streisand sang 'I'll Tell the Man in the Street.'

Margery wasn't home. Mullica got some ice in a rocks glass, picked up the scotch decanter, and sat in the living room with the lights down. He sipped and looked out through the glass doors and past the wrought-iron balcony railing, at the lake. Below his line of sight were the tops of the as yet unbudded famous elms of Shoreview. Far down the lake shore curving out to his extreme right were the tall lighted embrasures of the Gold Coast high rises in Chicago.

He took a deep breath. What will happen? he thought. Let's put it together. He began systematically reviewing the events on the Borrow Street platform. Then he pictured a detective in his trenchcoat kneeling beside the facedown body in the headlight from the stopped five-fifty train. He put dialogue in the detective's head to indicate what the detective might make of what there was to see. He listened critically. The ice cubes were cold against his upper lip.

The detective saw that Selmon had been electrocuted. He saw nothing to show that the dead man had been the victim of an assault. So it was clearly something that had happened by itself, an accident or suicide, and there was no need for an autopsy. Now the detective went through the dead man's pockets. If he'd done that to Jack Mullica, he wouldn't have found any connection to any abandoned bog iron works.

Selmon's identity wouldn't be particularly thin. He'd have a Social Security card so he could work, and probably a driver's license. He surely had a checking account, and it was practically impossible to convert checks into spot cash without a driver's license, even if you never drove.

Now the detective moved to Selmon's apartment. Again, there'd be nothing of any significance. Unless Selmon still had parts of his first-aid kit and was stupid enough to store them where he lived. But after more than twenty-five years, what would he have left, no matter how healthy he looked? No, it wouldn't be the presence of anything that bothered the detective. It would be absence. No military service records, no school diplomas.

Would that matter so much? It was just a routine investigation into a casual accident. What the hell? Still, they might get curious and push it some.

Barbra Streisand sang 'Who's Afraid of the Big Bad Wolf?' Mullica refilled his glass.

If they were curious, how long would curiosity persist? Selmon hadn't been shot, or robbed, or hit behind the ear. All he was, really, was one of what had to be thousands of perfectly settled-down citizens who had chopped themselves free of something in their pasts that might make them unemployable. It seemed to Mullica that in a society where a high school marijuana bust or a college Red affiliation could haunt you to your grave, a lot of that had to be going on. Once you had figured a way of getting a set of papers in a new name – crime novels were full of ways that worked – you rarely had to stand up to a real bedrock investigation. Ordinarily they didn't check your identity; just your identity's credit.

The wife. Selmon's wife. Would he have talked to her? Would he have told this woman he was Engineering Officer Selmon, and that Navigator Arvan lived right up the tracks?

Well, did Margery have any inkling that Engineering Officer Selmon was riding the train with Navigator Arvan? And if she did, could she put a face to either name? No – Mullica shook his head – it was Jack Mullica that Margery knew dangerous things about.

Barbra Streisand sang 'Soon It's Gonna Rain.'

Mullica swallowed, and the cold, sweet scotch made his palate tingle. He refilled his glass.

Out beyond the elms and the floodlit, strut-supported balls of the Lindheimer Observatory on the Northwestern University lakefront campus were stars whose names he did not know in constellations he had never learned. From where Arvan sat now, he could see that the Shieldmaiden was as lanky as a *Vogue* model and the Howler's paws were awkwardly placed. All of those suns blazing in the night out there had names and catalog numbers in the local astronomy tables, but he had never learned them, except for the little bits that everyone knew. He knew the Big Dipper, and he knew how to find what they called Polaris. But let the locals come and wring him for how to find the places of his folk. If they ever became aware enough to do that, let them also learn to translate.

Jack Mullica felt that he looked out into the night sky only at controlled times.

Who said there was even a Mrs Selmon? Would a married Selmon have moved so easily from Oakland just like that? Oh, hell, he'd even said he was alone in Oakland, hadn't he, and the Selmon trying to make himself invisible on Loop CTA platforms didn't seem the type to go courting around here.

Funny how the mind had registered that and yet not registered it. Face it, it was only because Mullica was married, of all unlikely things, that he had put his mind on that track. He couldn't imagine how one of them could get married except under the most extraordinary circumstances. It was funny the tricks your mind could play … Oh, shit! Eikmo was married, too! – Eikmo and his fish-store lady – Mullica, what the hell good does your mind do you? But the important thing was they were probably in the clear – Navigator Arvan, and Hanig Eikmo, and Ditlo Ravashan, all three. Ravashan, he thought, would be in the clear in a cage full of tigers.

Barbra Streisand sang 'Happy Days Are Here Again.'

Still, he thought briefly of taking a personal ad in the Denver and San Francisco papers. 'Olir Selmon RIP Chicagoland. All O.K. Dwuord Arvan.' Something like that.

But when he thought about it some more, his lips and the tip of his nose pleasantly numb, it became clear that he was playing with his mind again. All he was trying to do was give the poor bastard an obituary notice, and none of them could have that.

He could point a high-frequency antenna upward and broadcast the news; all he had to do was go to Radio Shack and buy the hardware, with a promise to apply for the FCC license. And then if there happened to be somebody along the line of transmission, it might be one of his people who heard it, instead of a Methane-Breather or a local in the local 'space program' monitoring a local satellite.

No, it was going to happen to each of them, in its own time, silently far from home and in a land of cool-blooded foreigners.

Poor clumsy bastard. Engineering trades graduate, exploration volunteer, parents living at last report, farm boy, originally – didn't like shoveling manure, one would guess, and turned his mind to ways of getting out of it. If you weren't in one of the academies, the only way to make officer status and then have some hope of getting up the promotion ladder was to go the route they'd all gone. And the bonus pay made a difference. But you didn't have much to talk about in letters home from the slick, modern metropolitan training center to the rural little outpost of your birth. Still, the parents were there at the graduation ceremony. Stolid folk with callused hands, their eyes wet and alive in the lights from the podium where you came up in your brand-new dress reds and held out your hand for the certificate. And now he was an accident among people who couldn't ship the body home.

Well, have another scotch alcohol, Jack Mullica, he said to himself, and turned up the light beside his chair.

Margery came home about eight o'clock. She was a good-looking, slim, long-legged frosted brunette just past forty but didn't look it, pointy-breasted, and she seemed a little flushed and swollen-lipped. She found Mullica sitting in the den with glossy photographs of a car model line spread on his desk beside the rocks glass.

'Hello. Did you eat?' she asked.

'I thawed something. You?'

'I'll make a hamburger, I guess. See the paper?'

'Read it on the train.'

'They found something in the bog near where you first turned up.'

'I saw that.' He looked at her and let his smile widen crazily. 'It's a piece of flying saucer, all right. For you see, darling, as I slip off this outer skin, you will know that you have come to love a being from another Solar System.'

She snorted. 'Oh, God.' She came forward and tousled his hair. 'I do love you, you know,' she said fondly. 'I really do.' She raised an eyebrow, then looked at the pictures on his desk and the blank piece of paper in his type-writer. 'Will you be up late?'

He nodded. 'Detroit's having a rash of midyear models. Low-displacement engines, stick shifts, high rear-axle ratios. Arab-fighter product. Won't carry luggage, won't climb a hill, but we'll talk gas mileage. Detroit wants all the stops out with the local press; I've got to flange up some release copy, here, and start planning a junket out to a test track. Be in bed about midnight, I guess.'

'All right. I'll watch TV for a while and go to sleep.'

'Fine.'

She stayed in the doorway for a moment. 'When will the press conference be?'

'Soon. Has to be, if it's going to do any good for the summer. Do it up at Lake Geneva, probably – Playboy Hotel.' He looked down at his hands. 'Be gone four, five days. Finish up on a Friday.' He waited.

She said: 'I asked because Sally and I were talking about going out to Arizona to that ranch she talks about. If you were going to be out of town anyway, that would be—'

'A good time for it. Right. I'll let you know as soon as we have firm dates.'

She'd look good in tight jeans and a western shirt. Not as good as she'd have looked in her twenties, but there was a limit to how soon promotional copywriting could lead a man's wife into the habits of affluence. And it was immaterial how she might look in a Playboy Hotel room on a Friday night with a good week's work under your belt. 'Good night. See you in the morning,' he said.

'Night.' When she turned to go, he could see that her petticoat was twisted under her tailored black skirt, and the eyelet at the top of her zipper was unhooked at her neck. Her gleaming hair almost hid that.

He had met Margery's only woman friend, Sally. She was all right – a steady-eyed keypunch pool supervisor with a four-martini voice – and she was the type who always returned favors. Sally had a lot of contacts, a busy social schedule, and a life plan that wasn't anything Margery couldn't cover for her with a few alibi phone calls to Sally's various fiancés and good friends.

He went back to culling together specifications and making notes on a scratch pad. After a while, he turned to his typewriter and wrote, 'Sporty but thrifty, the exciting new mid-year XF-1000 GT features the proven inline 240 C.I.D. six-cylinder Milemiser engine with ...'

With what? With the simple fuel-saving carburetor and the uneven mixture distribution in the intake manifold, or with the space-age solid-state ignition that was the only thing that let the engine run at all with all those emission controls fucking over the power curve? He frowned and decided to list the electronics ahead of the single barrel; after a tongueful like Milemiser you wanted to come back fast with something sexy.

He went on with his work. He concentrated on being the best there was in Chicago. In his trade, the name of Jack Mullica meant something.

'Designed to take the Chicagoland family to even the most far-flung summer destination with a minimum of fuel cost, the XF-1000 GT's comfort features sacrifice nothing ...'

THE RATIONALE*

We don't retrieve people. It's a good policy. You have to assume the down vehicle was being tracked. If another one now goes in after it, you're liable to lose both. There are things that happen to delay the locals – your grounding field disables their spark-gap engine ignition systems and often knocks out utility power. But if you then go ahead and lay a lot of additional technology on the locals to hold them back beyond that, that could escalate on you.

Once you've gotten that tough, you might as well start in with your armed landing parties, your bridgeheads, garrisons, embassies or armies of occupation or both, and the next thing you know, the Methane-Breathers want Jupiter, to 'maintain the balance of power.' And for what? What's the power?

These people have nothing for us except potential. Someday, yes, they're going to be valuable, and that's why the Methane-Breathers keep hanging around, too, refilling their air tanks in the petroleum swamps at night and making funny lights when they're not careful. This is going to be a highly civilized manufacturing center someday, with factories all over the asteroid belt and on some of the bigger natural satellites, like the Moon, that'll have really significant installations. There'll be freighters and businessmen coming and going. Once you start getting that kind of traffic, you almost have to have a dockyard and maybe an actual military base – the Moon would be good for that, too – to keep a little order. There's always maintenance and repair work to be done, and there's always contraband to check for.

I keep thinking how cannabis will grow almost anywhere; one shipload of seed could make you a fortune in half a dozen places I can think of, and I don't even have a criminal mind. But the minute that kind of thing starts, you're into a commerce-regulating and immigration service kind of thing, and that's armed vehicles and men. That disturbs the Methane-Breathers, and it would disturb me if I were them. It's too easy to call a battleship just a coast guard cutter, and a regiment an inspection team. And there you go again; next thing, you've got two fleets eyeball to eyeball. And that stinks; any time you get the career armed services faced off, you're going to get actions in aid of prestige. That produces debris.

* Beginning the night he wrote the XF-1000 GT story for the press kit, Jack Mullica began sleeping badly and mumbling into his pillow. A few clear sounds emerged. None were comprehensible to the average ear.

And that's apart from the fact that if the locals get on to you and resent you, you're into a big thing with them. A slug thrower may not kill you as elegantly as a laser, but it will kill you, and these locals also have lasers. And fission and fusion and demonstrated willingness.

Then there's the fact that the tactical position of a planet-sited military force fighting off an attempted landing from space is both hopeless and unbeatable. They can't do much to you while you're aloft, but the moment you start landing they can lob all sorts of stuff at you from too many places to suppress. If you keep coming, they throw more. Pretty soon, what you're trying to land on can't be lived in. It's no good to them anymore, either, but that scores no points for you.

The same sort of thing applies if you try to destroy their military resources beforehand. At about the point where their industries might be worth taking over, locals are generally in possession of a well-dispersed, well-dug-in arsenal. That's a lot of firepower, and it takes tons more to knock out a ton of it. If we could afford to bring that much suppression to someplace out on the ass end of nowhere, we wouldn't need their damned industry in the first place.

So we don't shoot. That leaves you two alternatives. One is to poison them off – short-lived radioactives, or biologicals. Could be done, no problem with the delivery systems. Then you've got a lot of real estate, free for the burying of an entire ecological system, including the management and the work force you thought was going to sell you the produce of the factories. What you've got for your efforts is something that's turning hand over fist into a planetary desert. Thank you very much. And I, for one, would keep looking over my shoulder, and hearing whispers.

The only choice, really, is the one we make. You hang around as inconspicuously as possible, learning as much as you can from listening to and watching their electronics and so forth. You can learn a lot, by direct observation and by inference. Any intelligent race you can hope to someday relate to is going to have come up essentially the same developmental roads and dealt with the physical laws of the Universe in about the same way. So you keep tabs on them until they come out to meet you; then you can sit down right away and work things out; draw up your contracts.

If they're Methane-Breather types, of course, that's one thing; that's strictly business, and no hanging out together after working hours. If they're anthropomorphic, that's another, and welcome, brethren, into the family of spacefaring, oxygen-breathing, aspiring intelligent life, granted that's more true if it doesn't nauseate us to look at you. You also want to consider there's a lot of evidence – they say – that both the Methane-Breathers and we have found traces of some other types nosing around our corner of the Galaxy. Under those circumstances, everybody wants to be as friendly and businesslike as possible with anybody that'll have you. It could be a funny feeling to be trying to go it alone while something really exotic was undermining your back fences.

So we don't retrieve people. If something loud got triggered off in the process, it would upset too many future arrangements. We're a pretty self-reliant kind of animal, and we also take our service oaths seriously. We knew all the possibilities before we were assigned. And besides, hardly anything ever goes wrong.

ABOUT THE CHAPLAIN

Well, sometimes you get catastrophic failures. You're working off a propulsion system that can get crosswise of a planet's magnetic field in a hurry if things go out of kilter back among the rectifiers and sorkin felkers in the mome-divider, and the most common type of failure produces a high-speed fireball that disintegrates before it hits the ground.

There was a scandal about that; some clown approved an engine design that was cheaper, easier on fuel, and, it turned out, an almost certain time bomb. It produced a mass display over the southwestern United States that they're still talking about. They claimed later they'd gotten the bugs out of it with a few modifications, but once, driving up the Merritt Parkway in Connecticut in the middle of the night, I actually saw one go up like that – brilliant and green as hell, from the copper in the hull alloy burning in contact with the air. I think they'd better put out another set of modifications.

But every so often you just hit a snag, so to speak, and that's what happened to us. So, instead of working to keep you aloft at a controlled speed, the energy gets trapped inside the system and things start to soften and drip, and it gets pretty warm in the cabin.

Ravashan grunted and began hitting switches. Hanig turned up the cabin coolers and began clearing his side of the instrument board. I picked up the communicator and yelled to Selmon to hurry up and get the after bulkhead hatch shut and never mind trying to get to the engine-compartment controls. He was searing his hands on the hatch coaming; how did he expect to work the engines? With potholders? A big gob of stuff came roaring and spitting out from the blazing light beyond the hatch before he got it shut, and I put out the standard distress call.

It's all drilled into us – the entire procedure. Except for Ravashan, who had a choice between killing the engines or trying to get enough ergs out of them to land this beast, none of us had any optional moves. Unless it was the chaplain. He was staring directly back into my eyes in horror, and he was dealing with the fact that the half-molten transformer array that had come in from the engine room had hit him in the lower belly as he sat there. But none of us had the option of helping him.

I reported five men and one reconnaissance coracle with critical engine trouble over the U.S. Eastern Seaboard; took one glance at the engine temperature repeaters and added a note about no expectation of recovering control; gave the altitude, present course and speed, one crewman injured, no detectable local traffic; saw that Ravashan was heading us for the one black area in the seaboard's endless swath of light; reported that we were attempting to set down in a suggested emergency ditching area and gave its code name; and kissed my ass good-bye.

Selmon finished beating at the hatch clamps and threw himself into his chair, blowing blindly on his hands while he stared out forward over Ravashan's shoulder. I reached over and fastened his crash straps for him, and cranked our two chairs into the three-quarter angle prescribed in the hard-landing procedures manual. He and I were the two spectators. The chaplain was moaning down at his lap, which was fountaining little popping globules of flame and swirls of soot for an instant before he got to the chair-arm toggle that released his fire extinguisher, and then he was wrapped in a pressure-foamed cocoon of yellowish white gel. He looked like a monster, writhing against his straps in there.

Selmon and I watched Ravashan and Eikmo perform. I had always thought they were pretty good, for mustang officers. But I had never seen them work for their lives before. They danced fingertip ballets on their controls – Ravashan slapped Hanig's hand away from a switch at one point, never missed a beat himself, and then grabbed the copilot's wrist and guided it back to the same switch an instant later – and I knew we were going to live through it.

Even with the smoke and stink, the alarm hooter, and the wild yawing of the coracle, I had time to regret it for a moment. When you're young and you suddenly have that big block of time ahead of you to fill, drastic solutions have a certain appeal. But that's a transitory feeling that only occurs in the rational part of your mind; the animal wants to live.

Then you start worrying about being hurt in some serious way. There's only so much your survival kit can do for you. Unfortunately, from what we knew of the local culture, that was as much as their medicine could do, too. They knew how to prevent sepsis, set bones, and bypass damaged organs. And they knew immunology and antibiosis. That about summed it up. They couldn't regenerate destroyed organs and all they could do for motor nerve damage – a lacerated spinal cord, say – was to make you comfortable as much as possible.

But that was all fantasy anyway. It was a worry your mind gave you to help you ignore the possibility of outright death; it was an attempt to comfort yourself.

And then I remembered that one of us really was crippled.

It made no difference what I was thinking. Ravashan was setting us down almost as gently as a baby's kiss, sideslipping in over a bunch of scrub pines, using the cushion of some thick brush to take more of the speed off, and then down into some sort of body of shallow water hemmed in by bushes. We skipped once, snapping and drumming inside, bottomed on the mud with brown water and bits of vegetation and a smashed turtle foaming back over the viewport, swirled around in concentric spirals that threw up one last big sheet of liquid mud, and came to a crumpled stop with the radar altimeter still going ka-blip … ka-blip … ka-blip until Hanig Eikmo sighed and shut it down. The crew compartment had passed its crashworthiness test as advertised. 'Well, gentlemen,' Ravashan said in what I thought at the time was a pretty good American accent, 'welcome to your new home.'

What you want in that kind of situation is speed.

Ditching areas are preselected and coded for what we call min-time: a computer-calculated optimum average of the length of time it should take for a critical-sized team of locals to get to the impact site. Critical size is defined in numbers – three – and weight; one law-enforcement person, which is anyone in any uniform, equals three civilians. You have to assume a group of three will be able to contact reinforcements while making enough trouble to distract you, unless you act fast.

And there were other factors. There was a lot of air traffic in the area, even though the Friendship and Dulles patterns barely existed yet and even what they were then calling Idlewild was almost brand-new. They had a pretty comprehensive air traffic control system, most of it radarized, and there was military air at Atlantic City, and at Floyd Bennett and Mitchell on Long Island. I don't think McGuire AFB existed yet.

It wasn't like it would be a few years later, when the SAC and NORAD systems got into full bloom, but it was good enough; they'd seen us, for sure. They nearly always see us – our radar search receivers tell us that – but all the systems have to be designed for tracking air-breathing aircraft or ballistic missiles, and our maneuvering styles slip us off and on their screens in ways they can't really read. Still, this time it was a question of how far down they'd been able to follow us before ground return scrambled up their scopes, and how soon they'd get a search organized if they came to a decision that this time it might be worth it.

Anyway, min-time was short. We melted hell out of the controls, vaporized our charts and data storage, carved off peripheral structures and undermined the hull with lasers set at emergency overload, and tossed the guns into the bog when they got too hot to hold. They went off like small depth bombs, shattering from thermal shock as they hit the cold water.

All of that was in the procedures manual, too, and it worked like a charm. Four of us stood on some sort of clay dike overlooking a cranberry bog, with nothing but our iron rations, our survival kits, fatigue coveralls, and sweat on our faces. The guns were scattered chunks of crystal, aluminum hydroxide and copper sulfate. The pressure hull was twenty feet down, already full of silt. The stars shone on unruffled water and four wet, muddy men full of adrenaline and ignorance.

Atop the dike, the chaplain lay wordlessly on his back. Trying to fathom his injuries, we had peeled off the gel and dropped it in the water to dissolve. Ravashan had given him some tablets of painkiller – not too many – and cut away some of his half-melted coverall below the waist. But a lot of it had amalgamated into his muscle and sinew. I remember his feet jerked constantly and his heels drummed against the ground.

I stared into Ravashan's face. Ravashan looked back at me, at Selmon, and at Eikmo. 'I'll take him with me,' he said.

I saw the look cross Selmon's and Eikmo's faces. How far and how long would even Ditlo Ravashan carry a dead weight?

But now we didn't have to.

The chaplain lay there, his lips moving. His name was Inava Joro, and he was about my father's age. He had done his job all during the long hours and days of our flight, keeping our heads straight, doing his best to moderate the tensions that build up among aggressive, apprehensive, finely honed young men locked up elbow to elbow in a barrel swirling toward unfriendly shores. You can't assign a woman, or even four women, to our kind of crew. That's been tried, and it turns into a zoo. And then a madhouse. So they put a little something in the food, and they do a chaplain to be a sort of umpire: a neutral party among the crew; someone who speaks and listens, and is never one of you.

I couldn't hear what he might be saying to himself. Ravashan said: 'Well, Navigator?' We were running out of min-time.

I glanced up at the stars for the last time in my official capacity. A thing that's hard for locals to understand is that the constellations are composed of stars which are, generally, so far away that with a few distortions it tends to look almost the same – but wrong – from almost any planet we or the Methane-Breathers know about. When you're in flight, of course, you get the tachyon inversion effects beyond C velocity, so constellations are of purely academic interest to a navigator until he gets near dirt. But I knew enough to jerk my thumb over my shoulder. 'That's west,' I said, and we all said 'Good luck' to each other in our native language and dispersed, each mumbling something to the chaplain as we turned our backs. Ravashan was squatted down to pick him up.

The procedures were fixed and conditioned into us. A crew must destroy what it can of its vessel and conceal the rest. Complete destruction depends on making a certain, cross-connection in the engines, and that had been forestalled, but we'd done well enough. Then, after concealment, you take no artifacts with you but your rations and your survival kit, which are designed to look the way you'd expect packaged local stuff to look. On our mission, the food said Nestle's and Borden's on the wrappers, and the survival kit was a blue and white box that said Johnson & Johnson, although there wasn't any fine print and none of them were duplicates of what you'd see in a store. And then you scatter, and make every attempt to never be seen with another member of your race again.

Ravashan put the chaplain over his shoulder and moved off eastward. The chaplain's head lolled. Then he raised it briefly, and moved one arm as if he were waving.

Eikmo, Selmon, and I fanned out, the angles of our separate paths diverging, the whole nighted continent ahead of us. I moved generally westward, and after a while I couldn't hear anyone else. I heard forest noises I assumed were normal, and I heard my breathing.

You go on your own. For one thing, if the locals get on to you, you're going to be interrogated and maybe vivisected. That would put a crimp in any plans you might have for remaining in charge of your life. You can probably pass for a slightly off-brand local if you're alone; get together in a bunch, and it draws attention to little peculiarities that were going disregarded. So it's common sense, and it's in the service oath, too.

There's the catalyst phenomenon. In the Recon Service you're usually dealing with locals who are right on the brink of going off-planet. There's a good possibility you might give them technology they can replicate. Suppose some bright local figures out the principles behind one of the artifacts he drags out of your knowledge. Maybe he has some ideas of his own to add to what he learns. Then he comes up with some unique development your own people never thought of. That kind of thing can land right between your eyes, or, if they start building ships that will go faster than C, right up your family's whatsis.

By and large, it would make more sense if the services issued plain instructions to commit suicide in some way that disintegrated everything, and when you think about it, they come as close to that as they can. But if they made it an order, who would sign for it? Who'd contract-up the recon jobs? So they brief us well, drill us in the procedures, and, no doubt, hope very hard for whatever it is you'd hope for if you were in charge of the big picture.

And of course there's always your hope that you'll outlive the situation – that someday, when the papers are being signed in United Nations Plaza or Red Square or that big plot of ground in Peking, or whatever ... well, Peking would be awkward if you didn't have the epicanthic fold around your eyes, which most of us don't ... anyway, there'd suddenly be these two or three individuals in the surrounding crowd who'd push forward and start speaking in tongues.

But this is not a realistic hope. We don't exactly gather in new planets every year; it hasn't happened in my lifetime, and at the turn into the 1950s it seemed to me these particular people were being damned slow about qualifying.

Moon rockets don't count. That's all chemical stuff; it's like firing yourself out of a cannon. The circus crowd applauds, but it's just a piece of entertainment. Of course, Neil Armstrong and his cohorts are much braver men than I am. They have to be, to chance it in those getups. But none of us – not even poor, lonely Selmon, who actually knew something about what goes on inside a starfaring engine – is going to try to help with that.

I guess it was different in the old days here, when what you had was some finder crew stumbling into a place that was still hundreds of generations away from being ripe. It's against procedure and it's not something you'll find recognized in the official histories, but everybody knows a certain amount of hanky-panky goes on under those circumstances. The only people who'll be finders are the kind of people who'd rub themselves raw against the rules and constraints of civilization. That's why they can fly without destinations, hoping to turn up useful planets before they trip on a black hole or their toilets go into reverse. The bounty for finding a likely world is enough to suit most independent lifestyles, but sometimes there just has to be a temptation to stay and do magic for the savages.

Well, what the hell, it must be fun, being a god, and it isn't going to do a lot of harm to run off a few simple tricks for the admiring multitude in some simple corner of the world. Might even kick 'em a few steps up the ladder, though it's amazing how self-perpetuating ignorance is. Sowing a few judicious hints at that stage might even be all to the good, if it's done discreetly. But if I read the local books correctly, some of those early boys got a little out of hand. I think they attracted the fuzz and got dragged away to a reward they hadn't counted on. And it's different now; these people really are on the brink, and if I screwed things up at this critical point, you'd find my name in the books, and featured where my family and my family's friends could find it offhand. There wouldn't be much point in my going home by that route.

So we went our separate ways. I followed the dike at first, keeping my footing as best I could in the starlight. The dike and the bog terrain petered out into rising ground that was loose underfoot and difficult walking. This country was sand with a thin top layer of rotting needles and leaves. Nothing tall or sturdy could grow in it. I was constantly pulling my coveralls through underbrush and getting smeared with sap from trash pines. I wasn't sure what it was or what it might be doing to me; it smelled corrosive and felt as though it might never come off. Eventually I turned onto a crude road, keeping my eyes out for lights, listening for voices and motor noises. All I heard were insects, and I saw nothing.

The road was narrow – two ruts and a weedy strip between them. Underbrush encroached on it. It was better than the woods for forward progress, and the soil was so loose I couldn't be backtracked, so I stayed on it and didn't try to check whether I was really still headed west. I was still numb. Not much time ago, I'd been an ultracivilized man cruising airily over the patchwork lights and distorted broadcast voices of promising but unpolished folk. Now I tripped over things in the dark and wanted my mommy. I practiced my American. I said into the dark: 'Any landing you can walk away from is a good landing.'

NOTE ON DOTHAN STABLITS

Gouldville, in northern Indiana, is the sort of city reached by driving over railroad grade crossings. Dothan Stablits has been chief of police there since 1974, in charge of a department of about eighty-five persons, including civilian employees. In his dozen or more years of service, Chief Stablits has given the citizens of Gouldville no actionable reason to feel dissatisfied with his department, and he has been circumspect with and trustworthy to the other municipal authorities.

Stablits is a rawboned, awkwardly constituted, very large middle-aged man with a jutting jaw, slate-blue eyes, and sparse black hair. He has a tendency to stay on his feet and grip things with his gnarled hands – the back of a chair, by preference – as he speaks to visitors asking questions in his small, orderly office. He stands behind his chair, in constant incomplete motion, as if trying to find exactly the proper location to push the chair into but not sure it's not already in the right place. He chooses his words with the same sort of effect:

I was never – I never thought I'd get into enforcement work. Law enforcement. I come from Mennonite people, you know, from around Millersburg and Honeyville. Farmers; always been farmers. There's Stablitses living on their farms yet in Kutztown, Pennsylvania. There, we're *platdeutsch* – what they call Pennsylvania Dutch. We don't believe in engine-powered machinery, would you believe it, and the best job I had before I went on the cops was driving a gasoline tanker truck for Standard Oil of Indiana.

I was – I don't know, I was never the kind of person who sits down and says here I am, here's where I want to be, this is what I'll do. I've moved around a lot. I'm not the kind of person who says I don't understand it so I won't look at it, I'll never do it. A lot of us – there's just so much land, you know, and there's always a lot of brothers and sisters – there's no room on the place to feed us, a lot of us had to get jobs, and in the way it worked out, later, most of your RVs – your travel trailers and pickup truck camper inserts, your motor homes; your recreational vehicles – was Mennonite-built in factories all over this part of the state. The women would sew the curtains and make the cushions, and the men would be the cabinetmakers and body builders. And every once in a while, when the elders weren't looking, some of the younger men would run a forklift in the lumber shed or actually go out on the road with a unit for a test run. Well, you know, you do that kind of thing when you're young. Then you get older. I think maybe most of the elders know all about that. They see but they don't say, because they know everybody gets older.

I was – well, I was taken with this one girl. And she went to Chicago; her aunt there died, and her uncle needed somebody to cook and clean, he was old. I went and looked for work up there so I could live and call on her. Well, the uncle died and it came out at the wake she was expecting.

Then she had – she got the idea to be a barmaid. There are people who will get into that because they can sleep while the kid is in the day-care and work while the kid is sleeping. And there are then people who will like that kind of life, and I have never seen one of those change away from it until they got too crippled up for the action. So I went on the Chicago PD with a fellow I met delivering gasoline in the middle of the night. But that was no work for me, it was in the Summerdale District, maybe you heard about that, and I quit there before that burglar testified and it all blew up. I went to Shoreview, the next town, because they were making a lot of sergeants up there fast and I liked the work, basically. I still like it. It's good.

I, well, I was getting along, and this guy went down on the CTA tracks. I have to tell you, I worried about that. But I couldn't handle – I couldn't get a handle on it. There was – well, look, it's not like Sherlock Holmes. I have never seen a case solved yet by adding up all the clues and dividing by logic. You don't say 'solved.' You say 'cleared.' You don't say 'clue.' You say 'lead' – you get a lead to somebody who saw something, or heard something, and you get that person to tell you what they saw or heard in such a way that it gives you the next lead. And I couldn't get any. But – but I knew – I know to this day – there're leads out there somewhere.

Are you trying to tell me the man fell? Then he fell when there were still people around who had been on the train with him. If they were within a hundred yards, they must have seen something; I mean, there's a flash, and there's noise. Where are they? Or else he waited until they were a ways off.

Do you want me to think he was a jumper? What the dickens did he go all the way up to Borrow Street to jump for? Was he trying to leave a message for somebody lived around there – see what you made me do? Then where is that person?

Was he pushed? Then that person knows what happened. He remembers. He could tell me. Or he could tell somebody. You don't forget a thing like that; it lives in you. It makes you move in ways different from the way you'd move if it had never happened. Little ways, maybe, at first. But they add up, and someday you put your feet entirely different from how you would have if you hadn't pushed him. And that will be a lead. Anybody knows me, knows I can wait a long time for a lead.

At this point, Chief Stablits shrugs and looks around his office as if discovering it was some other room; his arms rise and fall, his hands slap his thighs.

But there's just so long you can keep a file active when your commander says it was just some guy on the tracks, it wasn't dope or bets or the Mafia; it's not something the city manager's going to feel heat, the town's going to the dogs, do something. And there's just so much time in a day, and sometimes these things can take years … well, a lot of them never come to anything, really – you can't be sure, they could just as lief pop open on you, I have to admit that. But you can't hang your hat on it. And one day there's a letter from here, from Gouldville, it's the town council, they say they're looking for a new chief and I've been recommended. Well, there's the pay, and there's the being the commander, and, tell you the truth, there's the getting away from the man on the tracks and all the other open files. So I came here and talked to them, and I got hired.

Do I wonder how they got my name, in particular? You mean, why would they write to a sergeant in Shoreview, in particular? No, there's nothing to wonder about that. They had a list made up by this company, and I was on it, that's all. Yeah, it took me off that case; it took me off a lot of cases.

He pushes the chair to a new place and shortly thereafter the interview is over.

Stablits's name did, indeed, appear on a list prepared by an employment search agency specializing in municipal positions. A similar list was furnished to a number of other communities within reasonable distance of Shoreview. The list was accompanied by brief dossiers on the subject individuals. It was sent to every community with a high-rank opening in its police department, and Stablits's is the best dossier in every instance. It is also the only one common to all the lists, which contained no other duplications. I have been able to establish this much by examination of records stored by those municipalities.

The lists were volunteered. The firm had not been contacted, but apparently had some means of compiling a roster of openings. The firm was not one of the leading agencies specializing in this sort of work, and has long since gone out of business without a trace. And therefore there is no way to tie it back to whoever is behind the National Register of Pathological Anomalies.

– A.B.

DITLO RAVASHAN'S STATEMENT ON EVENTS IMMEDIATELY FOLLOWING THE CRASH

I am Ditlo Ravashan. On the night in question, I succeeded in making a forced landing in the New Jersey cranberry swamps. With me were Hanig Eikmo, Olir Selmon, Dwuord Arvan and Inava Joro. Joro was severely wounded by the breakup of the engine; the others sustained no wounds.

After we had disposed of the ship, we set out in different directions and I did not ever see my crewmen again. I carried Joro for a time, but he was getting worse and worse despite everything I could do for him, and shortly he died.

I buried the body deep, and not even I could find it again. It has never been found. I managed to reach a highway, and in due course was able to hitch a ride to Atlantic City Naval Air Station, where I entered the service of the United States, to which I have been completely loyal from that day to this.

This is a true and accurate account, and it is complete.

– Ditlo Ravashan

A TRUE AND ACCURATE, COMPLETE ACCOUNT BY DITLO RAVASHAN FOR HIS OWN FILES

Unlike the others, I had an exact idea of where I was, and a fair outline of what I would do if possible. I waited until the other three had gotten over their first confusion, waiting as usual with perfect patience since it cost me nothing, and after a time the three of them set out in different directions, as they had been taught.

Once we had parted company, I moved off in the direction of a two-lane highway, carrying Joro for a time. I remember that except for Joro's incessant moaning the night was still and clear. 'I don't – don't think I can – stand the pain!' he said at one point. What did he expect that to do – make the pain go away? In truth, I was sick and tired of him since considerably before the crash. I would certainly have left him – would have never picked him up in the first place – but he was needful for my plan, and so I carried him patiently. But after a time I laid him down, for his gasps had grown both more frequent and more shallow, and it was obvious that soon I would be alone.

Joro lay staring blindly up at me, his hands hugging his belly. 'What's going to become of me?' he asked.

'Chaplain,' I said, 'you're going to die. If I had all of a military hospital here to help, I think you'd still die. And that's the truth.'

'But I don't want to—'

'Chaplain, you have the choice between going down a whimpering, puling babe, or dying like a man. That's your only choice.'

'Oh, Ravashan, why – why did we come all this way?'

'Chaplain, we really don't have time for this. Be useful. There is a question I hope you can answer.'

'Wh-what do you want to know?'

'What is the meaning of life?'

'Wh—' He did not answer at first, so I struck him lightly in the face. 'Chaplain Joro.'

He stopped his moaning, but did not otherwise respond. I struck him a little harder. 'Chaplain. Answer the question.'

Joro looked at me, and it seemed some sort of remission were temporarily taking place, for his breathing steadied for a moment. 'Ravashan,' Joro said. 'You're crazy.'

312

'Chaplain, there is nothing I or anyone else can do for you. You *are* dying. Tell me, if you can, the meaning of life.' I struck him again, but all he did was weep.

'Ssss ...' His eyes had closed and his head drooped. I struck him again.

'Chaplain – what *is* the meaning of life? Do you hear me? What is the meaning of life?' I crouched over him in the darkness, repeating the question tirelessly, but all he said was 'Hurt—' and then he lapsed into incoherent gibberish until he died.

Somehow, the night did seem a little more alien with him gone, for a moment or two. But I was ... buttering no parsnips ... where I was, and I wanted to be far away from the swamp by the time dawn occurred. So I shouldered my burden – it was a dead weight now, but on the other hand it was quiet – and in due course found the highway, a clear cut through the countryside, with soft sand shoulders. There was no appreciable light, but there were stars, and by the starlight I could tell that I had happened upon country in transition from the bogs and trees to bullrushes. I was not really near the coast, as yet, but I could expect estuaries, and creeks running to meet them.

The highway was deserted. Well, at that time of the morning it would be, for the most part. But somebody was bound to come along. I set Joro down on the shoulder and waited.

I remember what I thought. Two things, leading up to a third:

From time to time, birds went by overhead, on their own errands. Birds as such were not known on my home world, though they were on some others – including this one, obviously. We had, instead, creatures that navigated the air using the displacement of their bodies, distended by digestive gases. These were capable of a slow sort of dirigibility, enough to eat seeds and insects, and at the higher end of the chain, predatory types that ate lesser flying creatures. So they served the same purpose.

I have heard it said that the lack of birds on my home world can be explained by the fact that birds are actually descended from dinosaurs, or the equivalent. And dinosaurs, or the equivalent, were unknown to my people's paleontology. The theory is that *we* are the dinosaurs – that in due course, we shall devolve into birds. So I followed the flight of these Terrestrial birds with some interest.

I watched the man-made air traffic, too, wondering if they were attempting a search for us. But I noticed nothing concentrating on the swamp. In fact, I noticed nothing out of the ordinary: propeller planes, almost exclusively, and mostly commercial, judging by their height and size. One or two jets went by overhead; those were military, but none of them showed any interest in my particular part of the darkness below them.

And the upshot of these thoughts, for what it's worth, was that this was a relatively primitive world, and so I was comparatively safe from anything the natives might do. And at the same time it was a world sufficiently advanced for me to enjoy myself upon it. I was not at all sure that I would have been as happy on my own world, all things considered. There were quite a few Ditlo Ravashans back there. Here there was only one, and I was he, and this planet would support me in the style to which I intended to become accustomed. It was not an unpleasant thought.

After a while, the lights of a car began to glow in the distance, and I stepped out into the road. I reckoned that a uniformed man, which I was, so soon after the war, in trouble – which I was – would be able to flag down most forms of transportation. I was almost wrong, as it turned out. The car swerved and slid, and almost made it around me, in which case it might have sped up again and gone, but in the end it did stop, and the driver rolled down his window and poked a pale and bewildered face at me. 'Wha-what do you want?' he said in a breathless and slightly drunken voice.

He was a middle-aged man, with his tie undone, who was probably returning home to wife and children after a night partly spent with another woman. There was a smell to him of cheap perfume, and there was lipstick on his left ear. And he could not make up his mind about me, as I suspected he could not make up his mind about many other things as well.

I said, as he looked at me with his mouth slightly open and his eyes trying for sharper focus: 'Get me to Atlantic City Naval Air Station as fast as you can. My buddy's hurt bad.' I said it just like that, and if my accent wasn't quite right, my uniform wasn't, either; it was just a coverall with a couple of badges sewn on. But I didn't expect either one of these things to give me trouble with this man, and they didn't.

He demurred only about the destination. He looked for a moment at Joro, lying huddled on the shoulder, a dim figure in the backscatter from the headlights, and said, 'But there's lots of places closer than Atlantic City.'

Not with military personnel. Not that I knew of. 'Atlantic City is where we have to go.'

'Well, all right, I was just—' But I was gone away from his window, opening his offside door, wrestling Joro into the backseat, and settled in beside the driver, before he could complete the thought. And if he was a little amazed at how fast I did all that, he did not speak of it. He craned his neck to look at Joro again, and I said, 'Let's go.'

He nodded uncertainly, but put the car in gear, and began climbing up the ladder of speeds until he had the car up to highway velocity. 'You got it,' he said, having decided that, really, it was all his idea.

It was too much to hope, of course, that the Earthman would just drive and do his job. He was a man who thought of himself as being different from other men because he had a woman on the side, and he was a man who, underneath that, realized that he was overweight and over age and not especially lovely to look at, so that some small but vital part of him knew that his woman on the side was either desperate or playing him for a fool, or perhaps both, and therefore he actually got no pleasure from his pleasure. So every opportunity to open up his life, to give it meaning and texture, was, necessarily, exploited. So about ten minutes into it, he began talking. 'Can't get much more than seventy out of this bucket without goin' all over the road,' and 'Boy! Have I got a story to tell my wife!' and similar expressions. Well, Joro wasn't in any kind of a rush, actually. As for the Earthman's wife, whatever he told her wasn't going to be believed. 'Your buddy doesn't look too good, what I could see of him. What kind of outfit you in?' was closer to the mark.

'Brazilian Naval Air Force,' I said. 'We're allies of yours. Night flying exercise. Couple of things went wrong.'

'Oh.' There was a pause. 'Hadn't you better check on your buddy?'

'My buddy's as all right as he needs to be.'

'Oh.' More thought. 'What about your plane?'

'I know where it is. The naval station will send out a recovery vehicle, have it back at the air station by dawn.'

'Oh.' I could see him pondering that. The next thing out of his mouth might be *You know, there's something fishy about this story*, so I said: 'Sooner we get to the authorities, the better,' and he remembered that we were, after all, headed for the authorities. Which meant, I suppose, that no matter how fishy the story, it had the official sanction of the United States government; which meant, since he was too clever to be taken in by it but it was the story the government wanted told, that he could tell the story without feeling like a fool, and with the feeling he was on the inside of something. It never occurred to him, I reckon, that somebody would head to the authorities who didn't belong to the authorities.

We pulled up, finally, at the main gate of the naval air station. It was before you actually got to Atlantic City, on the highway that ran through the cattails, and though it was off to one side it was easy enough to direct him to it … it was, really, the only thing that looked like a naval station, and one of the few things that were lit up at night.

The gate was a guard shack with the highway dividing to run to either side, and two guards in it, except that they came out, carrying rifles, as the car came toward them but then turned partway to go back, and yet stopped. The guards looked at us … like we had two heads … and they pointed their weapons at us.

I reached into the backseat and pulled Joro out. Rigor had set in; he was like a wooden dummy, and very cold to the touch, even though he was at the ambient air temperature or even above it. He sprawled on the tarmac, one leg in the air, hands over his belly, and this was the first I'd seen him that way in the light; he was dirty, pieces of foam clung to him, pieces of coverall were blended with scorched flesh, and his mouth was ruined.

The guards were not combat veterans. One of them choked down an out-cry. The other reacted to the thump of Joro's body on the tarmac by firing his rifle automatically; that was how I learned the weapons weren't loaded, for all I heard was the click of the firing pin. I turned to the driver of the car. 'You can go now.' And he did, with one glance at Joro, sick dismay beginning to dawn on his face, backing the car until he could complete turning it around and go, where the first thing he would have to explain to his wife would be the lipstick, which would mean he might never have to explain anything else. I turned to the guards, who were very young. 'Let me speak to your com-manding officer,' I said, and let the military routine take over.

There was a great deal to it, of course, and I did not speak to the commanding officer until I had worked my way up the chain of command. But eventually I spoke to an adjutant, and explained that Joro's body wasn't getting any sweeter-smelling, and at that stage they put it on ice somewhere. And then I did get to speak to the commanding officer, and explained to him that what he was wanted for was to relay my demand to speak to a government official.

And by then there was enough mystery about me, what with my uniform badges that looked real only at first glance, and my first-aid kit, which had Johnson & Johnson on it but just wavy lines where smaller letters should go, and only slightly comprehensible things inside, and as luck would have it, spending the night at the naval station was a young congressman who until recently had been in the Navy. They got him up; in truth, he undoubtedly was up by then, and possibly even had had breakfast, but they told me they got him up, and they brought him to my room, with a couple of really armed guards to keep him safe. And so this man who was to be wedded to me in so many ways over the years to come came into the gray room where I sat. He looked at me, and sat down in a chair opposite mine, across the plywood table. He cocked his head and watched me. He did not, at first, speak.

I explained about Joro's body – that it would require a confidential autopsy which would prove my bona fides. The congressman nodded – he was quick, and that was far from the last time he would display that quality – and waved the military personnel out of the room, although they were very uncomfort-able with that. I could hardly blame them, but the congressman was right – he was utterly safe from me, because he was the key to what I wanted.

I told him what I was. And he believed me. And we worked out a deal, which has been very good for me and not bad for the congressman, either.

An early part of the deal, as we worked it out across the plywood table, was that he would call me by a nickname, and I would call him by a nickname, and avoid what might happen if our real names became known at some time. It was only the first of myriad precautions we would take, in the end. It has been so long, now, that I have trouble thinking of him as anyone but Yankee. And I think that is for the best.

– Never revealed.

HANIG EIKMO, Part One

Retracing Hanig Eikmo's path has not been easy. Not because it was so complicated but because it was so simple. Hanig seemed to be a man of direct action, a man who would solve problems characteristically with his hands, not with his mind. Therefore, it became at times infuriatingly difficult to reason out what he would have done next, because what he did next was often spur-of-the-moment.

Too, he was by far the weakest speaker of American, barely advanced beyond the mandatory classes at the trade school he went to instead of the Academy, and barely having learned any more from the radio and television during the trip. He seemed uninterested in most things, even things almost anyone else would have thought vital. Therefore, he did not interact as much with Americans as his fellow crewmen did, and tended to live by himself. This was particularly true during the early years of his exile, but it was always true to a large extent.

But in the end it did not matter, as it turns out. But I am getting well ahead of myself. Best to tell Hanig's story simply as it unfolded, for him, to the best of my ability to reconstruct it.

After the crew split up, Hanig went on through the night, very steadily, looking little to the left or right, until he came, in due course, to a creek. There he stopped long enough to put a hand in the water. Determining in which direction the water was running, he proceeded along the bank, downstream. And again in due course, he came to an estuary. Technically, it was a river, for the creek emptied into it, but the water was plainly salt when he tasted it; the tide came up this far. And now he had a choice to make.

At this point, he would leave solid ground; the cattails grew on either side from a base of water, the soil that nourished them being submerged. But it was not a real choice. To stay with relatively firm footing, he would have to divert, and divert into a land of which he knew very little. If he stayed with the estuary, he was in much more familiar territory, for his youth had been spent in country much like this. A little testing showed that he could follow the water at least for a time without having it close over his head, so he proceeded to do that. And though in time the water did become too deep for literal wading, it was calm, so that he was able to half swim, half gain a foothold and jump forward in the water, and continue to move downstream at a good pace.

A more cautious person might have given thought to marine denizens of various kinds – the more troublesome because largely unknown to Eikmo. But as it happens, with the exception of sharks – which did not normally penetrate this far inland, and, if they did, were only liable to attack under the most extraordinary circumstances – Eikmo had in a manner of speaking picked a climatic range in which the water was free of that. Farther south he would not have been as lucky, but he was not farther south. He made his way through the night, taking as much care as practical to keep reasonably quiet, and that was that.

And in due course he came upon a sailboat, tied up to the dock/veranda of a shack built on stilts. It was a bit of a shock; one moment he was moving onward, with nothing to either side but the dim shadows of cattails, and the next he had rounded a turn and found this. But he was not truly surprised. In fact, he had been looking for it, and considered that it was only a matter of time until he made his way close enough to the sea to come upon the home of a waterman.

There were no lights – not in the shack, not on the boat, not even running lights. Levering himself out of the water onto the dock, he listened. There was someone sleeping in the shack, but that did not immediately disturb Eikmo. He slipped aboard the boat, a twenty-four-foot yawl, and found it perfect; certainly showing signs of wear and tear, but the sails were apparently whole, being loosely gathered at the base of the mast with a few turns of cordage to keep them so, and the hull was sound. With that learned, he examined the ties to the dock and found that one of them was a padlocked chain, despite the fact that access to shack and boat was limited to water. He examined the chain and found it strong, and fastened to an eyebolt through the dock, the other end of the eyebolt with its threads apparently damaged deliberately so that the nut could not be backed off – at least not by Eikmo's hand. Shaking his head, he now entered the shack and stood over the sleeping occupant.

The interior of the shack was dim, and he could not make out much detail, but it was one room, plus the veranda/dock from which, undoubtedly, the occupant fished from time to time, and the occupant was alone. He was a man of thirty or so, who had gone to sleep with his clothes largely on, and judging by the smell which fountained up from his mouth – he was on his back – he had gone to sleep drunk. Eikmo killed him swiftly, by breaking his neck, and searched his clothes until he found the key to the padlock.

He now had transportation. It did not take long to puzzle out the mysteries of the yawl rig. In a matter of several hours, he was down through the increasingly broad estuaries and on the ocean, and then around Cape May into Delaware Bay. Full daylight saw him headed in the general direction of Dover, Delaware.

The bay was not, even then, the loveliest of spots; the water that sometimes literally foamed back from the hull was liberally laced with chemicals and detergents, and yellowish; nor was it helped by Eikmo's having to tack, again and again, against a quartering breeze. But he forged on, ducking the tankers and freighters that occasionally cut across his path.

In due course, he found a landfall in the form of a long, deserted, weather-beaten dock poking out into the bay, flanked by an obviously abandoned building and some distance from a highway he could see. That was the extent of civilization at this point, Dover being inland by a few miles, but for Eikmo the highway was the important thing, with its traffic proceeding more from left to right than from right to left.

He scrambled onto the dock, taking a few things with him and lashing the wheel of the boat. He watched the boat start to sail away, and then he turned shoreward. He made his way over some broken concrete and then through a scrub field to the shoulder of the highway, which was the main coastal artery but was two-lane, if concrete. He studied the traffic flow, and then he began to walk in the direction of Dover. In due course the highway became a street. And so he proceeded, gradually seeing signs of life in the form of decaying houses and stores, and then somewhat less decayed structures, and the occasional human, and being passed by cars, and in a little while he was walking down an undoubted human street in an undoubted human city, with humans here and there, and he betraying no sign that he was any different from them or did not belong there.

He had, aside from his iron rations and his first-aid kit, a compass, a chronometer, and a portable marine band radio. He had also changed from his uniform into paint-spattered jeans and a T-shirt, which, though somewhat skimpy for the weather, and short, were of course far safer than his uniform. The latter was at the bottom of the bay.

He found a pawnshop in due course, probably simply going along until he came to a store window full of all sorts of things with only portability in common. But remember that he had the items in the first place; he knew there was someplace where you could get money for items without clear title. True, he traded in the stolen goods for a very little amount of money – he could not bargain, of course, though I doubt he would have even if fluent in American – and with that little bit of money bought some clothes at a secondhand store; a better-fitting pair of jeans, and much cleaner; and the same for a T-shirt, which he topped with a blue chambray shirt and a pea coat. He kept his issue socks, underwear, and shoes. In fact, he still had the shoes, years later, and though they were like no pair on Earth at the time, neither were they outlandish, and he saw no point in discarding them. (It is also possible he wanted something to tie him back to the world of his birth.)

Outfitted, so to speak, he next waited beside one of several saloons, and, picking his victim judiciously, relieved a sailor of his pay, which came to several hundred dollars. He killed again, yes.

With that much for a stake, he moved to the Greyhound station, where he bought a ticket to Denver … quite possibly because it was the easiest city name to pronounce. Practically every city name has a variety of possible pronunciations, except Denver. And in due course he arrived there.

In Denver he lived for many years, working as a day laborer, getting paid at the end of each day, sleeping in flophouses and eating in diners, distinguished from his fellow denizens only in that he did not drink. He really seems to have been content with his lot, and if he hadn't accidentally seen Ravashan on a stopover on his way to Colorado Springs, he might be there yet, and reasonably happy, and out of this story entirely.

But he is not out of it.

– A.B.

JACK MULLICA

The sand road gradually widened and became firmer. I was conscious of piled trees, and clear-cut patches in the growth. Apparently someone intended, or had intended, some form of enterprise here. Whether it still proceeded, during the day, or not, I had no idea. But certainly it was abandoned by night.

I came to a road bridge – concrete, as I later confirmed – lichened, partially eroded away, but still sound enough. It was not very long. An enameled sign, very worn, proclaimed MULLICA RIVER, and, in truth, there was some water in the bed below, but if this was a river, it was a poor excuse for one. And in any case the road kept on going, a track through the quiet and the darkness, until finally up ahead I could hear something. I stopped.

I strained to hear anything that would give me a clue to what lay ahead. But none of it made sense to me. There was something that sounded like muffled laughter, and the sound of glass on glass, but I could make nothing of that. I stood for a while in the darkness, and then I moved forward, toward the sounds, very slowly.

Gradually, they grew clearer; they were the sound of two or three males, drinking and carousing. They were also the sound of one female, and though at first hers had blended in with the male voices, now it was in an increasingly different tone: less companionable, more argumentative. And the male voices grew less festive.

I moved forward again, and now I could see the shadowed form of a parked car, and cigarettes, and increasingly tense voices. 'Goddamn, Margery, what the hell?' suddenly came clear.

'I want to go home,' said the woman.

'Margery, we ain't through here.'

'Yes, we are. I have to get up early in the morning and work. You've had all the fun you're going to have for one night.'

There was a giggle, and a different male voice said: 'I ain't so sure about that. How 'bout the rest of you fellers?'

Margery's voice was suddenly cold. 'The only way you're going to get more is to commit rape. And if you do that, you'd better kill me afterward.'

'Rape!' The voice was incredulous; it was the giggler. 'Rape!' But the other males were more thoughtful. And just as cold; one of them, the leader, I suppose, said:

'All right, Margery,' in a calm voice. 'All right.' And suddenly the back door of the car flew open, and for a moment there was light, so that I could see the woman come tumbling out, to fall heavily to the ground, grunting. 'All right, Margery. And good night.' The door closed and the light went out. The car started and the headlights flicked on. 'Enjoy the walk home.' And the car pulled away, all revelry gone, and in a little while it was dark again except for the starlight, and I could hear Margery cursing softly as she got to her feet and stood in the road, looking after it.

She didn't know I was there only a few steps away. She moved, an awkward, twisting motion, and it was obvious to me that she'd been hurt by her fall. And she began to walk up the road, each step slow and unbalanced; she was limping badly.

'Miss?'

'Holy Jesus, Mary, and Joseph! Who the hell is that?'

'Jack,' I said, taking the name of the all-American boy. 'Jack … Mullica. I was walking along a minute ago, and I saw—'

'Jesus H. Christ! You were walking along?'

'That's right. And I—'

'You scared the shit out of me!'

'Well, I'm sorry. Look, can I help you? You look like you're walking hurt. I've got a first-aid kit, and—'

Her sudden chuckle was both amused and bitter. 'It'll take more than first aid to help that. A lot more.'

I didn't understand. But that was not as important as reaching some sort of accommodation with her. 'Well, look, whatever you say – will it help you to lean on me as we walk?'

Her chuckle this time was rueful, and still bitter but not as much. 'Yes, it will help. Especially considering that we have over two miles to go. Bastards. All right – come on.' She moved over next to me, on the left. She was almost as tall as I. I noticed that she smelled of perfume – some artificial scent. And we began to walk along the road through the dark, slowly and, for her, painfully. But she settled in against my hip, and I thought to myself, abruptly, about her as a woman, not as an Earth person, and I didn't know what to make of that, but it was better than not thinking of her as a woman.

She asked, almost immediately: 'Where'd you come from?'

'I got lost,' I said at once, having anticipated that I would have to account for myself to someone. 'I was hitching a ride, and they let me out in the dark, and I got lost.'

'Uh-huh. And what kind of an accent is that?'

'Indian. East Indian.'

'Uh-huh.' She seemed disinclined to pursue this line any further. We walked along in silence for a while. Then she said: 'I don't suppose you have a place to stay.'

'Well, no.'

'Yeah. All right – you can stay with my father and me, for a while. Sleep in the barn.'

I thought that over. 'All right. Thank you; it's kind of you.'

'You're helping me get home. Helping a lot. This leg of mine hasn't been good for much since I was a little girl. Polio. So it's a fair exchange.' Her voice was flat – there was not a trace of her feeling sorry for herself. But, of course, she'd had time to prepare the statement. 'My name's Margery Olchuk, by the way. And yours is Jack Mullica.' Again, her voice was flat.

'That's right. Jack Mullica.'

'All right.' And after that she concentrated on walking. Even with me to help her, it was no picnic for her.

> – Reconstruction, as best as possible,
> of various bits and snatches Mullica
> mouthed in his sleep

OPENING STATEMENT BY YANKEE

The Navy man shaking me by my shoulder and saying my name over and over was apologetic. And he was very cautious: 'We have a man here who turned up in the middle of the night. We don't know who he is. The C.O. thinks we should wake you.' And he retreated across the room while I woke.

And awake I did, slowly – that is, externally I was slow. But I was processing the information quite rapidly. Paramount was the fact that instead of handling it routinely, the C.O. was awakening me. So the odds were overwhelming that the man was not mental; the odds were overwhelming that the C.O. at least felt that with a member of Congress on the base, he had to include him in whatever it was, or risk censure for not having done so. That made it serious. So I woke up slowly, but by the time my feet hit the deck, I was ready for anything.

After a quick shower and hasty breakfast, I followed the Navy man to the door of the mystery man's room, where we were met by an armed party. After my nod, we went in.

The man seated there had a definite air about him. He was dark, handsome in a hawkish way, dressed in some sort of fatigue uniform, and as he stood up I saw that he was tall. He extended his hand. 'Hello.' His voice was almost accentless, but a little stiff, as though he were first thinking out his phrases in some other language. 'My name is Ditlo Ravashan. Captain Ravashan, I think you would say, except that I have no vessel any longer.' He said that, and then he smiled.

I studied his hand. Then I took it, and as I took it, I felt for the first time the incredible power of the man. It was as if steel – warm steel – had closed around me. If he did not want to give my hand back, I simply could not take it. But he gave it back.

I looked at him. And I knew – I don't know how, but I *knew* – what he would claim about his origins. I gave him my name and my position in the U.S. Congress, while looking directly into his eyes. They were brown, and there was little to see that was different, though they tended more toward the maroon than was common in a white man. And they were as steady as mine. And he grinned suddenly, a sharp broadening of his smile into something else entirely. 'You've guessed,' he said approvingly. 'You've actually guessed! From very small clues indeed! Bravo! But to remove any lingering doubts,' he said, 'I brought in a body – another of my crew. It won't take much cutting to determine we are different from you, inside.'

'No, I don't doubt you,' I said, making up my mind. If it was true about having a body, there was no longer any doubt. He'd brought it to us to spare the need for cutting him. I could hardly blame him. 'All right – leave us alone,' I said to the Navy party. 'All of you,' to the C.O. It wasn't that I didn't trust them. It was a matter of need to know, that's all. And they went, although the C.O. was frowning and hesitating. A better man would have stayed, but the better man had been discharged after the end of the war.

Ravashan and I looked at each other across the room. Then we sat down on opposite sides of the table. 'What do you want, Ravashan?'

Ravashan grinned. 'Don't you want to know how I got here, where my ship is, and so forth?'

'I'll learn all that, in time,' I said. 'You obviously didn't plan it; you're improvising. That's the primary fact.'

Ravashan sat silently for a moment, looking at me. And in that look, I read him for what he was – an uncommonly clever individual, sizing me up, and not realizing that I was more clever than he. And he *was* clever – far cleverer than any man I knew, in his situation. I respected him for that. More important, I prepared to enjoy our association, and he did not disappoint me for a long time.

He began to speak; of long voyages, at first:

'We range,' he said, 'over a fair part of the immediate Universe. Well, we should – we've been at it for a long time. Long time. You have got to understand that, nevertheless, we haven't even scratched the surface of the stars in this immediate vicinity. There are very many of them. But in those stars, we have found only one race that was in space before us. Those are the Methane-Breathers. We … traffic … with them. We are not enemies. But we are not friends, either. If we had an interest in the same worlds, I think we would be deadly enemies. But never mind that for now.

'We explore the stars for many reasons, but the main one is commerce. Natural resources. And the occasional customer.'

'Oh?' I said.

He laughed. 'We have, as you can imagine, things for sale. Machinery, technology packages, even gadgets. All, of course, more advanced that anything your race possesses. In return, we take a certain spectrum of natural resources. Sometimes, too, we find articles of native manufacture for which there is a market … much as your more advanced nations will buy certain goods from less advantaged cultures, because they are cheaper for the disadvantaged to make, or because the goods are somehow cute. I'm sure you know what I mean.'

'Yes.' But I barely noticed the insult. Why should I? I had already established that I was more intelligent than he. What was important was his talk of advanced machinery and consumer goods. True, they would collapse the domestic manufacturing capability if introduced at random. But they did not have to be introduced at random, if one were careful. And the man who controlled the flow ... the man who controlled the flow would become the most powerful man on Earth. The most powerful man on Earth. But all I said was 'Yes.'

He said: 'There's a catch, unfortunately.'

'And what is that?'

'It's illegal. Even my telling you this is illegal. We take an oath. We are not, under any circumstances, to communicate the truth of ourselves to the natives. We are not for a moment to even consider it. It's too soon in your development.'

I looked at him. He looked back. I said: 'Why, then, are you breaking your oath?'

'Well, wouldn't you? If you were me, and faced years of a wasted life now?' He took a breath. 'When I obviously was born to engage life?'

I grinned mirthlessly. In some ways, we were very much alike. He went on: 'So I need protection not only from your people but from mine. Oh, not for a while. But if we are to do each other any good, then in time I may have advanced the Earth to the point where an official commercial envoy lands. And at that point, I had better not be the individual who took so many risks with the secret of our existence.' He grinned wryly. 'Precisely because I would have gotten away with it. That they dare not forgive.'

I stopped him then and called the C.O. I could not, of course, exercise any duress over the commanding officer, and I could not keep him from informing his superiors ... in fact, he had so informed them even before waking me. What he had informed them of was that he had an unaccounted-for personnel who had told a good enough story to get on the base ... with a corpse. That had been enough for the Navy to send a specialist, who was on his way and would arrive shortly, and depending on what the specialist recommended, further action would be taken. Presumably, that included giving the C.O. a discharge if he had pulled the wrong chain frivolously. Well, that was right, proper, and did not perturb me – though it obviously perturbed the C.O. I did not think the story that this man might be from off Earth had gotten beyond the confines of the base as yet, and even on the base the number of persons who knew even a wildly distorted version was minimal.

Furthermore, I did not know if an un-Earthling had ever previously been encountered, but that did not mean much; you can trust any branch of the service above a certain level of rank to keep its secrets. But a secret like this had the quality that, except in very special circumstances, it could be bandied about and still it was too huge to be believed.

What I wanted to make sure of, nevertheless, was that all the enlisted men were not in communication with the news media. Enlisted men have an almost unique ability to make trouble, in a clumsy, sloppy way that is almost impossible to deny because you can't be sure what it is about, so muddled does it become. And as for the news media – even in those early days I regarded it with suspicion on the one hand and contempt for its manipulability on the other. And, as I rather thought, the C.O. had secured the base, and would only gradually release the men who had seen or heard anything, transferring one to Alaska and one to Hawaii, one to Norfolk, and so forth. And really, what did they know; what hard facts did they possess? Good. With that assurance, I dismissed the C.O. and returned to my un-Earthly man.

We reasoned on what sort of questions the investigating officer would ask when he got there, and how my man would respond. And also I thought it likely I foresaw what I would do next. So that was that.

Ravashan would be loyal to me, I thought, above all other things on Earth … and for that matter, when push came to shove, above all things off Earth, too, though I did not make that clear to him. I did not at once know exactly how he could best serve me. But serve me he would. Plainly he was too precious to let slip away, and I could always think of something later. And so, in that room, the two of us struck a bargain that endured for many years. It did not, of course, endure forever. But nothing is forever.

– From a private tape

OLIR SELMON

I was terrified. Every noise of the night seemed monstrous. I saw nothing in the dark; I collided with a hundred things in the first five minutes, and to this day I can only guess at what they were.

I blundered on. And as I blundered, I went through the first of what I would go to sleep with every night for the rest of my life. I conducted an enquiry: *Why* did the engines suddenly begin to fail? *What* did I do wrong in attempting to restore the balance? *When* had they actually begun to fail … was it, for instance, as soon as we started them up at home? Had they *never* actually been right, and I, fool, had not noticed? Had we in fact been lucky to reach this planet at all, before the trouble became too catastrophic? Could I, in short, have done *anything* differently; and if I had, would it have made a difference? I could not know … all my life I would continue to ask these questions.

And I tried to convince myself that in fact it had not happened – that I was sleeping aboard the ship, and would waken at any time now, and shake my head ruefully, and go on about my duties, safe and sound. But I was not safe and sound, and I knew it.

I blundered on. And on. It seemed to me that I would never get out of this trackless maze of sharp objects in the dark, of unknown voices crying who knew what, in response to what, with the object of what. And *why* did the engines fail? And Joro. Poor, luckless Joro.

It was dawn, gradually filtering through the trees, that brought a measure of a sort of calm. First of all, I could see the trees, at last, and pick my way among them, so that the innumerable bristlings of branchlets and twigstickers lessened to almost nothing. I was bleeding, lightly, from a hundredfold pervasions of my skin, and my coverall was punctured and stained with blood and sap, but all of me was functioning, and with dawn the quality of noises, too, went through a diminishment, so I found that I was clearly less nervous, and that, too, helped calm me. But what was I to do? Where was I to go?

Indeed, my options seemed so few. So very few. Here I was, stranded for life, with nothing beyond what I could carry, and who would give me shelter, who would give me a place of livement, when the situation would produce questions I could not answer? What was I to do? Where was I to go? And, asking myself these questions, I moved on, with neither plan nor direction, with no purpose beyond sheer survival, and what good, really, was that?

I confess it freely – if I had had a weapon, at certain points on that first morning, I would have, indeed, turned it on myself … if I could have thought of a way to do so and yet conceal the weapon after my death. It is good that doctrine does not allow us to salvage weapons, for surely a weak being might not, in the last extremity of despair and spiritual debility, take as much care for the last part as he should, and would leave a mysterious and rankling corpse, and beside it a weapon of great puissance and intrigue; it was good that the doctrine did not permit us to salvage weapons, I repeated to myself, and sobbed.

It became clear to me, too, that we had fallen into a very peculiar part of the planet. It was good for nothing. Fenced off on the seaward side by cranberry bogs, fenced off on the west by unguessable territory that eventually became America as most people knew it, ending to the north but where the trees were short and spindling, the soil was essentially sand; I could understand, I suppose, why it was the only stretch of the Eastern Seaboard for hundreds of miles in either direction that showed almost no lights at night – a blotch of darkness upon the lacy webworks that otherwise adorned the edge of this continent. We were come upon a wasteland … as was calculated, true, when emergency landing areas were designated, but in fact 'emergency landing area' was a sort of joke, wasn't it, intended to somehow give the impression that things were somehow under control somehow even after a crash, but they were not under control, were they? No, they were not under control; nothing was under control.

I came to a field, in the midst of nowhere. I had been moving through scrub pine, precisely – tedious, unsatisfactory stuff, surely useless for any purpose but to break the hearts of people who tried to find some purpose in it. And suddenly, without warning, I came to a clearing.

Thunderstruck, I barely managed to keep myself back in the trees, and peered out at what this might be. And what this might be was an opening in the pines – not so much a field as an opening, unlinked to anything, really, at one margin of which was a small dwelling place that seemed to be cobbled together of whatever came to hand rather than planned, and a truck, very old and badly dented, and motionless forever, I suspected, for the tires were flat, and the windshield was opaque with fractures. It sat at the end of two ruts that disappeared among the trees; only that much road had sufficed to bring it here, to die.

I looked at this, not knowing what to do. I was afraid: to commit, finally, to having intercourse with these people; to having to speak their language; to masquerade as one of them. That was very hard to contemplate. Anything – almost anything at all – and I would delay the moment. And then a dog began to bark, and I retreated back into the woods, and went around the field, and went on; I went on I don't know how long, and came to another place, somewhat like the first but even smaller, in a bare clearing, no truck, no dog, no road at all leading up to it that I could see, and I circled around it and drew closer, eventually: a hovel, without any sign of life – perhaps, I thought, abandoned; a place, I thought, where I might rest and plan my next move, and I pulled aside the rotting blanket that hung over the entrance and ducked quickly inside.

There was only the one room. In the little bit of light that came in the one window, I saw a camp stove, very old and battered, and a chair, and a rickety old chest of drawers, and a cot, bare except for a stained uncovered pillow and a blanket only marginally newer than the one which hung in the doorway. There was no one inside – perhaps had been no one in a long time, I thought, but I suddenly did not care. I think I realized, somehow, that if I were asleep it would not be my fault what happened from then on.

I laid myself down on the cot, and wrapped the blanket around me, and thought that it had been such a long time since I had slept, and so much had happened, so much had changed forever since the last time I had closed my eyes ... and I slept.

I do not know how long it was before I heard a voice say: 'Wake up. Wake up, now.' I opened my eyes, hardly knowing where I was, or who, and peered across the tiny room in a growing heart-stopping panic, and saw an old man sitting calmly in the straight chair. He held across his lap a rifle – a single-shot .22, I later learned, with which he hunted small game – and despite this he did not look particularly menacing. He was very old, really, to my far younger eyes. He looked at me and said again, 'Wake up, now.' And then he laughed, and though technically I could not be sure, because laughter after all might be subtly different here, in fact I was positive, from the first moment I saw him, that he was hopelessly crazy; and I was right ... the laughter was too free, too delighted by very small things; he was as ... batty as a bedbug.

Which is not to say that most of the time he was not as sane as anyone. It was, however, to say that his bridges were down, and had been replaced by extravagant structures which were much more daring, if less well able to carry a load, than normal.

His name was Jack English, and he was of an indeterminate age but probably sixty-five or so. He had lived in this spot in the pine barrens for a very long time, as far as I could tell, and I believe at one time he had had a wife, but twenty or twenty-five years ago she had disappeared, and he did not expect to see her again. He laughed again.

He lived, as I said, in the pine barrens, and like most people who lived there he lived on land that was not his own, but did not seem to belong to anyone else, either, and he lived in a house that, basically, he could walk away from in ten minutes, move a mile in any direction, and duplicate in very short order. He had no power or running water, of course; the result was the only constraint on him – that he live near a creek. But he had not actually moved in over twenty-five years.

He told me this, and more, as the morning wore on. I sat on a box, and he sat in a chair.

We conversed. That is, he asked me who I was and what I did; what had brought me to the pine barrens – which was the first I knew of them – and what had brought me to his dwelling place in particular. But when I tried to tell him – that my name was Charlie Mortimer, that I was part of a special Army detachment, that I was lost – he would laugh and call me a liar. Maybe my name was Mortimer, though he doubted it, but that I was part of the U.S. Army he doubted very much, for I carried no military gear, and he doubted if I could be so lost as to be completely separated from the rest of my group; he doubted if I was lost at all. What did I want with him, specifically; why had I come to his dwelling place? And when I tried to tell him I had not come to his dwelling place except by accident, he just laughed and laughed. And finally he said, in his crazy way: 'You know what I think, Mr Mortimer? I think you came down in a flying saucer, and you're trying to fool me. That's what I think. Either that, or you're an escaped prisoner. That's what I think. And you know what, Mr Mortimer? I don't give a shit, really, as long as you don't pull nothing stupid.'

So passed my first morning on Earth. And this is hard to explain, but after a while he showed me how to cook a meal out of a dead squirrel and some flour, and we ate it, from a plate and a cardboard thing like a plate, with a knife for him and a fork for me, and it tasted delicious. Of course, I had not eaten in a long time, but it tasted delicious. And we drank some wine from a glass jug he had, and in due course it was time to go to sleep, the sun going down. And he showed me a corner of the hut where I could bed down, apparently not being at all afraid of me.

And the next day was much the same, and in about a week he went off and came back with a fresh jug and a loaf of bread and some other necessities, though we continued to depend on squirrel and other small creatures for our main dishes, he being very good with the rifle, and the weeks became months and somehow we managed. Sometimes we went days without speaking, once the initial freshet of lies and half-truths was exhausted. I cooked, and did not ask for anything, and this seemed satisfactory to him. That and the occasional night I spent on the bed with him.

And in due course – in a year or two – he let me go to the general store several miles away, on the edge of the barrens, and trade various things, such as cranberries or various things we found in the woods – axes and saws and such, if we were careful, for their owners might notice – for the staples we needed. By then I was wearing a pair of bib overalls, of course. At least, I recall I was ... there was a certain mistiness to the entire experience ... and in a few more years, one morning he died. But by then I was acclimated pretty well to life as an Earthman, and in a few weeks I left, with the contents of a buried jar of cash – a hundred and twelve dollars it was, which he had finally shown me the day before he died.

I worked as a dishwasher in a diner for a while, coming out of the barrens, and then I was a day laborer for a while, and then I wrote away for my birth certificate, living in a town called May's Landing. What you do is, you scan the back files of the newspaper until you find an infant that died about the time you want to be born, and you write away for a copy of the birth certificate, and from then on it's you. On the outside.

I think that was the bravest single thing I did. Suppose somebody else had already written for that particular certificate? I got a post office box and everything, and let it lay in the box for a week, and snatched it at last, and left town immediately. Even so, I went clear across the country, by train to Oakland. There I got a job drafting, and living in a room, and thought I would spend the rest of my life in Oakland, which I liked as much as I liked anything. But Eikmo ran into me, or I ran into Eikmo, and I moved to Chicago ... or, to be precise, Shoreview. And there I ran into Dwuord Arvan, and I knew it was no good, and then eventually I read the paper, and I couldn't help but confront Dwuord, and that was the last straw; it really was.

You must understand that I turned my head and saw that my hand was going to make contact with the third rail, and I could have stopped myself – I thought about the postmortem, but I suddenly realized I would not care.

You understand? It had come down to that. To hell with the whole game. And I reached out my hand deliberately, and died in violet fire.

– Never revealed. A.B.

JACK MULLICA

We came, eventually, to her father's farm – Nick's farm – on the edge of the barrens. It was not much of a farm; the buildings were old, and even the house was swaybacked with age. Nor was it large. But on the other hand, the soil was a little better, there was grass, there were some towering trees which were clearly different from the barren pines. There were outbuildings, including a barn.

The whole layout was not large, but then, Nick Olchuck had long ago given up on the idea of actually making a living from it. There were a few animals – a pair of goats, a hutch full of rabbits, a dog, enough chickens running around to provide eggs for Nick and Margery, and of course cats, which were essentially wild. I knew little of this in detail, as I stood at the edge of the road, supporting a sweaty Margery in the first light of dawn, but one did not need detail to grasp the essentials. The dog, Prince, had come out of the barrel lying on its side beside the barn, where he was chained, and was barking furiously at me.

'Home, sweet home,' Margery said. She called to the dog: 'Shut up, Prince. I said, shut up!' and the animal subsided, stood beside his barrel, and regarded me stiffly. Margery turned to me. 'All right. You can sleep in the barn. I'll get you some food before I go to work. Now I've got to go inside and explain you to my father.'

I looked at her. Up to now, she had been body coolth and bulk and smells, and occasional glimpses, but this was the first time she had stood a little apart from me. Perhaps I had been much the same to her, because she took a minute to look me up and down, too.

She was about my height, and, except for a tendency to too much makeup, not bad-looking. I stood peering at her face for a moment, trying to figure out what was off about it; when I saw her again later, it was less vivid, and her eyes in particular looked much blander, and then I realized it had been makeup. What I did not realize, for years, was that I never actually saw her; she always had some makeup on. But that's beside the point for the time being.

She had a slim, long-legged figure. But it was canted off to one side, and one of her legs was much thinner than the other. She was wearing a dress made out of a chicken feed sack – feed was sold in print sacks, with no company markings, for that express purpose – and she looked out of focus. I found out later that she was only nineteen when I first met her, and one of the purposes of the extreme makeup was to make her look older, but now it was smeared and awry.

'All through?' she said.

'What?'

'Are you all through looking at me?'

I tried a smile. 'Yes. You're not bad to look at, you know.'

'Bullshit,' she said, and turned to go into the house. It was painful to watch her make her way, especially since she knew I was watching her. I went to the barn and lifted the wooden latch, and went inside.

The barn had not been used for anything in particular for a long time. It smelled of something vaguely unpleasant – I learned later it was mildew – but not overwhelmingly so. There were some spots where other odors did overwhelm – cat turds and rat turds – but these were localized, and I avoided them with almost perfect success. There were some feed sacks along one wall, and there were several cats that looked up from sleeping in various nooks as I came in, but that was all. The barn was essentially an empty space enclosed by four walls and a roof. I went over to the feed sacks, and they made a respectable bed. That was my main concern. I was tired enough, God knows. And without further ado I lay down. I thought to myself that life on Earth was a little stranger than it ought by rights to be, and then I was asleep.

I woke up a long time later – late afternoon, it was, by the light that came in through the cracks – and beside me, on the floor of the barn, was an upside-down box that had not been there. I lifted it, and there was a sandwich and a glass of something, red and sweet. Kool-Aid, it turned out. I put the box back down over it and went to the back door, which was jammed shut and hadn't been opened in years. But by tugging on it I got it to open an inch or two and managed to urinate outside. And it struck me funny, for a minute; here was water that had never been on Earth before. But I was not the first, and I went back to the food, which the cats were trying to figure a way into, and smiled, and chased them back, and ate every scrap, including draining the Kool-Aid, which I have not done very often after the first few occasions, for it almost always gives me indigestion. But I was pretty thirsty at the time.

I took stock. There was not much to take. I was in Margery Olchuck's barn after abandoning my crashed flying saucer and the rest of my crew. I had on my issue fatigue uniform, which tended to resemble a coverall jumpsuit, my fatigue shoes, which looked only vaguely Earthlike – until Adidases came along, which was much later – but would pass, and my first-aid kit and my iron rations, which were in two of the patch pockets on my uniform pants.

The iron rations you could keep; we had all eaten one meal of them, in accordance with shipboard drill, and no doubt they would keep body and

soul together in a dire emergency. Nobody ever complained. They couldn't –
not the ones who actually had to live on the things. The first-aid kit had all
sorts of goodies in it, but I did not need any of them. And that was it – oh, I
had an identity, Jack Mullica, which was both woefully thin and too well
established to abandon. I promised myself that if I were ever to be in a crashing flying saucer again, I would do much better next time.

And that really was it. I considered going into the house to talk to Nick,
and felt a mild curiosity that he had not come out to investigate me, but he
was too much of a cipher for me to pursue that seriously. I didn't even know
his name. So I sat down on the feed sacks, and watched the cats lick the plate
and the glass, and scratched one of them behind the ears when it cautiously
came over, before it jumped away. And that was it. I wondered what Margery
might have in store for me. If not then, then I wondered very often later. I see
no reason not to assume that I began that habit in that barn, without knowing it, or at least without knowing what it would cost me, over the years.

It hasn't been that bad.

She came in the evening, carrying more food – a hamburger – and another
glass of Kool-Aid. She was wearing jeans and a white T-shirt over a bra. I
liked her breasts. She looked tired. She did not look sweet, or girlish. She
looked all business. She handed me the food and sat down on the feed bags
beside me. 'He didn't come in here?" she asked, and I nodded my head, and
then remembered and said, 'No.' She looked at me patiently. 'Which is it?'
and I said 'No' again, and she nodded. 'I didn't think so.' She shook her head.
'He drinks. I drink, too, but he drinks.'

'What else does he do?'

'Well, that's about it, really. We're lucky to keep the farm. But he had the
mortgage paid off before he started drinking, and my job with the glass company looks pretty solid.'

'Glass company?'

'Kimble Glass. In Vineland. I ride the bus. I work in the office; payroll clerk.'

Vineland, I presumed, was a town. 'What does Kimble Glass do?'

'Medical glassware. We're a division of Owens Corning.' I didn't know
what that was, but it didn't matter. 'When are you planning to move on?'

Move on. I was reluctant to move on. 'I don't know. Do you want me to go
soon?'

'Eat your supper before it gets cold.' Then she looked me right in the eyes
and said: 'We can't afford to keep you for any length of time.'

Well, that had been pretty obvious. I bit into the hamburger. 'Is there some
kind of work I could do?'

'Where did you say you were going when you bumped into me?'

'I don't believe I said. Nowhere, really.'

She nodded. There was infinite knowledge in her eyes. Not judgment; just knowledge. It was hard to face. 'You don't have anyplace to go on this continent, do you, Jack Mullica?' And before I could formulate a reply to that, she said: 'It's okay. Some of us who were born here don't have anyplace to go, either.' She grinned crookedly. 'I don't know. I've got a few people around here who owe me things. Maybe we can find you a job. We'll see.'

I had finished my meal. 'Look.' I had thought this over very carefully. 'Look,' I said again, 'I want you to do me a favor.'

'A favor.'

'That's right.'

'What kind of a favor?'

'I want you to let me try something with your leg.'

She stared at me incredulously. Then she burst out laughing. 'With my *leg*?' It was not frank and open laughter. After the first instant of genuine shock, it was harsh and mechanical, echoing back from the walls of the barn in sarcasm and anger. She twisted around to face me with her whole body, and the leg was thrust out toward me. 'My leg. I've done a lot of favors in my life,' she said. 'But not with my leg.' Then she grinned crookedly. 'Or did you mean my good leg?'

I went on doggedly. It was the only way I knew to eventually get through to her at the time, and the time was what I had to work with. So I persisted. 'I want to use my first-aid kit on your leg.'

'Your what?'

'My first-aid kit.' I took it out of its pocket. 'I don't know if it'll do any good. But it won't do any harm. I want to try it.'

'Oh, yeah. I forgot. Your first-aid kit,' she said. 'First-aid kit!' She began to laugh again. She reached out and took it. 'First-aid kit.' She shook her head, then looked more closely. She looked back at me. 'I can't read any of the words except Johnson & Johnson.'

I shrugged.

She bit her lip momentarily, then looked at me again. 'Do you really think it will do any good?' And I heard the faint note of hope underneath everything else she put into the question, which was loaded with carelessness, ninety-nine percent.

'I don't know,' I repeated. 'It's worth a try.'

'Well, what do I have to do?'

I looked down at the floor. 'Take your pants off.'

She began to laugh again, and I turned on her. 'Look, take your pants off or don't; I think I can do you some good, but I may be wrong; if I wanted to copulate with you, I'd at least wait until tomorrow, considering that you haven't even gotten any sleep after your last time; is that clear?'

She had started some reaction, but my choice of words choked it off before it got started. 'Copulate with me?' She giggled and put her hand over her mouth, but it did no good; the giggle grew, and turned into a guffaw. She looked at me as if I'd just gotten off the boat, and she couldn't stop laughing. Still laughing, she stood up and opened the belt of her jeans, opened the buttons of the fly front, and pushed the jeans down. She was wearing white cotton panties. She stepped out of the jeans and kicked them aside, and said 'Now what?' still laughing a little, seemingly unaware for a moment how thin and wasted the leg looked in contrast to the good one, and then I saw that in fact she knew exactly how it looked, and she stood there like a young, if tired, queen, and she was utterly in command of the situation. The two of us faced one another in the barn and the relationship cemented itself, right there, nor has it changed to this day, whenever this day is. I pointed to the bags. 'Sit down,' I said, and she sat, but not as a favor to me – as a favor to herself – and waited.

I opened the kit and took out the tin of muscle stuff. It was intended to help bruises heal faster. It did not work miracles, but it did cut down healing time dramatically. Maybe it would do something for her. 'Stretch the leg out,' I said, and took two fingertips' worth of the ointment. 'Now. Just relax.' I wiped the fingers over the outside of the upper thigh, and worked them around. The muscle felt strange, not like a usual muscle at all. But in half a minute the fingertips of my opposite hand, on the inside of her thigh, were slick with the ointment that had come through her leg. I wiped them on the peculiar-feeling muscle there, and worked them, and in a very short while the fingertips of my first hand were slick again. It was working back and forth, a little less emerging out the other side each time, until finally it was gone.

She was looking at me peculiarly. 'It's as if I could feel it going all through me,' she said. I nodded. 'And I taste garlic.'

'You taste what?'

'Garlic,' she said, a little impatiently.

'Interesting.' So now I knew what garlic tasted like. 'All right; now we do the rest of the leg.' We did the rest of the leg. About a fifth of the ointment had been used. I looked up. 'That's all.'

She did not move the leg. Her voice was carefully neutral. 'Just exactly what do you mean, that's all?'

'That's all I can do, for now. You should feel something – a flush of heat, probably; less impediment to motion; perhaps a little growth in the flesh – within hours. It won't be much, at first. It may never be much. In either case, we'll do some more in twenty-four hours. And maybe something permanent will happen. That's all.'

She got off the feed bags, feeling the ground with the toes of her bad leg, twisting it a little, looking down at it. Then she got back into the jeans. 'It feels warm,' she said.

'That might just be the massage.'

338

'I – don't think so.'

'Let it go,' I said. 'Let it go. It'll start healing or it won't, and what you think of it doesn't matter. What I think of it, too. Just let it go.' I stood there, putting the cap back on the ointment, realizing that I had started something from which there was no drawing back. I looked at her, just drawing her belt together, getting ready to button up the fly on her jeans. 'All right?' She had her head down; the wings of her hair fell around her face, and I couldn't see her expression. 'All right.' Then she said: 'Come on in the house; you could use a wash.'

'All right,' I said.

I met her father. He was sitting in the kitchen, a half-empty glass in front of him, and a bottle beside that. He looked blankly at me as I came into the house. He was in his fifties, I imagined, a square-headed man gone bald on top, with bad teeth and washed-out blue eyes, in an undershirt and work pants. Without changing his expression or raising his voice, he said to his daughter: 'I thought I told you to keep your men out of this house. I said to you, very clearly—'

'He's not one of my men,' Margery said.

'You expect me to believe that?'

'I'm not a liar.'

He frowned thoughtfully. Than he nodded. 'No. You're not.' He frowned. 'You're not,' he repeated. He looked at me. 'That's all right, then. What's his name?'

'My name's Jack Mullica,' I said. 'I'm pleased to meet you, Mr Olchuck.' I stuck out my hand.

He ignored it. 'Are you? Pleased to meet Margery's drunk of a father? I wouldn't be.' He drank from the glass. 'Go on about whatever business you have here. Don't bother being friendly. I don't really take to it.' He took another sip. 'On the other hand, I'm not nasty. Count your blessings.' He looked thoughtful. 'Yes. All in all, I'd say count your blessings.'

'Come on, Jack,' Margery said, and tugged at my arm. And I went. What, pray tell, else would I do?

The bathroom was crowded – a sink, the John, and a bathtub with a shower attachment competed for space that left very little bare floor – but it was no worse than the analogous facility on the ship. In fact, it was a little more spacious. In any case, I didn't complain. Earlier that evening, I'd been forced out of the barn long enough to crouch down behind some bushes, and then wipe myself with leaves; that experience makes you appreciate indoor comforts very quickly.

She looked me up and down. 'I think some jeans and a shirt of my father's will fit you. And underwear. That'll have to do. All right, I'll leave you now.' And she did, with a little flirt of her head that might have meant anything,

But when I was through in the shower – and, oh, it was a *good* shower, once I figured out what it was, and how to work it – there are things you can't learn adequately from television; not even the television of today, and in those days it was much worse – she opened the door a crack and passed through a small heap of clothing which turned out to be as described, with a pair of white cotton socks thrown in. 'Pass me your old clothes,' she said. 'I'll wash them the next time I do laundry.'

I did, after taking my iron rations and first-aid kit out of the pockets, and passed my clothes to her. Which left me with the first-aid kit exposed, because it wouldn't fit in any of the jeans pockets. It didn't really matter, I supposed, but I found myself staring at it, and wondering if it was doing her leg any good, and then realizing that it was the only thing, now, that was still mine to control from before the crash. It was an old friend, suddenly. And its content was waning. I stood there with the kit in my hand, looking at the lettering, and the lettering that wasn't lettering, and suddenly I realized I had been down on this planet less than a day, and already I was more Earthman than not. Which was exactly what the people back on my home planet wanted, under these special circumstances. Everything was going well. Everything. I stood there in a bathroom in a marginal farmhouse in borrowed clothes, dependent on a very marginal girl and to some extent on an over-the-edge father; I had no job, no real place to sleep, no money, and everything was going well.

I spent another day in the barn, coming into the house only for a little bit of time at night. The father ignored me. Margery looked at me warily; she seemed, in what few glimpses I had of it, to be setting her leg a little differently, experimentally. But I couldn't be sure, and she seemed to be almost hiding it. After dinner she went back out to the barn with me. 'If you want to work on my leg some more, it's all right,' she said casually.

'That's right, it *is* twenty-four hours since the last time, isn't it?' I said.

'Yeah.' She opened her pants, dropped them, and sat down on the bags. I got out the first-aid kit, and the container of muscle ointment out of the kit, and went over to her. The leg was measurably better. It was less wasted, felt more like a normal leg, and seemed more responsive to stimuli. I did not comment on any of this. I simply applied the ointment, and she simply stared over my shoulder at the wall, her expression completely neutral. The only way you could tell, really, that there was something going on was the fact that she wept, silently and not very hard, but steadily, so that her cheeks were wet when we were finished and she got up and put her pants back on.

'Your hands are warm,' she said. 'Your whole body's warm. I noticed that from the first. You sick?'

I shook my head, getting it right. I had noticed that she was cold; not much colder than normal, but still … 'No. It just is that way.'

She looked at me for a long time. Then she shrugged and left the barn.

The next day, after work, she came out to the barn, looking at me narrow-eyed, swinging her leg. She walked a lot closer to normal. We neither one of us said anything. It was either working or it wasn't. It appeared to be working. What could you say beyond that, really? Finally she said 'Come on' and jerked her head toward something outside the barn. She stood with a hand on the door, and I went over to her.

'What's happening?' I said, and she said, 'Get in the car. ' I looked in the yard, and there was a car there.

– Mullica's recollections, reconstructed

INTERPOLATION, DWUORD ARYAN

It took me a while to get used to the animals – the cats, the dogs, the chickens, and whatnot. They fit their ecological niches in understandable ways, but they weren't the same as the animals we had at home. And it isn't the same to see them on TV and then have them actually rub up against you. It is, as a matter of fact, horrifying at first. Particularly the cats.

But it doesn't take long to acclimate to them; to realize that a cat is profoundly innocent. A chicken has no brain to speak of. A dog seems to have some concept that he is doing something bad, or good, depending on the action. But a cat does everything the same – kills and purrs, plays with a ball of string or a moribund mouse, the same in either case. We have no such thing on my home world; it is unsettling to think too much about cats, and thank your stars they are not larger. But one grows accustomed to them, particularly if one realizes they live pretty much without reference to human beings ... or us.

What persisted in strangeness was the smells.

That is something for which radio and TV do not prepare you. And it is pervasive; there is nowhere on Earth you can go to escape the smell of Earth.

When we first landed, there was the rich smell of the bog, and then the scent of pines. The one was thick, and clogged the nostrils, and was deceptively familiar, for it was largely the smell of decay. The pines were more difficult: astringent, so that the mucus membranes dried up and tingled, and the throat felt peculiar. But the smell of her, thick with human sweat, cigarette smoke, and liquor, was exotic and oddly titillating, whereas the smell of the farm, with its dog, cat, and chicken feces, its odor of mold and dust in the barn, was hard to take at first.

But it was the cars that really struck me as exotic. They were so different from what we had: different fuel, odd cooling systems, pervasive lubricants. I loved it. I purely loved it. Cars seemed to me to speak more clearly of Earth than any single thing else, and I was going to be of the Earth. I was. It was the only course of action that made sense. Soon enough, I promised myself, no one would be able to tell me from an Earthman ... at least on the inside.

COURTNEY MASON DOWRIGHT

It is a riverfront home in Maryland. It is not a large home, and the grounds are not extensive. Nevertheless, it is a riverfront home in Maryland.

It is the retirement home of Commander Dowright, who is not yet so frozen by old age that he cannot get up at dawn and, with a gun under his arm and a dog coursing along before him, go for long walks-cum-casual-shootings. But Commander Dowright does not actually do that very often. Most of the time, he sits out on his back porch and broods, bitterly. When I found him, he was glad to talk. He raised the tape recorder to his lips and said:

My name is Courtney Mason Dowright, and I was, at the time of my assignment to determine exactly what was going on at NAS Atlantic City, a commander in the United States Navy. I am now retired, of course.

There were several peculiarities about the call to Philadelphia Naval District Headquarters. Minor in themselves, they led to the inevitable conclusion that, once again, Fred Andrews was doing nothing to disprove the grading that had made him graduate almost dead last in his year at the Academy. (Frederick Mayhew Andrews was a captain in the U.S. Navy at the time, and commanding officer of NAS Atlantic City, not a plum job. He was scheduled to retire later that year, still a captain, and would have been retired earlier if the opening at Atlantic City had not needed a man for a short while, until his successor had completed certain courses. For that matter, it is problematical that he would have been a captain in the first place if so many other better men hadn't been killed or invalided out in the war.)

But a three A.M. telephone call from a commanding officer to a district headquarters – any commanding officer, any district headquarters – leaves the district headquarters with few options. So I in turn was knocked out of bed and told that something worth my time was going on down at NAS Atlantic City, though no one at Philadelphia was sure what. That was the first thing I was to find out for sure. And in due course after that I was helicoptered down to NAS Atlantic City, where in due course after *that* I learned that a congressman had somehow gotten involved.

Upon learning that he was a Navy veteran, I at first took this for an encouraging sign. But I am getting ahead of myself.

Upon landing, I was taken to Fred Andrews. In his office, alone with him, I learned that the base might have a visitor from another planet. It might almost equally well have a convincing madman, or some third possibility, but whoever or whatever he was, he was wearing badges that could not be read, and he had brought with him a similarly attired corpse who was not the world's prettiest sight.

I sat back and looked at Captain Andrews for a while, making up my mind tentatively. This was after the first big rash of reported flying saucer sightings – we had not yet learned to call them UFOs – in 1947 and '48, including quite a few by Navy personnel. And I was as aware as he that there were persistent rumors the Navy, or somebody, actually had some corpses, possibly even some live crewmen. But nothing solid; only reports of rumors, and I, of course, no more actually knowledgeable than anyone else in the Navy as far as I knew.

Well, that was what you would expect. If some base somewhere had solid evidence, that base was now buttoned up pretty good. In fact, that base was leading two lives: one, that nothing had ever happened there, and two, that for the few personnel that knew different, life was very complicated indeed.

Because anybody who thought the United States was going to make off-world visitors – we had not yet learned to call them extraterrestrials – public, or even private, didn't have his head screwed on right. And the same for every other government on Earth.

Why? Because if it was a small government, it knew perfectly well the big governments would take an immediate, intense, and personal interest, which could not possibly be good for the small government. And if it was a big government, then it knew it was at the top of the technological heap on Earth, the visitors were bound to be advanced beyond that, so, ipso facto, the big government could do nothing real to protect its citizens, or say it was protecting them, from whatever. And that inevitably leads to anarchy, which is the thing governments like least of all.

So, inasmuch as the visitors, if any, had somehow chosen not to announce themselves to Earthpeople so far, the best course was to hunker down and pray they would turn out to be an illusion, would at the very least continue to play coy, or we would, in the fullness of time, surpass them technologically. I suppose. Frankly, the last possibility struck me as unlikely in the extreme, since presumably the visitors weren't obligingly standing still developmentally, either. On the first two choices, I had at that time an opinion divided exactly fifty-fifty.

But be that as it may, the immediate question was, what was Captain Andrews going to do? So I quickly pointed out that Captain Andrews was only an inch or two away from safe retirement, and Captain Andrews huffed and grunted that of course he knew that and he was of course turning the entire matter over to me as the representative of the Philadelphia Naval District and I said no other thought had crossed my mind for even a moment,

and that was that. Then I said let's go look at the corpse and then let me interview this man you've got, and that was when I learned about the
congressman.

The congressman was young, junior in rank, and many miles from his
home district. But he was indefatigable, in the sense that he was rapidly
developing a reputation for going anywhere and doing anything that would
inch him up the ladder, and heavyweights in the system had cautiously
marked him as a comer.

He was at the base on a visit with some servicemen from his home state, having brought one of them a medal for heroism in a fire, said heroism having been
performed while the serviceman in question was home on liberty. An innocu-
ous errand having nothing to do with the congressman's being a junior member
of the House Armed Services Committee, and I looked at Captain Andrews
with almost open incredulity when I heard that. But then I remembered that
the congressman was ex-Navy, and I almost relaxed for a moment. After all,
too, this was not the first congressman to think up some excuse for enjoying
the free perks of a service installation instead of paying for a hotel room.

So I let that one go by. And apparently that *was* the congressman's motive –
or else whatever his motive actually was, it was derailed in favor of the one he
had been presented with this morning. Because I never heard of any other
trouble at the base as a result of the congressman's visit. Not that – ah, hell
with it; I never heard of any other trouble, there is no reason to think there
ever was any other trouble brewing, and what I'm saying is that life's too short
for some people to keep up with all the possibilities the congressman presented over the years. But now I'm getting beyond myself, and certainly
beyond the point you're interested in, right?

So. We went down to where the corpse was, in among the gray narrow corridors, the captain and I, and found him in the morgue. We dismissed the
morgue attendant, and I pulled out the drawer.

I did not learn much. He did not look any different from a man to me, he
was dressed in coveralls which were slightly different from those one normally saw, but not outlandishly so, and they were marked with badges I could
not read and did not look like they were in any language I had ever seen –
and I have seen quite a few, as have most people who have served in the Navy
for any length of time. But there were several explanations for my not recog-
nizing the language, and most of them did not require that the lettering be
part of a coherent system in use on some other world.

The man *had* died hard; the middle of his body was not a pretty sight.
There remained enough, however, to assure us he was a man. Frankly, it was
difficult to believe in him being off-world after seeing his genitals; blackened and burned, of a good size, rather they cried out pitifully that a man like

ourselves lay there, in worse case than we fervently prayed we would ever be. I turned away. 'That's enough,' I said. 'I'll come back for him later,' and we left.

We moved up one flight to where the prisoner was. And on the way we were joined by the congressman.

It was my first meeting with him, and I was immediately struck by his intensity, and by the fact that it was not in particular directed at me. Rather, he seemed to have an invisible opponent in play, and I – and everyone else – was not as important. Other than that, he was pleasant and polite. I got the distinct feeling that he would always be pleasant and polite as long as he did not feel compelled to study you closely. I wondered what I could do to keep him that way.

Fat chance.

Anyway, there we were, in the corridor outside the prisoner's room, with an armed guard at the door, and the congressman seemed to have materialized out of thin air, although actually he had simply stepped out of an adjacent room. How he knew it was us, and not more casual traffic, was easy – he had kept one eye to the crack in the slightly open door. But until you realized that, there was something just a bit disconcerting about it.

'You're going to speak to him now?' the congressman asked, and when I allowed that yes, indeed, that was what I was there for, he nodded. 'Of course. Well, you'll speak to me afterward. Correct?'

Well, not correct, exactly. There was no reason in the world for me to speak to him – or the commanding officer, for that matter – afterward. My report was technically for the admiral commanding the naval district. But I could see now that this would lead to a confrontation with the congressman, and one thing the admiral did not want was a confrontation with any congressman. And certainly not this one, on brief acquaintance. The fact was that the Navy was, as usual in peacetime, fighting to keep every friend it had in the House and Senate. So I smiled frankly and openly, and said 'Of course, sir,' and he did his best to smile openly and frankly, too. 'Very good,' he said, and I went in to the Martian or whatever he was with a definite feeling of unease.

He was behind his table and yawning into his hand when I came in, and gesturing in embarrassment with his other arm as his jaws gaped wider and wider and his eyes screwed themselves shut. 'Sorry,' he said a moment later, collecting himself. 'It's been a while since I slept. And your name is …?'

'Court Dowright. And yours is what?'

He grinned. 'Well, so far I've been claiming it's Ditlo Ravashan, and I say I am a member of a civilization that takes in more than just your Sun.'

'Ah.' I pulled out a chair and sat down opposite him. 'And is this true?'

'Which? That I claim it, or that my claim is true, or both?'

I looked at him. If we were going to play that sort of verbal game, we could be here a long time. On the other hand, the longer we played it, the likelier it was that the man was, simply, a man. Frankly, looking at him, I found it quite difficult to believe he had come out of a flying saucer. 'Both,' I said.

'Well,' he said with a faint twinkle in his eye, 'I have claimed it. And it might be true.'

That eye – those eyes – were a peculiar shade of brown. I wondered if he might not have on a pair of tinted contact lenses, which were just coming into limited use at the time.

'Are you crazy?' I asked.

He threw back his head and laughed. 'Well, if I am – and I might be – I'm not really the right person to ask, am I?'

'Where is your ship?'

'If there is one, it's lost in the bogs.' He waved as if he knew which way the room faced; in actual fact, he waved at the North Atlantic. 'Somewhere out in the bogs. We would have hidden it, and we would have done a good job.'

'We?'

'Oh, the other man and I.'

'The other man was moribund.'

'But he would have been alive at the time.'

'Would have been.'

He laughed again. 'Yes. Would have been.'

'You're really not saying anything, are you?'

'Well, yes and no.'

I was not prepared to take any more of that. The man had an accent, and he had somewhat peculiar eyes, but the rest of him as far as I could tell was as normal as normal could be. We could have spent a year in that room together, and if he wanted to keep playing verbal games, and if I kept to playing verbal games, we would be no further along at the end of that year than we were right that minute. I pushed back my chair. 'This really isn't very satisfactory. I'll be back,' I said, and left. The man was smiling at me as I went.

They had taken away his first-aid kit; the armed guard outside his door had it. I examined it. It had several things in it which were obviously machine-produced, and the lettering was (A) machine-produced and (B) unreadable except for the Johnson & Johnson. But that, too, could easily have been produced on Earth. Nothing said the gadgets actually had to do anything. All it told me, really, was that someone had gone to a great deal of trouble and expense to create the kit.

But that, too, depended on the scale of size. For a national government, for instance, or even one considerably down the ladder from that, it would have been nothing. Perhaps more important, even for one man with hidden motives, if it had to be consistent with his story, it could certainly be done. In other words, the first-aid kit, for me in my situation, answered no questions definitively; rather, it perhaps raised a few additional ones. Or perhaps not.

I gave it back to the guard, a little annoyed that I had ever looked at it at all.

'What do you think?' the congressman said to me.

We were sitting in the adjacent room, just the two of us, not much different from the room with the man in it – except that I was facing the door, I suddenly realized, and the congressman was between me and it – and the congressman was pretending it was just a casual question. Well, I'd tell him the truth. Anything else was too dangerous. 'I don't know,' I said. 'I know less, I suppose, than I did before I got here.'

'You suppose. Yes. It all has a tendency to raise more questions than it answers, doesn't it?' The congressman suddenly turned a smile on me, and I felt peculiar. Later, I finally decided it was because it was a perfectly friendly smile, and it chilled me to the bone.

'You know what I think? I think you will give him to me.' The congressman was quite serious.

'What?'

'Look at it from all sides,' the congressman said reasonably. 'This isn't really a Navy matter. It would be different if the Navy knew more, perhaps. But all that happened was that the man turned up at your main gate in the middle of the night. He said only the minimum to the enlisted personnel, he said only enough more to the officers to work his way swiftly up the chain of command, and he still isn't saying much, is he?'

'Not now, no.'

The congressman waved his arm – in much the same way that the man had. 'That's as may be. The fact is, he isn't talking.'

'Sir, I—'

'The chances are excellent he's a man with a hidden agenda. Period. The chances that he's actually the captain of a flying saucer are—'

'That's not the point! He's—'

The congressman steepled his fingertips and looked at me. 'That is the point, Commander. That's very much the point. The man might be any number of things, of which the least likely is that he's the captain of a flying saucer. Furthermore, he's begun backing away from that claim. I think you should go back to Philadelphia, report to your admiral that the man was unbalanced – which he almost certainly is, wouldn't you say? – and let it go at that. I'm sure the Navy has a great many other things on its mind. For instance, the next appropriations bill.'

'Sir, I don't think that's quite the truth.'

'Oh?' The congressman looked down at his hands. 'Do you know what the truth is? Suppose I told you that in fact Congress has a subcommittee devoted to investigating flying saucer claims, and that the duty of every member of Congress is to bring in any scrap of evidence he happens to come across?'

'Is that true, sir?'

The congressman spread his arms. 'You see?'

I shook my head. I felt I was getting deeper and deeper into a morass. 'I don't know—'

The congressman looked at me as if I were not too bright a child but he was choosing not to point that out to me. 'Commander,' he said, 'there are only two basic explanations for the man. One, he is what he at one time was saying that he was. In which case, do you suppose the Navy is superior to the national legislature in dealing with it? Or the man is a hoax, in which case the Navy wants to be rid of him as soon as possible. Now, isn't that a fair summary of the situation?'

'Congressman, I—'

Now the congressman looked closely at me, and I knew I had crossed a line I devoutly wished to get back to the safe side of as soon as possible. 'Commander,' he said softly, 'do you perhaps have a hidden allegiance which makes you so stubborn?'

This was the late 1940s, remember. 'A hidden allegiance' meant the Soviet Union, and there was no surer way to spend the rest of one's life essentially as a hunted animal than to become identified with that. You think it's bad now; that was the day of Joe McCarthy. I straightened up as though jolted with an electric current, and said 'No, sir!' as brightly and innocently as I could manage. And on that question, I made it my business to manage every volt that I could, plus some extra I usually didn't use.

'Then what's the problem, Commander?' The congressman was looking at me hard.

'Sir, I have a responsibility to my mission—'

'And how would you be failing to meet it?'

'Sir, I came down here—'

The congressman shook his head in mild exasperation. 'And you will go back up, and make your report. The base commander certainly won't contradict it. A couple of enlisted men will be transferred, but in fact they don't know – nobody knows – what actually transpired here. The junior officers he talked to don't know for sure. The base commander doesn't actually know for sure. And *you* don't know, do you? Do you, Commander?'

He was right. I didn't know. I suspected. And what I suspected was that the man was playing some game far beyond me; that he hadn't come down in a flying saucer, which was ridiculous, but that he was playing some elaborate game. Which, in fact, was more properly in the hands of the national legislature than it was in the Navy's.

'And what do I do with the corpse?' I asked.

'Why, you give it to the man. He'll know what needs to be done with it. Give it to the man, packed in dry ice. Give us the use of an ambulance for a few hours, and it'll then be as if it had never been. The water will have closed seamlessly.'

And that is how it was. The driver returned with the ambulance from National Airport in Washington, the man and the congressman and the corpse having gotten out there and from there could have gone anywhere, and it was not until I was in the helicopter going back to Philadelphia that it gradually dawned on me my Navy career was irretrievable blighted. Because the admiral commanding the Philadelphia District could not know for certain that I was telling him the whole truth, but on the other hand he did not dare put me on trial to determine that fact. So he made sure I never advanced beyond commander, because a man who might know as much as I did could not be trusted with higher command. Oh, I might in fact be under the protection of persons in the Navy higher than he, but if they moved to intervene on my behalf, they would show their hand. So they would not move to intervene on my behalf.

And so forth. You see what I'm saying? It was impossible for *anyone* to deal with Ravashan – or whatever his name was – and remain untainted. And it was impossible to get at the truth of the man. And that was that. The base commander died a long time ago, of old age, and the junior officers have many other things to think about, and the enlisted men are scattered, and none of us is getting any younger.

For that matter, you don't know that what I've told you is the truth, the whole truth, and nothing but the truth, do you? It is, but you don't *know* that, do you?

And Commander Dowright smiles bitterly.

– Statement taken in 1973. A.B.

FOOTNOTE

Commander Dowright was quite correct. Whereas up to then his fitness reports had been outstanding, they show a peculiar shift after his visit to NAS Atlantic City. It is not something one can put his finger on legally; the words of praise are still there. But when you put them all together, they give a sense that they add up to 'a loyal and thoughtful officer, considering what he is.' It is not necessary, of course, for the reports ever to say exactly what he is.

– A.B.

CARS

It was a '39 Chevrolet, I found out later, four-door, with the six-cylinder inline nailhead engine – stick shift, of course – a car there, with a man behind the wheel, watching me as I walked up.

'It's all right,' Margery said to me. 'He's a friend.' That seemed hardly likely, since he didn't even know me. What she meant was, she was willing to vouch for him. The other thing was that she had uttered an undoubted cliché; I had heard it issue from the mouths of actor after actor, and if I had heard it so often, how many additional times must it have been uttered? But then I realized something else. Margery was no dummy, but she was a rustic, and I was going to get just so much a range of utterances out of her. Well, so be it. There are worse things to be than a rustic.

'All right.' I nodded; that was twice I'd gotten nodding right. As for whether she was trustworthy enough to vouch for anyone, that was an order of question that was beyond me to judge. 'Okay,' I said. 'And?'

'He wants to talk to you about a job.'

'Really?' He was in his middle twenties, I found out, a spare, blue-jawed man with black hair that hung over his forehead in oily spikes. He was wearing farm clothes – a blue chambray shirt and bib overalls – and a cigarette dangled out of a small, thin-lipped mouth. I went around to the driver's window. 'Hello,' I said, watching him carefully. 'I'm Jack—'

'Mullica,' he said. His mouth twisted into a mirthless grin. 'My name's Roland Lapointe. Get in.' He gestured toward the passenger seat in front and waited for me, his eyes appraising me while I made up my mind. I finally walked around to the other side of the car and got in. Margery got into the backseat, and Lapointe drove out of the farmyard. The engine ticked over flawlessly; Lapointe, or somebody, had taken very good care of it during the war.

'That's the ticket,' Lapointe was saying. 'I like my people to do what they're told.'

I glanced at him. 'Your people.'

'When you work for me, you're my people.'

'And what makes you think I'll work for you?'

'Haven't got much choice. Can't expect Margery to keep feeding you for free. Can't expect to live in the barn forever – it's all right now, but winter does come.'

'I could get another job.'

'Not if I say no. Nobody'll give you a job if I say not to. Now, suppose you sit and think about that until we get to where we're going.' His voice was flat; he might have been giving the time of day.

I glanced at him again. As far as I could tell, he also hadn't changed expression once while speaking. I got the definite impression Lapointe was a genuinely tough man. Maybe not the brightest. But his outstanding quality would always be his toughness; it would carry him far. Doubtless, it had carried him far already. The important thing was, he was tougher than I.

Well, come to that, Margery was tougher than I. The jury was out on Margery's father, but the likelihood was that he was at least as tough as I. So as far as I knew, every single inhabitant of Earth was tougher than I. It made a fellow proud to be a soldier.

We drove along. Lapointe turned several corners, and we left unpaved surface and pulled onto a main road, though it was still only two lanes of asphalt. We passed several farms. Then we came to a corner. We pulled up outside a structure I recognized as a garage.

There were two things out front that were gas pumps, obviously, and then there were actually a couple of buildings – a small one in front and a much bigger one about twenty-five yards back from both roads, set behind the small building and separated from it by a drive way. The small building had a window with oil jars in it, and in front of the building were several oil drums.

I studied it with some intensity. We don't depend anywhere near as much on individual transport as Earthpeople do, though there was a time when we did. Now our cars and trucks run on a modification of a spaceship engine. The roaring, stinking, polluting Earth car was utterly foreign to me. And utterly intriguing. The idea of getting into your own vehicle and roaring off at speeds of about a hundred miles per hour and going on for miles – far more miles than apparently made sense in a culture with plentiful trains, planes, and buses – and having a garage on practically every street corner in most parts of the nation ... well, it was grotesque. And it was quaint. And it was, in its own way, glorious.

We forget, now; so much is different. But that was the time when America was the undoubted leader in the world, and gasoline was twenty-five cents a gallon, and cars – new cars – cost a thousand dollars, and the United States was about to buy a highway system that would cover the country from one end to the other, *replacing* a highway system that was the envy of all other nations. I understood, even then, that without question the best way to understand these people was to understand their infatuation with cars. And apparently I was going to get my chance.

'All right,' Lapointe said. 'What I'll want you to do is tend the garage. Pump gas, fill tires, hand out road maps, tell people the John is out of order. You won't be a mechanic. I'll take care of that. You'll sleep inside at night, you'll get three meals a day, and a dollar a day. Sundays we're closed.'

'You're offering me that job.'

'Yes.'

'I don't know how to drive.'

Lapointe turned in his seat and looked back at Margery.

'So teach him,' she said. 'How hard can it be?'

Lapointe looked at me. 'Um.'

Lapointe had gone into the other building. Margery and I were alone. 'Listen,' Margery said to me, 'he's all right. He's hard. But he's all right.' And she had brought my kit; the coveralls, and the kit. She sat on the corner of the battered desk in the garage, with her pants down around her ankles, while I worked on her. There was something a little bit evasive about her all of a sudden, and that had to be Lapointe, but she flexed and moved the leg almost normally, and she spoke to me in a tone that was much gentler than the one she used to use.

'You keep your nose clean, and you'll be all right,' she was saying. 'Don't jump to any hasty conclusions. And I'll be around. You got any questions, you ask me first. Got that?'

I cocked my head. 'What's wrong?' I said.

'Nothing's wrong unless you screw up. And you won't screw up all the way; you've got sense, even if it isn't horse sense.'

'Look, Margery—'

'I owe you more than you can imagine,' she said, sliding off the desk and pulling up her pants. 'You can't dream how much what you're doing to my leg means to me. But that's not the only thing in the world. Anyway, I got you the best job you could possibly get. You'll learn to drive, you'll get a Social Security card, pretty soon you'll blend right in with us Americans.'

'What do you mean?' I asked with a sinking feeling.

'Jack,' she said, looking at the floor, 'you wouldn't fool a four-year-old right now. There's only one place you could have come from, and that's a Russian ship. Probably a submarine. All right? Get this through your head – we don't care. You obviously aren't here to commit sabotage. Chances are you're glad to get away. I know I would be – it doesn't sound like a decent way for the ordinary guy to live, communism. All right; fine. We'll help you. And if some of the things we ask in return aren't exactly legal, well, what's legal?'

It was my turn to look down at the floor. 'I see.'

'So you keep your nose clean, and we'll gradually make an American out of you.'

'Yes.'

'And I really do thank you for my leg. I didn't know you people could do that. I'm grateful.'

'Yes, well.'

'And if you want to bed me, that's all right, too.' Both of us were looking at the floor.

Things were going too fast for me. 'I – what about Lapointe?'

'Lapointe is my brother. Half-brother. We've got the same mother. Came out of the barrens, settled with old man Lapointe first, when he died she moved in with my old man. One day Pop woke up and she was gone. Found out she hitched a ride on the highway. Last anybody here has seen of her.'

'My God.'

Margery shrugged. 'It was a long time ago, now. She wasn't the first funny thing that came out of the barrens.' She looked at me. 'Wasn't the last. Though I will say, it wasn't usual for somebody from the barrens to name themselves for the Mullica River.'

Things at Lapointe's Garage settled into a routine very quickly.

Roland did teach me how to drive, by the simplest method, which was to sit me behind the wheel in the middle of a large open field, point out the accelerator, brake, and clutch and the functions of each, and then stand back and let me stall out a few times, swing around wildly a few times, damned near run into a tree a few times even if this meant wandering far afield, and fairly soon learn to coordinate everything. I did not, of course, tell him that I knew how to drive our ground cars. He, on the other hand, did not tell me that I was a good driver, which I very soon was.

The name of the town, if it can be called a town, was Phyllis. The name of the next town was Wertenbaker. The name of the town three miles down a side road, fronting a lake, was Serena Manor. At some early point in our relationship, Margery explained this to me. Daniel Wertenbaker had named Phyllis for his daughter, and Serena Manor for his wife. There was no particular reason for the towns in the first place; of the combined population of about three hundred, two hundred fifty were engaged in raising chickens, one of the few crops that would grow profitably on the soil. The narrow spaces in the woods that the three towns represented were crammed with two-and three-story chicken coops, housing well over a million chickens, and they smelled like it. At night you could hear the chickens snoring. During the day you could hear them eating, and pecking weaker chickens to death.

Margery came to see me every day after work, and I used up all of my muscle balm. By the time I did that, she was walking normally, and it would have taken a very sharp eye to detect the difference between her legs; in effect, there was none.

She had to account for it somehow. At first, it had been a sort of miracle, but one that could fail. The leg could go back to what it had been. The whole thing might have been some kind of illusion born of hope. But now it wasn't failing, and if she didn't find some way to account for it, there were too many questions to ask about me. And she saw me every day, and I worked in a garage. What could be mysterious about me?

'It's the Sister Kenny treatment, isn't it?' she said, referring to a long, hard course of hot towels and massage that only worked sometimes, and only if it was started the minute the paralysis set in. 'Some variation on the Sister Kenny treatment.'

'Yes,' I said. 'A variation on it,' as if I really knew what I was talking about. And she brightened up.

'That explains it,'

'Absolutely.' As long as you didn't question it. And what do you suppose the chances were of her ever questioning it once she had hit upon Sister Kenny in the first place? She flirted the leg back and forth, feeling the power and the weight-carrying capacity of it. If she spoke of it skeptically, ever, might not the charm be broken? She licked her lips and nodded.

'Yes,' she said very softly. The offer to bed her was still good, I knew. I wanted to, but somehow I felt that it was too soon, and that Lapointe would hear us, and that – in truth, I wanted to, very much, but the thought of interspecies ... well, I would get to it, but it would take some getting used to – I was scared. I was scared green. I'd had one or two women, not many, and I was afraid of all the usual things, plus giving myself away. I had no idea what the sexual appendage of an Earth male looked like. Whereas Margery knew very well. It would take special circumstances, and they had not yet occurred. And so we each had a secret thing between us.

I know it puzzled Margery that I did not take her up on the offer. But she was too polite to come out and ask me directly. I also presumed that the creation of a good leg meant, among other things, a change in her sex life ... more discrimination, certainly; perhaps even complete abstinence until she could fully assimilate the change, and fully assimilate the idea that she could be choosier than in the past.

I gradually learned Lapointe's real business. Once or twice a month a tow truck dragging a car would pull up to the other building in the middle of the night, and once or twice a month a car would emerge from the building, a different color and usually with different accessories than when it went in at the end of a hook. The car would be driven away by Christie, Roland's right-hand man, and the following day, late, Christie would come back on the bus.

Christie was about five feet three inches tall, and I presume the lack of height weighed on him; he was muscular, young, and handsome, but didn't have a sense of humor at all. He kept to himself and handed Roland his tools.

In due course – it was the spring – Christie did not come back. Well, it was a weak point in Roland's system; there was nothing to compel Christie to come back, if he chose instead to keep the car, or the money from the car, and go and do something else thereafter. There was really little likelihood Roland would spare the time and trouble to find him. And if he found him, the money would likely already be spent.

Roland went around in a black rage. Finally I said to him: 'Roland.'

'What?'

'Roland, what if I were to deliver the cars?'

Roland gripped me by the upper arm in a hold that bruised flesh. 'What the hell do you know about it?'

The hold was not comfortable. But I pretended not to mind it. 'I've got eyes. I know Christie takes the cars somewhere. I know he didn't come back. If the authorities had him, they would have been here by now. The other possibility is he's in cahoots with whoever receives the cars, but that makes no sense because that man would cut off his source of supply if he offended you. So Christie did this on his own. All right – from now on, I'll be Christie. The difference is, I'll always come back.'

'Will you?' Roland frowned. 'Why?'

'Because Margery's here,' I said, and it was the truth. Somehow, without really meaning to, I had built up too many ties to cut.

Roland grinned mirthlessly. 'Yes. Little Sis Margery. Little Margery that's no longer crippled. I wonder how much I believe in Sister Kenny. I wonder, if it's that easy, why don't more people use it.' His eyes were very sharp on my face for a minute. Then he shrugged. 'All right,' he said, and it was a moment before I realized he had okayed the deal. 'All right,' he said again. 'You gonna stick with the Mullica name?'

'It's my name,' I declared, because, after all, what else could I do?

'Right,' he said.

'What difference does it make?' I asked a little testily.

'Gonna show up on your driver's license, that's why,' he said, and walked away to use the phone.

And that is how I got a birth certificate, and then a Social Security card, and a driver's license in the name of Jack Mullica: on the strength of one phone call from Roland Lapointe to someone who could forge the basic document.

To this day, nobody ever checks back to the original issuing authority for the validity of the birth certificate. If you present the purported certificate in another state, the odds are very low of the particular clerk's even knowing what a genuine certificate should look like. For that matter, states themselves change the appearance of their birth certificates from time to time. I presume the appearance of my certificate is actually genuine for its time frame. I don't actually *know* – no one has ever questioned it, and I have never seen another one.

I took it, when I got it, to the Social Security office in Mays Landing, and to the driver's license station in Atlantic City, and in about as much time as it takes to tell, I was a valid citizen of the United States of America. Eventually I got a fake draft card, and that was a bit of a risk, but not as much of a risk as a physical examination would have been. I had to explain to Roland that I was a bit old to just take the exam in the regular way. He grumbled, but he saw the sense of it. In any event, no one has ever asked to see it. I marvel at such a country – I don't complain.

– Reconstruction. A.B.

FOOTNOTE

A check of records bears out that Mullica obtained them as just outlined. The documents all either are forgeries or emanate from forgeries. The birth certificate is in fact rather crude, containing inks not available at the time of the supposed birth, and being countersigned by the wrong names. But no one subjects the ink and paper to analyses, and who knows what the right names are?

The draft card is rather good. It would have to be, since it was required by law to be carried on the person, and was subject to inspection at any time. But Mullica was never asked for it, apparently. From time to time he would have to record the pertinent data on work applications and the like, but in that case the persons asking for the data did not ask to see the draft card. Nor, given the nature of the times, did anyone ever check the data; they simply filed it together with the rest of his employment data.

Until I began the research for this book, I had no idea how porous the systems of identification really are in this country. No wonder Americans are forever getting into trouble on visits overseas, where there are much stricter controls no child of Uncle Sam will tolerate well.

– A.B.

STATEMENT, DITLO RAVASHAN

The Navy truck let off Yankee at one end of National. Then it drove to the other end, and the driver helped me with the crate with Joro and the dry ice in it. There were no benches; I sat on the crate and watched the truck go around a turn and disappear from this account. It was a little chilly. The crate fumed CO_2 gas through its narrow bottom slots. Once a man going by eyed the crate thoughtfully. 'Lobsters,' I said, and the man nodded and went on his way, without saying, 'On dry ice?'

I watched the women. I had plans. Most of the women were dogs, but every once in a while a good-looking one went by, her physical attributes evident even in her topcoat. I pictured them at my feet, beside themselves, crying out like the animals they were, and this helped pass the time.

After about an hour, a plain station wagon came cruising down the ramp and stopped in front of me. Henshaw – he introduced himself – was driving it: an ugly, appealing black man, well dressed, in his early thirties, who did not waste my time with small talk. He looked me in the face, and when he shook my hand, he looked at my wrist. Something behind his eyes nodded to itself. But he didn't say anything. He took his end of the crate, we wrestled it aboard, and were on our way.

We crossed the river and stopped at a motel. 'You've got a reservation,' Henshaw said. He told me the name. 'It's already paid for. All you have to do is get your key. Tomorrow, or the next day at the latest, we'll have an apartment for you. And some clothes. Meanwhile, I strongly suggest you get some sleep. And order your food in from room service.' He reached behind him and handed me a brown paper shopping bag. 'Razor, toothbrush, and so forth.' He looked at my jaw again. What he said was 'Good luck,' and he and Joro's corpse drove away. I went into the motel, and commenced my life as an American.

I had been right, when I carefully misused the engines on my craft – it would be a very good life for me here. Much better than it would have been on my home world. I had seen the retired captains on my home world; they did not look happy. They looked as though they had lost something, out in the stars. As indeed they had; they had grown old, out among the stars, and had had to come home, finally, and gradually dry up, and blow away.

It was a long run on Earth for me, and I enjoyed it immensely. We got me an apartment in Georgetown, and I enjoyed its amenities. I did not go out of town and leave it very often; I did not need to, and I did not want to. Why take chances?

We also acquired a very nice house in Georgetown, quite nearby, and that is where the National Register of Pathological Anomalies settled in after we got government funding. I ran it with a phone at first, and then computers, and I never set foot in the NRPA offices. Why should I? The NRPA occasionally sent a message to its 'parent organization,' and I would answer it, and that was that – the NRPA was staffed by conscientious civil servants, and they ran the routine daily in an exemplary manner. They even did a lot of good for pathology departments across the nation; well worth the taxpayer's dollar. And meanwhile I took in the recreational delights of Earth.

Not to put too fine a face on it, I had no qualms about using prostitutes, often black and in pairs, which I did with imagination and gusto. A permanent attachment seemed much too risky to me. It meant I would never have a wife, but that hardly mattered; I was not going to have children in any event, and I counted that, as a matter of fact, among my advantages. For one thing, I did not have to go through the stultifying mechanics of contraception.

Prostitutes are cheaper, and one does not have to entertain them with small talk. I met them in hotels all over town for years, and many a memorable time we had. It really is amazing what you can get the animals to do if you make the rewards big enough for them. And I had plenty of reward to distribute.

I proceeded to make Yankee very rich, you see, a procedure he took to very well. I began by having him manufacture shoes like mine, through a dummy corporation, and though there were imitators very soon, that was to be expected – and Yankee owned some of the imitators, too. Then there was the deceptively simple aerosol valve, which alone would have sufficed to make him a multimillionaire if he hadn't had to split it with the front man. And the new way to make a milk carton, the razor that was a continuous strip of razor-sharp steel in a compact head, and so on.

Several things were to be remarked on about all this. For one thing, I got my split, of course, and not even I could spend it as fast as it came in. For another, Yankee, no matter how wealthy he became, did not lose his primary drive, which was not for power, which he soon had to a nearly incalculable point, and not so much for a public awareness of his actual power, which awareness wavered with his fortunes and was never very accurate. Rather, it was for public awareness that he commanded mysterious and fundamentally, deliberately unknowable power. *That* was more important to him than any other single thing on Earth, by far. It created a peculiar aura around him. Nobody liked him. Nobody loved him – and this bothered him. But everyone kowtowed to him, and that, it seems, was what he held most precious.

And for a third, it would take an inspection team from my home world about thirty seconds to determine that this was too much to be a coincidence; someone was feeding Earth this information. So there was some risk, but it was on the order of requiring Earth to be the subject of an inspection, and then it required the inspection team to find me. I thought I had made that rather difficult for them. But in any case you will notice that none of the information was strategic or tactical.

Well, actually, when I gave him the secret of the transistor, it was a close call. But in fact several laboratories on Earth were about to discover it for themselves, and all we did was jump the gun by, literally, months. And I did not so much give him the secret of the transistor – which I did not fully know – as alert him to the possibility. He was the one who found the work at Bell Labs and elsewhere much advanced. So that was all right. And of course the patents were quickly superseded, and improvements on the original design came thick and fast and were patented by others. But I'm sure you will agree that with a device as fundamental as the transistor, you can spill ninety-nine parts in a hundred, and still realize quite a nice profit. As we certainly did.

As I say, it was a generously nice run. For a time, Yankee restlessly wanted more information about my home civilization, and data such as the engineering behind the spaceship engine drive. But the fact is I couldn't have given him the latter if I had wanted to – what would a pilot have to know about engineering, as distinguished from inconspicuous unbalanced use of the engines? – and the former, he quickly realized, could have been made up or couldn't have been made up, and how was he to know? So our arrangement was not quite what he had expected, but it did make him filthy rich, and he quickly accommodated to it.

And he found ways to use it, nevertheless. I'm sure he told very selected people about me, and what I represented. What else accounts for his rise in American politics? Other people were easily on the same side as he on the Communist question, and other people were this, that, and the other thing as he was, but only Yankee wove the web of obligations and fear, the 'natural' aristocracy of the person who came up through the ranks in a certain way, and only he presented his particular solutions to problems that frequently did not exist, although he said they did, and beat the drum for years until they were well entrenched. It was a lovely performance, and I frequently chuckled over it. Even the times he was defeated, temporarily, would have been a permanent setback for any lesser man, but he just soldiered on, and whispered whatever he whispered to his corporate sponsors, and lo! there he was again, as if he had never been gone.

And nobody, as far as I know, ever questioned the source of his wealth. Remarkable. Only in America.

And then one day, after about twenty years, things changed. I had come back from one of my various trips around the country, to inspect various odd bits that proved never to actually be flying saucer wreckage, and I noticed that I was more tired than usual, and that my arms tended to go to sleep. Then a while after that I began to get dizzy spells, and shortly thereafter the dizzy spells became quite noticeable; I could hardly stand up without feeling the effects. Lying down became an exercise in increasingly careful motion. And my legs cramped at night. At first I could solve this by slipping out of bed and standing up for a minute or two, but then the cramps moved out of my calves into my thighs and feet, and did not yield to simple remedies. I began to seriously lose sleep.

I did not know what to do. I could not, I at first told myself, go to a doctor. I became very worried when it proved more and more difficult to get up from a chair – often it took me two or three tries. I was only glad that no one observed me; I did fire the cleaning woman. I did, in short, as much as I could, and when this proved insufficient, I thought to call in Henshaw.

Henshaw, whom I had not actually seen since that one day long ago, was a peculiar person. He was black, first of all, and that tended to isolate him; he was a doctor of veterinary medicine, and that tended to isolate him further, from the ordinary run of black man. Then, his interests were very broad, and he acted on them; he had traveled to many parts of the world, he had studied far beyond the basic requirements of the DVM degree, he loved grand opera, he painted with quite a bit of skill and had studied painting – in short, and I have just touched on the high spots, he would have been thoroughly hated by the average person even if he hadn't been black, which he was, and which he rubbed your nose in if he got the idea this made him in your eyes in any way inferior to you, honky.

Of course, nevertheless, Yankee had chosen him to dissect Chaplain Joro because he was much less likely to be believed than a white man if he attempted to … spill the beans. That was many years ago, when Henshaw had first turned up, with the barest beginnings of a private practice among the poodles and kitties of Georgetown. He was Yankee's family animal doctor, and of course had had his measure taken early by Yankee, as all who came in repeated contact with him did. I was taking a chance in contacting him with my problem, but I really had no choice. He was the only man besides Yankee who knew about me, and he was the only man who was a medical practitioner.

I called a taxi, making my selection at random, and had myself driven out to his house in the middle of the night. I left a note in his mailbox while the taxi waited and had myself driven to the Willard Hotel, from which I took another taxi home. It was the best I could do. I did not think Yankee detected me. Then it was wait for Henshaw to come to me.

He did. DVMs are not ordinarily asked to make house calls, so he had to presume that after all these years I had another corpse to dissect. The arrangement was that he would be on call in case we ever found another one. The fact that we never did was beside the point.

We sat in my living room, I behind a desk, Henshaw draped over an upholstered chair, a black bag at his feet. I had not seen him since that day at National, long ago now. He had not much changed. He was a large man, who gave a sense of power and vitality, and who, besides his wife and six children, took an occasional flier on other women, very discreet. Every time he did it, he put himself further into my power; I kept a tap on his phones, of course. And Yankee must have done something analogous to that, from before the very beginning – kept the man on a string, until he needed him, and then one day called him and suggested he get in his station wagon and go out to Washington National Airport.

And the man had gone, because he had no choice. But that was not why he had thereafter stayed a contingency employee of the NRPA all these years; no, not once he had seen me. Wild horses, I think, could not have kept him away. But of course I kept the phone taps anyway.

I said: 'Doctor, something serious is wrong with me.'

He raised an eyebrow. 'And that's why you chose such a roundabout method of getting in touch with me? And asked me not to talk about it, on the phone or otherwise?'

'Yes.'

He sucked his front teeth. 'Interesting.'

'Doctor, I want you to examine me and determine what's wrong, if you can.'

A peculiar look come over his charmingly ugly features. 'You don't want the services of a physician? Ah.' Henshaw sat back and looked at me. He folded his hands on the knee presented by his crossed legs. 'You know,' he said, 'it's been a long time coming. Your calling on me in this way. I didn't know if you ever would. I wasn't even sure I was right about you. But if I hadn't gambled, would I have this opportunity now?' He smiled without it getting to his eyes, which remained speculative and searching. 'The opportunity to get his hands on a living one of you? How many men could say they had done that? No, I've waited' – and now he did smile, genuinely – 'patiently. And now I'll have my reward.' He reached down for his black bag. 'All right, take off your clothes.' And we began. 'You know,' he remarked, 'it'll be quite a novelty, having a patient who can talk.'

Finally he was done, and I put my clothes back on. He toyed with the vials of blood he had drawn. 'Fascinating,' he said in a distracted voice. 'Altogether fascinating.' He put the vials away, carefully, in his bag. He looked up. 'We'll have to wait a few days until the lab results come back, before I can be sure. Even then, how sure can I be?' He closed his bag and sat down in the chair again. 'Systemically, you're sort of human, but not very much. I don't think we have to worry about what the lab will make of your blood. They'll think it's some kind of exotic animal – which, of course, is what it is, from the human point of view. And I can't tell now what abnormalities are present, not that it'll help a great deal when the results are in, because neither you nor I will ever know what the normal structure is – unless, of course, in the fullness of time I get a healthy one of you to examine, but I don't think that'll ever happen.'

'I really don't care about any of that.'

'I didn't think you did. I'm stalling for time.' He pulled at his lower lip. 'All right. You've got some sort of severe circulatory problem. I can't tell how severe, because I don't know what your normal blood pressure is ... and neither do you. Shame you weren't a doctor. On the other hand, you wouldn't be here, would you? The point is it's obviously severe, or you wouldn't have those symptoms. And those symptoms are incapacitating you. Now – what's causing the symptoms? That's much more interesting. And even less ponderable, for the moment at least.'

He got up from the chair and walked around my apartment, while I watched him with every fiber of my being. He cupped his hands together behind his back and went from wall to wall, without ever really seeing them. 'You're a very sick boy,' he said to the empty air. 'Very sick. And I don't know how much I'm going to be able to help you.' He turned back to me. 'Not that anyone else could help you as much as I can. But that may turn out to be cold comfort.'

'I may die.'

'Yes,' he said, 'you may die. But you knew that, or you would not have called even me.'

– Never revealed.

STATEMENT II, DITLO RAVASHAN

The next several days were not pleasant for me, waiting. And the dizzy spells and cramps were worse than they had ever been. When Henshaw arrived at my office, I was more than ready for him.

He sat down, taking a sheaf of paper out of a file folder – the lab report. He flipped it open and read it silently – again, I presumed – and then looked me in the face.

'You know what a T-cell is?' he asked, and before I could say no, he shook his head. 'No, you don't.' He put the laboratory report aside. 'All right. About five years ago, a doctor happened to mention a peculiar thing to another doctor. He had begun getting a number – small, but a number – of examples of a mysterious viral infection from Haitians, hemophiliacs, homosexuals, and h'infants. He mentioned it because he had thought of this cute way to describe the correlation. What was not so cute was that the disease resisted all attempts to handle it; his patients, every one of them, were either already dead or were dying. And actually he was a little bit scared.

'So you can imagine how he felt when the other doctor said he was seeing the same thing.

'They were at a medical convention, so they checked as best they could. And a significant number of other doctors said they were seeing it too.

'The other thing was, it wasn't the disease itself that killed people. There didn't seem to be a clear-cut disease, as a matter of fact, although their blood work-ups all showed the same pattern. But the patients died of half a dozen different diseases; cancers and lung diseases, mostly – not particularly frequent cancers. What the viral infection could do, it shut down the immune reaction. After that, it was just a matter of time. The first disease that came along after that, the person died.'

'How many died?' I asked.

He shook his head wearily. 'All of them. After a time, all of them die. There are no survivors.'

'None at all?'

'None. At all. Nobody knows much about it yet. But nobody survives it. And we can't be sure, but I think it attacks h'aliens, too. I think you've got it.'

I looked at him incredulously. 'You think *I've* got it? Why? Surely you must—'

'Be mistaken? Maybe.'

There was something about the way he said it, the way he looked at me. 'But you think I've got it.'

'I'm afraid so.'

'How did I get it?'

'Well, I gather your sexual habits—' He shrugged. 'Sex seems to have something to do with it.'

'Jesus Christ, if that's all it takes, this town ought to be a hecatomb!'

'No argument. Perhaps in time it will be.' He shook his head. 'I know you won't take much of an interest, but this does look very bad for the future of the human race.' He laughed without humor. 'And I can't tell anybody about it. Well, it'll emerge among the more sensitive part of the human community soon enough, I'm sure. It'll be among the heterosexuals; white male Anglo-Saxon Protestant heterosexuals. That'll take care of it … raise an outcry like you couldn't believe.'

'How long have I got?'

He shook his head. 'I don't know. A month, maybe. Maybe a week. Whatever your particular disease is, it seems well advanced.'

'A week.'

'It's hard to tell.'

'A week,' I repeated. I looked around the office. 'Well.' The thing was, how did we do a funeral in which the corpse was totally destroyed? Because if it wasn't, some medical examiner whom we did not control would grow very interested.

'Henshaw, you've got to help me.'

'Yes, I do,' he agreed. He shook his head. 'Funny how it leads you to this day. Life. I decided I was different, and I *was* different, but it didn't help after all.'

'What are you taking about?'

'I didn't take any precautions while examining you. Why should I? But the fact is, just by some minor action I don't even remember, I may have contracted it. On the other hand, maybe not. But we can't be sure. I called the lab and made careful inquiries, though, and none of their technicians got any of your blood in a cut. So *that's* probably all right.'

'Wait a minute—'

'Oh, it's not as bad as all that,' Henshaw said. 'For example, you apparently had a long interval between exposure and reaching a critical stage. And someone exposed to you might have even longer – after all, you *are* an alien, and any number of things might have happened. No, I might not have been exposed at all. But on the other hand—' He shrugged, not too casually. 'On the other hand, we're not even sure what to look for, exactly, in the blood of someone who hasn't reached criticality. So I can't be sure. So I can't stick it in my wife or anybody else, anymore, forever.' He laughed, not amusedly. 'Ain't that a bitch? Of course, your case is considerably worse than that, so I don't expect you to sympathize.'

And I don't suppose I did. His case was even funny, in a way … spending the rest of his life wondering when the disease would break out in him, nagged by the thought that he might not have it at all. But not daring to take the chance. Yes, it *was* funny. But I thought it best not to laugh. The wave of dizziness would have been overwhelming.

'Listen,' he said, 'we don't want to tell [and he gave Yankee's real name].'

No, we didn't. I had been very right to take precautions. But I said: 'Well, that's interesting. Why not?'

'I've thought about it,' he said. 'All I can see coming from it is a million questions, including among others what in the hell I was doing visiting you in your apartment. I'm not supposed to know you, beyond one contact a long time ago. And of course that was true, until recently.'

'I see.'

'I don't have to tell you what he's like.'

No, he didn't. He was right. The questions would never stop. The trust, once thought to be broken, would not be restored. It was even possible an accident would befall Dr Henshaw. I had no reason to believe that – but in the case of Yankee, the fact that I also had no reason not to believe it was something to be considered. 'All right. Makes sense. And it certainly makes no difference to me, at this point.'

So we left it at that. I sank back in my chair, and the world whirled and spun.

And the time came. I could not walk anymore, and my body would convulse in cramps that were indescribably painful. It was more than a week after the last time Henshaw and I spoke. It was less than a month.

Henshaw came for me. I looked around the apartment one last time. Then I emptied my pockets, because when I left this apartment for the last time, I would disappear without a trace. Disappear permanently, but in any case, without a trace.

I hoped Yankee would reason that my people might have come for me. I chuckled a little bit.

The NRPA would go on; in time, it might even develop a new parent organization. I laid my wallet down on top of the little pile on my desk, patted my pockets, and extracted one last item – a Democratic National Committee matchbook. I looked at it, smiled briefly, and laid it down. It gave the address – the Watergate complex – and a phone number.

Henshaw looked at it. 'What the hell are you doing with one of those?' he asked, a little incredulously. 'I didn't think you gave a damn about our politics.'

I laughed. 'I didn't get a chance to try it. There's a hot rumor around that a call girl ring is operating out of one of the spare offices there.'

'You're shitting me.'

I shrugged. 'That's the word. But what's the difference? Neither one of us is ever going to give it a try.' I turned to leave the apartment, and stumbled into his arms.

We drove to a Virginia farm, long abandoned, the track running through shrubbery and fallen fences, until we stopped at what remained of the yard. Henshaw shut off the engine and looked at me. Then he said 'No point stretching it out' and opened his little black bag. He took out a hypodermic and a bottle, and filled the hypodermic. 'Cyanide,' he said. 'It'll kill you very quickly.'

'All right,' I said.

'Anything you want to say?'

Was there anything I wanted to say? To have come all this way, and to end like this. I remembered the chaplain, and how I had questioned him as he was dying. 'What is the meaning of life?' I had asked him, and he had finally answered, 'Hurt.' Or perhaps not. Really, it occurred to me, it was a question to ask a child, not a dying man.

'No,' I said. It hadn't been a bad life, everything considered. I was beginning to recall one of its more pleasantly outrageous moments, with a woman beneath my face and another kissing her while I fingered – but that was when I felt the needle go into my arm, and very soon thereafter I was dead.

Henshaw pushed me out of the car, and drove it a little ways away. Then he got out, opened the trunk, and took out the two five-gallon cans of gasoline. He doused me with one of them, and set it alight. Then he retreated to the car until the flames died down, and poured the second can over what remained of me, and lit that, going back to the car again. Finally he came back and stirred the remains, until you could not have said what it was that had burned there. There were some bone fragments, but beyond seeing to it they were scattered, Henshaw did nothing further. He did not need to. And so I departed this life, far from home. But whether I was home or not, I had had a good life. A somewhat shorter one than I had anticipated, but I had had the money, I had had the girls, and nobody told me what to do. Is there, really, anything else? Are you sure?

– Never revealed. A.B.

CONVERSATIONS BETWEEN FUNCTIONARIES

#1: I don't get it. I went into the apartment, and there's nothing unusual there but a pile of clothes, with the stuff piled on top.

#2: You've got no clue as to where the occupant's gone?

#1: None whatsoever. Everything's got a light film of dust on it, so he's been gone at least a week.

#2: All right. Inventory the stuff, and come back in. Then I'll pass the word up.

#2: Well, the shit hit the fan when I made my report. He wants you to get together a crew of trustworthy guys, break into the Watergate, and scour Democratic National Committee Headquarters ASAP.

#1: You're kidding.

#2: No, I'm not.

#1: Christ, there's never anything in a national committee headquarters! It's a clerical office, for Christ's sake!

#2: Buddy, you know that and I know that, but apparently he doesn't. So I suggest you do exactly as instructed. Put together a crew – get a bunch of those Cuban exiles or somebody else that'll tend to be loyal. And get in there!

#1: Jesus Christ. Jesus Christ.

MORE CARS

So for a while, I was Christie. Once a month, or sometimes twice, I drove into Newark, and parked the car in another garage, and a man handed me a sealed envelope which I took back to Roland, riding the bus.

The trips fascinated me at first. There was so much to see – the farms, and the gradually larger and larger villages, and finally the city, which was actually a whole group of cities, of course; the only way you could tell you were in Newark, finally, was by a sign on one side of a street. This was before they finished the New Jersey Turnpike – in fact, it was before they finished a whole bunch of things. The Adams Burlesque Theatre was still going in downtown Newark; ah, it was all right. They stripped down to nothing sometimes. And the comics were great; really great. I even saw Joe Yule, who was Mickey Rooney's father.

But truth to tell, it began to wear thin after a while. I wasn't getting anywhere. I got to Newark once or twice a month, but it was as if I were on an elasticized string; I always went back. And the thought of spending the rest of my life on the edge of the barrens was more than I could comfortably live with.

My English got good; I was reading a lot. My favorite was the car magazines, of course. I even wrote some letters, and they printed them; it was mostly pointing out errors in the journalism, at first.

I wasn't getting anywhere with Margery, either. I began necking with her, timidly at first and later with considerable warmth, and she enjoyed it as much as I did, but that was all. Roland Lapointe just shook his head. 'Look, you do know what it's for, don't you?' was as far as he went in commenting. I nodded, my face flaming, and he threw a bolt into a bucket on the other side of the garage and walked out.

One thing I learned from the burlesque was that Earthwomen had essentially the same equipment I was more or less familiar with. And I finally got my hands on one of Roland's nudist magazines, and found out my equipment was not essentially different from what Margery was accustomed to. But somehow … I don't know. It just … well, it might have gone on forever, I suppose, but one time I came back from Newark at dawn and found the light on in the back garage.

It was dawn. Roland never got up at dawn; he worked mostly at night. So the chances of the light having gone on recently were very low. But it was just as unusual for Roland to work *through* the night. In fact, he had never done it.

I looked at the window for a long time. Then I cautiously opened the door, and first thing that struck me was the smell. It reminded me, in a way, of the spots in Nick Olchuck's barn where the cats and the rats had been. But this was fresher. I went around the stuff piled in the front of the garage to look harmless through the window, and there was Roland, dead.

He *was* tough. The car had slipped off a jack and put a brake drum in the center of his chest. If the wheel had been on the drum, he might have lived. Even then, from the blood and the torn-up fingers it was clear he had been hours dying, his chest all concaved, but trying to push the car off to the end, dying, finally, in the small hours of the night, alone and thinking God knows what. I looked at him for a long time, and a lot went through my mind.

But really my choices were very few. I couldn't keep the operation going, and I couldn't expect to keep the garage … I couldn't expect anything. And I realized it was my big chance.

I backed out of the garage and closed the door. Then I went over to Roland's car, and the keys were in it, as they always were. I drove over to Margery's, and threw pebbles at her window. When she finally opened the window, tousle-headed and with her breasts falling out of her nightgown, I said: 'Let's go.'

She blinked. 'What?'

'You coming with me?'

She blinked again. Her glance grew sharp. She took in Roland's car, and the sealed envelope sticking out of my pocket, and she bit her lower lip, but she nodded. Twenty minutes later we were on our way, headed for the Pennsylvania Turnpike, and I was explaining. It didn't take much. 'All right,' she said, 'I've got it.'

'One more thing.'

'What's that?'

I carefully did not look at her. 'Will you marry me?'

She said nothing for quite a while. Then she began to laugh. 'Sure. Why not? Somebody's got to make an honest man out of you.'

'I didn't mean to make a joke,' I said.

She bit her lip. 'No, I don't suppose you did.' She looked at me in the morning sunlight while the car zipped along. 'Neither did I, really.' Her eyes were grave. 'Yes, I'll marry you. For richer or poorer. For better or for worse.' Her mouth quirked up. 'I'll even throw in till death do us part; how about that, Jack, my Mullica Jack?'

I studied her. 'I hope to make you happy.'

She shook her head, staring off at nothing. 'I think you've already done as much about that as you could,' she said. 'It's quite a bit, you know. Don't try to do any more than you can.'

I didn't say anything. We would see.

We were married in a little chapel in Sandusky, Ohio.

'You may kiss the bride,' the beaming JP and the beaming witness said, and I did. Then we moved to the Lake Vista Motel, and there the pattern of our life together was established forever. I looked at her bleakly in the morning light, and she looked back at me and shook her head slightly.

'It doesn't matter that much, Jack,' she said.

'Maybe it'll be better as I get used to you.'

'Maybe. The big point is, I'm warm, I'm comfortable, and I know you love me.'

I smiled a little. We were on the bed, stark naked, and she looked so desirable, so much the woman— Well, it wasn't as if I hadn't satisfied her, because I had. And it wasn't as if I hadn't ejaculated, because I had. But it was also true that I had no idea how she felt to be inside of, which made me practically unique among the men she had known.

'Jack—'

I let my grin widen. 'What the hell? It wasn't so bad.'

She laughed in turn. 'No. No, it wasn't.' She wriggled on the bed. 'In fact, if you felt like some more, I could use—' Well, that's as much of that as you need to know. Gradually, over time, we accommodated. The time also came when she stayed out a little late, and after that, for all the years we were together, there were times when she stayed out. But she always came back. It was all right. Really.

We settled down in Detroit. I got a job in a garage – just cleaning up, at first, but eventually I got to be the lead mechanic – and she got a series of jobs as a supermarket cashier and so forth. Nobody ever came for us. What happened to Nick Olchuck we never knew, but the assumption is he vanished into a bottle. Roland's car we left on the street, miles away from the first apartment we got, and nobody ever connected us to it. I went by it a couple of times, and first the tires were gone, and then the hood and trunk were open, and then the engine was gone, and in about a week – this was before Detroit got real bad, which was why it took so long – all that was left was the frame and the body shell. So that was all right. And we lived.

We lived not badly. Both of us were making good money. I was making a bit on the side; *Automotive News* ran some of my fillers, and some of the other magazines. And then one day, in the classified section of the *News*, was an ad for an entry-level position in the public relations department of the number three carmaker. I was I guess a little bit older than most of the other applicants, but I had a track record established, and the man who would be my boss liked the way I wrote, and so I became an automotive PR man.

It was not glamorous. All the glamor is on the outside. It was cranking out press releases about the new rear axle ratio, and the rejetted carburettor, and like that, and you had to go to the engineers for the raw data. Engineers do not particularly like PR men. The senior PR men got to stand around test tracks in suits and ties without a spot on them; we grunts had to find someplace that would wash a car at six in the morning in some godforsaken hole on the day of a press conference. More than once, I've mopped off a boss's car with the T-shirt torn from my own body, hosing down the piece with a hotel loading dock hose. And turned up at eight A.M. impeccably dressed, except I wasn't wearing an undershirt, handing out press kits to contemptuous automotive journalists, and secretly wondering if the engineers had actually had time to get the units into halfway decent shape. I remember the time we sent off the automotive editor of a major magazine to drive back to Long Island and test the hot new brakes on a completely new model; after he was gone, it turned out the engineers hadn't gotten delivery on the hot new brakes, so they substituted a set from the old model. We heard about that – we heard about that a great deal, and oddly enough it wasn't the engineers' fault, somehow; it was the PR department's.

But everything that doesn't outright kill you will eventually go away. One day they offered me the top job in the Chicago shop of the PR department, and I took it, because it was a good deal of money, and Margery and I moved to near the Borrow Street El stop in Shoreview. We lived in a nice condo overlooking the lake, and not even Selmon's eventually turning up really spoiled it, though I will admit I began hitting the bottle a little harder. But even that wasn't bad enough to really matter. I had made it – I was an American named Jack Mullica, I had a good job, a wife, Margery, and I was home free.

Even after Selmon died – God, I felt sorry for the poor dumb son of a bitch! – I was home free.

– Reconstructed. A.B.

THE END

It was August, and Jack Mullica was home, idly watching TV. He was on sick leave. At a press conference in Lake Geneva, Wisconsin, at nine at night or thereabouts, he had been out on an airfield, checking the lineup of cars for the next morning's exhibition. Somehow one of the cars had been left idling, and somehow it had dropped into gear. (The PR department of course denies that ever happens, so the incident was tightly suppressed.) At any rate, the car had brushed Jack while he was paying attention to something else, and he had a badly bruised shoulder and arm. He was wearing a home-style sling on the arm and was doped up on Margery's Darvon now; that was all right – there wasn't anything to that, although he didn't much care for the close approach to getting something broken and being taken to a doctor. But he was convinced it had been a simple accident, and was not liable to be repeated.

Margery was out somewhere. Jack was watching President Richard Nixon getting into a helicopter in the middle of the day, and thrusting his arms out to each side with his fingers spread into a V. His family was around him. Jack frowned. Where was Nixon off to now, when he ought to be staying in Washington and putting down this Watergate scandal? Jack was about to bring more of his attention to the whole business – he thought the TV had made a reference to President Gerald Ford; what they must have meant was Vice President – when the doorbell rang.

Margery's forgotten her keys or something, Mullica thought as he made his way to the front door. Came into the building on someone else's ring, and now she's standing outside, waiting for me to let her in. He opened the door, and there was Hanig Eikmo. He gaped at him, and Eikmo, who was bent a little oddly, and wearing a suit from K Mart or someplace like that, and needed a shave, said in a hasty voice: 'Can I come in?'

'Well – well, sure,' Mullica said, and stepped back. He could not close his mouth. How in the hell had Eikmo – it was Eikmo, wasn't it? – he peered at the man as he came in and pushed at the door behind him, Mullica giving ground – yes, of course it was Eikmo, and somewhere in his system Mullica realized the Darvon was affecting him more than he had thought.

'Can I sit down?' Eikmo was saying, and once again Mullica said 'Why, sure,' and Eikmo sat on a straight chair, ignoring the overstuffed sofa.

'How are you, Dwuord?' Eikmo said. 'Things going well for you?' And Mullica belatedly realized Eikmo was speaking in their old language.

He pushed the language forward, speaking it for only the second time in years. 'I – how did you find me?' Mullica was gathering himself, getting his presence back.

'Well, Selmon was writing to me once a month – payments, sending back the money he owed me. In the course of that, he told me you were here. Crazy. Policy violations like the plague, around here. Why the hell didn't he move away? But then the letters stopped coming.' Eikmo looked around. 'You alone? Nobody lives or visits here except for your lady?'

Mullica nodded. Eikmo looked around him again, and relaxed to a great extent. 'Nice. I was settled in pretty well, too, but not like this. Wife died a little while ago. Not too much of a surprise; she was a lot older than me.' Eikmo's voice grew softer for a moment. 'I liked her a lot. Came from some-place near where we originally crashed. Funny. Coincidence. But she left the barrens years before we got there. Well, anyway – I came out here looking for Selmon. Had to know what had happened to him. And I found out what happened. Finding you wasn't that hard. I've been following you for about a week. When I saw your lady go out a while ago, I came up.'

'Look, Eikmo, it's nice to see you, but policy—'

Eikmo laughed. 'Policy! You haven't sold them the shoes and a dozen other things? The razor?'

'Christ, I use an electric shaver. What are you talking about?'

Eikmo laughed. 'Sure. You don't know a thing about it.'

'Oh, come on, Eikmo—'

Eikmo stood up. 'It doesn't really matter what you say, does it? I'll take care of you. Living high on the hog. Killing Selmon.' He slipped a long, sharp knife out of his sleeve. 'What's the matter with you?' he shouted suddenly. 'Killing a poor harmless man like Selmon!'

'I didn't kill Selmon!' Mullica cried out in protest, but at the same time he turned his body, and so the knife, which should have gone into his belly, sliced instead through his right forearm muscle, glanced off his equivalent to a radius and ulna, continued upward to the elbow, and jammed there, caught in the joint.

'Jesus!' Mullica cried, and fell back, spouting blood, confused, conscious that he could not bend either arm now, seeing the blood painting the corridor walls, stepping back farther.

'Leave me alone!' he blurted, falling into a couch, trying to find the pressure points in his forearm with the fingers of his left arm, which were dreadfully weak.

'You killed Selmon,' Eikmo repeated, grappling for the knife.

'No! It was an accident. Why would I kill him?' It was a nightmare. Mullica turned his head this way and that, trying to find something that would help him, insanely watching Nixon's helicopter fly away. He didn't know if he should stop the flow of blood before he stopped Hanig Eikmo somehow; probably. Things came and went in his head with unnatural speed. He tried to hold on to one thought, any thought, and he couldn't, he couldn't.

Eikmo had his hands around Mullica's throat; Mullica was vaguely conscious that Eikmo had his knee in Mullica's lap.

'No! This is ridiculous, Eikmo! Help me stop the blood—'

'No. I'm not gonna help you stop the blood.'

Mullica, in a panic, threw Eikmo off. He backed away from Eikmo, across the room. Eikmo came after him – an older Eikmo than Mullica remembered, but Eikmo, Jesus, Eikmo, he was supposed to be in Oakland, and instead— 'Why, Eikmo?'

Eikmo had another choke hold. 'What the hell did you kill him for?'

'I didn't—'

Now they were crashing through the doors to the balcony. And now he felt the railing pressing into his back. And now he was going over, and Eikmo was leaning on the railing, looking down at him, and getting smaller.

Margery came home. The front door was pushed shut, but the lock hadn't quite found the striker plate. The apartment wall was covered in blood. She dropped the grocery bag and sprang forward. She saw a man leaning over the balcony rail. She cried out, or rather, she sucked in air, and the sound of it was a voracious rattle in her throat. She was on the balcony in a split second, and as a startled Eikmo began to turn, she placed both hands flat on his chest and pushed. No one on Earth could have resisted that push. Eikmo went toppling into space, only moments after Mullica, and crashed down through twelve floors of emptiness before impacting on the concrete sidewalk, almost exactly on the spot where Mullica lay. And finally Margery cried out; it floated down, hard on the sodden thump of Eikmo's body. 'Jack! Oh, Jack Mullica!'

Mullica saw the sidewalk coming up at him at an amazing rate of speed. Then there was a moment's blackness, and then he was looking up, and Eikmo was hurtling down at him. Jack rolled out of the way. His sling and the knife were gone. He looked up, and Margery was standing there, many floors above the street, shouting something, and then he was up there, holding her in his arms, and she was looking at him with all the love in the world, and he was taking her in his arms, and she was crying with joy, saying 'Oh, Jack Mullica! Oh, Jack Mullica,' so he took her into the bedroom and took her in his arms, and she was tearing off her clothes and his, and he was huge, he was godlike, and they made love, and they made love, and they made love, while she kept murmuring 'Oh, Jack Mullica!' over and over again, wild and wanton, in his arms, beautiful in love.

– Never revealed. A.B.

Henshaw shook his head imperceptibly. He had told the widow he was with a government agency, which was true enough. Still, one had to be careful.

It was some days after the double death. The blood in the apartment had been partly cleaned up. There was new glass in the balcony doors, though the doors themselves were splintered in places and only temporarily repaired. The widow did not look good, which Henshaw found a fleeting moment to regret, because she was basically a fine-looking woman. But he was still not certifiably clear of the disease. They still didn't know much about it. They were beginning to suspect a long incubation period. It really didn't matter, to him; he was going to play with nothing but his hand for the rest of his life, and that was that. And, besides – well, besides.

The widow sat at one end of the couch, very small, somehow, very much in need of something she would not get. She looked at nothing. An open decanter of scotch, mostly used up, sat on the end table. A glass, mostly drunk, was in Margery Mullica's hand. She cried and she looked at nothing.

A television set was on, ignored, just something to fill the room a little. Henshaw actually looked for a moment, and saw that Gerald Ford had pardoned Richard Nixon. He shook his head incredulously.

'Mrs Mullica,' Henshaw said gently.

She looked at him with faint interest.

'Mrs Mullica, I'll be going in a minute.' And leaving you completely alone. 'It's self-defense. That's clear. You'll be all right. But can you tell me *why* you pushed the stranger over the rail? Can you tell me that?' There were so many other things she could have done. True, most of them wound up with the stranger killing her, too. But still—

She smiled wanly, and looked at the drink in her hand. Then she looked at Henshaw. 'I loved him,' she said. 'I didn't care. He fixed my leg. And he was the most decent man I ever knew. Or ever will know. Even if he was a Russian deserter. I didn't care where he came from.' She was sort of smiling, and sipping at her glass, but she had not actually, at any time, stopped crying. 'I didn't care where he came from,' she said again. 'I cared what he was. I will never find a man like him again,' she said softly. 'Never, never, never.' And she continued weeping.

– From Henshaw's unwritten novel.

Well, there you have it. I began to research this book after the media story came out about two men falling off a condominium balcony. The TV and the papers covered it, of course, *but* something about the story didn't quite ring right. I figured it was worth a look. And the first thing I found, of course, was the blood all over the apartment wall – which nobody else had mentioned, and which I saw only because the superintendent happens to be my cousin. With that much to go on, I was off.

I'm sorry the book isn't more definitive. Actually, much of what precedes this closing note had to be made up. Well, all right, call it a docudrama, instead of the documentary that'll never be written because there's just plain so much that *has* to be conjecture. I mean, all five of them are dead, and were dead before I started on the book. Marjorie finally told me what she knew, for the most part, but when you look at it, she didn't really know very much, did she?

In fact, I could have made up the *whole* thing, couldn't I?

– A.B.

If you've enjoyed these books and would
like to read more, you'll find literally thousands
of classic Science Fiction & Fantasy titles
through the **SF Gateway**

For the new home of
Science Fiction & Fantasy . . .

✳

For the most comprehensive collection
of classic SF on the internet . . .

✳

Visit the SF Gateway

www.sfgateway.com

Algis Budrys (1931–2008)

Born in East Prussia in 1931, Budrys and his family were sent to the United States when he was just five. After studying at the University of Miami and Columbia University, Budrys turned his hand to both writing and publishing science fiction. Over the years he worked as an editor, manager and reviewer for various publishing houses, while maintaining an impressive output of fiction and editing his own magazine, *Tomorrow Speculative Fiction*. He was shortlisted for numerous awards, including the Hugo and the Nebula, for his fiction and critical non-fiction. He died in 2008.